Doors and Mirrors

Doors and Mirrors

Fiction and Poetry
from Spanish America
1920–1970

Selected and Edited by
Hortense Carpentier
and Janet Brof

Grossman Publishers
New York   1972

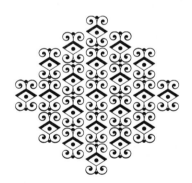

ACKNOWLEDGMENTS
All the care possible has been taken to obtain permission from the copyright owners to re-
print articles and selections protected by copyright; any errors or omissions are unin-
tentional and will be rectified in any future printings upon notification to the editors, who
wish to express their gratitude for permission to publish or reproduce the material in this
anthology to the following:
    for José María Arguedas: "El Ayla" from *Amor Mundo y todos los cuentos de Jose
Maria Arguedas.* © 1967 Francisco Moncloa Editores, S.A. Lima, Peru, by permission of
Syvila Arredondo de Arguedas;
    for Roberto Arlt: "Esther Primavera" from *El Jorobadito* by Roberto Arlt, © 1968
Compañia General Fabril Editora, S.A., Buenos Aires, by permission of Mirta Arlt;
    for Miguel Angel Asturias: "El espejo de Lida Sal" from *El espejo de Lida Sal* by
Miguel Angel Asturias, © 1967 Siglo XXI Editores, S.A., Mexico, D.F., by permission
of the author;
    for Jorge Luis Borges: "The Dead Man" from the book *The Aleph and Other Stories,*
English translation © 1968, 1970 by Emece Editores. S.A. and Norman Thomas di
Giovanni, published by E. P. Dutton, Inc., reprinted with their permission. "Delia Elena
San Marco" from *Dreamtigers* English translation © by Jorge Luis Borges, published by a
special arrangement with the University of Texas Press. "To a Saxon Poet," translated
by Norman Thomas di Giovanni, copyright © 1969 by the New Yorker Magazine, Inc.
The poem originally appeared in *The New Yorker.* "Parting," translated by W. S. Merwin,
copyright © 1968 by Emece Editores, S.A. and Norman Thomas di Giovanni. The poem
originally appeared in *Selected Translations 1948–1968* by W. S. Merwin (Atheneum Publishers). "Page to Commemorate . . .", translated by Alastair Reid. The poem originally
appeared in *Encounter,* April 1969. These three poems will appear in *Jorge Luis Borges:
Selected Poems 1923–1968,* edited and with an Introduction by Norman Thomas di
Giovanni, to be published in 1972 by Delacorte Press/A Seymour Lawrence Book. Used by
permission of the publisher;
    for Ernesto Cardenal: Selections from *Gethsemany, Ky.* and *Epigramas,* reprinted by
permission of the author. The translation of "Someone Told Me" by Quincy Troupe and
Sergio Mondragón, reprinted by permission of Mundus Artium;

for Alejo Carpentier: for "Los Fugitivos" from *Narrativa Cubana de la Revolución,* © 1968, Alianza Editorial, S.A., Madrid, by permission of the author;

for José Coronel Urtecho: Selections from *Pol-La D'Ananta Katanta Paranta* © 1970 Editorial Universitaria de la U.N.A.N., Leon, Nicaragua, by permission of the author;

for Julio Cortázar: "Silvia" from *Último round* by Julio Cortázar, © 1969 Siglo XXI Editores, S.A., Mexico, D.F., by permission of the author;

for Salvador Elizondo: "Puente de piedra" from *Nardo o el verano,* by Salvador Elizondo, © 1966 Ediciones Era, S.A., Mexico, D.F., by permission of the author;

for Eduardo Escobar: Selections from *del embrión a la embriaguez,* 1969, by permission of the author;

for Jaime Espinal: "Sobre migranas y fantasmas," by permission of the author;

for Norberto Fuentes: "Capitán Descalzo," "Para la noche," "Orden número 13" from *Condenados de Condado* by Norberto Fuentes, © 1968 Casa de las Américas, La Habana, Cuba;

for Gabriel Garciá Márquez: "Balthazar's Marvelous Afternoon" from *No One Writes To The Colonel and Other Stories* by Gabriel Garciá Márquez. Translated from the Spanish by J. S. Berstein. Copyright © 1968 in the English translation by Harper & Row, Publishers, Inc., reprinted by permission of the publishers;

for Juan Gelman: Selections from *El juego en que andamos,* 1959, and *Gotan,* © Ediciones La Rosa Blindada, 1965, by permission of the author;

for Adriano González León: "El arco en el cielo" from *Hombre que daba sed* by Adriano González León, © 1967 Jorge Alvarez, S.A., Buenos Aires, by permission of the publisher;

for Felisberto Hernandez, "El cocodrilo" from *Las hortensias,* by Felisberto Hernández, © 1967 ARCA Editorial s.r.l., Montevideo;

for Vicente Huidobro: Selections from *Obras Completes de Vicente Huidobro* © Empresa Editorial Zig Zag, S.A. 1963, Inscriptión No. 26915, Santiago de Chile 1964, by permission of the publisher;

for Roberto Juarroz: Selections from *Cuarto poesía vertical* © (1969), Aditor, Buenos Aires, by permission of the author;

for José Lezama Lima: from "Paradiso", a novel by José Lezama Lima; the present selection © 1967 *El Corno emplumado,* Mexico, D.F.;

for Enrique Lihn: "Agua de arroz" from *Agua de arroz* by Enrique Lihn, © 1968 Centro Editor de América Latina, S.A., Buenos Aires, "Gallo," and "Cementerio de Punta Arenas" translated by Miller Williams, by permission of the author. Selections from *La Pieza Oscura,* Editorial Universitaria, S.A. © Enrique Lihn, 1963, by permission of the author. The translations © 1968 by Miller Williams from *Chile: An Anthology of New Writing.* Kent State University Press, by permission of the translator;

for René Marqués: "En la popa hay un cuerpo reclinado" from *Cuentos Puetorriqueños de hoy,* Selection, prologue and notes by René Marqués, Club del Libro de Puerto Rico, © 1959 René Marqués, by permission of the author;

for Luis Palés Matos: Selections from *Poesía 1915–1956.* Copyright 1968. Universidad de Puerto Rico. The translations are from *Nine Latinamerican Poets,* © 1968 by Las Americas Publishing, by permission of the translator, Rachel Benson;

for Daniel Moyano: "Artistas de variedades" from *El monstruo y otros cuentos* by Daniel Moyano, © 1967 Centro Editor de América Latina, S.A., Buenos Aires, by permission of the author;

for Alvaro Mutis: for selections from *De Los Trabajos Perdidos,* © Ediciones ERA, S.A., by permission of the author;

for Pablo Neruda: "Oda Con un Lamento" and "Solo La Muerte" from *Residencias en Tierra II,* "Las Furias y Las Penas" from *Terrera Residencia* and "Alturas de Macchu Picchu, VI" from *Canto General,* Editorial Losada, S.A., copyright by Pablo Neruda, by permission of the author. The translation "Ode with a Lament" by W. S. Merwin from

Selected Translations 1948–1968 by W. S. Merwin, Atheneum Publishers, copyright ©
1959 W. S. Merwin, reprinted by permission of the translator. The translation, "Nothing
But Death" by Robert Bly from *Neruda and Vallejo: Selected Poems* edited by Robert Bly,
Beacon Press, 1971, copyright 1964 and 1968 by The Sixties Press, reprinted with their
permission. The translation "Furies and Sufferings" by Nathaniel Tarn from *Selected
Poems of Pablo Neruda,* © 1970 by Nathaniel Tarn, Jonathan Cape Ltd., by permission
of the translator;
    for Ricardo Ocampo: "El Indio Paulino" from *Narradores Bolivianos* edited by Mariano
Baptista Gumucio, © 1969 Monte Avila Editores, C.A. Caracas;
    for Juan Carlos Onetti: "Un sueño realizado" from *Cuentos completos* by Juan Carlos
Onetti, © 1968 Monte Avila Editores, C.A., Caracas, by permission of Monte Avila
Editores and the author;
    for Carlos Oquendo de Amat: "Madhouse Poem" from *Contemporary Latin American
Poetry,* Dudley Fitts, ed., copyright 1942, 1947 by New Directions Publishing Corporation,
reprinted by permission of New Directions Publishing Corporation;
    for Nicanor Parra: "La Trampa" from *Poems and Antipoems,* translated by W. S.
Merwin, copyright © 1967 by Nicanor Parra, reprinted by permission of New Directions
Publishing Corporation and Lawrence Pollinger, Ltd;
    for Octavio Paz: Selections from Octavio Paz, *Configurations,* copyright © 1971 by
New Directions Publishing Corporation, reprinted by permission of New Directions Publishing Corporation and Lawrence Pollinger, Ltd;
    for Roberto Fernández Retamar: Selections from *Poesía Reunida.* La Habana, Cuba, by
permission of the author;
    for Augusto Roa Bastos: "La tumba viva" from *Madera quemada* by Augusto Roa
Bastos, © 1967 Editorial Universitaria, S. A., Santiago, Chile, by permission of the publisher;
    for Juan Rulfo: "El día del derrumbe" from *Cronicas de Latinoamerica* Prologue and
notes by Ricardo Piglia, © 1968 Editorial Jorge Alvarez, S.A., Buenos Aires, by permission of the author;
    for Jaime Sabines: Selections from *Recuento de Poemas* © 1962, Universidad Na-
cional Autonoma de Mexico, by permission of the author;
    for Sebastián Salazar Bondy: Selections from *Sebastián Salazar Bondy: Obras,* pub-
lished by Francisco Moncloa Editores, S.A., "Olographic Testament" © El Corno emplumado, Mexico, D.F.;
    for Antonio Skármeta: "Una vuelta en el aire" from *Desnudo en el tejado* by Antonio
Skármeta, © 1968, Casa de las Américas, La Habana, Cuba, by permission of the author;
    for César Vallejo: "Agape" from *Neruda and Vallejo: Selected Poems* edited by
Robert Bly, Beacon Press, 1971, copyright 1964 and 1968 by The Sixties Press, reprinted
with their permission. The other selections from *Poemas Humanos: Human Poems,* translated by Clayton Eshleman, copyright © 1968 by Grove Press, Inc., by permission of Grove
Press, Inc. and Jonathan Cape Ltd;
    for Mario Vargas Llosa: "La Literatura es fuego," by permission of the author;
    for Cintio Vitier: Selections from *Testimonios* (1968), UNEAC, La Habana, Cuba,
1968, by permission of the author.

To
Ralph, Wil & Jill

PREFACE

There are times when you stand at the water's edge intending just to put your foot in and suddenly you are swimming in deep water. We never intended an historical survey of these fifty years of Spanish American literature; it happened as a series of meetings, sometimes accidental, in a vast geography.

The stories and poems that follow are, of course, those meetings, 44 writers from 14 countries, a wide range of themes and styles. These works are connected by a unity of language and history in which there are more similarities than differences. But what is most striking is the spirit which animates each work—if *spirit* seems too vague a word, then let us say conviction or energy or even attitude. It races through the stories and poems, a particularity of the Spanish American soul, uniting the literary entities so that they seem to complete each other. This spirit, however, is not ephemeral, for these writers, in digging out their roots have touched what is essential in themselves. In searching for reality they have extended to boundaries where dreams are. And in searching for dreams they have walked with the wretched.

This anthology had many friends, but there are those without whose generous help it could not have been done, now and in this form. The knowledge of the Espinals—Marcia, Jaime and Luis,—Carlos Suarez, Alvaro Medina, Luisa Valenzuela, and Ernesto Mayans directed our attention to many of the present selections: their love of Spanish American literature and belief in the anthology helped develop our own. We are grateful for the gentle and intelligent presence of George-Anne Roberts, who gave endlessly of her literary and linguistic resources. It was our good fortune to have the editorial expertise of William Rose on questions of language and history. We could rely on the friendly interest and fastidious judgment of Norman Thomas di Giovanni, Hardie St. Martin, W. S. Merwin, Electa Arenal and Alastair Reid (whose translations would have appeared but for the early 1971 British mail strike). Natalie Hahn, Daisy Jacobs, Virginia Ridlehoover, Carlo Grossman, Allen Planz, Michael Barrett, Cecilia Espinal and Marta Fernandez were friends who helped in many different ways, and this included everything from translating difficult passages to typing manuscript.

But finally it is the authors themselves we thank, for it is truly their book which we now leave with you.

Hortense Carpentier
and Janet Brof

CONTENTS

Poetry

Doors and Mirrors

INTRODUCTION
Angel Rama

To Readers, Friends and Strangers

The Spain of "bullfights and castanets" invented by nineteenth-century French romantics had a correspondingly distorted reflection lasting well into this century, in a folkloric Spanish America of *gauchos, charros, huasos,* and *llaneros,* all costumed from the same London theatrical wardrobe. The falseness of these images stemmed from their being the progeny of a foreign imagination. They expressed the eager hankerings of Frenchmen, Englishmen and, soon after, of North Americans, who sought refuge from the benefits of their industrial society through the invention of fierce natural creatures.

Legitimate descendants of the *"bon sauvage"* with which Rousseau had already populated our American jungles, these creatures were copied faithfully by Spanish Americans for the pleasure of those who had dreamed them up, and who were, besides, lords and masters beyond the ocean. Nevertheless, like the Indians of Cuzco who created an original school of painting while copying Spanish religious imagery with absent-minded industriousness, Spanish writers occasionally forgot the foreign literary models and faced their own truth, giving us sparkling texts, such as Sarmiento's *Facundo,* or Hernandez's *Martín Fierro,* or Martí's *Nuestra America,* or Rivera's *La voragine.*

Our nature remained as ascribed to us by Hegel, without the possibility of redemption, for we lacked the social synthesis that generates culture. Consequently, the imitation of European models, the steadfastness of folkloric elements, and provincialism—countless scattered regions each with its own customs and petty vanities—seemed unchangeable.

Coherency demands an elaboration of a dynamic system rather than just a simple series of books. Incorporation into western culture and the building of a coherent literature from its urban structure and rationalized tenets was the intellectual program explicitly formulated by the writers of the end of the nineteenth century. Because they thrust us into the modern world, we call these writers "the modernists."

Since then, we have been in the mainstream, sailing in it, although it is only in the last decade that we have sent abroad a body of works stamped with creative autonomy instead of works in which the European's fantasy is returned to him with an appearance of reality. Now the reader finds a reality related to his own, but different. Thus, he is able to experience "otherness" simultaneously with "humanity." We are "others," but of the same species, by God!

When different literatures come abruptly into contact with each other, as they have in the last half century, the degree of misunderstanding almost exceeds the degree of enlightenment. We are speaking of fame, in Rilke's words, the sum of all misunderstandings. Works and writers become little heads for the photomontage of a Parnassus; their profiles—brilliant and timeless—are stamped on the album-museum-anthology in which they are collected. They are dislodged from affiliations, cultural fields and periods in which they flourished. Structuralist thinkers would be pleased to say that they are all joined within "literaturity," a notion passable in this case, since we are dealing with works written over the past fifty years and corresponding to the same literary movement—one might say to the same general stylistic sweep. They all adhere to a world-view in which contemporary man can recognize himself.

The new association through thematic or stylistic networks corresponds with Malraux's belief that museums reorganize criteria in order to unify and categorize disparate works of art. The intemporal, the formal, the thematic measurements are no doubt legitimate, even convincing, with their faintly metaphysical airs. But they do not do justice to an art as notoriously anti-museum as is contemporary Spanish American literature, nor to the multiplicity of roles assumed by its authors who, as

Wright Mills theorized, are still conceived by their people as potential heroes of great deeds and not merely litterateurs. Their words can be likened to burning coals; they hold the fire of the historic and artistic process in which they were forged. At the same time they perform an extraliterary task not expected to such an extent in literature of other countries: the ceaseless constitution of a nation, the nation of Spanish America. Yet such an entity has existed only in the revolutionary proclamations of its heroes from Bolívar to Guevara, and in the intercommunicative efforts of literary works. Abhorring the geographical dismemberment—multiple frontiers—these works wove its single body with an hallucinated fervor. For long historical periods only books kept alive the concept of a single continental nation. But, as in a Borges story, a dream cannot become a reality if the dreamer is unreal, himself a dream. The present systematic formation of a Spanish American literature coincides with the formation of a Spanish American nation.

It was in 1881 that José Martí clearly located the problem: *"From an undefined people, an undefined literature. But as soon as a people begins to coalesce, the elements of its literature approach and condense into a great prophetic work. Let us decry our lack of this great work, not because of that lack but because it is a symbol of our lack of the great country of which it is to be a reflection."* This assertion corroborated Martí's programmatic statement: *"There are no letters—which are expression—until there is an essence demanding to be expressed. Nor will there be a Spanish American literature until there is a Spanish America."*

It is no coincidence that the sudden eruption, a boiling over, of Spanish American literature has occurred in the past decade, the decade of the revolutionary eruption of the continent. The attention the world has paid since 1959 to this forgotten part of the globe brought into prominence a literature which had existed for decades. It is now read with an awareness of its contemporary history.

In 1887 the same José Martí, then living in New York, went to hear Whitman thunder his elegies to Abraham Lincoln. In an explosive article, Martí introduced to the Spanish-speaking world the poet who, he said, was *"the most intrepid, all-embracing, and unencumbered of his time."* In this memorable essay, he reflected: *"Each social state carries its own expression to literature in such a way that its diverse phases tell the history of the people more truthfully than chronicles and journalistic profiles."* So we may say of today's Spanish American literature, as it is found in the pages of this anthology: it is the living history of a people and, to use Verlaine's disdainful phrase, the rest is literature.

In the ninety years since Martí's prophecy, we have witnessed an uninterrupted flow of interior dialogue within which the autonomy and originality of Spanish American literary creation has become consolidated. The external corroboration lies in the abundance of narrators and poets and in the amplitude of their esthetic orientations. Into an anthology of consistent artistic calibre, Hortense Carpentier and Janet Brof have collected almost fifty writers of the last half century. Not one name should be scratched from the list. On the other hand, we might continue to add names of the same quality until we composed another volume of the same dimensions. I am already listing suggestions for that second volume: among prose writers, Manuel Rojas, Carlos Fuentes, Salvador Garmendia, Fernando Alegría, Mario Benedetti, David Viñas, José Donoso, Juan García Ponce, Reynaldo Arenas; among poets, Ramón López Velarde, Enrique Molina, Idea Vilariño, Gonzalo Rojas, Tomás Segovia, Eliseo Diego, Antonio Cisneros, Heberto Padilla, Julia de Burgos, Rafael Cadenas, Noé Jitrik.

This literature has developed through a cumulative process and it is useless for writers to feign unfamiliarity with it, saying that they have nothing to do with their parents, that they hate either the regionalists or the avantgarde or the neobaroque. Underneath irate manifestos and paper parricides—the foam of these tumultuous years—the great waves continued forming the enduring sea. We see that the conquests raised as banners by one generation are absorbed by the following, which handles them as professional tools. It is not a matter of a tradition, but of a process.

But the cumulative process had still more refined internal effects in literature. To it we owe the establishment of a specific literary language, a change which took place in the second decade of this century, after prodigious efforts, partial solutions, and failures. It was the poets who first gave this language articulation, utilizing the contribution of the two preceding modernist generations, at a time when prose writers tarried with the enunciative, logical speech of regionalism. With Ramón López Velarde, César Vallejo and Vicente Huidobro, the specific literary language is achieved. Avoiding fixation at the lexicographic level, they based it on a taut syntax capable both of devouring the most common words and jointly of appropriating surrounding reality. That language ramifies immediately into variations represented by Carlos Pellicer, Pablo Neruda, Jorge Luis Borges, Nicolás Guillén, León de Greiff, Luis Palés Matos, before becoming sire and practically midwife to the novel. For neither Miguel Angel Asturias, nor Alejo Carpentier, nor Arturo Uslar Pietri, nor Agustín Yañez, nor Borges the narrator, would have been possible without this conception of poetic writing in light of which they revised the ideas of character, narrative structure, and invention dominant at the time.

The contacts of principal avantgarde prose writers with poetic experience (several of them have been poets as well as masters of prose) were as basic to the reorientation they brought about in Spanish American fiction as their relations—often direct—with the French surrealists. In Paris in the twenties, the Paris of Breton, Soupault, Aragon, Desnos, lived Miguel Angel Asturias, Ernest Hemingway, Vincente Huidobro, E. E. Cummings, Ezra Pound; César Vallejo, Henry Miller, Alejo Carpentier. They did not all meet each other, but Paris was for all of them a "moveable feast" at which they came into contact with a major shift in the world's culture taking place at that meridian. And in Paris, confronted by an "other-reality," they reencountered themselves. The London of Henry James remained behind; even further behind was Madrid, where the "ultraista" spark paid fleeing attention to Borges' presence.

This so-called "lost generation" is in truth the "recovered generation" of Spanish America, the one which finally disengages itself from the marginality complex which had been suffocating its authors. They now dedicate themselves to a clear task: participating with their own

Spanish American responses in the cultural dialogue of the modern world. All contribute to the labor, regardless of ideology or esthetic position: Alejo Carpentier discovers that the search for the unique reality of magic must take place in Spanish America and not in the surrealist's rumpled deck; Pablo Neruda makes of land, metal and wood a poetic residence, even before his reencounter with another at Macchu Picchu; Borges invents a monstrous city named Buenos Aires, that imitates, in the south, a syncretic Europe; Asturias undertakes the first Spanish American social archetype, *El señor presidente.* And there is yet room for the interstitial figures of that generation: Felisberto Hernández, Julio Garmandia, Enrique Labrador Ruiz, who move toward those whose lives are lived in obscurity and handle them with humor, recreating the spoken language of the streets.

Novels make the most delayed appearance. Not until the decade of the forties do they accumulate, inverting the generic sign of Spanish American creativity: it would seem as if the novelists succeed the poets. But it is a false impression, derived from the fact that there are at last novelists. By this time, we find a new generation on the march, today's intellectual leaders of the continent. And following them, the rapid footsteps of at least two more generations are heard. "They follow, like a storm/youths, children, newcomers," as in Amanda Berenguer's poem.

If one were to baptize that generation on a continental level, one would say its members are "universalists"; and needing to employ a prototype, one would point to two figures, one from the south and another from the north, who share the same artistic line, the same mastery. They are Julio Cortázar and Octavio Paz, the first more a prose writer, the second more a poet, both multifaceted, men of wide culture, rooted at the same time in a modernity that begins by not wanting to be cultural; a modernity ordained by Rimbaud, defined by the endless and tragic anguish of the search for forms—their discovery and immolation—the speculative turning inward in order to see and devour oneself. This can be observed in a poem like *Blanco* or in a novel like *Rayuela.* It is a conception of literature as a cognitive adventure in which each discovery is a clue.

One might say that rather than rupturing with their heritage, Paz and Cortázar made a conscious acceptance while departing from it. The extension of their activities throughout the world, which led, especially for Paz, to the absorption of oriental thought and the assumption of an ongoing avantgarde spirit (a sign of perennial artistic youth) are factors placing Paz and Cortázar as leaders of the universalist generation and masters of the literature of the continent.

In this vein they are accompanied by José Lezama Lima, to whom, not surprisingly, Cortázar had paid homage, perceiving the iconoclastic and universal spirit pervading Lezama Lima's chaotic, book-filled jungle.

But the predominant role of this generation lay in poetic and at times critical realignment with Spanish American reality, what we might call a getting-under-the-skin of a continental culture in order to explain it intimately. That role implies a drastic questioning of social values, which has enabled us to define these writers as members of a critical, even hypercritical generation. It would suffice to evoke, after the early prose of Juan Carlos Onetti, that of José Revueltas, Ernesto Sábato, Carlos Fuentes, Mario Monteforte Toledo or Carlos Martinez Moreno, all of whom coincided in demystifying their society.

The inquiry can also be detected, although on a level of greater complexity—in the works of a group of profound writers who, playing an observer's role, reconnected forgotten zones of culture to the universalism of the hour: Juan Rulfo, José María Arguedas, Augusto Roa Bastos, had to call upon diverse poetic modes to realize this artistic project which actually represented acts of transculturation.

In all likelihood this unearthing of forgotten cultural roots explains to what extensive influence of surrealism in Spanish America may be attributed. South America, it can be said, is and has been, since the first Spaniard set foot on it, a surrealistic continent. Surely, the surrealist technique of literary montage by the conjunction of disparate elements— what a South American named Lautreamont described as the fortuitous encounter of an umbrella and a sewing machine on a dissecting table—is a valid description of the continent. Since 1492, it has lived as an assemblage of different cultures, antithetic cultures corresponding to widely varied levels of development and historical periods. Furthermore, it has been shaken for the past fifty years by a violent urbanization that compresses millions of people from ancient rural cultures into houses, streets, and life styles adapted from the latest fashionable blueprints of industrial societies. Even before Breton employed the term, this was surrealism to the restless eyes of Nerval and Lautreamont; and in this way it is relived by Spanish America—as the law of violent contrast and as a yearning to recapture the world of magic. That is how it is portrayed in literature, if one draws an arc from *El señor presidente* by Asturias to *Cien años de soledad* by García Márquez, and from *Las cosas y el delirio* by Enrique Molina to *Delante de la luz cantan los pájaros* by Montes de Oca, including the work of entire groups, such as "La Mandragora" of Chile, or the firebrands of "El Techo de la Ballena" of Venezuela. But Spanish American writers of the latest generations seldom handle those explosives to invent phosphorescent dances in the jungles of America, but rather to promote the progress of humanity, putting them at the service of a rational delving into knowledge, within a complex but severe artistic structure.

In spite of the euphoric proposals made in the '20's in favor of a "magic realism," and in spite of its development into "literature of fantasy" of the '40's centering around the magazine *Sur* of Buenos Aires, the following generation preferred a cautious shift to realism. They controlled the irrational impulses so dazzling in the previous period, defined by Lukacs as the climax of the assault on reason. This shift was prefigured in the stories of Cortázar (as compared to the intellectual schemes of Borges, the older master), in which the magic world dwells within daily life, and that was "miracle enough." As always, the first to know it were the poets of the '40's. Witness the intimist formulations cultivated by Cintio Vitier, Eliseo Diego, Juan Cunha, César Fernandez Moreno; the dramatic and individualist alienation from surrealism by Nicanor Parra, Idea Vilariño, Gonzalo Rojas, Enrique Lihn; the critical grasping of a social world, of an inherent mass appeal, by Sebastián Salazar Bondy, Mario Benedetti, Ernesto Cardenal, Roberto Fernandez Retamar, Juan

Gelman, Noé Jitrik, Milton Schinca; the handling of human passions by Alberto Girri or Jorge Gaitán Durán. Colloquialism, prosaism, straightforward street talk, baroque twists, mistrust of images, flowing rhythms of speech: is poetry surviving? Fernández Retamar, who writes poetry of today, a poetry of constant risk, distilled from age-old poetic traditions, answered this eternal question: "Everything to be possible, that's what poetry is."

Next to the poets came the prose writers, marked by the experiences of a decade that saw the successive fall of Spanish American dictators: Peron, Rojas Pinilla, Perez Jimenez, Batista. These writers will be seen as a generation serious from the start. Possessing a creative liberty they would attribute perhaps to their elders, they reinvestigate riverbeds of the old social realism.

We could select six representative figures to cover the continent: Carlos Fuentes (Mexico), Gabriel García Márquez (Colombia), Salvador Garmendia (Venezuela), Mario Vargas Llosa (Peru), José Donoso (Chile), and David Viñas (Argentina). They are the new literature of Spanish America. Their individual evolutions, occasionally unexpected and full of sudden artistic detours (Fuentes, García Márquez) may have estranged them from their first attempts. Yet at the core of their works is the will to know the world, unmask it and remake it.

For a time it was thought that in accord with the pendular rhythm of Spanish American culture, a new regionalism would respond to the universalism of the '40's, although on a higher artistic level. Something of the sort came about with the award of the Rómulo Gallegos Prize to Mario Vargas Llosa in 1967. It was not only a distinction given to an exceptional novel, *La casa verde,* but it proposed that Vargas Llosa carry on the tradition of the regionalist master Gallegos.

Nevertheless, even more significant than the thematic terrain or the realist attitude, was the experimental trend adopted by a majority of these writers who set themselves up as heirs to Cortázar and Paz, whose leadership they recognized. Cortázar's idea on the need to realize the revolution within literature was taken up throughout the continent. An alternative or at least an enrichment of the previous position that demanded logically and deliberately useful thematic support of social revolution, this idea appears, then, as one of the new, unexpected modes. This new approach, partly a response to the rising demands of present-day readers, has raised literary creation to a more complex structural level, at the same time opening a new field of tensions in the social body of Spanish America, already torn by ideological propositions and disparity of cultural development.

The experimentalist framework becomes autonomous in the scrupulous writing of Elizondo, seems to dissolve in the programmatic narrative of González León, and strikes a median note, immersed in subject matter, in the stories of Antonio Skármeta, the most recent promise of Spanish American short story writers. The same general framework governs the poetry of the Colombian Alvaro Mutis; the Argentine Roberto Juarroz, and the Mexican Jaime Sabines. All these experiments of a structural nature reveal the ever more complex propositions confronted by writers of the continent.

The date of an anthology, like that of a prologue, abruptly cuts across the flowing river of literature. Instead of a cinematographic sequence, we are presented with a still photograph. This is the case with two of the younger writers: Javier Heraud, who bears a mythic halo since his tragic death in the Peruvian guerrilla struggle, and the Cuban, Norberto Fuentes, whose whole production is related to the fierce battle waged by the regular army against the counter-revolutionary bandits in the mountains of the island. In one way or another, revolution has obsessed, hallucinated and shaped them. If we reread the poems Heraud wrote before entering guerrilla life, we find a song to life in simple and tense verses, which convey a naked naming of the world. Reading Norberto Fuentes' *Condenados de condado,* we find a concentrated vision, devoured by action itself; men and objects in a contest which seems, as in his teacher Babel, more cosmogonic than social. The intensity of the writing and the terrible violence of the images sets the struggle as mythic combat. Both still-shots offer the before and after of the experience of action, a preview of the incessant revolutionary cataclysm that rocks Spanish America and sets its literature aflame.

Universidad de Montevideo, 1971

TRANSLATED BY MARCIAL RODRIGUEZ
AND ELECTA ARENAL DE RODRIGUEZ

DE *Altazor de Canto I*

Altazor morirás Se secará tu voz y serás invisible
La Tierra seguirá girando sobre su órbita precisa
Temerosa de un traspié como el equilibrista sobre el alambre que ata las
                    miradas del pavor
En vano buscas ojo enloquecido
No hay puerta de salida y el viento desplaza los planetas
Piensas que no importa caer eternamente si se logra escapar
¿No ves que vas cayendo ya?
Limpia tu cabeza de prejuicio y moral
Y si queriendo alzarte nada has alcanzado
Déjate caer sin parar tu caída sin miedo al fondo de la sombra
Sin miedo al enigma de ti mismo
Acaso encuentres una luz sin noche
Perdida en las grietas de los precipicios

Cae
        Cae eternamente
Cae al fondo del infinito
Cae al fondo del tiempo
Cae al fondo de ti mismo
Cae lo más bajo que se pueda caer
Cae sin vértigo
A través de todos los espacios y todas las edades

Vicente Huidobro

FROM *Altazor, Fragment of Canto I*

Altazor you will die
   Your voice will dry up & you will become invisible
The earth will continue to turn in its precise orbit
In terror of tumbling like an acrobat out on a wire
       its rope ends tied to the wide eyes of fear
You will hunt in vain for some maddened eye
But there's no way out & the wind displaces the planets
You think it doesn't matter falling forever
      if you somehow escape in the end
Don't you see that you're falling already?
   It's time you were rid of morals & prejudice:
If you try to rise & you stumble towards nothing
Let yourself fall without stopping
      without fear to the deep end of darkness
To the baffled cry of your Self
Maybe you'll find a sun that can't set
Lost in the fissures of cliffs

Fall
   Fall forever
Fall to the depths of the infinite
Fall to the depths of time
Fall to the depths of your Self
Fall as low as you can
Fall without dizziness
   Into all spaces & ages

A través de todas las almas de todos los anhelos y todos los naufragios
Cae y quema al pasar los astros y los mares
Quema los ojos que te miran y los corazones que te aguardan
Quema el viento con tu voz
El viento que se enreda en tu voz
Y la noche que tiene frío en su gruta de huesos

Cae en infancia
Cae en vejez
Cae en lágrimas
Cae en risas
Cae en música sobre el universo
Cae de tu cabeza a tus pies
Cae de tus pies a tu cabeza
Cae del mar a la fuente
Cae al último abismo de silencio
Como el barco que se hunde apagando sus luces

Todo se acabó
El mar antropófago golpea la puerta de las rocas despiadadas
Los perros ladran a las horas que se mueren
Y el cielo escucha el paso de las estrellas que se alejan

Into each soul each longing for land each shipwreck
Fall
    Scald the stars & the seas as you pass
Scald the eyes that watch you the hearts that await you
Scald the wind with your voice
    The wind that's trapped in your voice
And the night growing cold in its cave filled with bones

Fall into childhood
Fall into age
Fall into tears
Fall into laughter
Fall into music all over the universe
Fall from your head to your feet
Fall from your feet to your head
Fall from the sea to its source
Fall to the final abyss of silence
Like a sinking ship drowning its lights

Then it's all over
The man-eating sea beats the doors of those merciless cliffs
Dogs bark at the death of our hours
And the sky hears the footsteps of stars trailing off

TRANSLATED BY JEROME ROTHENBERG

Tenemos un Cataclismo Adentro

Los años suben como ramas a la punta
Suben al cielo y las montañas cruzan las manos a la muerte
Entre campanadas de especie desconocida
Los entierros siguen a ciertos pájaros
En la noche de las flores sonámbulas
Y los brillos hipnóticos llenos de lágrimas

Por qué voy tras el viento de los sueños
Que agita mis cabellos rumorosos encima de la noche
Por las rutas solitarias como tristes palabras
No te pude encontrar
Ni siguiendo los rastros de una flor
Y sin embargo estás en algún sitio
Entre tu andar y la muerte
Con una alegría planetaria a flor de ojo

Nada recuerdo pero el sentimiento vive
Llevo en la carne los tiempos infantiles
Y los antes de los antes con sus ruidos confusos
Las épocas de los grandes principios
Y de las formaciones en fantasmagorías imprevisibles
Cuando el mar apenas aprendía a hablar
Y los árboles no sabían lo que iban a ser
Y la vida se estrellaba entre las rocas

Despiértame y grítame que estoy viviendo en hoy
Sé muy bien que si hubiera comido ciertas hierbas
Sería paloma mensajera
Y podría encontrarte a la sombra de esa flor que es la tarde
Pero el murmullo nada indica
Los barcos han partido hacia sus pájaros
Ya no es tiempo

There Is a Cataclysm Inside Us

The years burgeon at their tips like branches
They burgeon toward the sky and the mountains fold their hands in
                                    death
Between the sounding of uncharted bells
Funerals trail certain birds
In this night of sleepwalking flowers
                and the hypnotic spotlights full of tears

Why do I follow the wind through my dreams
As it stirs my murmuring hair on the roof of this night
Down deserted roads like sad words
I never could find you
Not even tracing the print of a flower
And yet I know you are somewhere
                between your footsteps and death
With the planetary joy of a flower emerging from each eye

I remember nothing but the feeling still lives
I bear my earliest days in my flesh
Day before the befores with their turbulent noises
The epochs of mighty beginnings
And formations into blind phantasmagorias
When the sea scarcely knew how to speak
And the trees couldn't tell what they would become
And life smashed itself on the rocks

Awaken me shout at me tell me I live in the present
I know damn well that if I'd eaten certain herbs
                I'd be a carrier pigeon
And I'd be able to find you in the shadow of that flower called evening
But the whispers don't tell me a thing
The ships have sailed off toward their birds
Time is all gone

Esto es lo único seguro entre los huracanes dados vuelta
Ya no es tiempo
La tarde se entierra seguida de sus selvas

Algo brilla en el aire
Sobre ese trozo de la tierra donde tú estás durmiendo
En donde las raíces ponen flores y otoños desgarradores
La vida se estrella en la cima de los montes
O no se estrella Para la noche es lo mismo

Todo es lo mismo para la noche
Y a veces para mí también
Ah ese cielo sereno con toda su eternidad
Y todo lo que se forma en sus entrañas
Y todo lo que palpita antes del amanecer
Ah la sed de infinito en relación a mi pecho
Desatad el árbol que tiene ansias de espacio
Recoged las velas de los astros cansados

Y tú anuncia la vida con tus ojos
Mira que el doble sueño no quiere terminar
Mira que el fantasma pudiera deshacerse
Y yo aún tengo palabras retenidas
Tengo cosas dolientes y cosas que susurran
Mira que las estrellas continuadas
Son como la voz que te canta y quiere ser interminable

Pero otros suben otros bajan
Ah cielo lleno de días y de noches
Amigos en dónde estáis amigos
Saliendo de palomas viene la muerte

This is the only sure thing in these cycles of hurricanes
Time is all gone
The evening buries itself alongside its forests

Something glows in the air
In that parcel of earth where you sleep
Where the roots hatch flowers and severing autumns
Life smashes itself on the summits of mountains
   or doesn't smash itself
     But the night doesn't care

The night doesn't care about anything
And sometimes I don't care either
Ah that patient sky with all its eternity
And all that takes shape in its belly
And that throbs before daybreak
Ah the thirst for the infinite pressing my chest
Untie this tree that longs after space
Shorten the sails on those played-out stars

Proclaim life with your eyes
See how the double dream doesn't want to be over
How the phantoms could really be sloughed
And I still keep words in my throat
I keep painful things and things full of whispers
See how the stars that endure
     are like the voice that sings you
And wants to keep living forever

But others burgeon others decay
Ah sky full of days and of nights
Friends where are you friends
Scattering pigeons
    Here comes death

TRANSLATED BY JEROME ROTHENBERG

La Poesía Es un Atentado Celeste

Yo estoy ausente pero en el fondo de esta ausencia
Hay la espera de mí mismo
Y esta espera es otro modo de presencia
La espera de mi retorno
Yo estoy en otros objetos
Ando en viaje dando un poco de mi vida
A ciertos árboles y a ciertas piedras
Que me han esperado muchos años

Se cansaron de esperarme y se sentaron

Yo no estoy y estoy
Estoy ausente y estoy presente en estado de espera
Ellos querrían mi lenguaje para expresarse
Y yo querría el de ellos para expresarlos
He aquí el equívoco el atroz equívoco

Angustioso lamentable
Me voy adentrando en estas plantas
Voy dejando mis ropas
Se me van cayendo las carnes
Y mi esqueleto se va revistiendo de cortezas

Me estoy haciendo árbol Cuántas veces me he ido convirtiendo en otras
                    cosas . . .
Es doloroso y lleno de ternura

Podría dar un grito pero se espantaría la transubstanciación
Hay que guardar silencio Esperar en silencio

Poetry Is a Heavenly Crime

I am absent but deep in this absence
There is the waiting for myself
And this waiting is another form of presence
The waiting for my return
I am in other objects
I am away travelling giving a little of my life
To some trees and some stones
That have been waiting for me many years

They got tired of waiting for me and sat down

I'm not here and I'm here
I'm absent and I'm present in a state of waiting
They wanted my language so they could express themselves
And I wanted theirs to express them
This is the ambiguity, the horrible ambiguity

Tormented wretched
I'm moving inward on these soles
I'm leaving my clothes behind
My flesh is falling away on all sides
And my skeleton's putting on bark

I'm turning into a tree How often I've turned into other things . . .
It's painful and full of tenderness

I could cry out but it would scare away the transubstantiation
Must keep silence Wait in silence

TRANSLATED BY W. S. MERWIN

Monumento al Mar

Paz sobre la constelación cantante de las aguas
Entrechocadas como los hombros de la multitud
Paz en el mar a las olas de buena voluntad
Paz sobre la lápida de los naufragios
Paz sobre los tambores del orgullo y las pupilas tenebrosas
Y si yo soy el traductor de las olas
Paz también sobre mí

He aquí el molde lleno de trizaduras del destino
El molde de la venganza
Con sus frases iracundas despegándose de los labios
He aquí el molde lleno de gracia
Cuando eres dulce y estás allí hipnotizado por las estrellas
He aquí la muerte inagotable desde el principio del mundo
Porque un día nadie se paseará por el tiempo
Nadie a lo largo del tiempo empedrado de planetas difuntos

Este es el mar
El mar con sus olas propias
Con sus propios sentidos
El mar tratando de romper sus cadenas
Queriendo imitar la eternidad
Queriendo ser pulmón o neblina de pájaros en pena
O el jardín de los astros que pesan en el cielo
Sobre las tinieblas que arrastramos
O que acaso nos arrastran
Cuando vuelan de repente todas las palomas de la luna
Y se hace más obscuro que las encrucijadas de la muerte

El mar entra en la carroza de la noche
Y se aleja hacia el misterio de sus parajes profundos
Se oye apenas el ruido de las ruedas
Y el ala de los astros que penan en el cielo

Monument to the Sea

Peace over the singing constellation of the waters
Jostled like shoulders in the crowd
Peace on the sea to waves of goodwill
Peace over the shipwreck's slab of stone
Peace on tambours of pride and tenebrous eyes
And if I am translator of the waves
Peace also over me.

And here the die full of destiny's fragments
The die of vengeance
With its furious words unsealing lips
And here the die full of grace
When you are sweet and hypnotized there by the stars
And here death unending since the world's beginning
Because one day no one will walk through time
No one through time paved with extinguished planets.

This is the sea
The sea with its own waves
With its own senses
The sea trying to break its chains
Wanting to imitate eternity
Wanting to be lung or mist for birds in grief
Or garden of stars hanging heavy in the sky
Over the gloom we drag along
Or that perhaps drags us
When suddenly all the doves of the moon fly
And it is darker than the crossroads of death

The sea enters the coach of night
And recedes toward the mystery of deepest regions
The rumble of its wheels barely heard
The wing of stars in the heavens grieving

Este es el mar
Saludando allá lejos la eternidad
Saludando a los astros olvidados
Y a las estrellas conocidas

Este es el mar que se despierta como el llanto de un niño
El mar abriendo los ojos y buscando el sol con sus pequeñas manos
tremblorosas

El mar empujando las olas
Sus olas que barajan los destinos

Levántate y saluda el amor de los hombres

Escucha nuestras risas y también nuestro llanto
Escucha los pasos de millones de esclavos
Escucha la protesta interminable
De esa angustia que se llama hombre
Escucha el dolor milenario de los pechos de carne
Y la esperanza que renace de sus propias cenizas cada día

También nosotros te escuchamos
Rumiando tantos astros atrapados en tus redes
Rumiando eternamente los siglos naufragados
También nosotros te escuchamos
Cuando te revuelcas en tu lecho de dolor
Cuando tus gladiadores se baten entre sí

Cuando tu cólera hace estallar los meridianos
O bien cuando te agitas como un gran mercado en fiesta
O bien cuando maldices a los hombres
O te haces el dormido
Tembloroso en tu gran telaraña esperando la presa

Lloras sin saber por qué lloras
Y nosotros lloramos creyendo saber por qué lloramos
Sufres sufres como sufren los hombres
Que oiga rechinar tus dientes en la noche
Y te revuelques en tu lecho

This is the sea
Greeting a far-off eternity
Greeting forgotten stars
Familiar stars

This is the sea awakening like a child's cry
The sea opening its eyes and seeking the sun
            with its small trembling hands
The sea pushing the waves
The waves shuffling destinies

Rise and greet the love of men

Listen to our laughter listen to our cry
Listen to the footsteps of millions of slaves
Listen to the ceaseless protest
Of that anguish named man
Listen to the ancient ache of flesh bone and blood
And to the hope each day reborn in its own ashes

We also listen to you
Ruminating on the many stars trapped in your nets
Ruminating forever on shipwrecked centuries
We also listen to you
When you toss in your bed of suffering
When your gladiators fight among themselves

When your fury explodes meridians
Even when you stir like the great market at carnival
Even when you curse mankind
Or fake sleep
Trembling in your giant web awaiting the prey

You cry not knowing why you cry
We cry believing we know why we cry
You suffer suffer as men suffer
May your teeth grind in the night
And you toss in your bed

Que el insomnio no te deje calmar tus sufrimientos
Que los niños apedreen tus ventanas
Que te arranquen el pelo
Tose tose revienta en sangre tus pulmones
Que tus resortes enmohezcan
Y te veas pisoteado como césped de tumba

Pero soy vagabundo y tengo miedo que me oigas
Tengo miedo de tus venganzas
Olvida mis maldiciones y cantemos juntos esta noche
Hazte hombre te digo como yo a veces me hago mar
Olvida los presagios funestos
Olvida la explosión de mis praderas
Yo te tiendo las manos como flores
Hagamos las paces te digo
Tú eres el más poderoso
Que yo estreche tus manos en las mías
Y sea la paz entre nosotros

Junto a mi corazón te siento
Cuando oigo el gemir de tus violines
Cuando estás ahí tendido como el llanto de un niño
Cuando estás pensativo frente al cielo
Cuando estás dolorido en tus almohadas
Cuando te siento llorar detrás de mi ventana
Cuando lloramos sin razón como tú lloras

He aquí el mar
El mar donde viene a estrellarse el olor de las ciudades
Con su regazo lleno de barcas y peces y otras cosas alegres
Esas barcas que pescan a la orilla del cielo
Esos peces que escuchan cada rayo de luz
Esas algas con sueños seculares
Y esa ola que canta mejor que las otras

May insomnia keep you from quieting your pain
May the children stone your windows
May they pull your hair
Cough cough burst your lungs in blood
May your coils rot
And may you see yourself trampled as grass in graveyards

But I am a vagabond I fear you'll hear me
I fear your vengeance
Forget my curses tonight let us sing together
I say become a man as I sometimes become the sea
Forget the deadly prophecies
Forget the explosion of my prairies
I offer to you my hands like flowers
Let's make peace I tell you
You are the most powerful
Let me take your hands in mine
And may there be peace between us

Near my heart I feel you
When I hear your violins sighing
When you lie there like the cry of a child
When you are thoughtful facing the sky
When you are aching on your pillow
When I feel you crying behind my window
When we are crying without reason as you cry

And here the sea
The sea where the odor of cities comes crashing in
Its lap full of boats and fishes and other happy things
Those boats fishing at the edge of the sky
Those fishes listening to each ray of light
Those sea weeds of secular dreams
And that wave singing better than the others

He aquí el mar
El mar que se estira y se aferra a sus orillas
El mar que envuelve las estrellas en sus olas
El mar con su piel martirizada
Y los sobresaltos de sus venas
Con sus días de paz y sus noches de histeria

Y al otro lado qué hay al otro lado
Qué escondes mar al otro lado
El comienzo de la vida largo como una serpiente
O el comienzo de la muerte más honda que tú mismo
Y más alta que todos los montes
Qué hay al otro lado
La milenaria voluntad de hacer una forma y un ritmo
O el torbellino eterno de pétalos tronchados

He ahí el mar
El mar abierto de par en par
He ahí el mar quebrado de repente
Para que el ojo vea el comienzo del mundo
He ahí el mar
De una ola a la otra hay el tiempo de la vida
De sus olas a mis ojos hay la distancia de la muerte

And here the sea
The sea which stretches and grasps its shores
The sea embraces the stars in its waves
The sea with its martyred skin
And the shock of its veins
With its days of peace and nights of hysteria

And on the other side what is on the other side
What are you hiding sea on the side
The start of life long as a serpent
Or the start of death deeper than yourself
Higher than all the mountains
What is on the other side
The ancient will to create a form and a rhythm
Or the eternal whirlwind of shattered petals

And there the sea
The sea open wide wide
There the sea suddenly broken open
So the eye can see the world beginning
And there the sea
Between one wave and the next the span of life
Between those waves and my eyes the distance of death

TRANSLATED BY ELECTA ARENAL

Felisberto Hernández

The Crocodile

On one humid and hot autumn evening, I went to a city which I scarcely knew; the dim light in the streets was diffused by the dampness and some leaves on the trees. I entered a café which was near a church, sat down at a table in the rear, and thought about my life. I knew how to isolate the hours of happiness and lock myself in them; first, I abducted with my eyes any stray thing from the street or from the inside of houses, and then I would take it to my lonely retreat. I enjoyed examining it so much that if people had known this about me, they would have hated me. Perhaps I hadn't much time left for happiness. Before, I had passed through those cities giving piano concerts; the hours of happiness had been few, for I lived the anguish of organizing people willing to approve putting on a concert; I had to coordinate them, get their cooperation, and try to find someone who might be helpful. That was almost always like struggling with slow and inattentive drunkards: when I managed to get hold of one, the other would slip away. I also had to study and write articles for the daily papers.

It had been some time since I had had that preoccupation: I managed to get a job with a women's hosiery firm. I thought that stockings were more of a necessity than concerts and it would be easier to sell them. A friend of mine told the manager that I had a lot of female contacts because I was a concert pianist and had traveled through many cities and could, therefore, make use of the prestige of the concerts to sell stockings.

The manager made a sour face; but he accepted, not only because of my friend's influence, but because I had won second prize for the advertising slogan for those stockings. Their brand name was "Illusion." My slogan had been, "Today, who doesn't cherish an Illusion?" Selling stockings also proved difficult for me, and from one moment to the next, I expected they would call me from the home office and take away my meal ticket. In the beginning, I worked hard. (The sale of stockings had nothing to do with my concerts: I only had to do business with merchants.) When I met old friends, I would tell them that representing a great commercial house permitted me to travel independently and there was no obligation on their part to patronize concerts when they were not convenient. My concerts had never been convenient. In this very city I had been given some unusual excuses: the president of the club, in a bad mood because I had made him get up from the gambling table, told me that a person with many relatives had died and that half the city was in mourning. Now I was telling them: I shall be here for a few days to see if the demand for a concert comes about naturally; but the fact that a concert artist was selling stockings made a bad impression on them. As for selling hosiery, every morning I worked up courage and every night I lost it; it was like dressing and undressing. It was an effort to constantly renew a certain brute strength necessary to keep facing merchants who were always harried. By now I had become resigned to waiting for them to fire me and I tried to enjoy the meal ticket while it lasted.

Suddenly, I realized that a blind man with a harp had entered the café; I had seen him in the afternoon. I decided to leave before losing the will to enjoy life; but as I passed near him, I looked at him again in his hat with the badly crushed brim, his eyes rolling toward the ceiling as he made an effort to play. Some strings on the harp were added on, and the light-colored wood of the instrument and the entire man were covered with a grime that I had never seen. I thought about myself and felt depressed.

When I turned on the light of my hotel room, I saw the bed I was sleeping those days. It was pulled down, and its nickel-plated frame made me think of a foolish young girl who gave herself to anyone. After lying down, I turned out the light but I couldn't sleep. I turned it on again and the bulb stared out from under the shade like an eyeball under a dark lid. I quickly turned it out and tried to think of the hosiery business, but for a moment I continued to see the lampshade in the darkness. It had changed to a light color; then, its form, as if it were the ghost of the shade, moved off and became lost in the darkness. All this happened in the time it would take a blotter to soak up spilled ink.

On the following morning, after getting dressed and working up courage, I went to see if the night train had brought me any bad news. I had neither a letter nor a telegram. I decided to make business rounds on one of the main streets. At the end of that street was a store. As I entered, I found myself in a room filled to the ceiling with cloth and trinkets. There was only a nude mannikin, partly covered with red cloth which, instead of a head, had a black pear-shaped cushion. I clapped my hands and the cloth immediately swallowed up the sound. From behind the mannikin, a girl of about ten years appeared, who said to me in an ugly tone, "What do you want?"

"Is the proprietor in?"

"There is no proprietor. My mama is the one who runs it."

"Is she in?"

"She went to see Doña Vicenta and she'll be right back."

A boy around three years old appeared. He grabbed hold of his sister's skirt and they stood in line for a moment, the mannikin, the girl and the boy. I said, "I'll wait."

The girl didn't answer. I sat down on a box and began to play with her little brother. I remembered I had a chocolate candy which I had bought in the movie theater, and I took it out of my pocket. I quickly offered it to the little kid and he took it from me. Then I put my hands up to my face and pretended to sob. I had my eyes covered but I opened the cup of my hands just a crack and looked at the boy. He observed me without moving, and I cried louder and louder. Finally, he decided to put the chocolate on my knee. I laughed and gave it back to him, but at the same time I noticed my face was wet.

I left that place before the proprietress could return. As I passed by a jewelry store, I looked into a mirror and my eyes were dry. I sat in the café after lunch, but I saw the blind man with the harp roll his eyes upward and I left immediately. I went to a lonely plaza in a deserted neighborhood and sat down on a bench opposite a vine-covered wall. There I thought about the morning's tears, intrigued by the fact that they had come from me. I wanted to be alone, as if I were hiding to play with a toy which, unintentionally, I had made work a few hours ago. I was a little ashamed of myself for beginning to cry for no reason, even if it were a joke, as it had been in the morning. I wrinkled my nose and squinted rather timidly to see if the tears would come; but then I thought I shouldn't expect to squeeze out tears as if I were wringing out a rag; I would have to become more sincere. I put my hands to my face. There was something serious about that pose; unexpectedly I was moved; I felt a certain self-pity and the tears began to flow.

I had been crying for a while when I saw that a pair of women's legs in glossy "Illusion" stockings moving down the wall. I immediately noticed a green skirt which blended into the vines. I had not heard the ladder touch ground. The woman was on the last step and I quickly dried my tears; but I lowered my head again as if I were lost in thought. The woman approached me slowly and sat down at my side. She had come down with her back turned to me and I didn't know what her face was like.

Finally, she said to me, "What's wrong? You can trust me . . ."

A few moments passed. I frowned to hide my tears and stall for time. I had never made that facial expression before and my eyebrows were trembling. I made a gesture with my hand as if I were about to speak but nothing occurred to me that I could say to her. She took the initiative again.

"Talk, just talk! I've had children and I know what sorrow is."

I had already imagined what that woman's face and that green skirt

were like, but when she spoke of children and sorrow, I began to imagine someone else. At the same time, I said, "I need to think a little
longer."

She answered, "In such matters, the more one thinks, the worse it
gets."

Suddenly, I felt a wet rag fall near me. It turned out to be a large
damp banana leaf. After a little while, she questioned again, "Tell me
the truth, what is she like?"

At first I thought it was funny. Then I remembered an old sweetheart. When I didn't want to accompany her in a walk along the banks
of a stream where she had walked with her father when he was alive,
that sweetheart of mine would cry silently. Then I would comply, although I was bored walking over the same path again and again. Thinking of that, it occurred to me to tell the woman who was now at my
side, "She was a woman who cried often."

This woman put her large and reddish hands on her green skirt and
laughed as she said, "You all always believe in women's tears."

I thought about my own. I felt a little disconcerted and got up
from the bench saying to her, "I think you're wrong, but thanks for the
consolation anyway."

I went off without looking at her.

Rather late in the morning on the following day, I went into one of
the most important stores. The owner unfolded my stockings on the
counter and stroked them with his square fingers for quite a while. It
seemed he wasn't listening to me. His sideburns were as gray as if he
had left shaving soap on them. In those moments, several women entered; he, before walking away, gestured with one of those fingers that
had stroked the stockings that he wouldn't buy from me. I remained
calm, intending to be persistent; perhaps later I could talk to him
when there weren't any customers; then I would tell him about a powder
which, dissolved in water, would tint his sideburns. The customers were
not leaving and I was unusually impatient; I would have liked to leave
that store, that city and that life. I thought about my home town and
many other things. Suddenly, when I was already calmed down, I

had an idea: "What would happen if I began to cry, here, in front of all of these people?" That seemed very violent to me; but for some time now I had wanted to test the world with some unusual act; besides, I wanted to prove to myself that I was capable of violent emotions. Before I could change my mind, I sat down on a little stool next to the counter and, surrounded by people, I put my hands to my face and began to sob noisily. Almost simultaneously a woman shouted, "A man is crying!" I heard spurts and pieces of conversations: "Baby, don't go too close . . ." "He must have received some bad news . . ." "The train just arrived and there's been no time for mail delivery . . ." "He must have heard by telegram . . ." Through my fingers I saw a fat woman who was saying, "It's hard to believe the state the world is in. If my children wouldn't see me, I'd cry too!" At first, I was desperate because the tears wouldn't flow; I even thought they would take it as a hoax and arrest me. The anguish and the tremendous effort that I made choked me up and the first tears became possible. I felt a heavy hand rest upon my shoulder and when I heard the voice of the owner, I recognized the fingers which had stroked my stockings. He was saying, "But, friend, a man must have more courage . . ."

I sprang up; I took my two hands from my face and the third one that was on my shoulder, and I said, with my face still wet, "But everything is all right! And I am very courageous. It's just that sometimes this comes over me; it's like a memory . . ."

In spite of their anticipation and the silence they observed for my words, I heard a woman say, "Ah! He is crying because of a memory . . ."

Then the owner announced, "Ladies, it's all over."

I was smiling and wiping my face. The group of people stirred and a little woman with mad eyes appeared, who said to me, "I know you. I think I saw you somewhere else and you were upset." I thought that she might have seen me at a concert, leaving in disgust before the end of the program; but I kept my mouth shut.

All the women burst into conversation and some of them began to leave. The one who recognized me remained. She came closer to me and said, "Now I know that you sell stockings. Once I and some of my friends . . ."

The owner interrupted, "Don't concern yourself, Madam," (and turning to me) "Come back this afternoon."

"I'm leaving after lunch. Do you want two dozen?"

"No, half a dozen . . ."

"The company doesn't sell less than one . . ."

I took out the sales book and began to fill the order blank, writing on the window of a door, staying away from the owner. I was surrounded by women talking loudly. I was afraid the owner would change his mind. He finally signed the order, and I left with the others.

Soon it was known that "that thing" came over me which was like a memory at first. I cried in other stores and sold more stockings than usual. When I had cried in several cities, my sales became as large as those of any other salesman.

Once they called me from the home office—I had cried all over the northern part of that area—I was waiting to talk with the boss, and I heard another salesman from the other room say, "I do all that I can, but I'm not going to cry so that they'll buy!"

The sickly voice of the boss answered him, "You must do anything, and cry for them too . . ."

The salesman interrupted, "But I can't work up tears."

And after a silence, the boss, "What? Who told you that?"

"Yes! There is one who cries like a faucet . . ."

The sickly voice began a forced laugh and coughed intermittently. Then I heard mumbling and muffled steps.

Soon, they called me and made me cry before the boss, the divisional managers and other employees. At first, when the boss asked me to come in and the details were clarified, he laughed painfully and his tears were flowing. He very politely asked me for a demonstration; I had scarcely agreed when several employees who were behind the door entered. There was a lot of commotion and they asked me not to cry yet. I heard a voice from behind a screen say, "Hurry, one of the salesmen is going to cry."

"Why?"

"How should I know?"

I was seated next to the boss, at his great desk; they had called one of the store owners, but he couldn't come. The boys wouldn't be quiet and one of them shouted, "Have him think about his mommy, he'll cry quicker." I said to the boss, "When they are silent, I'll begin to cry."

With his sickly voice he threatened them, and after a few moments of relative silence, I looked through a window at a tree-top—we were one flight up—I put my hands to my face and tried to cry. I was rather disgusted. Whenever I had cried before, other people were not aware of my feelings; but these people knew I was going to cry, and that inhibited me. When the tears finally began to flow, I took one hand away from my face to take out a handkerchief and so they could see my damp face. Some were laughing and others were serious; I shook my face violently and all of them laughed; but they immediately fell silent and then started to laugh again. I was drying my tears while the sickly voice repeated, "Very good, very good." Perhaps they were disillusioned. I felt like a dripping, emptied bottle; I wanted to react, I was in a bad mood and I felt like being bad.

I went over to the boss and said, "I wouldn't want any of them to use the same procedure for selling stockings, and I would like the company to recognize my . . . initiative and grant me exclusive rights for a while."

"Come back tomorrow and we'll talk about it."

On the following day, the secretary already had the document drawn up, and he read, "The company promises not to utilize and to respect the advertising and sales system comprised of crying . . ." At this point they both laughed and the boss said that didn't sound right. While they were editing the document, I walked up to a counter. Behind it was a girl, staring at me as if her eyes were painted on.

"So, you cry for the fun of it?"

"That's right."

"In that case, I know more than you. You yourself don't know you're sad."

For a moment I was pensive; then I said, "Look, it's not that I'm among the happiest of men; but I know how to get along with my grief and so I'm almost happy."

As I was leaving her—the boss was calling me—I noticed her gaze. It remained with me as if she had placed her hand on my shoulder.

When I returned to my selling, I was in a small city. It was a gloomy day and I didn't feel like crying. I would have liked to be alone in my room, listening to the rain, thinking that the water was separating me from everybody. I was traveling concealed behind a mask with tears on it, but my face was tired.

Suddenly, I felt that someone had come near me in order to ask, "What's the matter with you?" Then, like a worker caught idling, I tried to continue my work and, putting my hands to my face, I began to sob.

That year I cried until December. I stopped crying in January and part of February and began again after Carnival. That rest was good for me and I cried again willingly. Meanwhile, I was experiencing success with my tears and I began to take a sort of pride in my crying. There were many more salesmen, but only one actor who could perform without previous rehearsal and could convince the public with weeping.

That next year I began crying throughout the west and I arrived at a city where my concerts had been very successful. The second time I was there, the public had received me with an affectionate and lengthy ovation; I acknowledged my gratitude bowing next to the piano and they didn't let me sit down to begin the concert. Surely now at least they would give me an audition. I cried there, for the first time, in the most luxurious hotel; it was at lunch hour on a radiant day. I had already eaten and had coffee when, with my elbows on the table, I covered my face with my hands. In a few moments, some friends whom I had greeted approached me; I felt them standing there for some time, and meanwhile, a poor old lady—I don't know where she came from—sat down at my table and I looked at her through my damp fingers. Her head was bowed and she said nothing; but her face was so sad it made me want to cry . . .

The day on which I gave my first concert, I felt the nervousness that comes from fatigue; I was on the last work of the first part of the program and I took one of the movements too fast; I had intended to slow down, but I became clumsy and lost my balance and power. There was nothing I could do but continue; but my hands became tired, I lost my precision and I realized that I wouldn't get through to the end. Without even thinking about it, I took my hands from the keyboard and held them to my face; it was the first time I had cried on stage.

At first, there were murmurs of surprise and for some reason someone tried to applaud; but others mumbled and I got up. With one hand I covered my eyes, and with the other I grasped at the piano, trying to leave the stage. Some women shouted because they thought I would fall into the pit. I was about to exit through a doorway in the backdrop when someone from the upper gallery shouted, "Crooocoodiile!"

I heard laughter; but I went to the dressing room, washed my face, and immediately reappeared and, with refreshed hands, I finished the first part. At the end, many people came to greet me and we talked about the "crocodile" affair.

I told them, "It seems to me the one who shouted is right. To tell the truth, I don't know why I cry; crying overcomes me and I can't help it, it's as natural for me as it is for a crocodile. After all, I don't know why a crocodile cries either."

One of the persons they had introduced me to had an oblong head; and as he combed his hair letting it stand on end, his head made me think of a brush. Someone in the crowd pointed to him and said to me, "Here, this gentleman is a doctor. What do you say, doctor?"

I turned pale. He looked at me with the stare of a police investigator and asked, "Tell me, when do you cry most, in the daytime or at night?"

I remembered that I never cried at night because I wasn't selling during those hours, and I answered, "I only cry by day."

I don't remember the other questions, but finally he advised me, "Don't eat meat. An old case of poisoning is acting up."

Within a few days, they gave a party for me in an important club. I rented a full-dress suit, with an immaculate white vest and as soon as

I saw myself in the mirror, I thought, "No one will say that this croco-dile doesn't have a white belly. By God! I think that animal has a double chin like mine. And he's voracious . . ."

When I reached the club, I found only a few people. I realized I had arrived too early. I saw one of the members of the committee and told him I wished to work on the piano a bit. In that way, I would disguise my early arrival. We went through a green curtain and I found myself in a large and empty hall prepared for the dance. Across from the curtain, at the other end of the room, was the piano. The committee member and the janitor accompanied me there. While they opened the piano, the committeeman with black eyebrows and white hair told me the party would be a great success, that the high school principal, a friend of mine, would give a very pretty speech which he had already heard; he tried to remember some sentences, but decided it would be better not to tell me anything. I put my hands on the piano and they left. While I was playing, I thought, "This evening I shall not cry . . . it wouldn't look good . . . the high school principal might want me to cry to prove the success of his speech. But I won't cry for anything in the world."

In a little while, I saw the green curtain move; a young tall girl with loose hair came out from the folds, squinting as if she were near-sighted. She looked at me and walked over carrying something in her hand; behind her appeared a servant who caught up with her and began talking to her up close. I had a chance to look at her legs and I realized that she had only one stocking on. At every moment she made move-ments which indicated that the conversation was over, but the servant continued talking to her, the two again picking on the subject as if it were a delicacy. I continued playing the piano and while they were speaking, I had time to think, "What can she be doing with one stock-ing? Could one of them have a run and knowing that I'm a salesman . . . And so early in the party!"

Finally, she came to me and said, "Pardon me, sir, I wanted you to sign a stocking for me."

At first I started to laugh, but instead I tried speaking to her as if once again that request were being made of me. I began to explain that a stocking could not withstand a pen point; I had now solved that by autographing a label which the fan would later stick on her stocking. But while I was giving these explanations, I was revealing the experience of an old salesman who had then become a pianist. Anguish began to invade me when she sat down on the piano stool and, putting on the stocking, she said to me, "It's too bad that you turned out to be such a liar . . . you should have thanked me for the idea."

I had fixed my eyes on her legs; then I stopped looking at them and my ideas got mixed up. There was an unpleasant silence. She lowered her head and her hair fell about her shoulders; under that blond curtain her hands moved as if they were fleeing. I was silent and she was relentless. Finally, her leg made a dancelike movement; she slipped her foot into her shoe as she got up. Her hands gathered her hair together, she waved silently and departed.

When people began to enter, I went to the bar. It occurred to me to order whiskey. The waiter mentioned many brands and, as I didn't know any of them, I said, "Give me the last one."

I moved to a bar stool and tried not to wrinkle the tails of my jacket. I must have looked like a black parrot instead of a crocodile. I was silent, thinking about the girl with the stocking; the memory of her nervous hands was disturbing.

I felt myself being led to the dance hall by the high school principal. The dancing was stopped for a while and he recited his speech. Several times he uttered the words *duty* and *incarnation*. When they applauded, I raised my arms like an orchestra conductor before the attack, and as soon as they were silent, I said, "Now when I should cry, I cannot. Neither can I speak, nor do I wish to keep separated any longer those who should be joined together for the dance." I finished by taking a bow.

After my curtain call, I embraced the high school principal and over his shoulder I saw the girl with the stocking. She smiled at me and raised her skirt to the left, showing me the place on the stocking where she had glued a small portrait of me cut out of the program. I smiled, full of joy, but I uttered a bit of nonsense everybody repeated.

"Very good, very good! The leg with a heart."

Nevertheless, I felt happy and I went to the bar. I got up on the stool again, and the waiter asked me, "White Horse Whiskey?"

And I, with the gesture of a musketeer waving a sword, "White Horse or Black Parrot."

Soon a boy with one hand hidden behind his back came up to me. "Paleface tells me that you don't mind if they call you Crocodile."

"That's true, I like it."

He took his hand from behind his back and showed me a caricature. It was a large crocodile that looked like me: it had a small hand in its mouth where the teeth were a keyboard, and from the other hand a stocking was hanging; he was drying his tears with it.

When my friends took me to my hotel, I thought about how much I had cried in that area, and I felt an evil pleasure in having deceived them; I felt like a bourgeois from all the anguish. But when I was alone in my room, something unexpected happened to me. First, I looked at myself in the mirror; I had the caricature in my hand and alternately I looked at the crocodile and at my face. Suddenly, without my having resolved to imitate the crocodile, my face, all by itself, began to cry. I looked at it as I might look at a sister whose misfortune I was ignorant of. I had new wrinkles and the tears were flowing into them. I put out the light and went to bed. My face continued crying; the tears ran down my nose and fell upon the pillow. And so I fell asleep. When I awoke, I felt the sting of the tears that had dried. I wanted to get up and wash out my eyes, but I was afraid that my face would begin to cry again. I calmed down and rolled my eyes in the darkness, like that blind man who played the harp.

TRANSLATED BY ARTHUR BERINGER

Agape

Hoy no ha venido nadie a preguntar;
ni me han pedido en esta tarde nada.

No he visto ni una flor de cementerio
en tan alegre procesión de luces.
Perdóname, Señor: qué poco he muerto!

En esta tarde todos, todos pasan
sin preguntarme ni pedirme nada.

Y no sé qué se olvidan y se queda
mal en mis manos, como cosa ajena.

He salido a la puerta,
y me da ganas de gritar a todos:
Si echan de menos algo, aquí se queda!

Porque en todas las tardes de esta vida,
yo no sé con qué puertas dan a un rostro,
y algo ajeno se toma el alma mía.

Hoy no ha venido nadie;
y hoy he muerto qué poco en esta tarde!

César Vallejo

Agape

Today no one has come to inquire,
nor have they wanted anything from me this afternoon.

I have not seen a single cemetery flower
in so happy a procession of lights.
Forgive me, Lord! I have died so little!

This afternoon everyone, everyone goes by
without asking or begging me anything.

And I do not know what it is they forget, and it is
heavy in my hands like something stolen.

I have come to the door,
and I want to shout at everyone:
—If you miss something, here it is!

Because in all the afternoons of this life,
I do not know how many doors are slammed on a face,
and my soul takes something that belongs to another.

Today nobody has come;
and today I have died so little in the afternoon!

TRANSLATED BY JOHN KNOEPFLE

Voy a Hablar de la Esperanza

Yo no sufro este dolor como César Vallejo. Yo no me duelo ahora como artista, como hombre ni como simple ser vivo siquiera. Yo no sufro este dolor como católico, como mahometano ni como ateo. Hoy sufro solamente. Si no me llamase César Vallejo, también sufriría este mismo dolor. Si no fuese artista, también lo sufriría. Si no fuese hombre ni ser vivo siquiera, también lo sufriría. Si no fuese católico, ateo ni mahometano, también lo sufriría. Hoy sufro desde más abajo. Hoy sufro solamente.

Me duelo ahora sin explicaciones. Mi dolor es tan hondo, que no tuvo ya causa ni carece de causa. ¿Qué sería su causa? ¿Dónde está aquello tan importante, que dejase de ser su causa? Nada es su causa; nada ha podido dejar de ser su causa. ¿A qué ha nacido este dolor, por sí mismo? Mi dolor es del viento del norte y del viento del sur, como esos huevos neutros que algunas aves raras ponen del viento. Si hubiera muerto mi novia, mi dolor sería igual. Si me hubieran cortado el cuello de raíz, mi dolor sería igual. Si la vida fuese, en fin, de otro modo, mi dolor sería igual. Hoy sufro desde más arriba. Hoy sufro solamente.

Miro el dolor del hambriento y veo que su hambre anda tan lejos de mi sufrimiento, que de quedarme ayuno hasta morir, saldría siempre de mi tumba una brizna de yerba al menos. ¡Lo mismo el enamorado! ¡Qué sangre la suya más engendrada, para la mía sin fuente ni consumo!

Yo creía hasta ahora que todas las cosas del universo eran, inevitablemente, padres o hijos. Pero he aquí que mi dolor de hoy no es padre ni es hijo. Le falta espalda para anochecer, tanto como le sobra pecho para amanecer y si lo pusiesen en la estancia oscura, no daría luz y si lo pusiesen en una estancia luminosa, no echaría sombra. Hoy sufro suceda lo que suceda. Hoy sufro solamente.

I am Going to Speak of Hope

I don't suffer this pain as César Vallejo. I don't ache now as an artist, as a man or even as a simple living being. I don't suffer this pain as a Catholic, as a Mohammedan or as an atheist. Today I just suffer. If I were not called César Vallejo, I'd still suffer this same pain. If I were not an artist, I'd still suffer it. If I were not a man or even a living being, I'd still suffer it. If I were not a Catholic, atheist or Mohammedan, I would still suffer. Today I suffer from the depths. Today I simply suffer.

I ache now without any excuses. My pain is so deep it has no cause nor does it lack cause. What could be its cause? Where is that thing so important that its cause could cease to be its cause? Nothing is its cause; nothing has been able to stop being its cause. Why has this pain been born—for itself? My pain comes from the north wind, from the south wind, like those neuter eggs some rare birds lay in the wind. If my bride were dead my pain would be the same. If they cut my throat out by its roots my pain would be the same. If life were finally of a different order, my pain would be the same. Today I suffer from the heights. Today I simply suffer.

I look at the starving man's misery and see his hunger is so distant from my suffering, that if I were to fast unto death, a blade of grass would always sprout from my tomb at least. The same thing happens to the lover! How engendered his blood is compared to mine, my blood without spring or drinker!

I believed until now that all the things of the universe were inevitably fathers or sons. But behold, my pain today is neither father nor son. It lacks a back to darken, just as it has too much chest to dawn, and if they put it in the dark dwelling place it could not give light and if they put it in a lighted dwelling place it would cast no shadow. Today I suffer no matter what happens. Today I simply suffer.

TRANSLATED BY CLAYTON ESHLEMAN

Traspie entre Dos Estrellas

¡Hay gentes tan desgraciadas, que ni siquiera
tienen cuerpo; cuantitativo el pelo,
baja, en pulgadas, la genial pesadumbre;
el modo, arriba;
no me busques, la muela del olvido,
parecen salir del aire, sumar suspiros mentalmente, oír
claros azotes en sus paladares!

Vanse de su piel, rascándose el sarcófago en que nacen
y suben por su muerte de hora en hora
y caen, a lo largo de su alfabeto gélido, hasta el suelo.

¡Ay de tanto! ¡ay de tan poco! ¡ay de ellas!
¡Ay en mi cuarto, oyéndolas con lentes!
¡Ay en mi tórax, cuando compran trajes!
¡Ay de mi mugre blanca, en su hez mancomunada!

¡Amadas sean las orejas sánchez,
amadas las personas que se sientan,
amado el desconocido y su señora,
el prójimo con mangas, cuello y ojos!

¡Amado sea aquel que tiene chinches,
el que lleva zapato roto bajo la lluvia,
el que vela el cadáver de un pan con dos cerillas,
el que se coge un dedo en una puerta,
el que no tiene cumpleaños,
el que perdió su sombra en un incendio,
el animal, el que parece un loro,
el que parece un hombre, el pobre rico,
el puro miserable, el pobre pobre!

¡Amado sea
el que tiene hambre o sed, pero no tiene

Stumble between Two Stars

There are people so wretched they don't even have
a body; quantitative the hair
lowers inch by inch, the genial grief;
the mode, above;
don't look for me, the molar of oblivion,
they seem to come out of the air, to add sighs mentally, to hear
clear whipblows in their palates!

They slip from their skin, scratching at the sarcophagus
        they are born in
and rise up through their death hour by hour
and fall, the length of their frozen alphabet, to the ground.

Aie for so much! aie for so little! aie for them!
Aie in my room hearing them with lens!
Aie in my thorax when they buy clothes!
Aie of my white grime, in their united scum!

Beloved be the sanchez ears,
beloved the people who sit down,
beloved the unknown man and his wife,
neighbor with sleeves, neck and eyes!

Beloved be the one who has bedbugs,
the one who wears a torn shoe through the rain,
the one who keeps watch over the corpse of a loaf with two matches,
the one who catches his finger in the door,
the one who has no birthday,
the one who lost his shadow in a fire,
the animal, the one who looks like a parrot,
the one who looks like a man, the poor rich,
the pure miserable, the poor poor!

Beloved be
the one who is hungry or thirsty, but has no

hambre con qué saciar toda su sed,
ni sed con qué saciar todas sus hambres!

¡Amado sea el que trabaja al día, al mes, a la hora,
el que suda de pena o de vergüenza,
aquel que va, por orden de sus manos, al cinema,
el que paga con lo que le falta,
el que duerme de espaldas,
el que ya no recuerda su niñez; amado sea
el calvo sin sombrero,
el justo sin espinas,
el ladrón sin rosas,
el que lleva reloj y ha visto a Dios,
el que tiene un honor y no fallece!

¡Amado sea el niño, que cae y aún llora
y el hombre que ha caído y ya no llora!

¡Ay de tanto! ¡Ay de tan poco! ¡Ay de ellos!

11 octubre 1937

Palmas y Guitarra

Ahora, entre nosotros, aquí,
ven conmigo, trae por la mano a tu cuerpo
y cenemos juntos y pasemos un instante la vida
a dos vidas y dando una parte a nuestra muerte.
Ahora, ven contigo, hazme el favor
de quejarte en mi nombre y a la luz de la noche tenebrosa
en que traes a tu alma de la mano
y huímos en puntillas de nosotros.

hunger with which to satiate all his thirst,
nor thirst with which to satiate all his hungers!

Beloved be the one who works by the day, by the month,
by the hour,
the one who sweats from sorrow or from shame,
the one who goes at the command of his hands to the movies,
the one who pays with what he lacks,
the one who sleeps on his back,
the one who no longer recalls his childhood; beloved be
the bald man without a hat,
the just man without thorns,
the thief without roses,
whoever wears a wrist watch and has seen God,
who has an honor and doesn't perish!

Beloved be the child who falls and still cries
and the man who has fallen and no longer cries.

Aie for so much! Aie for so little! Aie for them!

October 11, 1937

TRANSLATED BY CLAYTON ESHLEMAN

Palms and Guitar

Now, between us, here
come with me, bring your body by the hand
let's eat supper together and pass life a moment to
two lives, giving a portion to our death.
Now, come with thee, please
complain in my name and by the light of the tenebrous night
in which you bring your soul by your hand
and we flee on tiptoes from ourselves.

Ven a mí, sí, y a ti, sí,
con paso par, a vernos a los dos con paso impar,
marcar el paso de la despedida.
¡Hasta cuando volvamos! ¡Hasta la vuelta!
¡Hasta cuando leamos, ignorantes!
¡Hasta cuando volvamos, despidámonos!

¿Qué me importan los fusiles,
escúchame;
escúchame, qué impórtanme,
si la bala circula ya en el rango de mi firma?
¿Qué te importan a ti las balas,
si el fusil está humeando ya en tu olor?
Hoy mismo pesaremos
en los brazos de un ciego nuestra estrella
y, una vez que me cantes, lloraremos.
Hoy mismo, hermosa, con tu paso par
y tu confianza a que llegó mi alarma,
saldremos de nosotros, dos a dos.
¡Hasta cuando seamos ciegos!
¡Hasta
que lloremos de tánto volver!

Ahora,
entre nosotros, trae
por la mano a tu dulce personaje
y cenemos juntos y pasemos un instante la vida
a dos vidas y dando una parte a nuestra muerte.
Ahora, ven contigo, hazme el favor
de cantar algo
y de tocar en tu alma, haciendo palmas.
¡Hasta cuando volvamos! ¡Hasta entonces!
¡Hasta cuando partamos, despidámonos!

8 noviembre 1937

Come to me, yes, and to thee, yes,
in step, to see the two of us out of step,
to mark time of the goodbye.
Until we return! Until the turn!
Until we read, ignorant!
Until we return, let's say goodbye!

What are the rifles to me,
listen to me;
listen to me, what's it to me
if the bullet's now circling in my signature's rank?
What are the bullets to thee
if the rifle's smoking now in thy odor?
This very day we'll weigh
in the arms of a blind man our star
and once thou sings to me, we'll cry.
This very day, beautiful, with thy in-step
and thy trust reached by my alarm,
we'll come out of ourselves, two by two.
Until we become blind!
Until
we cry from so much returning!

Now
between us, bring
thy sweet character by the hand,
let's eat supper together and pass life a moment to
two lives, giving a portion to our death.
Now, come with thee, please
sing something
and strum thy soul, clapping palms.
Until we return! Until then!
Until we part, let's say goodbye!

November 8, 1937

TRANSLATED BY CLAYTON ESHLEMAN

Los Desgraciados

Ya va a venir el día; da
cuerda a tu brazo, búscate debajo
del colchón, vuelve a pararte
en tu cabeza, para andar derecho.
Ya va a venir el día, ponte el saco.

Ya va a venir el día; ten
fuerte en la mano a tu intestino grande, reflexiona,
antes de meditar, pues es horrible
cuando le cae a uno la desgracia
y se le cae a uno a fondo el diente.

Necesitas comer, pero, me digo,
no tengas pena, que no es de pobres
la pena, el sollozar junto a su tumba;
remiéndate, recuerda,
confía en tu hilo blanco, fuma, pasa lista
a tu cadena y guárdala detrás de tu retrato.
Ya va a venir el día, ponte el alma.

Ya va a venir el día; pasan,
han abierto en el hotel un ojo,
azotándolo, dándole con un espejo tuyo . . .
¿tiemblas? Es el estado remoto de la frente
y la nación reciente del estómago.
Roncan aún . . . ¡Qué universo se lleva este ronquido!
¡Cómo quedan tus poros, enjuiciándolo!
¡Con cuántos doses, ¡ay! estás tan solo!
Ya va a venir el día, ponte el sueño.

Ya va a venir el día, repito
por el órgano oral de tu silencio
y urge tomar la izquierda con el hambre
y tomar la derecha con la sed; de todos modos,

The Wretched of the Earth

The day's going to come; wind
up your arm, look for yourself under
your mattress, stand again
on your head in order to walk straight.
The day's going to come, put on your coat.

The day's going to come; grip
your large intestine tight in your hand, reflect
before you meditate, for it's awful
when the wretchedness hits you
and your tooth falls out by its roots.

You have to eat, but, I keep telling myself,
you don't have to grieve, for the grief and sobbing
beside one's tomb don't belong to the poor;
mend yourself, remember,
confide in your white thread, smoke, check
your chain and keep it behind your portrait.
The day's going to come, put on your soul.

The day's going to come; they pass,
they've opened up an eye in the hotel
whipping it, beating it with a mirror that's yours . . .
are you trembling? It's the remote state of the forehead
and this recent nation of the stomach.
They're still snoring . . . What universe puts up with this snore!
How your pores agree, indicting it!
With so many twos, ay! you're so alone!
The day's going to come, put on your dream.

The day's going to come, I repeat
through the oral organ of your silence;
it is urgent to move further left with hunger
and further right with thirst; in any case

abstente de ser pobre con los ricos,
atiza
tu frío, porque en él se integra mi calor, amada víctima.
Ya va a venir el día, ponte el cuerpo.

Ya va a venir el día;
la mañana, la mar, el meteoro, van
en pos de tu cansancio, con banderas,
y, por tu orgullo clásico, las hienas
cuentan sus pasos al compás del asno,
la panadera piensa en ti,
el carnicero piensa en ti, palpando
el hacha en que están presos
el acero y el hierro y el metal; jamás olvides
que durante la misa no hay amigos.
Ya va a venir el día, ponte el sol.

Ya viene el día; dobla
el aliento, triplica
tu bondad rencorosa
y da codos al miedo, nexo y énfasis,
pues tú, como se observa en tu entrepierna y siendo
el malo, ¡ay! inmortal,
has soñado esta noche que vivías
de nada y morías de todo . . .

[*Fin de noviembre o primera
semana de diciembre 1937.*]

stop being poor among the rich,
stir
up your cold, for in it is mixed my warmth, beloved victim.
The day's going to come, put on your body.

    The day's going to come;
the morning, the sea, the meteor
pursue your weariness with banners,
and because of your classic pride, the hyenas
count their steps to the beat of the ass,
the baker's wife thinks about you,
the butcher thinks about you, fingering
the cleaver in which the steel
the iron and the metal are prisoners; never forget
that during Mass there are no friends.
The day's going to come, put on your sun.

    The day comes; double
your breathing, triple
your rancorous goodwill
and elbow the fear, the knot and emphasis,
for you, as anyone can see in your crotch and evil
being, ay! immortal,
you've dreamed tonight that you were living
on nothing and dying from everything . . .

End of November or first
week of December 1937.

                    TRANSLATED BY CLAYTON ESHLEMAN

Roberto Arlt

Esther Primavera

Just thinking of Esther Primavera, I am flooded by an overwhelming emotion. It's as if my face were suddenly struck by a gust of hot wind. And yet the whole range of peaks is lying under snow. White icicles glaze the crotches of a walnut tree below my garret room on the top floor of the Pasteur Wing of the Santa Monica Tuberculosis Sanatorium.

Esther Primavera! Her name heaps the past before my eyes. This red shock pales with one beautiful memory after another. Just to say her name is to have my cold cheeks suddenly hit by a gust of hot wind.

Stretched out on a deck chair, bundled up to my chin in a dark blanket, I go on thinking about her. For seven hundred days now I have been thinking about her night and day—Esther Primavera, the only living thing I have ever cruelly injured. No, that's not the word. I have not injured her, I did something even worse; I destroyed in her all hope of earthly goodness. Never again will she harbor an illusion, so brutally have I twisted her soul. And the infamy of this sends a pleasant sadness spreading through my flesh. I know now that I will be able to die. I never thought that remorse might acquire such pleasing depths. Or that guilt might be turned into a hideously soft pillow, on which—together with the anguish we ferment—we shall rest forever. And I know that she'd never be able to forget me, and that the fixed stare of this tall creature, walking with a slight motion of her shoulders, is the only thing of beauty that binds me to the world of the living, the world I left behind for this hell.

I still see her. Her delicate, long face drawn into a tormented expression, as if every time she came to me she had just torn herself loose from a huge block of hard life. And this effort helped preserve her briskness, so that when she walked, the flounced hem of her black dress swirled about her knees, and a wisp of hair swept back across the temple and baring the lobe of her ear seemed part and parcel of that headlong rush into the unknown which was her way of walking. Sometimes she wrapped her throat in furs, and seeing her in the street then you thought she was a foreigner returning from faraway cities. That was how she always made her way toward me. Her twenty-three years, which had slipped through all the planes of a perpendicular life—her twenty-three years contained in a lovely body—made their way toward me, as if at that moment I were her whole past's clear-cut reason for existence. Yes, that was it, she had lived twenty-three years for that—just to come down the broad sidewalk toward me with a look of torment on her face.

The Santa Monica Sanatorium. How nice to have put a gentle-sounding name on this red hell, where death has varnished all the faces yellow and where among four wings—two for men and two for women —we total about a thousand TB patients.

And oh, the times when one could cry his eyes out! And the rim of mountains there, topped by a ring of more distant peaks, where the glinting curve of tracks becomes lost and the trains slide along looking like a string of toys. And off the river, on sunny days, a sparkle of light among the greenery. And the distant crags, purple in the twilight and red as embers in the dawn. And higher up, Ucul; and farther along, Devil's Peak; and in between the tortuous slopes, the horizontal methylene-blue triangle of the dammed lake, always on the advance. And day or night, women coughing, men upright in their beds, numbed by fever hallucinations or the taste of blood that creeps to their palates from somewhere deep inside them. And God reigning over all our taciturn, guilt-ridden souls.

To the right of my deck chair is the mulatto Leiva. A wild profile and a swatch of black hair tumbling over the nut-brown forehead. To my left lies a red-headed boy, a Jew, who, so as to keep the TB from eating his larynx away, never speaks. Beyond him, in a long row that fills the covered porch, are deck chairs, and, lying on them, are boys, men, adolescents—all of them wrapped in the regulation dark blankets. And almost all of them with yellow skin stuck flat against their skulls, ears you can almost see through, burning or glassy eyes, and nostrils that throb with the slow breathing in and out of icy air that pours down from the mountains.

Between the lashes of all those half-shut eyelids, the trace of a memory languishes. But there are eyes still anchored in a recent vision, and, secretly, these are clouded with tears. This is the way we all are here in this "mountain-type" sanatorium—always remembering something. And I think about her. For seven hundred days now I've been thinking about Esther Primavera; I say her name, and that gust of hot wind strikes my cheeks. And yet, the gray snow lies deep on the crest of the mountains, while below, in the tunnels, everything is black.

The mulatto Leiva lights a cigarette.

"Want a smoke, seven?" he says.

"Sure."

We smoke cautiously because it's forbidden us. We let the smoke out under the blanket and, suddenly, the nicotine sets our stomachs swimming. From inside the ward comes continuous coughing. It's the man in bed number three. A ready-made dialogue is on our lips.

"Did he sleep at all last night?"

"Not much."

"Is his temperature still up?"

"Yes."

Or instead:

"When's he having his pneumothorax?"

"Tomorrow."

"Is he up to it?"

"And what good's his going on like this . . . ?"

A negro lies in a trancelike state on his deck chair. His charcoal-gray head is flattened against the pillow in an attitude of infinite weariness. Leiva looks at him and says, "He won't make it through the winter."

The noise of coughing comes from inside the ward. It's number nine now, number nine who hangs on and won't die, number nine who bet the doctor of our ward a case of beer that he wouldn't die this winter. And he won't die. He won't die, because he has the will to keep himself going until spring. And the doctor, who is an expert, is a bit put out with his patient. He says to him, for the sick man is almost a friend and knows everything, "But you can't live. Don't you see you haven't even this much lung left?" And he shows him the nail of his little finger.

Number nine, lying off by himself in a white, right-angle corner of the ward, wrapped in the acrid mist of his own decomposition, speaks with an almost subterranean gasping sound. "Nothing doing till spring, doctor. Don't get your hopes up."

And the doctor withdraws from his bedside, annoyed, intrigued by this case which, according to the X-rays, contradicts everything he knows. But before leaving, he laughs and says, "Why don't you die? Just to please me. Is that asking too much?"

"No, you're the one who's going to please me—paying for the case of beer."

The doctor has TB, too. "Just the apex of the upper left lobe—no more." So has the orderly—"a touch of necrosis in the right." And so all of us who move about like ghosts in this hell that bears the name of a saint—all of us know we are condemned to death. Today or tomorrow or next year—one day . . .

Esther Primavera! The sweet girl's name strikes my cheeks like a gust of hot wind. Leiva coughs; the Jewish boy dreams about his father's fur shop, where right now Mordecai and Levi are probably laughing over the samovar; and the chapel bell tolls a death. A train, looking like a toy, becomes lost along the shining curve of tracks that cut through the black tunnels. And Buenos Aires—so far, far away . . .

It makes you feel like killing yourself, but killing yourself there, in Buenos Aires, on her doorstep. I realized how much I was in love with

Esther Primavera when, on the streetcar that was taking us out to Palermo, I answered her question with these words:

"No, don't get your hopes up. I'll never get married—least of all to you."

"It doesn't matter. We'll be friends, then. And when I have a fiancé, I'll walk by with him so you'll know who he is. But of course I won't greet you." And with her eyes down, she gave me a sidelong look, just as though she had done something wrong.

"I take it you're used to this cynical game?"

"Yes, I once had a friend very much like you."

I began to laugh, and I said, "It's an odd thing. Women who go from man to man always seem to find a new one exactly like the last."

"How funny you are! Well, as I was saying, when the situation reached the danger point, I pulled back—just till I recovered my strength of course."

"You are delightfully shameless, did you know that? I really think you're fishing for something."

"You mean you don't feel safe with me?"

"Look into my eyes."

A strand of hair fell loose from her temple, and in spite of a devilish smile, her pale face wore an expression of weariness, as though it were rent with pain.

"And your fiancé—what did he think of your cynical game?"

"He never knew." Suddenly, she looked at me, serious.

"You are a wicked girl," I said.

"Yes, and I'm bored with all this nonsense. Have you any idea what it's like to be a woman?"

"No, but I can imagine."

"But why do you keep looking at me that way? You won't be angry if I tell you you look a little foolish, will you? Come on, what are you thinking about?"

"Nothing—I mean, you probably already know what I'm thinking about. But just you remember this. Play me dirty and I'll give you something to remember me by all your life."

My insolence pleased her. She gave a perverse smile and said, "Tell me—just out of curiosity—you won't be angry if I ask? You don't by any chance belong to that class of men who take a girl out for a week and then with big sheepish eyes tell her, 'Won't you give me some proof of your love, miss?' and ask for a kiss?"

I looked at her gloomily. "I'll probably never ask or give you anything."

"Why not?"

"Because I'm not interested in you as a woman who gives."

"And just how do I interest you, then?"

"As a pastime, that's all. When I'm fed up with your arrogant ways I'll leave you."

"Then you do think my soul is beautiful?"

"Yes, but nobody's going to understand you."

"Why aren't they?"

"We'd better not go into that."

We were walking in the green silence of trees now. With a voice like a child's, she spoke of faraway places, of early outbreaks of suffering. In Rome, she'd once visited a hospital for mutilated war veterans. She had seen faces that seemed to have been squeezed through a press, battered skulls which looked as if they had been cored by some huge drill. She had known lands of ice and whales. She'd been in love with a man who had gambled his whole fortune away among gold prospectors and murderers playing cards one night in a horrible tavern down south in Comodoro. And he left her with her trousseau so that he could go on living his frenzied existence among the gamblers of Arroyo Pescado.

We talked the whole morning long. The point of her parasol would linger in the patches of sun that lay across the red gravel paths. And I kept thinking of the peculiar contrast between the weight of the things she told me and her delicate tone of voice, so that her charm was enhanced by the several persons I discovered in her. The way she had of confiding her innermost secrets to me was that of a child, and yet her experiences were those of a woman. We addressed one another not as strangers but rather as people who have known each other for a long time and between whom the act of baring of their souls has left everything in the open, and no secret exists.

And as she entered into details, not letting on that they were painful, politely keeping to herself all that might not interest me, her voice became warmer and finer. In spite of myself, I knew I was in the presence of a lady. And this word, referring to her, took on a meaning of perfection as perfect and showy as the sprouting of a silver lily out of an iron rod.

We said goodbye—sadly. But before disappearing, she retraced her steps and said, "Thank you for having looked at me with eyes so free of desire. I'll always be able to tell you everything. And don't think ill of me."

Then, with that slight motion of her shoulders, and her skirt swirling round her quick-stepping legs, she disappeared.

Of the five of us who get together in the room at night, which is the worst scoundrel? Every night after dinner, two hours after dinner, we get together for a round of maté. The first to arrive is Sacco—onion head and boxer's chest, paler than a wax candle—who, back in Buenos Aires, had been a con man. His record is longer than a Ph.D. thesis. After him comes Pebre, the hunchback, who steals morphine from the emergency ward; then Paya, heavyset, bowlegged, his milky face always closely shaved, with a sour gleam deep in his brown eyes, and the magnificent physique of a weight-lifter.

They come into "our" room when the Jewish boy is asleep. Leiva the Bungler prepares maté, while Sacco tunes his guitar, almost covering the sound box with his huge chest. We all sip our maté through the same silver tube, no longer afraid of infection, and anyway what does one bacillus more or less matter. Conversation lags soon after starting and for the most part we keep silent.

Oh, yes, we call Leiva the Bungler. But he does not like to talk about the bungling he has done. He refers to his murders as bungled affairs. Only when he gets drunk in the bar at the Ucul stop, across from the sanatorium's gates, does he remember them. This happens on Sundays, when cockfights are put on and when everyone, from the local political boss down to the seediest character in town with a peso to bet, shows up. Leiva, elbows on the table, looking gloomily toward the rectangle of mellow distance framed by the door, his words veiled, recalls his good old days. He had been a cattle drover. "Somewhere around San Rafael" he made his first "blunder."

Under the blunt angle of the garret roof, the strings being tuned by Sacco leave octaves of slowly dying sound suspended in the smoky gray air. The hunchback lifts his slippers against the edge of the brazier and, with his face like a marmoset's, rocking his head, he follows the measure of sweet strident tones.

Paya, his neck wrapped in a silk scarf, takes refuge in a sullen silence off in one corner of the room, where the ceiling slopes down. He thinks, remembering the furnished apartment he had at the corner of Corrientes and Talcahuano, remembering . . .

Who is the lowest scoundrel of the five of us? We have all been through either frantic or tragic lives.

It was on a summer morning that I was taken unawares by the terrible pain in my lungs. Paya felt the blood come gushing to his lips one night in a poker session while he was betting two thousand pesos on a full house. Leiva had been hit by the flu; Sacco by a cough—a cough so persistent that it gave him away to another bus passenger whose pocket he was emptying.

Bored and taciturn, we gather around Leiva, who has now taken the guitar. Heads are bent forward, the faces showing an expression of virility that affirms our decision to live still more cruelly. Laryngitis sleeps with his face to the wall, and his red hair leaves a copper stain on the pillow. From the cigarette between Paya's lips, smoke curls up. He is remembering life—the times being picked up for questioning, the nights spent in the cooler. He remembers sunny afternoons at the racetrack, the grandstands jammed, the jockeys rounding the curve in a blur, their silks —green and red and yellow—ballooning out in the wind, while the mob sucked dozens of oranges and shouted their heads off as their favorites passed.

Leiva makes a tango bleed on the weeping strings of the guitar. Our fierce semblances disintegrate in a convulsive trembling of facial nerves. The way wild beasts smell the forest, we smell Buenos Aires—Buenos Aires that's so far away—and among the snowy mountains Esther Primavera's name hits my cheeks like a gust of perfumed wind, and Leiva's profile, made leathery by wind and sun, bends over the guitar. His eyes, too, are fixed on distant memories—the green and violet plain; the cattle moving like shadows in the mountain mist; the shot of rum drunk alongside the bar, a thumb hooked in his belt and the glass upraised "to your health."

Sacco, sitting on the edge of my bed, cleans his nails with a kitchen knife. He, also, is plunged in memory. With him it's Cellblock III; the petty thieves waiting around all morning for the visits of wives who bring clothes and the latest word from lawyers; the emotional meetings; late afternoon and the uneatable slop steaming in a pan. Then the night-long card games; the drives in the police car to the courtroom hearing; the stories of swindles; the preliminary questioning; the letter written to take in some sucker with a tale of bankruptcy; the joy of being set free, the flood of joy on hearing the jailer shout, "Sacco—with all your things, to the front office."

Like a gust of hot wind Esther Primavera's name hits my cheeks. The tango borders a land of sorrow, where women wear lilac shoes and men's faces are maps of welts and razor slashes. And suddenly, straightening up painfully, Sacco says, "The old bellows really hurt. They've been hurting for three days now."

A wince pulls a thin lip back over his crooked teeth.

"Are you in pain?"

"I'll say."

"Put on a poultice."

"I've had it. My back just won't take any more."

I saw her again the day after our meeting. I don't know what evil power ever led me to carry out my vicious experiment. Since then, I have often blamed it on my illness, which was already taking hold over me. I thought the evil streak starting to show in all my actions must be the result of a nervous disorder brought on by the poisons being generated by the bacilli. I was later to discover that perversity was common among TB patients, who, in their rankling, are out for the suffering of their fellows. This evil, found in all men whose blood becomes poisoned, is enriched by dark impulses, a kind of suppressed hatred of which the sick man is aware. But that does not prevent the evil from insinuating itself into relations with others. All this is accompanied by a sour pleasure, a morbid sort of desperation.

Well, anyway, I saw her the next night standing by the garden gate of her house. She could do nothing but stare at me; she obviously had a premonition that something was going to happen. I was mute, my words held back by the anguish I felt over the lie I was planning to tell her. It was proof of my madness. "I'm a married man," I said.

As if she had been struck on the chin, her head fell back. The outline of her face went into a contracted white burn. The skin over her jaw and lips tightened and trembled. A fine line creased her forehead, for an instant her eyelids blinked, and her soul seemed to be trying to escape through her eyes; then, for a moment, her stare was unswerving through the straight eyelashes that filtered a dying spark. At last she recovered, and in her frenzy said, "But it's not possible. Say it's not."

And, rather than take her anguish on myself, a gloomy sort of expectation steadied me. If Death itself had been at her side and her life had depended on one word from me, I would not have uttered that word. Was that not, perhaps, the most beautiful moment of our lives? Could we have compressed greater pain than that for the future? There we stood, a man betting a woman's love against himself before her very eyes. The rest was a lie—what was real was the grief of a girl who had forgotten who she was, who had forgotten appearances and, in doing so, became a creature of eternity. In that one moment I was not worthy of kissing the ground she walked on. Suddenly she drew back, saying, "No. This can't be. We have to meet again tomorrow."

And not only did we see each other that once, but many times over. She kept poking at my lie, which was the truth of another self, and I was unable to go back on what I had said.

I walked in the park with that lovely girl. With her gray parasol she traced lines in the sand, and under her airy straw hat she smiled like a convalescent. Oblivious of everything, we spoke about mountains, which I had never seen, and about cliffs at the sea's edge (which I did not even know existed), where the stench of seaweed makes me imagine the cold atmosphere of ice-floes on the other side of the globe.

She knew the faraway lands of the south, the loneliness of light-houses, the sadness of purple twilights, the tedium of dunes always blown about by the wind. And while I was listening to Esther Primavera, my short-lived happiness became more intense than any suffering, for this love was hopeless. And Esther Primavera understood what was happening to me, and to make me always remember her and those fleeting moments, she adorned them with infinite delicacy and childishness, so that the strong will which moved her to put an end to things between us seemed inconceivable under such a sweet and fragile appearance.

One day we said goodbye forever. Her eyes were filled with tears.

The guitar sounds rough in the hands of the mulatto Leiva. Sacco brews maté. The black mountain exhales the savage breath of a slow-breathing monster. Farther off are the lighted windows of all the wards. By flashlight, an orderly makes his way along a sanded path, his white uniform puffed out by the wind. He carries an oxygen mask in his hand.

Paya, sitting on Leiva's bed, slowly smokes. Nobody speaks; everyone listens to the tango—a tango that frames the dark alley of death in the body of a woman who returns from streetwalking. All at once, the Jewish boy wakes up in a panic. His hair matted, a shoulder against the headboard, he coughs and coughs.

"It's too smoky in here," Leiva says.

"Yes, it is."

Paya opens the window and a gust of icy wind roils the smoky air.

The Jewish boy goes on coughing, a handkerchief pressed to his lips. Then he looks at the handkerchief and smiles happily: it is still white.

"Any blood?"

The red-haired boy shakes his head no.

That is our obsession. And we always confer with one another. There's not one of us who does not know where his or his friend's lesion is located. We auscultate each other. Some have an awful ear for it, finding before the doctor that sort of whistling escape of wind which at certain points of the back and chest indicates a crevice of death. And we talk about the development of our disease with a morbid erudition. We even bet—yes, we bet—on those who lie dying in the wards. We bet packages of cigarettes to see who can guess the hour when one of the dying will pass on. It's a complicated and terrible game, for sometimes the dying man does not die but instead improves, enters a convalescent stage, is cured, and in turn has a laugh on those who bet against him. He may even get carried away to the point, ironically, of looking around for someone else to bet on.

And there are times when life and death seem to be worth less than the butt of the cigarette on which we sadly puff, so that I tell myself if it weren't for my memory of Esther Primavera, by now I would have killed myself. In the midst of this misery, her name strikes my cheeks like a gust of hot wind.

I see her now as out of time, as a woman who will never age or have gray hair or an old woman's sad, exhausted smile. Bound to me by my outrageous act seven hundred days ago, she lives in my remorse like a splendid, permanent brand, and my only happiness is in knowing that when I lie at the point of death and the orderlies pass my bed without looking at me, the torn image of that lovely creature will accompany me to my end. But how could I ask her forgiveness? And yet, it's seven hundred days now that I have been thinking about her.

Wrapped in an overcoat, I go out onto the porch carrying a blanket. Of course, this is forbidden, but I lie down on a deck chair in the shadows. So black is it that the sour smell of buckthorns is like the voice of the earth. A dark bulk rises opposite my face: it is the mountain. In the distance, twinkling like stars, strings of yellow lights outline the streets of Ucul.

It's so cold that the flesh hardens on my bones. Snowflakes come down, looking like tiny feathers turning over on themselves. And I think: Why was I so mean with that creature? And again I fall back into that hideous memory.

A month after everything was over between us, I met her in the street in the company of a certain man. He was smallish, had the look of an office manager, with a moustache like a cat's whiskers and a mulatto face. She shot me an ironic look, as if to say, "What do you think of this guy?" And I stood there on the streetcorner for a good fifteen minutes, gaping. But had I any right to be angry? Hadn't she already told me, "I'll marry the first man who shows me the least bit of love?"

And had that ironic look come from the same eyes that once looked at me so tearfully? Was that possible? Cold anger, rage led me to a café. It was a rage provoked by the violence buried in all men, which finds release in sudden action. I had to blot her out of my life, to overwhelm her with a situation that would make any further relationship between us impossible. I wanted her to hate me so much that in the future, even if I were to go down on my knees before her, all humiliation on my part would be of no avail. I would become the only man she would hate with everlasting patience.

Then I asked for paper, and I wrote the most despicable letter ever to come from my hand. My rage and my desperation piled outrage on outrage; I twisted events she had told me about; I underscored details of her life that to an outsider, who knew nothing of our relationship, would hint of an intimacy which had never existed; and I polished my insults so as to make them still more cruel and unforgettable. I did not use coarse language, but I mocked her nobility, twisting her ideas and shaming her for her generosity in such a way that I suddenly thought that if just then it were possible for her to read what I was writing, she would beg me on bended knee not to send it. And yet she was innocent.

Realizing that at that moment she was strolling along in the company of another man and could not be at home, I sent her the letter, sure that her mother or brother would lay their hands on it and that they would have no doubts about what it contained, since every fact I mentioned I could only have known through her.

I called a shoeshine boy and offered him a peso if he'd deliver the letter, asking him to make a lot of noise when he knocked at the door. That way the maid would not be able to hold the letter back, since the rest of them would be sure to ask what all the racket was about. The boy, shoving his box under the table, disappeared down the acacia-shaded street, skipping merrily along.

"It's all over now," I told myself.

Still, I didn't know what was happening to me. A new calm was settling my nerves. The boy came back and, from his description of the man who had received the letter, I knew it was her brother. I gave the boy the peso and off he went.

I headed along. I was walking calmly, watching the shadows of doorways and the green of gardens, until I stopped to pick up a child who, rushing out of an entranceway, had tripped and fallen. The child's mother thanked me. I was walking calmly, as if my whole being were alien to infamy. Nonetheless, something had happened that was as enormous and unavoidable as the path of the sun or the fall of a planet. And only by an effort of the imagination could I picture the grimy boy arriving and pounding on the door, and then the astonishment of the whole family on realizing that their daughter was receiving such—

And I couldn't help laughing, for I was so enmeshed in my daydream. I imagined a gentleman brandishing the letter in the midst of interrupted lectures on domestic morals and a Ciceronian tirade broken by the mother's fainting. I imagined the sisters' tears over the possible catastrophe, and the brother's loud questioning of the maid about me so that he could give me a beating. Meanwhile, the frightened maid kept an eye out for their darling's arrival, murmuring, "My goodness, the things that go on!" while the cook, among her pots and pans, rejoiced over the piece of gossip she would have to tell her husband that night, praising, the whole time, the morality of the poor and saying with grotesque sufficiency while hanging up a frying pan, "No, no, no—it's far better to be poor and honest."

My fit of laughter was so loud that passersby stopped to stare at me, sure I had gone mad, and a policeman ended up approaching me and asking, "What's the matter, friend?"

I gave him a defiant look, answering that, in the first place, I was no friend of his, and then saying, "What, is it against the law to laugh at your own thoughts?"

"No offense meant, mister."

Then my delirium passed. Nothing could take back what had been done. Night came, and I knew she was there in her room, suffering.

As the days went by, I suffered from every kind of remorse. In my mind, I saw Esther Primavera at sunset, alone in her bedroom. The pale creature, leaning back against her bronze bedframe and staring at the pillows, would be thinking about me. And she would ask herself, "Is it possible that I could have been so mistaken? Is it possible that such a monster was locked up in that man? Was every word he uttered a lie, then? Are all human words lies? How is it that I never saw the falseness in his face and eyes? How could I have spoken about myself? How could I have confessed so much and have given him my most intimate self without moving him? He has been the lowest of any man I've known. Why did it turn out like this?"

I had never seen her so sad as I saw her then in my mind. It seemed to me that all her dreams, built up in the shining morning air like slender prisms, were crumbling to pieces, covering her with the dust of this earth.

And as I reconstructed all the pain she was suffering because of me, even from a distance I felt bound to her, and if at that very moment Esther Primavera had come to kill me, I would not have stirred. How many times in those days I imagined the delight of dying by her hand! For I had thought that with my terrible infamy I would sweep her out of my consciousness and that her pale little face would never be with me again. But I was mistaken. By my cruelty, I placed her among my days more fixed and unshakeable than a sword pointed at my heart. And with every heartbeat, the wound widens, splitting bit by bit. And for a long time, the days and nights whirled their wings in my eyes as if I were drunk. Months later, I met her.

I was walking along with my head bent down, when by some instinct I looked up. Coming in my direction, Esther Primavera was crossing the street. I thought to myself, "How happy I'll be if she slaps my face!"

Did she guess what was going on inside me? With a slight movement of her shoulders, her face torn by suffering, her eyes fixed in a stare, she came toward me. Her black dress swirled about her quick-stepping legs. A wisp of hair hung loose from her temple and her neck was wrapped in a short black fur.

Her step became slower. She looked at me with soulful silence. I was the one who had caused her so much suffering. Then she was just a step away. She was the same person who had been with me that day we spoke of mountains, oceans, and cliffs. Our eyes met; in her face there was a lunar glow, a fine wrinkle lined her forehead, her lips trembled, and without a word, she vanished.

For seven hundred days now I have been thinking about her—always on the point of writing her, from this hell, to ask her forgiveness. The snow comes slanting down. An orderly appears from out of the darkness. All at once, from his right hand, a light flashes. Beaming its bright white cone on me, he says drily, "Seven, get back to bed."

"I'm on my way."

For seven hundred days now I have been thinking about her. The snow slants down. I get up from the deck chair and make my way back to the ward. But first I must skirt a banister that looks off to the south. There, five hundred miles away, is Buenos Aires. The endless night fills a space of desolation. And I think, "Esther Primavera . . ."

TRANSLATED BY NORMAN THOMAS DI GIOVANNI

DE *Los Animales Interiores*

I

Ese caballo está dentro de mí, ese viejo
caballo que la lluvia—mustio violín—alarga,
igual que sobre un lienzo crepuscular lo miro
proyectarse hacia el vago fondo de mi nostalgia.

A la fábrica en ruinas de su cuerpo la lluvia
se arropa mansamente como una hierdra elástica,
y al caer sosegado de las gotas, derrumba
la frente y las tupidas orejas se le apagan.

Sus patas, sus ollares, el ensueño perdido
que en sus ojos de bestia pura y simple naufraga,
toda esa mansedumbre derrengada y maltrecha,
ese sexo en silencio, esas crines chorreadas,

todo tiene una exangüe repercusión interna,
que la lluvia con blandos bemoles accompaña,
y me veo un caballo fantasmal y remoto
allá en una pluviosa lejanía de alma.

Luis Palés Matos

FROM *The Animals Within*

I

That horse is within me—that old horse
that the rain—sorrowing violin—draws out,
I see him projected on a twilight canvas
toward the restless depths of my nostalgia.

The rain wraps itself about the ruined factory
of his body like a supple ivy vine,
and at the quiet fall of the drops, his forehead
crumbles away and his clogged ears deafen.

His legs, his nostrils, the lost fantasy
that swims in his eyes—a beast's eyes, pure
and simple—all that abused and crippled mildness,
the silent sex, the dripping mane,

all have a pallid repercussion in me,
which the rain accompanies with soft B-minor chords,
and I see myself as a remote and fantasmal horse,
there in some distant rainy place of my soul.

TRANSLATED BY RACHEL BENSON

Falsa Canción de Baquiné

¡Ohé, nené!
¡Ohé, nené!
Adombe gangá mondé,
Adombe.
Candombe del baquiné,
Candombe.

      Vedlo aquí dormido,
Ju-jú.
Todo está dormido,
Ju-jú.
¿Quién lo habrá dormido?
Ju-jú.
Babilongo ha sido,
Ju-jú.
Ya no tiene oído,
Ju-jú.
Ya no tiene oído . . .

      Pero que ahora verá la playa.
Pero que ahora verá el palmar.
Pero que ahora ante el fuego grande
con Tembandumba podrá bailar.

      Y a la Guinea su zombí vuelva . . .
—Coquí, cocó, cucú, cacá—
Bombo el gran mongo bajo la selva
su tierno paso conducirá.
Ni sombra blanca sobre la hierba

Spurious Song for a Baquiné[1]

Ohé, nené!
Ohé, nené!
Adombe gangá mondé,[2]
Adombe.
Candombe[3] del baquiné,
Candombe.

See him sleeping here,
Ju-jú.[4]
All of him asleep,
Ju-jú.
Who has put him to sleep?
Ju-jú.
Babilongo was the one,
Ju-jú.
No longer can he hear,
Ju-jú.
No longer can he hear . . .

Except that now he will see the beach.
Except that now he will see the palm.
Except that now he'll be able to dance
with Tembandumba[5] before the great fire.

And his zombi returns to Guinea . . .
Coquí, cocó, cucú, cacá . . .
Bombo, the great river god of the Congo,
will guide his small feet through the woods.
No white shadow upon the grass

[1] Baquiné—an African ceremony for a dead infant.
[2] "Adombe gangá mondé" can be translated as "now we are going to eat" or "now we are going to dance."
[3] Candombe and calenda are both dances—the latter so lascivious that it was finally outlawed in Puerto Rico.
[4] Ju-jú—a witch doctor or a spirit.
[5] Tembandumba—a great African semi-historical, semi-mythological queen.

ni brujo negro lo estorbará.
Bombo el gran mongo bajo la selva
su tierno paso conducirá.
Contra el hechizo de mala hembra
cocomacaco duro tendrá.
Bombo el gran mongo bajo la selva
su tierno paso conducirá.
—Coquí, cocó, cucú, cacá—

    Para librarle de asechanza
colgadle un rabo de alacrán.
Será invencible en guerra y danza
si bebe orines de caimán.

    En la manteca de serpiente
magia hallará su corazón.
Conseguirá mujer ardiente
con cagarruta de cabrón.

    A papá Ogún va nuestra ofrenda,
para que su arrojo le dé
al son del gongo en la calenda
con que cerramos el baquiné.

    Papá Ogún, dios de la guerra,
que tiene botas con betún
y cuando anda tiembla la tierra . . .
Papá Ogún ¡ay! papá Ogún.

    Papá Ogún, mongo implacable,
que resplandece en el vodú
con sus espuelas y su sable . . .
Papá Ogún ¡ay! papá Ogún.

    Papá Ogún, quiere mi niño,
ser un guerrero como tú;
dale gracia, dale cariño . . .
Papá Ogún ¡ay! papá Ogún.

nor black witch doctor can hinder him.
Bombo, the great river god of the Congo,
will guide his small feet through the woods.
Against the spells of evil women
he will hold a stout hard stick.
Bombo, the great river god of the Congo,
will lead his small feet through the woods.
Coquí, cocó, cucú, cacá.

If you would have him safe from ambush
hang on him a scorpion's tail;
invincible both in war and dancing,
make him drink alligator piss.

With a bit of serpent's fat,
magic arts his heart will learn.
He will win an ardent woman
with a piece of he-goat's dung.

Our offering goes to Papa Ogún,
that he may make our baby brave
when the gong rings out and we dance the calenda
with which we close the baquiné.

Papa Ogún, the god of war,
shiny with blacking are his boots,
and when he passes the whole earth trembles . . .
Papa Ogún, ay! Papa Ogún.

Papa Ogún, implacable spirit,
who shines among the voodoo gods
with his spurs and with his saber . . .
Papa Ogún, ay! Papa Ogún.

Papa Ogún, my baby wants
to be a warrior like you;
show him your grace and your affection . . .
Papa Ogún, ay! Papa Ogún.

Ahora comamos carne blanca
con la licencia de su mercé.
Ahora comamos carne blanca . . .

¡Ohé, nené!
¡Ohé, nené!
Adombe gangá mondé,
Adombe.
Candombe del baquiné,
¡Candombe!

Now we are ready to eat white flesh,
with permission from your grace,
Now we are ready to eat white flesh . . .

   Ohé, nené!
Ohé, nené!
Adombe gangá mondé,
Adombe.
Candombe del banquiné,
Candombe!

TRANSLATED BY RACHEL BENSON

Miguel Angel Asturias

The Mirror of Lida Sal

I

As summer fades, the rivers begin to pant for breath. The soft hiss of the current is replaced by a dry silence, the silence of thirst, the silence of drought, the silence of films of water immobilized among islands of sand, the silence of the trees sweating leaves from the heat and the wind, baked by the ardor of summer, the silence of the fields where laborers sleep naked and dreamless. No flies. Sultriness. A piercing sun and the earth like a kiln for baking tiles. The enfeebled cattle drive off the heat with their tails and seek the shadow of the avocado plantations. In the scarce, dry grass, sedentary rabbits, deaf snakes looking for water and birds that scarcely get off the ground.

Not to mention, of course, how the eyes wear themselves out scanning so much flat surface of the earth. The gaze reaches to the horizon in all four directions. Only by staring intently can little groups of trees be distinguished, tilled fields and the kind of paths, created by much passing and repassing of the same spot, leading from there to hamlets containing the human attributes of fire, women, children and farmyards where life pecks at the contents of the day like an insatiable chicken.

During one of these desperate hours of breathless heat, Doña Petronila Ángela came home (some called her this, others Petrángela). She was the wife of Don Felipe Alvizures, mother of a boy, and some months pregnant. Doña Petronila Ángela acts like someone who does nothing for fear that her husband will grumble at her for doing things in her condition, and by that seeming to do nothing, keeps the house in order, everything the way it should be: clean linen on the beds, rooms, patios and corridors neat, an eye on the kitchen, her hands on her sewing or in the oven and her feet everywhere—in the chickenyard, in the room where the corn and the cocoa are ground, in the garden, in the ironing room, in the pantry, everywhere.

Her worthy husband quarrels with her when he sees her thus occupied; he would like to see her sitting still or stretched out carelessly and this is bad because the children might turn out lazy. Her worthy husband, Felipe Alvizures, is a man with a spacious interior which causes him to be slow in his movements and, from the outside, always stuffed into his ample drill suits. With little arithmetic, he still knows how to keep a running tally of the ears of corn; not very literate, he still knows how to read like many people who never open a book. And besides, the spaciousness within, as his wife is accustomed to say, is what makes it hard for him to put words together. It seems that he has to bring one from one place and another from somewhere much further off. Both inside and outside, Señor Felipe has had room to move quite deliberately, never doing anything hasty and thinking things out completely, completely. And when the time comes, God be with him, Petrángela is accustomed to say, if death doesn't take him, who knows what he may achieve?

The heat of the sun spreads throughout the house. A hungry sun which knew it was lunchtime. But under the clay-tiled roofs it feels quite cool. Contrary to his usual habit, Felipito arrived before his father, jumped his horse over the crossbars of the gate. He had only to get over two of the bars, the highest and most dangerous and, after terrorizing the chickens, setting the dogs barking and the pigeons whirling from the dovecote, after a coming and going at lightning speed, quieted his horse in a shower of sparks struck from its shoes on stones of the patio, and burst into laughter.

"What a way to act, Felipito . . . of course I knew it was you."

His mother did not like such showmanship. The horse stood with its eyes shining and foam on its mouth; Felipito already on the ground, embracing and pacifying his mother.

His father arrived a little later, astride a black stallion called Samaritano because it was quiet. He dismounted patiently, picked up the crossbars Felipe had knocked off the gate; he put them back and entered noiselessly except for the clatter of Samaritano's hooves crossing the cobblestones in front of the horseblock.

They had lunch mutely, looking at each other as if seeing nothing. Señor Felipe looked at his wife, she at her son, and the son at his parents devouring tortillas, tearing the meat from a chicken leg with sharp teeth, drinking large gulps of water to help down a mass of delicious dark yuca.

"God reward you, Father . . ."

Lunch was over, as always with few words, between a general silence and Petrángela's consulting her husband's face and the gestures of his hands to know when he was finished with one dish in order to ask the servant for the one that followed.

After thanking his father, Felipito approached his mother with his arms crossing on his chest, lowered his head and repeated, "May God reward you, Mother . . ."

And everything ended with Don Felipe in the hammock, his wife in a rocking-chair, and Felipito on a bench which he straddled like a horse. Each one had his thoughts. Señor Felipe was smoking. Felipito, who hadn't the nerve to smoke in his father's face, fixed his eyes on him through the smoke and Petrángela rocked in her chair, setting it in motion with one of her little feet.

2

Lida Sal, a mulatto girl giddier than a top, was eavesdropping, not on what was being done, but on the chatter of blind Benito Jojón and a certain Faluterio, who was in charge of the fiesta of the Virgin of Carmen. The blind man and Faluterio had finished eating and were ready to go. This made it easier for Lida Sal to hear what they said. The dishwashing sinks were almost at the street door of the restaurant.

"The Perfectantes," the blind man was saying, gesturing as if to remove cobwebs from the wrinkles of his face, "are magicians and how can what you've told me be true when no volunteers come, mainly because people are so stand-offish nowadays. Yes, friend Faluterio, there are many baptisms and few marriages, which is not good. Many single folk with children, many single folk with children . . ."

"What do you want? I'm asking you, face to face, to tell me your precise thoughts in this matter, and afterwards I can talk about it with the other members of the brotherhood of the Most Holy Virgin. It's almost time for the fiesta and if there are no women to take charge of the Perfectantes costumes then, like last year, we'll have to do without magicians . . ."

"Talk's cheap, Faluterio, action is hard work. If I take the trouble to concern myself with the Perfectantes, perhaps I'll find volunteers. There are a lot of marriagable women, Faluterio, a lot of women at an age when they ought to be married."

"It's difficult, Benito, it's difficult. Old wives' tales. With what people know today, who takes any stock in such junk. For my part and on the part of all the committee for the patron saint's festival, I think there will be no problem about giving you the necessary funds, seeing that you yourself can't work on the costumes of the Perfectantes because you're blind.

"Yes, yes and I'll take steps to distribute them; thus the old time customs won't come to an end."

"I'm off, I let it go at that, and you can assume my offer is firm."

"I take your word for it, Faluterio, I take your word, and I shall go look where God leads me."

Lida Sal's cold soapy hand abandoned the plate she was washing and came to rest on the blind man's hand, on the sleeve of his jacket which, from repeated patching, was all one patch. Benito Jojón responded to the affectionate gesture and stood still, although he, too, was going home, home being the whole plaza. He asked who was holding him.

"It's me, Lida Sal, the girl who scrubs the plates here in the restaurant."

"Yes, daughter, and what can I do for you?"

"You can give me some new advice . . ."

"Well, well, then you are one of those who believe there is old advice . . ."

"Just for that reason I want something new, advice that you'll work out just for me, that you haven't given to anyone else or even thought about before. New, you understand, new . . ."

"Let's see, let's see, if I can . . ."

"You already know what it's about . . ."

"No, I don't know a thing . . ."

"It's that I'm, how can I say it? I'm rather taken with a man and he doesn't even look at me . . ."

"He's unmarried?"

"Unmarried, handsome, rich . . ." Lida Sal sighed. "But who's going to look at me, scrubbing off leftovers, when he's such a big shot . . ."

"Don't worry about it any more. I know what you want but since you've told me you're a dishwasher, I wonder how you can manage to make a contribution for a costume for one of the Perfectantes. They're very expensive . . ."

"Don't let that bother you. I have a little something, if the contribution isn't too much. What I want to know is if you would go so far as to give me one of those magic garments and go and see to it that this ungrateful fellow puts it on the day of the patron saint. He must be dressed as a Perfectante in the costume I order for him, that's the main thing. The magic will take care of the rest."

"But, daughter, aside from being unable to see, I don't know where to find this gentleman you've promised yourself, which makes me doubly blind."

Lida Sal bent toward one of the large, wrinkled, dirty ears of the blind man and said,

"At the Alvizures . . ."

"Ah . . . ah . . ."

"Felipito Alvizures . . ."

"Now I see, now I see . . . you want to contract a good marriage . . ."

"God no! You're really blind in every way if you see nothing in my love but self-interest!"

"Then if it isn't self-interest, it's the call of the body . . ."

"Don't be a beast. It's my soul because if it were just my body I would perspire when I see him but, on the contrary, I don't feel like myself when I see him and I sigh."

"That's good. How old are you?"

"I'm going on nineteen but, you know, perhaps I may be twenty. Stop it, take your hand away from there . . . blind and all, feeling my breasts!"

"Just to make sure, just to make sure how you're built, little daughter . . ."

"Are you going to the Alvizures? That's what I want to know!"

"This very day. What is it that you've slipped on my finger? Is it a ring?"

"It's a gold ring, worth its weight . . ."

"How nice! How nice!"

"And I'll owe you what I have to pay for the contribution to the Perfectante costume."

"You're practical, child, but I can't go to the Alvizures without knowing your name . . ."

"Lida Sal . . ."

"A pretty name, but not a Christian one. I'll go where your heart sends me. We'll try the magic. Señor Felipe's carts are loading and unloading wood in the market right now, so I'll go sit in one of them. I've done it before and they will take me there for my visit to search out Felipito."

3

The blind man attempted to kiss Doña Petronila Ángela's hand, but she withdrew it in time and the smack of his lips was left hovering in the air. She didn't like kisses, which is why dogs didn't please her.

"The mouth is made for eating, talking and praying, Jojón, and not to go around eating people. Did you come to see the menfolk? They're over there in the hammocks. Give me your hand, I'll lead you so you won't fall. What can I give you for coming so far all of a sudden? Fortunately, you know that the carts are entirely at your disposal and that this is your house."

"Yes, God reward you, dear lady, and if I came without letting you know beforehand, it is because we haven't much time and must use what there is to properly prepare the fiesta of the Most Holy Virgin."

"You're right. We're on the eve of the great day and very soon we'll find it hard to realize that another year has gone by."

"And how much better than last year the preparations are being made. You can see . . ."

Señor Felipe was in one hammock, Felipito in another, rocking as the sun went down. Señor Felipe smoked fig-colored tobacco and out of respect Felipito contented himself with watching the smoke form clouds and disperse in the warm air.

Petrángela came close to them, leading Jojón by the hand, and when she was near the hammocks announced that they had a visitor.

"Not a visit," the blind man corrected her, "a nuisance . . ."

"Friends are never a nuisance," Señor Felipe hastened to say during the time it took to drag one of his short legs out of the hammock in order to sit up.

"Did the carts bring you, Jojón?" Felipito asked.

"That's it, my boy, that's it. Although I managed to come here, I don't know how I'll get back."

"I'll saddle a horse and take you," Felipito answered. "Don't worry about that."

"And if not, stay with us . . ."

"Ah, dear lady, if it were suitable I'd stay, but I talk and I know that guests who talk are always a nuisance."

Meanwhile, Señor Felipe took the hand of the blind man who was so full of ambiguities and led him to a chair which Felipito had brought.

"I'm going to put a cigar in your mouth," Señor Felipe said.

"Don't ask my permission, Señor, when you do me a favor, don't ask my permission . . ."

And now smoking and with a beating heart, Jojón went on.

"I told you mine was not a visit but a nuisance. And that's what it is, pure nuisance. I come as a messenger to find out if this year Felipito wants to be the leader of the Perfectantes."

"That's his affair," said Señor Alvizures, making signs for Petrángela to come close and, when she was next to him, he put an arm around the unembraceable waist to be close as they listened to what the blind man said.

"This is some scheme . . ." was Felipito's first reaction, spitting a gob of saliva which glistened on the ground. Whenever he became nervous, he spat.

"There's no catch to it," Jojón explained, "because there's time to think it over and then slowly make a decision, as long as you do it soon because the fiesta is coming. You must take into account, my boy, that the costume has to be tried on to see if it fits well and the braid of the Prince of Perfectantes has to be sewn on the sleeves."

"I don't believe there's much to think over," Petrángela, the executive, decided. "Felipito is dedicated to the Virgin of Carmen and what better way of rendering her devotion than to participate in her illustrious fiesta?"

"That's true . . ." Felipe, the son, muttered.

"Then . . ." said Felipe, the father, seeking words with which to arbitrate, "there isn't much to think over or more to say," and still not finding words for what he wanted to express, went on, "You see, you didn't make your trip in vain Señor Benito! And now, Felipito, if as you say, you'll take him back on horseback, when you get to the village you can try on the costume that fits you best and see if it needs any alterations?"

"At the moment only the Prince's braid—" Jojón said. "Afterwards I'll get the costume and bring it to you to try on because as yet they haven't given it to me."

"All right," Felipito said, accepting, "and to lose no time, I'm going to see if there's a nice quiet stallion before it gets dark."

"Wait a minute, Don Be-off-in-a-hurry," his mother stopped him. "We're going to see that Jojón has a nice cup of chocolate . . ."

"Yes, yes, Mother, I know, but while he drinks his chocolate, I'll find the stallion and saddle him. It's growing late . . ."

And he was already leaving for the stables. "It's getting late and it will be dark soon, although to a blind man it's all the same whether he travels by day or night . . ." Felipito said to himself.

4

The dining-room was inactive and silent. Few customers at night. All the activity was in the middle of the day. So there was plenty of room for the blind man, leaning on the arm of Felipito Alvizures, to enter and be seated at one of the tables. And for two dark eyes to fix their black pupils on him, bright with hope.

"Would you like something?" Lida Sal said as she approached with a napkin to wipe off the old wooden tabletop, weather-beaten and worn out by the years.

"Two beers," Felipito answered, "and if you have sandwiches with meat, give us two."

For a moment, the mulatto girl felt the ground unsteady under her feet and this was the only security there was. She was in a state which she could not successfully hide. Whenever she could, she rubbed her bare arms and firm breasts, which trembled under her blouse, across Felipe's shoulders. She did not lack pretexts to touch him: the glasses, the foam spilt from the blind man's beer, the plates with the sandwiches.

"And you," Alvizures asked the blind man, "where do you spend the night?"

"Right here. They sometimes let me sleep here in the dining-room, don't they, Lida Sal?"

"Yes . . . yes . . ." was all she could say and it was hard for her lips to utter the price of the beer and the sandwiches.

In the hollow of her hand, hollow as her heart felt, she squeezed the warm coins that Alvizures had paid her, warm from being in his pocket, in contact with his body and, unable to stop herself, she raised them to her lips and kissed them. After kissing them, she rubbed them over her face and slipped them between her breasts.

Through the darkness of her eyes—that nocturnal darkness which begins and ends black, the color of slate—trotted Felipito Alvizures' horse, followed by the gentle stallion on which the blind man had been mounted.

And how difficult it is to break through to speech in the midst of so much silence.

"Take it easy, blind man," she said as she finally got the use of her tongue, "You don't have to start feeling . . ."

"My hand would like to touch you (for all your thinking the worst) so that you will consider the ring you gave me this morning mine. I went to a lot of trouble and exercised ingenuity to earn it. Tomorrow you'll have here the Perfectante costume that Felipito will wear in the fiesta . . ."

"And what do I have to do . . ."

"Daughter, you sleep with the costume enough nights to impregnate it with your magic; when a person sleeps she grows magical and in this way, when he puts it on for the fiesta, he is overcome by the enchantment, seeks you out and then he can't live without you."

Lida Sal had to gasp for breath. Her head swam. She clutched the back of a chair with one hand, with the other she leaned on the table, a smothered sob on her lips.

"Are you crying?"

"No . . . no! Yes . . . yes!"

"Are you crying or not?"

"Yes, with joy . . ."

"But are you that happy?"

"Take it easy, Don Blind Man, take it easy!"

The mulatto girl's warm nipple was removed from the old man's hand as he felt the coins which Felipito had paid slide down from her breasts to her belly, as if her heart was emitting bits of warm metal to finish paying Jojón the contribution to cover the cost of the magic costume.

<h1 style="text-align:center">5</h1>

No costume was showier than that of the Perfectante. Swiss Guard trousers, archangel's hat, a bullfighter's jacket. Boots, braid, fringes, buttonholes and golden cord, brilliant and changeable colors, spangles, beads, fragments of crystal shining like precious stones. The Perfectantes glowed like suns among the masked troupes accompanying the Virgin of Carmen in the procession which passed through all of the streets of the town, from the most pretentious to the humblest, because none was too grand nor insignificant for the Great Lady to pass his house.

Señor Felipe moved his head from side to side. Thinking it over, he was not very pleased that his son should be involved in this gaudy display but to have opposed it would have offended Petrángela's religious sentiments, all the more intense now that she was pregnant, so he hid his displeasure with a joke which his wife found in bad taste.

"I was so mad about your mother when we got married, Felipito, that people said she had slept with the costume for seven nights, the one I wore as a Perfectante. I was twenty-seven, maybe thirty . . ."

"Your father never went as a Perfectante, my boy, don't believe it . . ." she contradicted timidly and mournfully.

"But then there would have been no use in your sleeping with the costume . . ." laughed Alvizures, a man who seldom laughed, not that he didn't like to laugh, it was good for you, but because after marriage, he said, laughter is left at the church door where you married, where the *via crucis* begins . . .

"This story that I cast a spell to make you marry me is a story you made up . . . If you did go as a Perfectante, who knows what other woman . . ."

"Other woman? Not within twenty leagues . . ." and he laughed cheerfully, inviting Felipito to laugh, too.

"Laugh, son, laugh while you're unmarried. Laughter and laughing are the privilege of bachelorhood. When you marry, when someone sleeps with the Perfectante costume that she gets you to put on for the fiesta, good-bye laughter forever. Married people don't laugh; we pretend, which isn't the same . . . laughter is an attribute of bachelorhood . . . of youthful bachelorhood, eh? Because old bachelors don't laugh either, they show their teeth . . ."

"Your father mixes everything up, son . . ." Petrángela objected. "Laughter is for young people, married or unmarried, and not for the old ones. He's growing old. How are we to blame? He's growing old . . ."

Petrángela couldn't fall asleep that night. On her conscience were those nights in which she had really slept with the Perfectante costume which Señor Felipe Alvizures wore in the fiesta thirty years before. She had to contradict him before her son because there are secrets which you don't reveal to your children. Not secrets; intimacies, little intimacies. Dawn wouldn't come. She felt cold. She tucked her feet into the warmth of the blanket. She pressed her eyelids together. It was impossible to sleep. As sleep continued to evade her eyes, she began to fear that at this very hour, on the eve of the fiesta of Our Lady of Carmen, someone was sleeping with Felipito's costume, impregnating it with her magical sweat and by this means seduce him.

"Oh Lady of Heaven, Most Blessed Virgin," she murmured, "forgive my fear, my superstition. I know they're stupid . . . they're just old wives' tales, tales with no basis . . . but he's my son . . . my son."

The best thing would be to prevent his appearing as a Perfectante. But how to avoid it when he had accepted and was to appear as the Prince of the Perfectantes? It would disorganize everything and then it was she, in the presence of her husband, who had pressed Felipito to accept.

Dawn wouldn't come. The cocks didn't crow. Her mouth was dry. Her hair was in a tangle over her face with so much searching in her pillow for sleep.

"What woman, oh God, what woman will be sleeping with the Perfectante costume my son is going to wear?"

6

Lida Sal, by day her cheeks more prominent than her eyes, by night her eyes more prominent than her cheeks, glanced from one side of her bedroom to the other and sure she was quite alone, that nothing but deep darkness surrounded her, that the door was as well barred as the small window which looked out on a completely sealed pantry, stripped herself naked in the cool air, passed her hands roughened by dishwashing along her slender body and, with moist eyes, throat dry with anxiety and muscles trembling, buried herself in the Perfectante costume before going to sleep. But more than sleep, it was deprivation which began to stiffen her body, deprivation and weariness which did not prevent her from carrying on an intense conversation with herself in a low voice, confiding her feelings of love to every thread of color, every spangle, to the beads and to every bit of gold.

One night, however, she did not put it on. She left it rolled up under her pillow, saddened because she did not have a full length mirror in which to see herself dressed in the costume. Not that it mattered whether it became her or was too short or too long, too loose or too tight, but because it was part of the foremagic to dress herself in it and to see herself so dressed, in a full length mirror. Little by little she went on pulling it out from under the pillow, sleeves, trousers, the back, the front, caressing it with her cheeks, putting it against her forehead, against her thoughts, kissing it with little cries . . .

Jojón came for his breakfast very early. Ever since he had become involved with her, he ate what he wanted, behind the back of the owner, who was not in the restaurant very often now since she went about making preparations to take care of her regular customers and the foreigners during the days of fiesta.

"The misery of being poor," the mulatto girl moaned. "I don't have a full-length mirror to see myself . . ."

"And that is definitely important," the blind man answered, "because without that, the magic might fail."

"And what shall I do? Creep into a rich home like a thief in the middle of the night dressed as a Perfectante? I'm desperate. Since last night I don't know what to do. Advise me . . ."

"I don't know . . . magic has certain rules . . ."

"I don't know what you mean . . ."

"Well, because magic consists in either this or that, but always in something and, in this case, dressing as a Perfectante and seeing oneself in a full-length mirror."

"Blind as you are, what do you know, what do you know about mirrors?"

"I wasn't born blind, daughter. I was already grown up when I lost my sight, when my lenses were destroyed and then the sickness went into the eyeball."

"Well, in big houses there are big mirrors . . . at the Alvizures' . . ."

"Yes, there's a beautiful big one at the Alvizures' and I've heard . . . no, it's just malicious gossip . . . Well, perhaps it might give you a little hope. That's why I tell you, not for fun but I'll make an exception because you're to be their daughter-in-law. They do say that when Felipito's mother, Doña Petrángela had no mirror in which to see herself when she was using magic on her husband, the day they got married she had the Perfectante costume on under her wedding dress and when Felipe told her to undress, she took off the white dress and instead of being naked, appeared as a Perfectante just to complete the rite, to complete the spell . . ."

"And married people strip like that?"

"Yes, daughter."

"Then you were married?"

"Yes, and since my eyes were not yet destroyed by the sickness, I could see my wife."

"Dressed like a Perfectante?"

"No, daughter, in Eve's costume."

Lida Sal took away the cup from which the blind man had been drinking his *café con leche* and he shook the crumbs off onto the table. The owner wasn't going to see this anyway.

"Don't ask me where to find it, but you must see yourself, at full-length, in a mirror somewhere," were his last words. This time he forgot to remind her that the moment to give up the costume was approaching and that it was almost time for the fiesta and that he had to bring the suit to the Alvizures'!

7

Stars almost drowned in the clarity of the moonlight. Dark green trees, farmyards smelling of milk and dew, haystacks in the fields yellower than the light of the full moon. It was very late in the fading afternoon, now no more than a reflection in the sky just where the stars were beginning to shine. And in this thin region, the afternoon was bluish, pinkish, pink, green and violet. Lida Sal's eyes were fixed, thinking that the time was coming to hand over the costume.

"Tomorrow is the last day I can give you," Jojón informed her, "because if it isn't delivered on time, everything will be ruined . . .

"Yes, yes, don't get upset, tomorrow I'll give it up. To-day I'll look at myself in the mirror . . ."

"In the mirror of your dreams, daughter, for I don't know where . . ."

The luminous edge of the afternoon still reflected in Lida Sal's eyes like a crevice in impossibility, a crevice from which the sky might peep out.

"You cursed insect!" cried the owner of the restaurant, pulling her hair. "Aren't you ashamed at the way you've left all the dirty dishes unwashed? For days you've been running around like crazy and you haven't lifted a finger!"

The girl let her hair be pulled and her arms pinched without answering. A moment afterward, as if by enchantment, the quarrel subsided. But there was worse to come, for after the wordy insults, there followed exclamations and lectures.

"Here the fiesta's coming and the young lady hasn't even asked me for new clothes. With what I have for you, you should buy a dress, some shoes and stockings. It's not decent to appear in church and in the procession like a poor sloven. I'm ashamed at what people will say about me, your boss—at least that I starve you or hold back your wages."

"Well, if you think I should, give me some money and tomorrow I'll go and buy something."

"Of course, child, one good turn deserves another. You take care of me by doing your work and I'll take care of you and buy what you need. What's more, you're pretty, not ugly. Who's to say that you won't find a good match among the people who come to sell cattle at the fiesta?"

Lida Sal heard her without listening. She scrubbed off the leftovers still thinking, reflecting on what she had imagined as she watched the last flicker of twilight. The hardest work was scrubbing out the pans and earthenware pots. What misery! She had to scratch them with a polishing bag and scouring powder to get rid of the butter at the bottom, then battle with the outside, also covered with greasy soot.

The brilliance of the moon made her feel as if it were not night; it was as if day had merely grown colder.

"It's not far away," she said, speaking her thoughts aloud. "It's a big pool, almost a lake."

She left her room quickly. She had to be back by dawn to give the Perfectante costume to the blind man so that he could bring it to the Alvizures' house . . . but, oh, she still had to see herself in a full-length mirror because magic has its rules . . .

At first, the open country startled her. But then her eyes became used to the trees, the stones, the shadows. She could see where she was going so clearly that it was like walking in subdued daylight. In her strange costume she met no one, so she did not put anyone to flight as if from a diabolical vision . . . She was afraid, afraid of being an apparition of fire, a torch of flaming spangles, a ripple of beads, of watery sparks integrated into a single precious stone in human form on the way to look into the lake, dressed in the costume which Felipito Alvizures would wear in the fiesta.

From the edge of a ravine, fragrant with the fresh earth turned up by landslides, among surface roots and moving stones, she stared at the broad green mirror, blue in its depths, between a film of low clouds, moonlight and dark shadows. She thought she looked different. Was she Lida Sal? Was she the mulatto girl who scrubbed dishes in the restaurant? Was it she who followed this road, on this night, under this moon, in this costume of flame and dew?

She moved from side to side to side, brushing her shoulders against the bark of trees; flowers somnolent with drowsy perfume moistened her hair and face with kisses which were drops of water.

"Let me pass! Let me pass!" she said, moving forward between clumps of maddeningly aromatic ginger trees.

"Make room! Make room . . ." she repeated, passing gigantic rocks and stones strewn about under the sky like meteors or perhaps recently erupted from the mouths of some volcano, or newly emerged from the earth.

"Let me pass! Let me pass . . . !" to the waterfall.

"Space, room to let beauty pass!" to the brooks and the ravines come, like herself, to see themselves in the great mirror.

"It swallows you up," she said to them. "It's not going to swallow me up. It's only going to see me, it's going to see me dressed like a Perfectante so that the rules of magic will be completely satisfied."

There was no wind. Moon and water. Lida Sal leaned against a tree that wept as it slept, but when she touched it, she shrank away horrified: perhaps it was bad luck to look into the mirror next to a tree that shed tears as it slept.

She looked up and down the shore for a spot where she could see herself full-length. She could not manage the whole image. Her whole body. Only by climbing onto one of the tall rocks on the other shore.

"If the blind man could see me . . . but what foolishness, how could a blind man see?" She had said something silly to herself; it was she who had to look for herself, look at herself from head to toe.

At last she was on a basalt rock looking at herself in the water.

"What better mirror?"

She slid one foot to the edge of the rock in order to enjoy seeing the whole costume she was wearing: spangles, beads, bright stones, braid, flecks and cords of gold. And then she moved the other foot to see better, and then she could not stop herself. Her body joined her reflection, a splash, after which there was no reflection and no body.

But she came up again. Tried to save herself . . . her hands . . . the bubbles . . . the choking . . . she had become the mulatto girl who fought for the unattainable . . . the shore . . . now the shore was unattainable . . .

Two immense moments of anguish.

The last thing to be extinguished was the enormous anguish of her eyes still able to distinguish the ever-more distant shore of the little lake, called Lida Sal's mirror from then on.

When it rains, with moonlight at the same time, her corpse floats. The rocks have seen it. The willows have seen it, weeping leaves and reflections. The deer and the rabbits have seen it. The moles telegraph the news with the beating of their little hearts before they return to their darkness.

Blinking silver nets of rain draw her image to the disturbed mirror and set it walking over the surface of the water in its costume of a Perfectante, the water which absent-mindedly dreams her.

TRANSLATED BY H. R. HAYS

Despedida

Entre mi amor y yo han de levantarse
trescientas noches como trescientas paredes
y el mar será una magia entre nosotros.

El tiempo arrancará con dura mano
las calles enzarzadas en mi pecho.
No habrá sino recuerdos.
(Oh tardes merecidas por la pena,
noches esperanzadas de mirarte,
campos desalentados, pobre cielo
humillado en la hondura de los charcos
como un ángel caído . . .
Y tu vivir que agracia mis anhelos
y ese barrio dejado y placentero
que hoy en luz de mi amor se resplandece . . .)

Definitiva como una estatua
entristecerá tu ausencia otros campos.

Jorge Luis Borges

Parting

Three hundred nights like three hundred walls
must rise between my love and me
and the sea will be black art between us.

Time with a hard hand will tear out
the streets tangled in my breast.
Nothing will be left but memories.
(O afternoons earned with suffering,
nights hoping for the sight of you,
dejected vacant lots, poor sky
shamed in the bottom of the puddles
like a fallen angel . . .
And your life that graces my desire
and that run-down and light-hearted neighborhood
shining today in the glow of my love . . .)

Final as a statue
your absence will sadden other fields.

TRANSLATED BY W. S. MERWIN

Página Para Recordar al Coronel Suárez, Vencedor en Junín

Qué importan las penurias, el destierro,
la humillación de envejecer, la sombrea creciente
del dictador sobre la patria, la casa en el Barrio del Alto
que vendieron sus hermanos mientras guerreaba, los días inútiles
(los días que uno espera olvidar, los días que uno sabe que olvidará).
si tuvo su hora alta, a caballo,
en la visible pampa de Junín como en un escenario para el futuro,
como si el anfiteatro de montañas fuera el futuro

Qué importa el tiempo sucesivo si en él
hubo una plenitud, un éxtasis, una tarde.

Sirvió trece años en las guerras de América. Al fin
la suerte lo llevó al Estado Oriental, a campos del Rio Negro.
En los atardeceres pensaría
que para él había florecido esa rosa:
la encarnada batalla de Junín, el instante infinito
en que las lanzas se tocaron, la orden que movió la batalla,
la derrota inicial, y entre los fragores
(no menos brusca para él que para la tropa)
su voz gritando a los peruanos que arremetieran,
la luz, el ímpetu y la fatalidad de la carga,
el furioso laberinto de los ejércitos,
la batalla de lanzas en la que no retumbó un solo tiro,
el *godo* que atravesó con el hierro,
la victoria, la felicidad, la fatiga, un principio de sueño,
y la gente muriendo entre los pantanos,
y Bolívar pronunciando palabras sin duda históricas
y el sol ya occidental y el recuperado sabor del agua y del vino,
y aquel muerto sin cara porque la pisó y borró la batalla . . .

A Page to Commemorate Colonel Suárez, Victor at Junín

What do they matter now, the deprivations,
exile, the ignominies of growing old,
the dictator's shadow spreading across the land, the house
in the Barrio del Alto, which his brothers sold while he fought,
the pointless days (days one hopes to forget,
days one knows are forgettable),
when he had at least his burning hour on horseback
on the plateau of Junín, a stage for the future,
as if that mountain stage itself were the future?

What is time's monotony to him, who knew
that fulfillment, that ecstasy, that afternoon?

Thirteen years he served in the Wars of Independence. Then
fate took him to Uruguay, to the banks of the Rio Negro.
In the dying afternoons he would think
of his moment which had flowered like a rose—
the crimson battle of Junín, the enduring moment
in which the lances crossed, the order of battle,
defeat at first, and in the uproar
(as astonishing to him as to the army)
his voice urging the Peruvians to the attack,
the thrill, the drive, the decisiveness of the charge,
the seething labyrinth of cavalries,
clash of the lances (not a single shot fired),
the Spaniard he ran through with his spear,
the headiness of victory, the exhaustion, the drowsiness descending,
and the men dying in the marshes,
and Bolívar uttering words earmarked no doubt for history,
and the sun in the west by now, and water and wine
tasted as for the first time, and that dead man
whose face the battle had trampled on and obliterated. . . .

Su bisnieto escribe estos versos y una tácita voz
desde lo antiguo de la sangre le llega:
—Qué importa mi batalla de Junín si es una gloriosa memoria,
una fecha que se aprende para un examen o un lugar en el atlas.
La batalla es eterna y puede prescindir de la pompa
de visibles ejércitos con clarines;
Junín son dos civiles que en una esquina maldicen a un tirano,
o un hombre oscuro que se muere en la cárcel.

1953

A Un Poeta Sajón

Tú cuya carne que hoy es polvo y planeta
Pesó como la nuestra sobre la tierra,
Tú cuyos ojos vieron el sol, esa famosa estrella,
Tú que viviste no en el rígido ayer
Sino en el incesante presente,
En el último punto y ápice vertiginoso del tiempo,
Tú que en tu monasterio fuiste llamado
Por la antigua voz de la épica,
Tú que tejiste las palabras,
Tú que cantaste la victoria de Brunanburh
Y no la atribuiste al Señor
Sino a la espada de tu rey,
Tú que con júbilo feroz cantaste las espadas de hierro,
La vergüenza del viking,
El festín del cuervo y del águila,

His great-grandson is writing these lines,
and a silent voice comes to him out of the past,
out of the blood:

"What does my battle at Junín matter if it is only
a glorious memory, or a date learned by rote
for an examination, or a place in the atlas?
The battle is everlasting and can do without
the pomp of actual armies and of trumpets.
Junín is two civilians cursing a tyrant
on a street corner,
or an unknown man somewhere, dying in prison."

1953

TRANSLATED BY ALASTAIR REID

To a Saxon Poet

You whose flesh, now dust and planet,
Once weighed like ours on earth,
Whose eyes took in the sun, that famous star,
You who lived not in the rigid past
But in a ceaseless present
At the topmost point and dizzying apex of time,
Who in your monastery heard the call
Of the epic's ancient voice,
Who wove words
And sang the victory at Brunanburh,
Ascribing it not to God
But to your king's sword edge,
You who with fierce joy celebrated swords hammered out of iron,
The Norseman's shame,
The banquet of raven and eagle,

Tú que en la oda militar congregaste
Las rituales metáforas de la estirpe,
Tú que en un tiempo sin historia
Viste en el ahora el ayer
Y en el sudor y sangre de Brunanburh
Un cristal de antiguas auroras,
Tú que tanto querías a tu Inglaterra
Y no la nombraste,
Hoy no eres otra cosa que unas palabras
Que los germanistas anotan.
Hoy no eres otra cosa que mi voz
Cuando revive tus palabras de hierro.

Pido a mis dioses o a la suma del tiempo
Que mis días merezcan el olvido,
Que mi nombre sea Nadie como el de Ulises,
Pero que algún verso perdure
En la noche propicia a la memoria
O en las mañanas de los hombres.

Gathering in your military ode
The ritual metaphors of your kin,
You who in an age without history
Saw in the present the past
And in the blood and sweat of Brunanburh
A mirror of ancient sunrises,
You who so much loved your England
And did not name her—
Today you are but a few words
That Germanic scholars annotate;
Today you are my voice
When it calls back to life your iron words.

Of my gods or of the sum of time I ask
That my days attain oblivion,
That like Ulysses I may be called No One,
But that some verse of mine survive
On a night favorable to memory
Or in the morning of men.

TRANSLATED BY NORMAN THOMAS DI GIOVANNI

Delia Elena San Marco

We said goodbye at the corner of Eleventh. From the other sidewalk I turned to look back; you too had turned, and you waved goodbye to me.

A river of vehicles and people were flowing between us. It was five o'clock on an ordinary afternoon. How was I to know that that river was Acheron the doleful, the insuperable?

We did not see each other again, and a year later you were dead.

And now I seek out that memory and look at it, and I think it was false, and that behind that trivial farewell was infinite separation.

Last night I stayed in after dinner and reread, in order to understand these things, the last teaching Plato put in his master's mouth. I read that the soul may escape when the flesh dies.

And now I do not know whether the truth is in the ominous subsequent interpretation, or in the unsuspecting farewell.

For if souls do not die, it is right that we should not make much of saying goodbye.

To say goodbye to each other is to deny separation. It is like saying "today we play at separating, but we will see each other tomorrow." Man invented farewells because he somehow knows he is immortal, even though he may seem gratuitous and ephemeral.

Sometime, Delia, we will take up again—beside what river?—this uncertain dialogue, and we will ask each other if ever, in a city lost on a plain, we were Borges and Delia.

TRANSLATED BY MILDRED BOYER

The Dead Man

That a man from the outlying slums of a city like Buenos Aires, that a sorry hoodlum with little else to his credit than a passion for recklessness, should find his way into that wild stretch of horse country between Brazil and Uruguay and become the leader of a band of smugglers, seems on the face of it unbelievable. To those who think so, I'd like to give an account of what happened to Benjamín Otálora, of whom perhaps not a single memory lingers in the neighborhood where he grew up, and who died a fitting death, struck down by a bullet, somewhere on the border of Rio Grande do Sul. Of the details of his adventures I know little; should I ever be given the facts, I shall correct and expand these pages. For the time being, this outline may prove of some use.

Benjamín Otálora, along about 1891, is a strapping young man of nineteen. He has a low forehead, candid blue eyes, and that country-boy appearance that goes with Basque ancestry. A lucky blow with a knife has made clear to him that he is also brave; his opponent's death causes him no concern, nor does his need to flee the country. The political boss of the district gives him a letter of introduction to a certain Azevedo Bandeira, in Uruguay. Otálora books passage; the crossing is stormy and the ship pitches and creaks. The next day, he wanders the length and breadth of Montevideo, with unacknowledged or perhaps unsuspected homesickness. He does not find Azevedo Bandeira. Getting on toward midnight, in a small saloon out on the northern edge of town, he witnesses a brawl between some cattle drovers. A knife flashes. Otálora has no idea who is in the right or wrong, but the sheer taste of danger lures him, just as cards or music lure other men. In the confusion, he blocks a lunging knife thrust that one of the gauchos aims at a man wearing a rough countryman's poncho and, oddly, the dark derby of a townsman. The man turns out to be Azevedo Bandeira. (As soon as he finds this out, Otálora destroys the letter, preferring to be under no one's obligation.) Azevedo Bandeira, though of stocky build, gives the unaccountable impression of being somehow misshapen. In his large face, which seems always to be too close, are the Jew, the Negro, and the Indian; in his bearing, the tiger and the ape. The scar that cuts across his cheek is one ornament more, like his bristling black moustache.

A fantasy or a mistake born of drunkenness, the fight ends as quickly as it broke out. Otálora takes a drink with the drovers and then goes along with them to an all-night party and after that—the sun high in the sky by now—to a rambling house in the Old Town. Inside, on the bare ground of the last patio, the men lay out their sheepskin saddle blankets to sleep. Dimly, Otálora compares this past night with the night before; here he is, on solid ground now, among friends. A pang of remorse for not missing his Buenos Aires nags at him, however. He sleeps until nightfall, when he is wakened by the same gaucho who, blind drunk, had tried to knife Bandeira. (Otálora recalls that the man has shared the high-spirited night with the rest of them, and that Bandeira had seated him at his right hand and forced him to go on drinking.) The man says the boss has sent for him. In a kind of office opening into the entrance passage (Otálora has never before seen an entrance with doors opening into it from the sides), Azevedo Bandeira, in the company of an aloof and showy red-haired woman, is waiting for him. Bandeira praises him up and down, offers him a shot of rum, tells him he has the makings of a man of guts, suggests that he go up north with the others to bring back a large cattle herd. Otálora agrees; toward dawn they are on the road, heading for Tacuarembó.

For Otálora a new kind of life opens up, a life of far-flung sunrises and long days in the saddle, reeking of horses. It is an untried and at times unbearable life, but it's already in his blood, for just as the men of certain countries worship and feel the call of the sea, we Argentines in turn (including the man who weaves these symbols) yearn for the boundless plains that ring under a horse's hooves. Otálora has grown up in a neighborhood of teamsters and liverymen. In under a year, he makes himself into a gaucho. He learns to handle a horse, to round up and slaughter cattle, to throw a rope for holding an animal fast or bolas for bringing it down, to fight off sleep, to weather storms and frosts and sun, to drive a herd with whistles and hoots. Only once during this whole apprenticeship does he set eyes on Azevedo Bandeira, but he has him always in mind because to be one of Bandeira's men is to be looked up to and feared, and because after any feat or hard job the gauchos always say Bandeira does it better. Somebody has it that Bandeira was born on the Brazilian side of the Cuareim, in Rio Grande do Sul; this, which should lower him in Otálora's eyes, somehow—with its suggestion of dense forests and of marshes and of inextricable and almost endless distances—only adds to him. Little by little, Otálora comes to realize that Bandeira's interests are many and that chief among them is smuggling. To be a cattle drover is to be a servant; Otálora decides to work himself up to the level of smuggler. One night, as two of his companions are about to go over the border to bring back a consignment of rum, Otálora picks a fight with one of them, wounds him, and takes his place. He is driven by ambition and also by a dim sense of loyalty. The man (he thinks) will come to find out that I'm worth more than all his Uruguayans put together.

Another year goes by before Otálora sees Montevideo again. They come riding through the outskirts and into the city (which to Otálora now seems enormous); reaching the boss's house, the men prepare to bed down in the last patio. The days pass, and Otálora still has not laid eyes on Bandeira. It is said, in fear, that he is ailing; every afternoon a Negro goes up to Bandeira's room with a kettle and maté. One evening, the job is assigned to Otálora. He feels vaguely humiliated, but at the same time gratified.

The bedroom is bare and dark. There's a balcony that faces the sunset, there's a long table with a shining disarray of riding crops, bullwhips, cartridge belts, firearms, and knives. On the far wall there's a

mirror and the glass is faded. Bandeira lies face up, dreaming and muttering in his sleep; the sun's last rays outline his features. The big white bed
seems to make him smaller, darker. Otálora notes his graying hair, his
exhaustion, his weakness, the deep wrinkles of his years. It angers him
being mastered by this old man. He thinks that a single blow would be
enough to finish him. At this moment, he glimpses in the mirror that
someone has come in. It's the woman with the red hair; she is barefoot
and only half-dressed, and looks at him with cold curiosity. Bandeira sits
up in bed; while he speaks of business affairs of the past two years and
drinks maté after maté, his fingers toy with the woman's braided hair. In
the end, he gives Otálora permission to leave.

A few days later, they get orders to head north again. There, in a place
that might be anywhere on the face of the endless plains, they come to a
forlorn ranch. Not a single tree or a brook. The sun's first and last rays
beat down on it. There are stone fences for the lean longhorn cattle. This
rundown set of buildings is called "The Last Sigh."

Sitting around the fire with the ranch hands, Otálora hears that Bandeira will soon be on his way from Montevideo. He asks what for, and
someone explains that there's an outsider turned gaucho among them
who's giving too many orders. Otálora takes this as a friendly joke and is
flattered that the joke can be made. Later on, he finds out that Bandeira
has had a falling out with one of the political bosses, who has withdrawn
his support. Otálora likes this bit of news.

Crates of rifles arrive; a pitcher and washbasin, both of silver, arrive
for the woman's bedroom; intricately figured damask draperies arrive;
one morning, from out of the hills, a horseman arrives—a sullen man
with a full beard and a poncho. His name is Ulpiano Suárez and he is
Azevedo Bandeira's strong-arm man, or bodyguard. He speaks very little
and with a thick Brazilian accent. Otálora does not know whether to put
down his reserve to unfriendliness, or to contempt, or to mere backwoods
manners. He realizes, however, that to carry out the scheme he is hatch-
ing he must win the other man's friendship.

Next into Benjamín Otálora's story comes a black-legged bay horse
that Azevedo Bandeira brings from the south, and that carries a fine

saddle worked with silver and a saddle blanket trimmed with a jaguar skin. This spirited horse is a token of Bandeira's authority and for this reason is coveted by the young man, who comes also—with a desire bordering on spite—to hunger for the woman with the shining hair. The woman, the saddle, and the big bay are attributes or trappings of a man he aspires to bring down.

At this point the story takes another turn. Azevedo Bandeira is skilled in the art of slow intimidation, in the diabolical trickery of leading a man on, step by step, shifting from sincerity to mockery. Otálora decides to apply this ambiguous method to the hard task before him. He decides to replace Azevedo Bandeira, but to take his time over it. During days of shared danger, he gains Suárez' friendship. He confides his plan to him; Suárez pledges to help. Then a number of things begin happening of which I know only a few. Otálora disobeys Bandeira's orders; he takes to overlooking them, changing them, defying them. The whole world seems to conspire with him, hastening events. One noontime, somewhere around Tacuarembó, there is an exchange of gunfire with a gang from Brazil; Otálora takes Bandeira's place and shouts out orders to the Uruguayans. A bullet hits him in the shoulder, but that afternoon Otálora rides back to "The Last Sigh" on the boss's horse, and that evening some drops of his blood stain the jaguar skin, and that night he sleeps with the woman with the shining hair. Other accounts change the order of these events, denying they happened all in the same day.

Bandeira, nevertheless, remains nominally the boss. He goes on giving orders which are not carried out. Benjamín Otálora leaves him alone, out of mixed reasons of habit and pity.

The closing scene of the story coincides with the commotion of the closing night of the year 1894. On this night, the men of "The Last Sigh" eat freshly slaughtered meat and fall into quarreling over their liquor; someone picks out on the guitar, over and over again, a *milonga* that gives him a lot of trouble. At the head of the table, Otálora, feeling his drink, piles exultation upon exultation, boast upon boast; this dizzying tower is a symbol of his irresistible destiny. Bandeira, silent amid the shouting, lets the night flow noisily on. When the clock strikes twelve, he gets up like a man just remembering he has something to do. He gets up and softly knocks at the woman's door. She opens at once, as though waiting to be called. She steps out barefoot and half-dressed. In an almost feminine, soft-spoken drawl, Bandeira gives her an order.

"Since you and the Argentine care so much for each other," he says, "you're going to kiss him right now in front of everyone."

He adds an obscene detail. The woman tries to resist, but two men have taken her by the arms and fling her upon Otálora. Brought to tears, she kisses his face and chest. Ulpiano Suárez has his revolver out. Otálora realizes, before dying, that he has been betrayed from the start, that he has been sentenced to death—that love and command and triumph have been accorded him because his companions already thought of him as a dead man, because to Bandeira he already was a dead man.

Suárez, almost in contempt, fires the shot.

TRANSLATED BY NORMAN THOMAS DI GIOVANNI
IN COLLABORATION WITH THE AUTHOR

Oda Con un Lamento

Oh niña entre las rosas, oh presión de palomas,
oh presidio de peces y rosales,
tu alma es una botella llena de sal sedienta
y una campanea llena de uvas es tu piel.

Por desgracia no tengo para darte sino uñas
o pestañas, o pianos derretidos,
o sueños que salen de mi corazón a borbotones,
polvorientos sueños que corren como jinetes negros,
sueños llenos de velocidades y desgracias.

Sólo puedo quererte con besos y amapolas,
con guirnaldas mojadas por la lluvia,
mirando cenicientos caballos y perros amarillos.
Sólo puedo quererte con olas a la espalda,
entre vagos golpes de azufre y aguas ensimismadas,
nadando en contra de los cementerios que corren en ciertos ríos
con pasto mojado creciendo sobre las tristes tumbas de veso,
nadando a través de corazones sumergidos
y pálidas planillas de niños insepultos.

Hay mucha muerte, muchos acontecimientos funerarios
en mis desamparadas pasiones y desolados besos,
hay el agua que cae en mi cabeza,
mientras crece mi pelo,
un agua como el tiempo, un agua negra desencadenada,
con una voz nocturna, con un grito

Pablo Neruda

Ode With a Lament

Oh girl among the roses, oh pressure of doves,
oh garrison of fish and rose-bushes,
your soul is a bottle full of dry salt
and a bell full of grapes is your skin.

What a pity that I have nothing to give you except
the nails of my fingers, or eyelashes, or pianos melted by love,
or dreams which pour from my heart in torrents,
dreams covered with dust, which gallop like black riders,
dreams full of velocities and misfortunes.

I can love you only with kisses and poppies,
with garlands wet with rain,
my eyes full of ash-colored horses and yellow dogs.
I can love you only with waves on the shoulder,
amid random blows of sulfur, and waters lost in thought,
swimming against the cemeteries which run in certain rivers
with wet grass growing over the sad plaster tombs,
swimming across the sunken hearts
and the small pale pages of unburied children.

There is a great deal of death, there are funeral events
in my helpless passions and desolate kisses,
there is the water which falls in my head,
while my hair grows,
a water like time, a black unchained water,
with a nocturnal voice, with the cry

de pájaro en la lluvia, con una interminable
sombra de ala mojada que protege mis huesos:
mientras me visto, mientras
interminablemente me miro en los espejos y en los vidrios,
oigo que alguien me sigue llamándome a sollozos
con una triste voz podrida por el tiempo.

Tú estás de pie sobre la tierra, llena
de dientes y relámpagos.
Tú propagas los besos y matas las hormigas.
Tú lloras de salud, de cebolla, de abeja,
de abecedario ardiendo.
Tú eres como una espada azul y verde
y ondulas al tocarte, como un río.

Ven a mi alma vestida de blanco, con un ramo
de ensangrentadas rosas y copas de cenizas,
ven con una manzana y un caballo,
porque allí hay una sala oscura y un candelabro roto,
unas sillas torcidas que esperan el invierno,
y una paloma muerta, con un número.

Solo la Muerte

Hay cementerios solos,
tumbas llenas de huesos sin sonido,
el corazón pasando un túnel
oscuro, oscuro, oscuro,
como un naufragio hacia adentro nos morimos,
como ahogarnos en el corazón,
como irnos cayendo desde la piel al alma.

of a bird in the rain, with an unending
shadow, a shadow of a wet wing which protects my bones:
while I'm plain to be seen, while
I stare at myself endlessly in the mirrors and window-panes,
I hear someone following me, calling me, sobbing,
with a sad voice rotted by time.

You are standing over the earth, full
of teeth and lightning.
You propagate kisses and you kill the ants.
You weep tears of health, of the onion, of the bee,
of the burning alphabet.
You are like a sword, blue and green,
and you undulate to the touch like a river.

Come to my soul dressed in white, with a branch
of bleeding roses and goblets of ashes,
come with an apple and a horse,
for there is a dark room with a broken candelabra,
a few twisted chairs waiting for winter,
and a dead dove, with a number.

TRANSLATED BY W. S. MERWIN

Nothing but Death

There are cemeteries that are lonely,
graves full of bones that do not make a sound,
the heart moving through a tunnel,
in it darkness, darkness, darkness,
like a shipwreck we die going into ourselves,
as though we were drowning inside our hearts,
as though we lived falling out of the skin into the soul.

Hay cadáveres,
hay pies de pegajosa losa fría,
hay la muerte en los huesos,
como un sonido puro,
como un ladrido sin perro,
saliendo de ciertas campanas, de ciertas tumbas
creciendo en la humedad como el llanto a la lluvia.

Yo veo, solo, a veces,
ataúdes a vela
zarpar con difuntos pálidos, con mujeres de trenzas muertas,
con panaderos blancos como ángeles,
con niñas pensativas casadas con notarios,
ataúdes subiendo el río vertical de los muertos,
el río morado,
hacia arriba, con las velas hinchadas por el sonido de la muerte,
hinchadas por el sonido silencioso de la muerte.

A lo sonoro llega la muerte
como un zapato sin pie, como un traje sin hombre,
llega a golpear con un anillo sin piedra y sin dedo,
llega a gritar sin boca, sin lengua, sin garganta.
Sin embargo sus pasos suenan
y su vestido suena, callado, como un árbol.

Yo no sé, yo conozco poco, yo apenas veo,
pero creo que su canto tiene color de violetas húmedas,
de violetas acostumbradas a la tierra,
porque la cara de la muerte es verde,
y la mirada de la muerte es verde,
con la aguda humedad de una hoja de violeta
y su grave color de invierno exasperado.

Pero la muerte va también por el mundo vestida de escoba,
lame el suelo buscando difuntos,
la muerte está en la escoba,

And there are corpses,
feet made of cold and sticky clay,
death is inside the bones,
like a pure sound,
like a barking where there are no dogs,
coming out from bells somewhere, from graves somewhere,
growing in the damp air like tears or rain.

Sometimes I see alone
coffins under sail,
embarking with the pale dead, with women that have dead hair,
with bakers who are as white as angels,
and pensive young girls married to notary publics,
caskets sailing up the vertical river of the dead,
the river of dark purple,
moving upstream with sails filled out by the sound of death,
filled by the sound of death which is silence.

Death arrives among all that sound
like a shoe with no foot in it, like a suit with no man in it,
comes and knocks, using a ring with no stone in it, with no finger in it,
comes and shouts with no mouth, with no tongue, with no throat.
Nevertheless its steps can be heard
and its clothing makes a hushed sound, like a tree.

I'm not sure, I understand only a little, I can hardly see,
but it seems to me that its singing has the color of damp violets,
of violets that are at home in the earth,
because the face of death is green,
and the look death gives is green,
with the penetrating dampness of a violet leaf
and the somber color of embittered winter.

But death also goes through the world dressed as a broom,
lapping the floor, looking for dead bodies,
death is inside the broom,

es la lengua de la muerte buscando muertos,
es la aguja de la muerte buscando hilo.

La muerte está en los catres:
en los colchones lentos, en las frazadas negras
vive tendida, y de repente sopla:
sopla un sonido oscuro que hincha sábanas,
y hay camas navegando a un puerto
en donde está esperando, vestida de almirante.

DE *Las Furias y Las Penas*

Recuerdo sólo un día
que tal vez nunca me fué destinado,
era un día incesante,
sin orígenes, Jueves.
Yo era un hombre trasportado al acaso
con una mujer hallada vagamente,
nos desnudamos
como para morir o nadar o envejecer
y nos metimos uno dentro del otro,
ella rodeándome como un agujero,
yo quebrantándola como quien
golpea una campana,
pues ella era el sonido que me hería
y la cúpula dura decidida a temblar.

Era una sorda ciencia con cabello y cavernas
y machacando puntas de médula y dulzura
he rodado a las grandes coronas genitales
entre piedras y asuntos sometidos.
Éste es un cuento de puertos adonde

the broom is the tongue of death looking for corpses,
it is the needle of death looking for thread.

Death is inside the folding cots:
it spends its life sleeping on the slow mattresses,
in the black blankets, and suddenly breathes out:
it blows out a mournful sound that swells the sheets,
and the beds go sailing toward a port
where death is waiting, dressed like an admiral.

TRANSLATED BY ROBERT BLY

FROM *Furies and Sufferings*

I remember no more than a day
which, who knows, was never destined for me,
an interminable day
which had never begun. Thursday.
I was a man put there by chance
meeting a woman by some vague arrangement.
We undressed
as if to die, or swim, or to grow old
and we put ourselves one into another,
she circling me like a pit,
I banging at her like a man
who would strike a bell
since she was the sound that wounded me
and the hard dome set on its own vibration.

It was some deaf science of hair and caverns
when, pounding piths and sweetnesses,
I rolled the great wreaths of her sex
between stones and tributes.
This is a story of ports

llega uno, al azar, y sube a las colinas,
suceden tantas cosas.

Enemiga, enemiga
es posible que el amor haya caído al polvo
y no haya sino carne y huesos velozmente adorados
mientras el fuego se consume
y los caballos vestidos de rojo galopan al infierno?

Yo quiero para mí la avena y el relámpago
a fondo de epidermis,
y el devorante pétalo desarrollado en furia,
y el corazón labial del cerezo de Junio,
y el reposo de lentas barrigas que arden sin dirección.
pero me falta un suelo de cal con lágrimas
y una ventana donde esperar espumas.

Así es la vida,
corre tú entre las hojas, un otoño
negro ha llegado,
corre vestida con una falda de hojas y un cinturón de metal amarillo,
mientras la neblina de la estación roe las piedras.
Corre con tus zapatos, con tus medias,
con el gris repartido, con el hueco del pie, y con esas manos que el tabaco
                    salvaje adoraría,
golpea escaleras, derriba
el papel negro que protege las puertas,
y entra en medio del sol y la ira de un día de puñales
a echarte como paloma de luto y nieve sobre un cuerpo.

Es una sola hora larga como una vena,
y entre el ácido y la paciencia del tiempo arrugado
transcurrimos,
apartando las sílabas del miedo y la ternura,
interminablemente exterminados.

where one arrives by chance and climbs the hills
and so many things come to pass.

Enemy, my enemy,
has love fallen to dust
and will nothing do save flesh and bone furiously adored
while the fire devours itself
and the red-harnessed horses rush into hell?

I want for myself oats and lightnings
in the folds of my skin
and the consuming petal unfurled in its fury
and the labial heart of the cherry tree in June,
and the repose of slow bellies aimlessly burning:
but I lack a chalk soil with tears
and a window to lean at waiting for waves.

That's life.
Run among the leaves. An autumn
black as soot has come down,
run in your skirt of leaves, with a yellow metal belt
while the hill-station mist corrodes the stones.
Run in your shoes, in your stockings,
in your gray divisions, with the hollow of your foot, and those hands
the wild tobacco would bless,
batter at stairways, tear down
the black paper blinds on these doors,
and come into the belt of the sun and the anger of a day of daggers
to throw yourself like a dove of mourning and snow upon a body.

There is one hour alone, long as an artery,
and between the acid and the patience of crumpled time
we voyage through
parting the syllables of fear and tenderness
interminably done away with, done to death.

TRANSLATED BY NATHANIEL TARN

DE *Alturas de Macchu Picchu*

VI

Entonces en la escala de la tierra he subido
entre la atroz maraña de las selvas perdidas
hasta ti, Macchu Picchu.

Alta ciudad de piedras escalares,
por fin morada del que lo terrestre
No escondió en las dormidas vestiduras.
En ti, como dos líneas paralelas,
la cuna del relámpago y del hombre
se mecían en un viento de espinas.

Madre de piedra, espuma de los cóndores.

Alto arrecife de la aurora humana.

Pala perdida en la primera arena.

Esta fué la morada, éste es el sitio:
aquí los anchos granos del maíz ascendieron
y bajaron de nuevo como granizo rojo.

Aquí la hebra dorada salió de la vicuña
a vestir los amores, los túmulos, las madres,
el rey, las oraciones, los guerreros.

Aquí los pies del hombre descansaron de noche
junto a los pies del águila, en las altas guaridas
carniceras, y en la aurora
pisaron con los pies del trueno la niebla enrarecida,
y tocaron las tierras y las piedras
hasta reconocerlas en la noche o la muerte.

Miro las vestiduras y las manos,
el vestigio del agua en la oquedad sonora,
la pared suavizada por el tacto de un rostro

FROM *Summits of Macchu Picchu**

VI

Then up the ladder of the earth I climbed,
through the atrocious tangle of lost forests,
up to you, Macchu Picchu.

Lofty city of laddered stones,
ultimate dwelling of all not wrapped
by earth in mantles of sleep.
In you as in two parallel lines
the cradle of man and lightning
rocked in a wind of thorns.

Stone mother, spume of the condors.

Lofty reef of the human dawn.

Shovel lost in the primal sand.

This was the home, this is the site:
here the broad kernels of corn rose up
and fell again as red hail.

Here from the vicuña came the golden thread
to clothe the loves, the tombs, the mothers,
the king, the prayers, the warriors.

Here men rested their feet at night
beside the feet of the eagle, in lofty carnivorous
lairs, and in the dawn
trod with feet of thunder the rarefied mist,
and touched the earth and the stones
unto recognition in the night or in death.

I look at the hands and the clothes,
vestige of water in echoing hollows,
the wall smoothed by the touch of a face

que miró con mis ojos las lámparas terrestres,
que aceitó con mis manos las desaparecidas
maderas: porque todo, ropaje, piel, vasijas,
palabras, vino, panes,
se fué, cayó a la tierra.

Y el aire entró con dedos
de azahar sobre todos los dormidos:
mil años de aire, meses, semanas de aire,
de viento azul, de cordillera férrea,
que fueron como suaves huracanes de pasos
lustrando el solitario recinto de la piedra.
la más alta vasija que contuvo el silencio:
una vida de piedra después de tantas vidas.

that watched with my eyes the terrestrial lamps,
that oiled with my hands the vanished
timbers: for everything, clothes, skins, pots,
words, wine, bread,
is gone, fallen to earth.

And the air came in with orange-blossom
fingers over all the slumbering ones:
a thousand years of air, months, weeks of air,
of blue wind, of ferrous mountain range,
like tender hurricanes of steps
burnishing the lonely habitation of stone.

TRANSLATED BY KATE FLORES

* The ancient fortress of Macchu Picchu, cradle of the Inca Empire, is located
more than 12,000 feet above sea-level in the most inaccessible corner of the Peruvian
Andes. Built some 3,000 years B.C., this oldest American city was lost for many centuries before it was uncovered and excavated by Hiram Bingham in 1912. Although
the roofs, which were thatched, are almost gone, the city is still virtually intact.

Augusto Roa Bastos

The Living Tomb

Much later—not in that moment when Fulvio Morel paled intensely upon looking upward—I understood that certain revelations of time are not mere caprice.

At that moment we did not know that the tree under which we found ourselves sitting—a banyan of unusual size—was a tree which had swallowed another tree. We still did not know that the cardinal, which had penetrated its foliage with the drowsy, dizzy flight of a humming-bird, was the indicator, seemingly chosen by chance to point out the spot with the fiery spark of its restless plumage. We still knew nothing of the mystery which had remained unsolved for more than fifteen years. In a word, we knew nothing yet of the whole story.

As far as the guests of Fulvio Morel were concerned, all that had gone on up to this time had been a few events of little importance: the tiresome and useless beating of the woods of the extensive property for game, the increasingly suffocating heat under the trees, the thirst, the small deer bagged almost exactly at midday and then sacrificed for steaks, the siesta afterward beneath the giant banyan with a shadow of more than eighty feet in diameter, the shouts and the diminishing chatter which sleep and sunlight finally ended. Then someone, a youngster, saw the cardinal hopping from branch to branch, perching at last on that twig, dry and white as a bone. At that moment the boy cried out: "Look, look at that there! Isn't it . . . ?" and he interrupted himself, trying, no doubt, to identify more precisely what he had so excitedly pointed out to the others.

We had only seen the red tassel of the cardinal among the leaves. But Fulvio Morel had already risen and was looking up as if struck by a sudden hallucination.

In the tenacious, secret passages which ascend from lead to gold or degenerate from rain to mud, from virtue to corruption, from crime to punishment, from indifference to desperation, every moment, even the most seemingly trivial, is predestined.

That moment certainly was. But only later did I understand. The accumulation of circumstances could have obscured the evidence at first. But afterwards everything was clear. And why it was Fulvio Morel and not his father who suffered the shock of that unique and inexorable moment also became clear to me later. Or I believe I sensed it. And it was the image of that incredibly voracious tree which subsequently suggested these reflections. That tree had swallowed another tree which was dry and dead within its knotty tentacles, lifting it as it grew with avid cannibal strength, lifting little by little over the years, imperceptibly, that dead and hollow trunk, as if to a vaulted niche, keeping intact its secret burden enshrouded in a thin, porous cape of bark which the wind and birds, the implacable erosion of time had finally uncovered.

As in the vigorous and voracious banyan, so in Fulvio Morel there remained intact and alive his father, who had been dead some years; that Spanish landowner with the hands and soul of the colonial gentry, who had been in his turn merciless and voracious and who, first by his widowhood, then by the strange disappearance of his daughter and finally, by the spiteful asceticism of his withdrawal into his feudal manor, had been converted long before his death into a mummy of bark around which the vitality of his only heir grew and upon which it fed.

Fulvio Morel *was* his father, with not only his own tentacles like a number of green capes, but also his greediness, his robust single-mindedness, his indifference, and the somber burden of family secrets.

I believed I knew Fulvio Morel pretty well. We had begun our studies in law school together and we left together in 1931 when the proximity of the Chaco War began to warm up the ancient and lazy atmosphere of Asunción.

In a way that even today I find hard to explain, my authoritarian classmate, rich, sensual and selfish, had succeeded in making me a complete slave of his caprices, to such an extent that his flamboyant title of lawyer—as well as mine—was partly due to my diligent reading. The other part was achieved by bribery and intimidation. At any rate, his gift of assimilation was truly fantastic. It was enough for him to hear something once; it remained engraved forever. On returning from his nights out, or as I brewed him maté in the morning, I had only to summarize what I had read or read him a few chapters for the first time. And I knew very well to what extent I was assuming the same servile attitude as that of the servant brushing the clothes and cleaning the boots of his master. But I could not do anything about it. The house, the books, the will to power belonged to Fulvio Morel.

The only concession he made to me was to consult me about how we should celebrate the end of our studies.

"We could stay and have some fun here or go hunting in the country."

He called it simply *the country,* that enormous rural estate of Ka'apukú, surrounded by ponds and mountains, situated a short distance from Lake Ypoá.

I don't know why this property and the old partly destroyed house there in the center of a hundred-year-old orange grove has always attracted me. So much so that without thinking twice and despite the expected discomfort of the trip, I said to him, "The country's better, Fulvio. You're sure to be bored here."

"True, there's nothing much new."

"A few healthy days in the country wouldn't be bad at all to dry you out a bit."

"Yes, but in any case we have to take along a few women for the drinking party. I can stand drinking alone less and less. I get the feeling I'm sucking my own blood. The spectacle of a drunken woman is the only thing that still makes my life more or less worthwhile." And Fulvio burst into harsh and gloomy laughter, celebrating his own destruction.

"Or better . . . yes. Perhaps . . . ," he said, after a pause, considering something which had evidently suddenly occurred to him, while I still had my thoughts fixed on the marble-columned portico of the ruined house where the old landholder had lived out his last years, withdrawn and ferocious, imprisoned in the immense circular orange grove in the middle of the estate, which even from a distance affected me with its disconcerting magic.

"Yes," he said, "I believe this will be a good time to get hold of that cute little Hebe Corvalán. We'll invite her with her mother. The old woman will come feeling perfectly safe. She'll plan to set her cap for me. And once there, a lot of things can happen. Am I right?"

"I don't know . . . I don't know . . ." I answered, a little upset at the rapid formation of the project. The lovely fine features of the scarcely seventeen-year-old Hebe Corvalán, all limpid charm and satin-skinned as a dark jasmine, appeared to me in the background, floating through the mansion among the trees while the bestial Fulvio Morel waited in ambush.

The daughter of an ex-minister who had been shot one night by an unknown assailant, heir to a bankrupt estate, unprotected except for her mother, a blonde ingenuous woman anxious to get the girl "settled" at all cost, she was the appropriate victim for Fulvio Morel. I knew that once she was in his clutches he would stop at nothing to sacrifice her to the whim of the moment, just as afterward he would shrug the matter off as casually as he rid himself of the shrivelled butts of his cigarettes, his eyes opaque and indifferent, his mouth wrinkled in that imperceptible twist of disdain and crafty cruelty which always hovered there at one side, like the trademark of his temperament.

Nothing could stop it from happening, and it did, on the second day after our arrival at the estate, in spite of my mad determination that it should not happen. But that event and its innocent victim were no doubt predestined.

Fulvio Morel carried out his plan the night before the hunting party. No one found out, no one suspected anything. I only came to know about it long after when, with the unpredictability of chance, years later Hebe Corvalán became my wife and in a moment of weakness, which became one of strength and rehabilitation for us both, she confessed to me what had happened on that night of pain, humiliation and shame. By then Fulvio Morel was no more than a sad memory while his bones rotted in some lost canyon of the Chaco where the war had caught him, destroying him and redeeming him at the same time in a truly inexplicable way.

Because of all this, I was not surprised when later I reconstructed the events whose location that cardinal had waited fifteen years to point out with its little red plume, waiting all this time to present the evidence to Fulvio Morel before all these people full of jovial hatred toward him, whom he himself had chosen to be witness to that revelation which he would have given everything he possessed to remain in ignorance of for the rest of his life.

I was not surprised that Hebe Corvalán, suddenly indisposed, had remained in the house with her mother.

For her, suffering and still full of profound resentment and despair from the outrage she had endured during the night, it would have been an incomprehensible, unpremeditated revenge, devised by a being superior to them both, to see him return that afternoon as he did, to see him, through the window, cross among the broken marble columns like a corpse which had lived on leaves until its death, until thus resurrected, pale and green as he was when he dismounted and buried himself in the most secret room of the ruined house, probably the same room in which his father died staring at the walls in whose cracks moss and dark bunches of parasitic weeds grew.

I was not surprised that it was a boy who discovered the cardinal and who, after two or three seconds of hesitation, finished the sentence he had begun.

"Look . . . look at that up there! Isn't it a . . . skeleton?"

Fulvio Morel had sprung to his feet and, looking upward, began to turn deadly pale while the boy was still climbing the tree. The red tassel of the cardinal had hidden itself in the foliage. The boy finally arrived at the top of the tree. His almost joyful shout fell upon the waiting faces.

"Yes . . . it's a skeleton! The skeleton of a child!"

His hands could be seen parting, groping between the leaves. Suddenly he shouted again:

"There's a chain around the neck!"

In the midst of the feverish, intense silence, the boy went on translating the secret message imprisoned in the bark shroud.

"There's a heart-shaped medal on the chain!"

The boy was spelling something out with difficulty.

"On the medal there's a name! It says . . . it says . . ."

Fulvio Morel flung himself against the tree. We all thought that he, too, was going to climb the thick hollow trunk, around which the tight, fibrous tentacles were coiled. The boy's voice, speaking the name, paralyzed him instantly as if he had been hit on the head by a stone.

"It says . . . *Alicia!*" the boy cried and, below, Fulvio Morel's stifled groan replied like a dull echo.

After fifteen years he had just encountered the remains of his little sister, Alicia, who had mysteriously disappeared, carried off by some monster, half-man, half-myth, when she was scarcely twelve and he one year younger.

It was probably not only the distant horror of the event, already transformed into a legend of his childhood, but also the circumstances of the discovery which had wrenched that groan from him: the moment, all that had just happened.

There was the living tomb of his sister; but the whole story went far back into the past.

It had begun when those poor pariahs who worked in the ricefields of the estate—something like half a hundred men and women who looked like copper-colored wraiths—came to advise Don Francisco Morel y Santillán of the mysterious disappearance of three children. They had vanished leaving no traces. The only clue they had noticed was the fact that the disappearance of the children, all between eight and ten years old, coincided with the first day of the new moon.

"And what do you want done about it?" the rude satrap of the white mansion, sitting in the gallery of the portico with his feet against one of the marble shafts, said to them. "While you're hunting around in the ricefields instead of working, am I to be nursemaid to your brats? If you don't look after them yourselves, I don't see how you can complain when they disappear . . . Bah, what do I know about it!"

"No, karaí, Don Francisco," a weeping woman murmured, "We've looked all 'round. Not there. Something stole ore memby . . ."

"All right, as I told you, look after them! You don't think I'm the one who stole them?"

"No, karaí, Don Francisco. But if something could be done . . . for this poor innocent . . ."

"I have enough to do keeping an eye on you people, you bunch of loafers, always sponging on my land! Go back to work and leave me in peace for once."

He shooed them out, clapping his hands vigorously as if they were animals which had threatened to invade the house. The copper wraiths went away silently, crushed back into the immense malarial puddle where the ricefields were. They had come to ask for justice, for protection. They got nothing but insults which simply poured out as the natural respiration of that enraged omnipotence entrenched in the mansion in the karaí-roga, as the people on the estate called it with timid respect.

A pair of childish eyes, the soft color of bluebells, watched the dark, ragged herd move off among the orange trees. They were the eyes of little Alicia Morel, who had heard part of the quarrel with those who had just left. A little later she burst into the gallery very much upset.

"What did those people want, Daddy?"

"Nothing, nothing, darling. The usual complaints, this, that, and the other thing. Ah!"

"They were talking about some children that got lost."

"It's nothing! Trifles! And you, when are you going to learn? I've told you never to listen behind doors and windows."

"They talked quite loud, Daddy. I listened without meaning to."

"All right, all right. Go inside. Where's Fulvio?"

"In the pantry, catching rats with a fishhook."

"A fine little rascal! Tell him I order him to stop his nonsense. Do you hear?"

"Yes, Daddy. I'll go and tell him though I'm sure he won't pay any attention to *us*."

The disappearances of the children continued methodically. The plague spread to the laborers in the cotton and corn. Altogether, eight children were lost within four months. Each disappeared in a different spot. Then the mysterious kidnapper gave himself a respite. And once more the kidnapping began, precisely on the first day of the new moon.

The natives were in despair at the truly diabolical ravages of this scourge. A superstitious fear fell upon them, a prophetic anguish confused with monstrous and terrible images, a black gust of mythology.

"It'll be the Luisón, dear God!"

"Or the Pombero!"

"Maybe the Pyta-Yovai!"

"Or the Mboi-yaguá . . ."

All the mythological fauna began to dance around the fires made nightly in the most wretched huts.

An old man stripped away something from the supernatural obscurity when he said: "Sometimes could be some leper steals a child to take a bath in its blood. There was one in Tavapy. He hung it by the middle of its legs in a tree. Then he got underneath, cut off its head so he got the hot stream over the ku-rú-vaí. They caught him doing this and they burnt him."

This alternative was no less awful. Some, certainly in the depths of their being, between two evils, chose the demonic one. Against this there was no remedy. But no one could imagine that the monster was a "Christian."

"Aní angá-kená, dear God!"

One day unexpectedly a clue, a trail was discovered. During the siesta someone saw a hunchbacked dwarf, furred with a long beard and thick red hair, run into the cornfield. On its back the enormous hump appeared like another head, but smooth and hairless. It was pursued hotly for a long distance but when they were about to overtake it, the monstrous dwarf, or whatever it was, disappeared mysteriously underground. It was seen two or three times subsequently and every time, in a flash, repeated the disappearance.

The fleeting apparitions coincided with nine new kidnappings of children so that now it was known to whom they should be attributed. The vision of the cannibal yasy-yateré then displaced the other mythological beasts and spread widely like the effects of a bad dream which nevertheless left real traces behind it: the tracks of the monster's deformed feet in the smooth earth of the plantations.

The intermittent nightmares ended by becoming a permanent reality. At first the monster's hump—not its face—its hairy red skin, its sinuous lizardlike movements, its mysterious disappearances underground, shone evilly only in the blinding fever of the fiestas, in the cornfields. Now they saw it all the time and everywhere: a black humpbacked sun burned in their retinas and imaginations like a fleeting firebrand.

The old man who cited the story of the invalid of Tavapy did not wish to share the impotent stupor of the others. He went on insisting:

"Maybe it isn't any yasy-yateré. Maybe it's some other wretch. Maybe we could get it with a good dog and a shotgun."

He ended by vaguely convincing them when a certain capybara hunter, wounded by a leopard, passed by and after hearing what had occurred, told them: "Could be. A dwarf like that one you are talking about disappeared a while ago in the lake at Ila Yakaré. He had a hump. He lived alone in the forest at the shore of the lake. He seemed to be sick. But nobody ever saw his face. One day we almost speared him thinking he was a capybara. He was in the water among the river plants. After that we never saw him again."

But still Yakaré Island was far away. That couldn't be it. The vision of the fabulous yasy-yateré continued to dictate the natives' superstitious fear.

Nevertheless, urged on by the old man, they went back to plead for the protection of the karaí of the mansion. He heard them impassively in the gallery of the mansion's portico, his feet against the white column, the robust shape a little blurred in the twilight which began to drain the scene of color as night fell. This time they only asked for the loan of a leash and a shotgun to try and capture the culprit. The old man explained: "If it isn't a yasy-yateré, at least we can catch it. We sprinkled a child with holy water and left it where the thing had been, to confuse the tekové vaí. But it took the child just the same. Maybe because we forgot to put a palmwood cross on its neck. Now we want to make sure what the trouble is. At least if we could catch it . . ."

Anxious blue eyes stared fixedly from the window. It was little Alicia Morel eaten up with anxiety on account of the fantastic story which emerged from among the orange trees from several lips at the same time in a harsh dialect mixture of Spanish and Guaraní.

"A cross around the neck . . ." Alicia made a mental note of this detail. Around her neck, next to the medal on the chain, she wore the gold cross that had been her mother's. Perhaps all she would have to do was to meet it and ask it to go away. If she were not so frightened, she thought that perhaps she might have dared. Those eight children cried out to her from the story she was hearing; their little dark decapitated heads, their little bleeding arms cried out to her in the harsh complaints of their parents. Maybe she ought to dare. The monster would see the gold cross and fly off snorting with the demon inside. The palmwood cross wouldn't work perhaps. It was a poor thing. That was why the yasy-yateré went on stealing and devouring their children.

The lusty clapping resounded again in the gallery, driving the natives out.

"If it's as you say, you'll get nowhere with dogs and guns. Pray and submit. God certainly won't punish you needlessly, you good-for-nothings. Go away and leave me alone. What cretins!"

Under no pretext was Don Francisco Morel y Santillán going to put a single cutting edge in the hands of simple people. You never knew about them. It was better to keep them crushed as they were, helpless, flattened against the earth. As for the lost children, he didn't give a damn.

"Those creatures are like rats, robbing you from the day they're born!"

The furious clapping drove the somber skeletons into the green night of the orange grove. A fragrant breeze blew between the white columns.

Alicia sought her brother and confided to him her secret project to confront the yasy-yateré with the gold cross.

"Of course you have to do it, Alicia," he encouraged her perversely. "You could easily do it. Papa sleeps during the siesta time. The monster only appears at that hour. We won't tell him anything. When you come back we'll have something to talk about . . . I myself will go with you to the edge of the cornfield."

The following day Alicia disappeared mysteriously.

Don Francisco got up from his siesta. He called Alicia. She didn't answer. She was never to answer him again as long as he lived.

"Where's Alicia?" he cried furiously.

Fulvio knew nothing, neither did the servants. No one knew anything. He beat the black woman who had been her wetnurse until she was half dead. Shouting curses and insults, he beat the other servants furiously. But nothing came to light. Fulvio, high in an orange tree, listened to his father's shouts and blows with an imperceptible and perverse smile. He knew where Alicia had gone but he was not going to tell unless they cut his back to ribbons. Afterward Don Francisco ran through the cornfield like a madman. He tore up bushes and ripped up the earth like a furious dog. His mouth was full of foam and curses. All he found were the tracks of the deformed feet of the yasy-yateré. It had come very close to the house. Where the tracks of the monster began, those of Alicia's little slippers ended. She had set out in the direction of Wonderland. He remembered the book with its richly colored illustrations that he had brought back from Asunción not long ago. He burst into hysterical laughter which died as sobs when he flung himself on the earth of the cornfield, burying his face in the dust as if he would search there for his eternally lost daughter. Yes, vanished forever, even if he did not know it at that moment, or at least refused to believe it. He arose from there sadder than ever, now silently overcome by a terrible and menacing paralysis.

He sent all his people up and down the estate from one end to the other, day and night. For a month it went on, the implacable, piercing and sonorous rhythm of dogs, shots and shouts. Once at siesta time they —and he, too—caught a fleeting glimpse of the monster in the dry corn-field. It lasted only a moment: a black gleam, red of hair, a hump and hellish eyes. It was a flash, a zigzagging noise. Nothing more. As soon as they were aware of it, it had vanished once again. The dogs barked and rushed on; the boss's gun resounded several times. But where it had disappeared only a few dark ashes remained.

Someone found the opening of a tunnel beneath a stone, evidently dug by some yurumí. It was considerably enlarged. The dwarf could well have slipped away through it. They excavated a large portion of the subterranean passage. In a sort of bend where the passage widened into an ovenlike cave, they found the remains of eight decapitated children, their rags and their bones. No remains of Alicia were found anywhere, neither the little blue dress nor the black patent leather slippers she had worn on the day she was kidnapped. Don Francisco gave the order to fill up this sepulchral hole in the earth. The copper-colored procession moved off, sobbing, toward the rice swamp with the remains of its children. Don Francisco Morel y Santillán did not have this much. He felt suddenly more wretched than his debased and miserable slaves.

The monster did not return to steal children. Alicia Morel had performed the miracle of driving it away.

After that Don Francisco took Fulvio to Asunción, where he shut him up in a church school. On his return, he cast out the house-servants and everyone else on his land and shut himself up in the house to live in taciturn isolation until his end.

From Asunción there arrived a veritable flood of steel traps of the sort used to catch foxes and jaguars; there were more than a thousand. He personally sowed them all over the property, camouflaging them with the obsessiveness of one possessed.

About four o'clock in the afternoon, after siesta time, he went out to visit them, one after another, mounted on his enormous grey. He knew all the spots, glanced sideways at them and passed on, his eyes gleaming with profound frenzied hate which stemmed from the very roots of his poisoned existence.

One afternoon he noticed an agitatedly moving shape in a distant thicket where one of the traps was situated. He approached at a gallop. Disappointment clouded his somber cadaverous face even more. It was not the yasy-yateré. It was one of the men who cut hay, struggling to rid his ruined foot of the jaws of the trap.

Don Francisco cried out accusingly, "You, what are you doing here, you dog, you thief? I told you all to go . . . all of you. Beat it!"

Don Francisco dismounted, more to open the trap and reset it than to help the victim.

Fifteen days later, a new thrashing in the underbrush caught his attention from a distance. But this time he did not hurry. From the desperation of the disturbance he supposed that the prisoner was again only one of the cretinous natives who had not departed. About three hundred feet before reaching the trap, he saw that the commotion had completely stopped. He supposed the captured man or animal had gotten free or would be dead. He dismounted and approached. Hatred, and above all astonishment, widened his eyes. Once more his obsession with revenge had partly missed its mark: caught in the trap there was only the bloody, deformed foot of the monster, not amputated by the teeth of the instrument, but cut a little higher at the ankle. The thing itself had cut it off with a machete or knife in time to escape the cadaverous-faced landowner approaching on his long-striding grey.

That hairy foot was a dripping portrait of the monster: the toes spread and protruding like stumps, truly the foot of a bear in which the human likenesses were the most monstrous. A broad foot, horny and flat, black with blood.

Nevertheless, Don Francisco Morel y Santillán did not have to wait long to see the complete destruction of his enemy. A few days later he was found dead at the edge of the ravine. Gangrene had eaten away the leg amputated at the ankle. Starvation and thirst had driven him in the direction of the ravine toward which he had dragged himself. He had not succeeded in wetting his leprosy-swollen lips in the crystalline water which only served him as a last mirror in which to see death overtaking his hairy and deformed red head, growing dimmer and dimmer in the shadowy night from which it had emerged.

In the duel that had taken place between these two sinister beings, no one could say who had conquered. The gloomy master of the mansion died soon after.

Only the incorruptible smile of Alicia Morel continued to float over the abandoned estate. Even now we could see it and breathe it from the perfumed bark as the summer breezes caused oranges to rain down around the ruined mansion.

And her childish blue eyes went on gleaming in the bluebells, when, of her angelic body which had erotically fascinated the monster, there remained only the little skeleton rising slowly in its frail shroud of bark toward the fiery spot of the cardinal that vindicated her fifteen years later, rising toward the secret reason for predestined revelations, rising toward the insane eyes of her brother.

TRANSLATED BY H. R. HAYS

El Apellido

Elegía familiar

I

   Desde la escuela
y aun antes . . . Desde el alba, cuando apenas
era una brizna yo de sueño y llanto,
desde entonces,
me dijeron mi nombre. Un santo seña
para poder hablar con las estrellas.
Tú te llamas, te llamarás . . .
Y luego me entregaron
esto que veis escrito en mi tarjeta,
esto que pongo al pie de mis poemas:
catorce letras
que llevo a cuestas por la calle,
que siempre van conmigo a todas partes.
¿Es mi nombre, estáis ciertos?
¿Tenéis todas mis señas?
¿Ya conocéis mi sangre navegable,
mi geografía llena de oscuros montes,
de hondos y amargos valles
que no están en los mapas?
¿Acaso visitásteis mis abismos,
mis galerías subterráneas
con grandes piedras húmedas,
islas sobresaliendo en negras charcas

Nicolás Guillén

The Name
Family elegy

I

From my schooldays on
and even before . . . From that dawn when I
was no more than a wisp of sleep and tears,
from then on,
they told me my name. A password
that let me talk with the stars.
Your name is, your name will be . . .
And then they handed me
what you see printed on my calling card,
what I put down at the foot of my poems:
fourteen letters
I carry through the streets on my back,
going with me everywhere at all times.
Are you sure it's my name?
Do you know everything about me?
Do you know the sailing waters of my blood,
my geography covered with dark forests,
with deep and bitter valleys
that don't appear on maps?
Did you ever visit my abysses,
my underground galleries
with immense seeping rocks,
islands jutting up out of black lakes

y donde un puro chorro
siento de antiguas aguas
caer desde mi alto corazón
con fresco y hondo estrépito
en un lugar lleno de ardientes árboles,
monos equilibristas,
loros, legisladores y culebras?
¿Toda mi piel (debí decir)
toda mi piel viene de aquella estatua
de mármol español? ¿También mi voz de espanto,
el duro grito de mi garganta? ¿Vienen de allá
todos mis huesos? ¿Mis raíces y las raíces
de mis raíces y además
estas ramas oscuras movidas por los sueños
y estas flores abiertas en mi frente
y esta savia que amarga mi corteza?
¿Estáis seguros?
¿No hay nada más que eso que habéis escrito,
que eso que habéis sellado
con un sello de cólera?
(¡Oh, debí haber preguntado!)

    Y bien, ahora os pregunto:
¿no veis estos tambores en mis ojos?
¿No veis estos tambores tensos y golpeados
con dos lágrimas secas?
¿No tengo acaso
un abuelo nocturno
con una gran marca negra
(más negra todavía que la piel)
una gran marca hecha de un latigazo?
¿No tengo pues
un abuelo mandinga, congo, dahomeyano?
¿Cómo se llama? ¡Oh, sí, decídmelo!

where I feel the pure stream
of ancient waters
pouring down from my steep heart
with a refreshing deep roar
into a place filled with burning trees,
monkeys like ropedancers,
parrots, lawmakers and snakes?
Does all my skin (I should have said)
all my skin come from that Spanish marble
statue? And my voice, like a ghost's voice,
the hard cry in my throat? Do all my bones
come from there? My roots and the roots
of my roots as well as
these darkened branches stirred by dreams
and these flowers in full bloom on my forehead
and this sap that makes my bark turn bitter?
Are you certain?
Is what you've written down all there is,
what you have endorsed
with a seal of anger?
(Oh, I should have asked!)

Well, I'm asking you now:
can't you see these drums in my eyes?
Don't you see these tight drums beaten
with two dry teardrops?
Don't I have
a night grandfather
with a long black scar
(even blacker than his skin)
a long black scar left by one lash?
Don't I have, then,
a Mandingo, Congolese, Dahomeyan grandfather?
What is his name? Oh yes, tell me!

¿Andrés? ¿Francisco? ¿Amable?
¿Cómo decís Andrés en congo?
¿Cómo habéis dicho siempre
Francisco en dahomeyano?
En mandinga ¿cómo se dice Amable?
¿O no? ¿Eran, pues, otros nombres?
¡El apellido, entonces!
¿Sabéis mi otro apellido, el que me viene
de aquella tierra enorme, el apellido
sangriento y capturado, que pasó sobre el mar
entre cadenas, que pasó entre cadenas sobre el mar?
¡Ah, no podéis recordarlo!
Lo habéis disuelto en tinta inmemorial.
Lo habéis robado a un pobre negro indefenso.
Lo escondísteis, creyendo
que iba a bajar los ojos yo de la vergüenza.
¡Gracias!
¡Os lo agradezco!
Gentiles gentes, thank you!
Merci!
Merci bien!
Merci beaucoup!
Pero no . . . ¿Podéis creerlo? No.
Yo estoy limpio.
Brilla mi voz como un metal recién pulido.
Mirad mi escudo: tiene un baobab,
tiene un rinoceronte y una lanza.
Yo soy también el nieto,
biznieto,
tataranieto de un esclavo.
(Que se avergüence el amo.)
¿Seré Yelofe?
¿Nicolás Yelofe acaso?
¿O Nicolás Bakongo?

Andrés? Francisco? Amable?
How do you say Andrés in Congolese?
What's the way you've always said
Francisco in Dahomeyan?
How do you say Amable in Mandingo?
Or no? Were they other names, then?
The name, then!
Do you know my other name, the one that comes
from that vast land, the bloodstained
captive name that crossed the sea
in chains, that crossed in chains over the sea?
Ah, you can't remember it!
You dissolved it in long-forgotten ink.
You stole it from a poor defenseless black man.
You hid it, believing
I would cast down my eyes in shame.
Thanks a lot!
I am grateful to you for it.
Nice people, thank you!
Merci!
Merci bien!
Merci beaucoup.
But no . . . Will you believe it? No.
I am clean.
My voice shines like polished metal.
Here's my coat-of-arms: it has a baobab,
a rhinoceros and a spear.
I am also the grandson,
greatgrandson,
greatgreatgrandson of a slave.
(It's the slave-master who should feel ashamed.)
Am I Yelofe?
Nicolás Yelofe perhaps?
Or Nicolás Bakongo?

¿Tal vez Guillén Banguila?
¿O Kumbá?
¿Quizá Guillén Kumbá?
¿O Kongué?
¿Pudiera ser Guillén Kongué?
¡Oh, quién lo sabe!
¡Qué enigma entre las aguas!

II

Siento la noche inmensa gravitar
sobre profundas bestias,
sobre inocentes almas castigadas;
pero también sobre voces en punta,
que despojan al cielo de sus soles,
los más duros,
para condecorar la sangre combatiente.
De algún país ardiente, perforado
por la gran flecha ecuatorial,
sé que vendrán lejanos primos,
remota angustia mía disparada en el viento;
sé que vendrán pedazos de mis venas,
sangre remota mía,
con duro pie aplastando las hierbas asustadas;
sé que vendrán hombres de vidas verdes,
remota selva mía,
con su dolor abierto en cruz y el pecho rojo en llamas.
Sin conocernos nos reconoceremos en el hambre,
en la tuberculosis y en la sífilis,
en el sudor comprado en bolsa negra,
en los fragmentos de cadenas
adheridos todavía a la piel;
sin conocernos nos reconoceremos
en los ojos cargados de sueños

Maybe Guillén Banguila?
Or Kumbá?
Possibly Guillén Kumbá?
Or Kongué?
Could it be Guillén Kongué?
Oh, who knows!
What an enigma in the waters!

II

I feel the immense night weighing down
on profound animals,
on innocent souls that suffer punishment,
but also on voices reaching up
to strip the sky of its suns,
its most obstinate ones,
to pin as decorations on fighting blood.
I know that distant cousins,
my remote anguish fired far into the wind,
will come from some burning country, run through
by the Equator's long arrow.
I know that pieces of my veins will come,
remote blood-relatives,
with hard feet crushing down the frightened grass.
I know that men with green lives will come,
my remote jungle,
with their pain opened like a cross and their red chests on fire.
We're strangers, but we'll recognize one another in hunger,
in tuberculosis and in syphilis,
in the sweat bargained for in the black market,
in what is left of chains
sticking to the flesh even now.
We're strangers, but we'll recognize one another
in eyes loaded down with dreams

y hasta en los insultos como piedras
que nos escupen cada día
los cuadrumanos de la tinta y el papel.

    ¿Qué ha de importar entonces
(¡qué ha de importar ahora!)
¡ay! mi pequeño nombre
con sus catorce letras blancas?
¿Ni el mandinga, bantú,
yoruba, dahomeyano
nombre del triste abuelo ahogado
en tinta de notario?
¿Qué importa, amigos puros?
¡Oh, sí, puros amigos,
venid a ver mi nombre!
Mi nombre interminable,
hecho de interminables nombres;
el nombre, mío, ajeno,
libre y mío, ajeno y vuestro,
ajeno y libre como el aire.

and even in the insults like stones
apes with ink and paper
spit at us every day.

Just what will my small name
with its fourteen white letters
matter then
(what does it matter now)?
Or the Mandingo, Bantu,
Yoruba, Dahomeyan
name of my sad grandfather drowned
in notary public's ink?
What does it matter, my pure friends?
Oh, yes, my pure friends,
come and look at my name!
A name that never ends,
made up of names that never end,
the name, mine, another's,
free and mine, another's and yours,
another's and free as the air.

TRANSLATED BY HARDIE ST. MARTIN

Alejo Carpentier

The Fugitives

I

The trail died at the foot of a tree. Sure enough there was the strong scent of a black man in the air each time the breeze stirred the flies working on the holes in the rotten fruit. But the dog, he had never been called anything but Dog, was tired out. He rolled around in the grass to get the kinks out of his back and loosen up his muscles. Very far off, the shouts of the band of men got lost in the gathering dusk. The black man's scent persisted. Perhaps Cimarron was hidden up there somewhere, astride a branch, listening with his eyes. And yet, Dog was no longer thinking of the hunting-party. On the ground covered with lianas, there was another scent that would perhaps be rubbed out forever by the next one rubbing up against it. Female scent. A scent Dog tried to pull off his back, writhing upside down, laughing through his fang to push it upward and stretch a tongue, that was much too short, toward the hollow separating his shoulder blades.

The shadows were becoming more damp. Dog righted himself, landing on his feet. The bells of the sugar mill, swinging slowly, made his ears stand up. In the valley, the mist and the smoke were one bluish stillness over which floated, each moment silhouetted, a brick chimney, a roof with huge wings, the church steeple and lights that seemed to go on at the bottom of a lake. Dog was hungry. But the female scent was over there. Sometimes the black man's scent enveloped him. But the scent of his own heat, claimed by the scent of another's heat, forced out everything else. Dog's hind legs stiffened, making him crane his neck.

At the base of his rib cage, his belly sank into the rhythm of a short, anxious panting. Heavy with too much sun, fruit plopped down here and there, with a wet sound, spraying warm pulp over the ground.

Dog started running with his head down toward the bush, contrary to his own sense of direction, as if he were being pursued by the overseer's whip. But the female scent was there. His snout followed a winding trail that doubled back on itself sometimes, left the path, grew more intense on a mimosa's thorns, was lost in leaves overly soured by fermentation, and sprang up again with unexpected strength on some dirt recently swept by a tail. Suddenly, Dog swung away from the invisible trail, from the thread that twined and untwined, to pounce on a ferret. With two shakes that sounded like a castanet inside a glove, he broke its spine flinging it against a tree-trunk. Dog stopped abruptly, leaving one leg suspended in the air. The sound of very distant barking came down from the mountains.

It wasn't the barking of the sugar mill's pack. The pitch was different, much harsher and bolder, coming from deep in the throat, muffled by powerful jaws. There was a fight going on somewhere between dogs that did not have a toothed brass collar with a numbered tag, like Dog. Before those unfamiliar voices, much more like wolves than anything he had heard till then, Dog was afraid.

He ran in the other direction, until the plants became tinted with moonlight. The female scent wasn't there any more. There was a black man's scent. And sure enough, the black man was there, with his striped pants, lying on his stomach asleep. Dog was about to pounce on him, carrying out a command given at dawn, in the midst of flying whips, back where there were boiling pots and straw litters. But up there, it was hard to tell where, the male fight went on. The bones of some gnawed ribs were beside Cimarron. Dog approached slowly, with alerted ears, determined to snatch some taste of meat away from the ants. Besides, those dogs barking so fiercely frightened him. For the time being, he had better stay at the man's side. And keep his ears cocked. But the wind from the south finally carried off the menace. Dog spun around three times and curled up, exhausted. His legs raced through a bad dream. At daybreak, Cimarron threw an arm around him, the gesture of a man who has slept with a lot of women. Dog snuggled up to his chest, looking for warmth. Both continued in full flight, their nerves shaken by the same nightmare.

A spider, that had come down to get a closer view, gathered its thread and disappeared into the top of the almond tree, whose leaves were beginning to slip out of the night.

2

From force of habit, Cimarron and Dog woke up with the ringing of the mill's bell. The discovery that they had slept together, body to body, made them get up with a start. Backing up against two trees, they stared at each other for a long time; Dog offering to take on a master, the black man anxious to have a friend again.

The valley was coming out of sleep. The urgent bell intended for the slaves was answered more slowly now by the melodious undersong of the chapel bell whose green tarnish swayed from shade to sunlight over a background of mooing and neighing, like an indulgent warning to those sleeping in tall mahogany beds. The cocks hovered around the hens to cover them early, expecting the little finger of the overseer's wife to make sure of the presence of unlaid eggs. A peacock circled the main house, lighting up, with a cry, at each sweep and turn. The grinding machine's horses were beginning their long circular journey. The slaves were praying in front of clay pots filled with bread and cane liquor. Cimarron opened his fly and left a stream of foam among the roots of a silk-cotton tree. Dog raised his leg over a sapling guava. Machete scars could now be seen on the felled cane. The bulldogs of the pack used to hunt blacks rattled their chains, impatient to be taken to the sugar plant.

"Coming with me?" Cimarron asked.

Dog followed him docilely. Down below there were too many whips, too many chains, for those who repented and went back. There was no female scent any more. But there was no black man's scent either. Now, Dog was much more conscious of a white man's scent, the scent of danger. Because the overseer smelled white, in spite of the ironed starch of his fancy guayabera shirt and the acrid polish on his pigskin leggings. It was the same scent the young ladies in the house had, in spite of the perfume their lace gave off. It was the scent of the priest, in spite of the stench of melted wax and incense that made unpleasant the shade of the chapel that was nevertheless so cool. It was the same scent the organist carried around with him, even though the bellows of the organ had blown so many puffs of moth-eaten felt on top of him. He had to get away from the white odor. Dog had changed sides.

3

During the first days, Dog and Cimarron missed their regular meals. Dog remembered the bones emptied by the bucketful at the sugar plant, as evening fell. Cimarron was homesick for the rice-and-beans brought in pails to the barracoons after the prayer bell or when the drums were put away on Sunday. That's why after oversleeping on mornings without bells or kicks, they fell into the habit of hunting at the crack of dawn. Dog would scent a rodent hidden among a cedar's leaves. Cimarron would bring it down with rocks. The day they ran into a wild pig's trail, they had their work cut out for hours and hours, until the animal, its ears in shreds, rattled by all the barking but still charging, was cornered at the foot of a large rock and beaten down with a stick. Little by little, Dog and Cimarron forgot the days when they had eaten regular meals. They wolfed down whatever they could grab, bolting as much as they could, knowing it might rain tomorrow and the water above would run down among the rocks to lay a thicker carpet over the bottom of the valley. Luckily, Dog knew how to eat fruit. Whenever Cimarron found a mango or a mamey fruit, Dog also got yellow or red smeared all over his snout. Besides, since he had always been an egg thief, he compensated with a quail's nest for his master's incomprehensible passion for the cray-fish that slept against the current at the end of the subterranean river that lit its way out with a mouth of petrified snails.

They lived in a cave, well hidden by a curtain of tree ferns. Stalactites dropped tears at regular intervals, filling the cold shadows with a sound like clocks. One day Dog started digging at the base of one of its walls.

His teeth soon came up with a femur and some ribs, so ancient they were flavorless, crumbling on his tongue like insipid lumps of dust. Then he carried a human skull to Cimarron who was making himself a belt from the skin of a majá snake. Although there were still pieces of pottery in the hole and some mortars they could have used, terrified by the presence of dead people in his home, Cimarron gave up the cave that same afternoon, mumbling prayers, heedless of the rain. They both slept among roots and seeds, wrapped in a single odor of wet dog. At daybreak they found a cave with a lower ceiling, which the man had to enter on all fours. At least here there were none of those bones that were useless and could only bring on sudden shocks and evil apparitions.

Since they had had no signs of any hunting parties in a long time, they both started venturing into the road. Sometimes a familiar cart driver went by, or a devout woman dressed in Nazarene habit, or a guitar player, or one of those who knows the big boss in every town, and they watched them from far off, quietly. There was no doubt that Cimarron was waiting for something. He would lie for several hours flat on his stomach in the Guinea grass, watching that dirt road, seldom used, which a bullfrog could span with one big jump. During those waits, Dog amused himself scattering flocks of white butterflies or leaping in a useless attempt to catch a sequinned humming-bird.

One day while Cimarron waited like that for something that never came, the rattle of hoofs got him up on his wrists. A two-wheeled carriage was coming pulled at a full trot by the sugar mill's gray pony. Standing on the shafts, Gregorio, the driver, snapped the whip, while behind him the parish priest tinkled the little viaticum bell. It had been so long since Dog had had any fun running faster than horses that he threw all caution to the winds.

He went down the hill full speed, stretched to full length, blue in the sunlight, caught up with the carriage and began barking at the pony's hocks, to the right, the left, in front, passing it again and again, baring his teeth at the driver and the priest. The pony broke into a full gallop, trying to shake off its blinkers and pulling at the bit. Suddenly, a shaft broke, snapping off the harness trace. Gesticulating like puppets, the parish priest and the driver pitched headlong into the small stone bridge. The dust was dyed with blood.

Cimarron came up running. He was brandishing a vine to whip Dog who was dragging himself along, asking for forgiveness. But the black man cut his gestures short, surprised by the thought that the accident was not all bad. He seized the surplice and the priest's clothes, the driver's jacket and high boots. In pockets and more pockets, there were almost five pesos; plus the little silver bell. The robbers returned to the bush. Wrapped in the cassock, Cimarron went into a dream of forgotten pleasures that night. He remembered the kerosene lamps filled with dead insects burning so late in the last houses in town, there where twice they had allowed him to ask for his Christmas bonus, to spend as he pleased. The black man, of course, had opted for women.

4

Spring surprised them both, at dawn. Dog woke up with an unbearable tenseness between his hind legs and a sickly look in his eyes. He was panting without feeling hot, stretching out between his fangs a tongue with a sharp-edged softness of barnacles on it. Cimarron was mumbling to himself. They were both in a nasty mood. They went out to the road early, but not with hunting in mind. Dog ran about helter-skelter, looking in vain for some scent he could pick up. He killed insects he had always found revolting, for the pleasure of destroying, he cracked open spears of wheat grass between his teeth, he pulled up young shoots. His exasperation reached its limit when a toad spit in his eyes. Cimarron was waiting, as he had never waited before.

But no one went by on the road that day. As night came down and the first bats flitted over the countryside like flying stones, Cimarron started walking slowly toward the houses around the sugar mill. Dog followed him, defying the same whip and the same chains. Following the dry stream-bed, they gradually approached the barracoons. There was a perceptible odor now, familiar from the past, of burning wood, lye, molasses, filings from horses' hoofs. They must have been making guava paste, because an interminable sweetness of marmalades was being blown about by the land breeze. Dog and Cimarron kept going in closer, side by side, the man's head down to the same height as the dog's.

Suddenly, one of the plantation's black women crossed the path to the smithy. Cimarron jumped her, bringing her down among the basil bushes. A broad hand smothered her cries. Alone now, Dog advanced to the edge of the sugar plantation. The English bitch, acquired by Don Marcial at a show in Paris, was there. She tried to run away. Dog cut her off, bristling from head to tail. His male scent was so enveloping that the English bitch forgot she had been bathed, hours before, with soap from Castille.

When Dog got back to the cave, day was breaking. Cimarron was asleep, muffled up in the priest's cassock. Down below, in the river, two manatees were playing among the rushes, muddying the current with leaps that fanned out clouds of foam over the slime.

5

Cimarron was getting more and more careless. He haunted the villages now, waylaying some lone washerwoman at any time of day, or a medicine woman who was out looking for coriander, broom or cactus for some exorcism. And from the night he had been daring enough to drink away the chaplain's pesos at a roadside inn, he had grown greedy for pieces of money. More than once, on the bypaths, he had made off with some peasant's money-belt, after knocking him off his horse and keeping him quiet with a stick. Dog accompanied him on those forays, helping as much as possible. Still, they ate worse than before and he had to satisfy himself more than ever with the eggs of quails, guinea hens and herons. Besides, Cimarron lived in constant alarm. At the slightest bark from Dog, he would grab his stolen machete or climb into a tree.

With the hard test of Spring over, Dog appeared more and more reluctant to go near the towns. There were too many children who threw rocks, people always ready to let fly with kicks, and all the dogs in the yards launched into war cries whenever they smelled him close by. Besides, on those nights, Cimarron returned stumbling and his mouth gave off an odor Dog detested as much as the odor of tobacco. That's why whenever his master went into a poorly lit house, Dog waited for him at a prudent distance. And so their life went on until the night Cimarron shut himself in a servant girl's room too long. The shack was quickly surrounded by stealthy men, carrying unsheathed machetes. Soon after, Cimarron was taken out into the street naked, letting out loud howls. Dog, who had just scented the sugar mill's overseer, ran off, down the cane path into the bush.

The next day he saw Cimarron passing on the road. He was covered with wounds cured with salt. There were irons on his neck and ankles, and he was being led by four members of the San Fernando police force, who hit him with a ramrod at every other step, calling him thief, drunk and a no-good bastard.

6

Sitting on a cornice of rock commanding the valley, Dog was baying at the moon. Sometimes a deep sadness came over him, when that huge cold sun reached its full roundness, spreading such gaunt reflections over the plants. The fires that used to light up the cave on rainy nights were over for him. He would no longer know the man's warmth in the approaching winter, nor would there be anyone to remove the copper-toothed collar that interfered with his sleep so much, even if he had inherited the priest's cassock. Hunting without let-up, he had, on the other hand, grown more tolerant of creatures that were no good as food. He used to let the majá snake escape between the hot stones without even barking, now that Cimarron was not there to sick him on, hoping to make himself a belt or put together fat for ointments. Besides, the smell of snakes sickened him. Whenever he seized one by the tail, it was because he felt impelled to, like everyone who needs someone else. Nor could he take the offensive with the wild pig any more, save in the case of extreme hunger. He was satisfied now with water birds, ferrets, rats and an occasional hen escaped from the village barnyards. Nevertheless, the sugar mill had been forgotten. Its bell had lost all meaning. Dog looked now for the shelter of bluffs almost inaccessible to man, living in a world of dragontrees the wind rocked with the sound of a new pack-saddle, a world of orchids, of creeping plants where green lizards with white earmuffs dragged themselves, the kind that taste so bad and, for that very reason, stay right where they are. He had lost flesh. The coat on his ribs, broken with hollows, caught wild plants that had no thorns now.

Spring came back in, with the agueweeds. One afternoon when a strange uneasiness kept him awake, Dog suddenly picked up the mysterious female scent, so strong, so penetrating, that had been the first cause of his flight into the bush. The sound of barking was also tumbling down from the mountains now. This time Dog took firm hold of the scent, picking it up again after swimming across a stream. He wasn't afraid any more. He followed the trail all night long, with his nose to the ground, dropping slaver over the edge of his tongue. At daybreak, the scent filled an entire gulch. A pack of wild dogs followed one who had picked up the scent. Several males with the profiles of wolves huddled there, their eyes shining, rigid on their legs, all set to attack. Behind them, the female scent had thickened.

Dog took one big leap. The wild dogs rushed him. Their bodies jammed together, one against the other, in a confused whirlwind of barks. But howls drawn out by the collar's teeth were soon heard. Mouths were filling with blood. There were ears in shreds. When Dog had the oldest one with his throat slashed open under him, the others backed off, growling with useless rage. Then Dog ran to the center of the field of action to do final battle with the gray stiff-haired bitch, who was waiting for him with her fangs out. The trail died in the shadow of her belly.

7

The wild dogs hunted in a band. That way they looked for big game, with more meat and more bones. When they ran across a deer, the job lasted for days. First, the chase. Then, if the animal managed to hurdle a ravine in one leap, the cut-off. Then, if a cave came to the aid of the prey, the siege. In spite of wounding and goring out eyes, the animal always died in the teeth of the dog pack that started cutting up the still living body, pulling out strips of brown hair and drinking blood, warm but fresh, from the neck arteries or at the base of an ear that had been ripped off. Many of the savage dogs had lost an eye, gored out by a horn, and all were covered with scars, sores and red raw places. On rutting days, the dogs fought among themselves, while the bitches waited, lying down, with surprising indifference, for the outcome of the fight. The sugar mill's bell, whose diapason was sometimes brought by the breeze, did not stir the slightest memory in Dog.

One day the wild dogs picked up a trail familiar in those jungles of lianas, thorns, and hellish plants that poisoned when they wounded. It was a black man's scent. The dogs advanced cautiously along the narrow passage of the snails, where there rose an old rock with a dead man's face. Men generally leave bones and scraps wherever they have been. But it's better to be wary of them, because they are the most dangerous animals, since they walk on hind legs and that allows them to make their gestures longer with sticks and objects. The pack had stopped barking.

Suddenly, the man appeared. He gave off a black man's smell. Broken chains, hanging from his wrists, kept time to his steps. Other, thicker links jangled beneath the fringes of his striped pants. Dog recognized Cimarron.

"Dog!" the black man rejoiced. "Dog!"

Dog went up to him slowly. He sniffed at his feet, but without letting himself be touched. He went around and around him, wagging his tail. Whenever he was called, he fled. And when he wasn't called he seemed to look for that sound of the human voice he had understood a little in other days, but which sounded so strange to him now, so dangerously reminiscent of commands he had obeyed. Cimarron finally took a step, putting out a soft hand toward his head. Dog let out a strange cry, mixture of a gruff bark and a howl, and leapt for the black man's throat.

He had suddenly remembered an old command given by the overseer of the sugar mill the day a slave ran away into the bush.

8

Since there was no female scent and times were peaceful, the wild dogs slept off their satiety for two days. Overhead, the vultures passed over the branches of the trees, waiting for the pack to leave without finishing the job. Dog and the gray bitch had more fun than ever, playing with Cimarron's striped shirt. Each one pulled at his end, to test the solidity of his fangs. Whenever a seam gave, they both rolled in the dust. And they would start all over again, with the rag getting shorter and shorter, staring into each other's eyes, their noses almost touching. Finally the order to depart was given. Their barking was lost at the top of the woody crests.

For many years, at night, hunters avoided that path spoiled for them by bones and chains.

TRANSLATED BY HARDIE ST. MARTIN

Autoretrato

Cuando al mirarme en el espejo
Veo en mi cara la de mi padre
Absurdamente tengo miedo.

Barbería

La brocha del arbol
hace nubes de espuma
en el jabon-azul del cielo.
Y sales colorado
lavado
afeitado:
SOL

José Coronel Urtecho

Self-Portrait

When looking at myself in the mirror
I see in my face the face of my father
Absurdly I feel some terror.

TRANSLATED BY JANET BROF

Barbershop

The soft brush of the tree
makes clouds of foam
in the soap-blue of the sky.
And you emerge reddish
washed
shaved:
SUN

TRANSLATED BY JANET BROF

DE *Oda a Rubén Darío*

Final (Con pito)

En fin, Rubén,
paisano inevitable, te saludo
con mi bombín,
que se comieron los ratones en
mil novecientos veinte y cinco. Amén.

Luna de Palo

Yo les mandé una luna de regalo
a mi madre, a mi hermana.
Plana.
De palo.

Era
la luna de los cortes de madera.
No la de miel de las alcobas
sino la luna de las tobobas.

Sólo era una carta mía
la que llevaba en su batea.
Una carta que decía,
que mi mujer era fea
pero que yo la quería. . .

Cuando la luna entró en la aldea
nadie la conocía.

FROM *Ode to Rubén Darío*

Finale (with whistle)

> And so, Rubén
> unavoidable countryman, I salute you
> with my derby
> that the rats ate in
> nineteen hundred and twenty-fi-
> ve. Amen.

TRANSLATED BY JANET BROF

Wooden Moon

> I sent a moon for a present
> to my mother, to my sister
> Flat.
> Of timber.
>
> She was
> the moon of wood slices.
> Not the honey one of boudoirs
> but the moon of vipers.
>
> There was only my letter
> in her flat bottomed boat.
> A letter which said
> that my wife was ugly
> but I loved her. . .
>
> When the moon came into the village
> no one knew her.

TRANSLATED BY JANET BROF

San Carlos

Esquina
del lago y del río.
Casas en zancos
trepando la colina como cabros.

Hasta las bombillas eléctricas parecen huevos de lagarto.
Huele a tabaco, a pescado salado.
San Carlos.
Puerto más puerto que los puertos de mar.
Asomado a sus aguas como la tripulación de un barco.
En cada estanco hay un fonógrafo desgañitado.
Una chica de cuerpo barato.
Y un chancho.

Yo me tomo un retrato
al estallido de magnesio de los rayos
(Noche empapada. Frío de Río Frío)
en el muelle de Gustavo U. Shión, el chino.

Bajo mi capote ahulado
Palpitando
Aspirando
Expirando
Mi corazón
como un pescado
Vivo.

1931

San Carlos

At the corner
of the lake and the river.
Houses on stilts
climbing the hill like goats.

Even the electric bulbs seem like alligator eggs.
It smells of tobacco, of salted fish.
San Carlos.
A port more port than sea ports.
Appearing over its waters like a boat's crew.
In each store there is a rasping phonograph.
A girl who sells herself cheap.
And a pig.

I take my picture
in the bulbflash of lightning
(Sopping night. Chill from the Río Frío)
on the dock of the Chinaman, Gustavo U. Shion.

Under my waterproof cape
Palpitating
Breathing in
Breathing out
My heart
Like a hooked fish
Alive.

1931

TRANSLATED BY JANET BROF

José María Arguedas

The Ayla

The Aukis, the community's priests, were singing in Quechua on the shore of the small lake. Hat in one hand and a small cross covered with red k'antu flowers in the other, they were chanting a very ancient hymn:

> *Aylillay, aylillay*
> *uh huayli*
> *aylillay, aylillay*
> *uh huayli.*
> *Gentlemen dignitaries*
> *gentlemen people*
> *beautiful word*
> *beautiful quiet please*
> *forgive me*
> *make me understand*
> *speak my father*
> *drive away wrath*
> *drive away sloth*
> *aylillay, aylillay*
> *uh huayli . . .*

They sang for a long time with their faces turned to the great mountain into whose snow no one had been able to nail a cross. It was the last ceremony of the ancient paschal feast with which they celebrated the conclusion of the cleaning of the aqueducts. The Head Auki had cut the throats of a sheep and a llama beside the well-spring on the slopes of the

Arayá. He had flung the yet living hearts of the sheep and the llama on to the water which drew colored sands from deep in the earth. Then he had spoken to the humming-bird living in a tiny chapel built with mountain stones, very close to the spring. The humming-bird glittered in the darkness of the chapel. The Head Auki passed on to him the complaints and the requests of the community and went out happily, bowing very low in the doorway of the small shrine. After that, they all went down the mountain, chanting hymns at various places selected about a thousand years before. They were received by the community at the entrance of the small lake. After they had adored the Head Auki's cross, they had all eaten ceremonially, and now they were going down to the town, to the neighborhoods of the capital of the district.

The evening sun not only makes the world beautiful, it also communicates with man. While the Auki sang, the light was spreading, coming down from the peaks without burning people's eyes. They could speak to the brightness or rather, the brightness vibrated in each body of the stone, in the body of the cricket, which was already growing impatient to sing, and in the spirit of the people.

When the chorus repeated the final strophe, the young single people, who had listened to the hymn standing beside a wall that was lost from sight in the ravine and on the peaks, joined hands and formed a chain. The women behind, the men at the head. They were all dressed in festive costumes. When the chorus stopped singing, the countryside was left in silence. And the girls began singing the difficult (outsiders said it was 'diabolic') cadence of the ayla. And the chain started out, downhill. The men were dancing. The Aukis and the older dignitaries, heads of family, had been drinking for two days. Their eyes looked dense, but the ayla was reflected in them. The Auki contemplated the file of single people going down to the town, as if he were the mountain itself. He was calm, without rage, stock-still, taking in with his heavy eyes in which the light was concentrated all the confines of the community's lands: mountains, gullies, canyons, summits, hawthorn forests, hay fields, terrains of many colors. The alfalfa fields belonged to the landed class.

Santiago followed the chain that was dancing the ayla. He was out of it, but he repeated within himself the music and the rhythm of its steps. The light had always helped him to understand.

Mestizos and gentlemen saw the file of the ayla passing through the streets at nightfall, and they talked among themselves:

"These Indians are going to carry on with their filth on the hill."

"The yearly orgy."

"And the priest doesn't object."

"He's the son of an unknown Indian father. The Bishop took him in."

"The priest also gets in on it too, later on."

"But out in the open, like animals, it's different. The priest doesn't go in for that."

"He's not a real Indian any more."

"Out in the open, like animals, just like pigs."

"What do they know about love!"

"All massed together, and yet many of them know how to read now . . ."

"No, those don't attend any more, so they say. They're ashamed of this filthy carrying-on."

"Some, some of them attend."

The great chain of the ayla split into four, according to neighborhoods, and headed in different directions. Santiago walked toward the square in Carmenk'a, the largest and most prosperous neighborhood. He didn't follow the dancers. He reached the square before the ayla did.

The married people danced in a circle near the four harps. Still in a chain, the single people went around the square several times, in an undulating line, like a very long serpent. The torches that lit up the harpists and the vendors of rum and *chicha* contributed a glimmer of light to the darkened square. Santiago went up to the tower to watch. The ayla moved like a single body. After the last time around, they formed a kind of jawbone at one end of the square. They advanced singing, all of them, not only the women, toward the place where the harps were playing and the married couples were dancing. Santiago came down from the church tower.

A few stray crickets could be heard right in the square where some dirty, dried-up grass barely managed to grow. The chorus of young people did not drown out the song of the crickets. The chain closed in like a curving fence around the four rings of married couples and then, undulating once more, it headed for the corner that led out to the road that climbed up the mountain. Santiago followed the ayla.

The moon came up as the ayla was crossing the creek. At the water's edge Santiago ran into a young man of the community leaning on a huge rock whose shadow fell across the current.

"Aren't you going?" he asked the young fellow in Quechua.

"You, Santiago, orphan, good man. I'm not going, my girl is working on the Coast. She hasn't been able to get here. I'm waiting. Maybe she'll still get here, pretty soon."

"They say filthy things go on in the ayla, ugly things with the girls. Right?"

The youth burst out laughing.

"They say. Who? The gentlemen in town, that's who. They don't go into the ayla. They haven't seen. Our hearts and the great father Arayá command us to play; we sow at night. Pretty. We know you. They say Don Guadalupe used to kick you, when you were little."

"He didn't kick me. He took me . . . to the torch in the cemetery."

"The torch in the cemetery in Don Guadalupe's town always leaves an ugly burn. That's what they say. You can't watch the ayla."

"Where are they going?"

"To the foot-hill, close by. We're going to play there. Maybe I'm not going to go. My girl hasn't got here. Sometimes people never come back from the Coast. She hasn't got here yet. I'm not going to sow, she's not going to sow . . ."

Santiago was going to say "torch in the cemetery," after listening to the young fellow's voice.

"Next year I'm going to sow. I'm going to lay down roots! It's better, maybe, if she doesn't come," the young guy went on talking. "Some come from the Coast, where there's factories, and more from Lima where, they say, ugly worms grow in the bonemarrow and in the heart too; those say that Arayá the father is nobody's father, that he's dead earth. The ones who've gone to school say that too. But they dance like the rest; some only make fun of . . . They stay in their homes like outsiders. That's how it is. They say ayla is animal game. Wait, Santiaguillo! Wait!"

The young member of the community didn't say Mister Santiago, he talked to him as an equal. And he stood still, looking at the uphill road. The moon lit up everything as if the world had actually turned into something transparent. The chorus of young people gave off more light than the very light of the moon and the stars.

"There's Felisa, my girl. She has come up from the Coast. She must have gotten off the truck up on the hill. This is where those of us who have to wait do our waiting."

She arrived exhausted.

"Santiago!" the girl said. Then she went on talking in Spanish, addressing the young man of the community:

"Santiago is not a gentleman, he is not a mestizo. His heart will be silent, his mouth will also be silent. Arayá the father is good for playing. He's not father. He is big little earth. *Ciao,* goodbye, Santiaguito . . . !"

She let out a sharp cry, the first note of an ayla song. She took the boy's hand, pulling him along, and they left Santiaguillo at the small river's edge. They climbed the hill dancing as they ran. The moon marked them out on the mountain and in the young fellow's breast.

Santiago decided to climb the hill. He left the primitive footpath and began to go up the mountain almost in a straight line. He went in through the shrubs. Digging his nails into the gravel, he went across the gullies.

He came to a shelf that had no weeds nor stones. The young people were dancing there. Santiago stood still, hidden behind a thin stone fence. A leafy black hawthorn grew next to the wall, on the shelf side. Its few red flowers stood out in the light. "I'm nervous, restless, I guess. I'm not tired, flower of *ankukichka,*" he spoke to the tree.

The girls in the ayla began screaming at this moment and dispersed waving their arms. Two were making for the hawthorn; they seemed to be flying low. Then the men shouted in hoarse voices, like the hawk as he gains height rapidly. And they started running in an undulating line. Two youths gave chase to the girls, near the hawthorn. The girls laughed and shrieked, the boys huffed and puffed, and whistled. Finally the young men let out a kind of buzz through their mouths and the girls stopped dead, a short distance from each other. When the men toppled on to them, they burst out laughing and hurling insults: "Twisted hawk, beaten hawk, one-eyed hawk, blind hawk, hawk with no chest . . ." The men were also shouting: "One-eyed pigeon, pigeon without eyes, pigeon without anything, I . . . I am going to give you baby chicks, in the name of the Father, the Mother . . ." And Santiago saw the boy who was nearest him lifting the girl's dress, while she made believe she was defending herself, then she was still, completely motionless, while the young man moved up and down on her. Whistles, screams, loud yells reached the place where Santiago was hiding, as if they came not from people, but from birds trying to talk like humans. Santiago watched the couple near him, and the screams kept him from feeling cold or smelling anything. Suddenly the couple got to their feet; they began to dance, screaming. They wheeled around for a moment, alone, then they joined the other couple. And the four moved, dancing the ayla, toward the center of the shelf. Other groups appeared from everywhere and formed the great chain once more. They went past the boy, all of them. He had never felt the cold and loving moon like this, the light of the world, like a river in which ducks flap around throwing off sparks from their wings and their beaks. He jumped out of his hiding place, yelling:

"I am Santiago, Santiaguillo!"

"Strange animal, unknown, happy animal!" the boy who was leading the ayla shouted in Quechua. *"Ciao,* goodbye!" he said the last words in Spanish. And he joined the dance again.

"Hot shit, dammit," another of the young people at the head of the line said, very distinctly.

They left the boy alone there, like a stone dropped from the sky. The young people started to sing and the chain headed toward other ground. The boy heard many voices like pumas and sheep talking, far off, mixing the tone of their voices, entangling it, making the ground tremble. He felt hot at that high altitude, all alone. "All this talking I hear is making me freeze," he said, getting confused.

"They didn't kill you," the priest told him in the confessional. "They didn't tear you to pieces because they took you for one of the animals on that accursed hill of Arayá . . ."

"Not at all, father! They recognized me. I . . . well, unknown, happy animal, I am. *Ciao,* goodbye, sir . . . !"

Once in the square where the sun was searing the helpless flowers, he didn't know which way to go.

"I've lost the bad smell, I think, I'm lighter, I think . . . Father Arayá, in the name of the Son, the Holy Ghost . . . I'm going off to the Coast . . . Let the worms eat my heart or else I'll eat them . . ."

He said goodbye to the mountain there in the square.

TRANSLATED BY HARDIE ST. MARTIN

poema del manicomio

Tuve miedo
y me regresé de la locura

Tuve miedo de ser

una rueda

un color

un paso

PORQUE MIS OJOS ERAN NIÑOS
Y mi corazón
un botón
más
de
mi camisa de fuerza

Pero hoy que mis ojos visten pantalones largos
veo a la calle que está mendiga de pasos.

1923

Carlos Oquendo de Amat

m a d h o u s e   p o e m

I was afraid
and I came back from madness

    I was afraid of being

        a wheel

            a colour

                a footstep

    BECAUSE MY EYES WERE CHILDREN

        and my heart
        one button
        more
        on
        my straitjacket

But today since my eyes wear long trousers
I look out at the street which goes begging for footsteps.

1923

TRANSLATED BY H. R. HAYS

film de los

Las nubes
son el escape de gas de automóviles invisibles.

       Todas las casas son cubos de flores

           El paisaje es de limón
           y mi amada
           quiere jugar al golf con él.

       Tocaremos un timbre
     París habrá cambiado a Viena.

   En el Campo de Marte
   naturalmente
   los ciclistas venden imágenes económicas

se ha desdoblado el paisaje

                    todos somos enanos

    Las ciudades se habrán construido
    sobre la punta de los paraguas

    (Y la vida nos parece mejor
       porque está más alta).

paisajes

un poco de olor al paisaje

somos buenos
y nos pintaremos el alma de inteligentes
>   *poema acéntrico*

>   En Yanquilandia el cow boy Fritz
>   mató a la obscuridad

>   Nosotros desentornillamos todo nuestro optimismo

>   nos llenamos la cartera de estrellas
>   y hasta hay alguno que firma un cheque de cielo.

Esto es insoportable
un plumero
para limpiar todos los paisajes
y quién
habrá quedado?
>   Dios   o   nada

>   *(VEASE EL PROXIMO EPISODIO)*

NOTA.—Los poemas acéntricos que vagan por los espacios subconcientes, o exteriorizadamente inconcretos son hoy captados por los poetas, aparatos análogos al rayo X, en el futuro los registrarán.

1925

m o v i e   o f   t h e

The clouds
are the exhaust of invisible automobiles

        All the houses are buckets of flowers

           The countryside is made of lemon
           and the one I love
           wants to play golf with it.

      We will press a bell
     Paris will have changed to Vienna.

     In the Campo de Marte
     naturally
     cyclists sell cheap images

the   countryside   has   broken   apart

              we all are dwarfs

    The cities will have been built
    on the tips of umbrellas

    (And life seems better to us
       because it is higher).

c o u n t r y s i d e

a little of the countryside aroma

we are good
and we will paint our souls intelligent

off-center poem

In Yankeeland Fritz the cowboy
shot the darkness dead

We unscrew all our optimism

we fill up a billfold of stars
and until there is someone who signs a check of sky.

This is unbearable
a featherduster
to clean up all the countryside
and who
will have remained?

God   or   nothing

(*WATCH FOR THE NEXT EPISODE*)

NOTE.—The off-center poems which wander through subconscious or outwardly in-
concrete spaces are today captured by poets, who are apparatus analogous to the X-ray
which in the future will register them.

1925

TRANSLATED BY JANET BROF

poema

Para tí
tengo impresa una sonrisa en papel japón.

Mírame
que haces crecer la yerba de los prados.

Mujer
mapa de música   claro de río   fiesta de fruta

En tu ventana

cuelgan enredaderas de los volantes de los automóviles
y los expendedores disminuyen el precio de sus mercancias

d é j a m e   q u e   b e s e   t u   v o z

Tu voz

QUE CANTA EN TODAS LAS RAMAS DE LA MAÑANA
1925

p o e m

For you
I have printed a smile on kite paper.

Look at me
You make the meadow grass grow.

Woman
map   light breaking   festival
of music   to the river   of fruit

     In your window

ivy hangs from the wheels of automobiles
and the dealers lower the prices of their merchandise

     l e t   m e   k i s s   y o u r   v o i c e

     Your voice

THAT SINGS IN ALL THE BRANCHES OF THE MORNING

1925

TRANSLATED BY JANET BROF

Juan Carlos Onetti

A Dream Come True

The joke had been thought up by Blanes; he used to come into my office when I had one—or into the café when times were bad—and motionless on the rug, leaning a fist on my desk, his bright-colored tie fastened to his shirt by a gold clip and his square clean-shaven head whose dark eyes seemed unable to fix on anything for more than a minute, soon blurring as if Blanes were falling asleep or remembered some pure moment of love in his life, doubtless imaginary, his head stripped of any superfluous detail leaning back against a wall covered with photos and posters, he would hear me out and then comment, mouthing each word: "Of course, you've ruined yourself producing Hamlet." Or else, "Yes, we know you've always martyred yourself for art and if it weren't for your insane love of Hamlet . . ." While I spent all these years putting up with those God-forsaken people, authors and actors, actresses and theater-owners, reviewers and my own family, friends, plus all their mistresses, all that time losing and making money that only God and I knew would again be lost the following season, existing with that drop of water falling on one's bare skull, that jab in the ribs, that bittersweet taste, that scoffing from Blanes that I couldn't quite understand.

"Yes, of course. You've been driven to acts of madness by that boundless love of Hamlet . . ."

If I had asked him what he meant the first time, if I had confessed that I knew no more about Hamlet than how to figure the cost of a play starting with its first reading, the joke would have ended right there. But I feared the endless digs my question would spark and I merely grimaced and sent him off. And so I was able to live twenty years without knowing what Hamlet was, without reading it, but reading in Blanes' face and the rocking of his head that Hamlet was art, pure art, great art and knowing also, although it slowly came to me unawares, that the play also had something to do with an actor or an actress, in this case it was always an actress wearing tight black clothes over absurd hips, a skull, a cemetery, a duel, vengeance, and a young girl who drowns. As well as with W. Shakespeare.

This is why now, only now, with my blond wig parted in the middle, which I wear even to bed, my false teeth which fit so poorly I lisp and babble like a baby, in the library of this rest home for penniless theatrical types, which they refer to by a more pretentious name, I found the book, very small and bound in dark blue with the word *Hamlet* inlaid in gold. I sank down into an armchair without opening the book, resolved never to open it or read one single line, thinking about Blanes, how in this way I could take revenge on him for his joke and remembering the evening Blanes came searching for me in that provincial hotel and after listening to me while he smoked and looked up at the ceiling or at the people wandering into the lounge, opened his lips in order to say, right in front of that poor madwoman:

"It's unbelievable. A man like you who went bankrupt producing Hamlet . . ."

I had asked him over to the hotel to offer him a role in some crazy one-nighter titled, I believe, "Dream Come True." The cast of that insane play called for some anonymous young man and Blanes was the only one who could play it since, when the woman came to see me, he and I were the only two left, the rest of the company having escaped to Buenos Aires.

The woman had stopped by the hotel at noon, but as I was asleep she returned at the hour the midday siesta ended in that hot province, when I had found the coolest corner of the dining room where I was eating some breaded cutlet and drinking some white wine—the only drinkable kind around. When I first spotted her, motionless within the hot curtained archway, her eyes widening in the darkened dining room, and after the waiter pointed out my table and she made a straight line for it, her skirt whirling the dust up, I had no idea what lay within that woman, no idea of that thing like a white and flabby ribbon of madness that she unravelled, gently tugging at it like some bandage on the wound of past, lonely years, which she now came to bind me in, like some mummy, me and a few of those days spent in that boring place, crowded with fat and drab people. But something in her smile even then made me uneasy, and I couldn't stop staring at her little uneven teeth which recalled some child asleep and breathing with its mouth open. Her hair, almost totally gray, was braided and wrapped around her head and her clothes were out-of-date, somehow befitting someone or something younger than herself. Her skirt, which reached down to her bootlike shoes, was long and dark and floated out as she walked, settling again only to tremble once more at her next step. Her tightfitting blouse had lace on it and a large cameo was pinned between her uplifted, young breasts; finally the blouse and skirt were both joined and divided by a rose at her waist, probably artificial, now that I think of it, a flower with a huge center and drooping on a stiff stem which seemed to threaten her stomach.

The woman was around fifty years old. What was impossible to forget, what I feel even now as I remember her walking towards my corner in the dining room, was that feeling of a young girl belonging to some past century who had fallen asleep and had just now awakened, her hair a bit rumpled, barely aged, but one who could at any time, in an instant, become her age and silently collapse before me, consumed by those innumerable days. Her smile was ugly to look at, for while it expressed her ignorance of standing on the edge of aging and sudden death, yet it understood—or at least those bared teeth expressed—the hideous decay that threatened her. It was all there, in the half-light of the dining room. I awkwardly settled my silverware beside my plate and stood up.

"Are you Mr. Langman, the theater producer?"

I nodded, smiled and asked her to join me. She refused to order anything. With the table now separating us, I glanced at the whole shape of her mouth and the lightly painted lips, from whose very center her voice hummed out, with a slight Castilian accent, slipping out between the unmatched teeth. Her small quiet eyes, widening to see better, revealed nothing to me. I could only wait for her to speak, and I thought that whatever kind of woman and life her words evoked would fit her strange appearance, and then the strangeness would disappear.

"I wanted to talk to you about a play," she said. "I mean I have a play . . ."

I thought she'd go on but she stopped and paused for me to say something, smiling and waiting for my words in an unshakable silence. She waited very calmly, her hands folded on her lap. I pushed my plate aside and ordered coffee. I offered her a cigaret but she motioned with her head and smiled, meaning she didn't smoke. I lit mine and began talking, trying to shake her off, gently, but at once and permanently, even though I felt compelled, I don't know why, to behave slyly.

"Madame, I'm so sorry. It's quite difficult you know. Is this your first play? Yes? Of course. And what is the name of your work?"

"No, it has no name," she answered. "It's so hard to explain. It's not what you think. Of course, one could call it *The Dream, The Dream Come True, A Dream Come True.*"

By now, I was certain she was mad and I felt more self-confident. "Good. *A Dream Come True.* Not bad. Titles are very important. I've always had, you might say, a personal yet selfless interest in giving a hand to beginners. Yes, to instill new values in our national theater. I need not mention that gratitude is the last thing I reap. Madame, there are many who took their first step on our major stages, thanks to me, many who now pocket unbelievable royalties from their plays in our capital city and yearly walk off with some prize. No longer do they remember how they came almost begging, to me . . ."

Even the young busboy standing way off in the corner of the dining room near the icebox, trying to fight off the flies and heat with his dishcloth, could see that my words meant nothing to that strange creature. Turning away from the warmth of my coffee cup, I threw her one last look, and said: "The point is, Madame, you've probably heard that our season here has been a catastrophe. We've had to close down and I've just stayed on in order to settle a few personal matters. I'll also be leaving for

Buenos Aires next week. I was wrong, that's all. Even though I gave in and gave them a season of farces, this place isn't ready for us—you see what has happened. So . . . Now, well we could do one thing, Madame. If you would give me a copy of your play, I'll see whether in Buenos Aires . . . Is it three acts?" I now played her game and fell silent, forcing her to say something. I leaned over, slowly rubbing the tip of my cigaret against the ashtray. She blinked.

"What?"

"Your play, Madame. *A Dream Come True.* Are there three acts?"

"No, there are no acts."

"Well, scenes. Yes, it's the new thing now . . ."

"I don't have a copy. It's nothing I've written . . ." she went on. The time had come to leave.

"I'll give you my Buenos Aires address and when you get it written down . . ."

Her body sagged and hunched over but her head lifted and I saw the same smile. I paused, positive that she would now go, but a moment later she brushed her hand over her face and continued. "No, it's not what you think. The thing is a moment, you could call it a scene, and nothing happens. Like this moment, here in this dining room, might be acted, I'd leave and that would be all. No," she went on, "there really isn't any plot, just some people on a street, some houses and two cars that go by. I'm there and a man, and some woman who comes out of the doorway of a store across the street and gives him a glass of beer. There's no one else, just us three. The man crosses the street towards the woman with the pitcher of beer and then crosses back and sits down near me at the same table he was at in the beginning."

She was silent for a moment and then smiling, neither at me nor at the half-opened linen cabinet behind me in the wall, she concluded: "Do you understand?"

I side-stepped again, remembering something about experimental theater, mentioning it and explaining how impossible it was to do anything like real art in such a place as we now found ourselves. No one would go to the theater to see something like her play. Perhaps I alone in the entire province was capable of understanding the meaning of her work, the sense behind the action, the car symbolism and the woman who offers a "tumbler" of beer to the man who crosses the street and then comes back to her, "near you, Madame."

She stared at me and there was something in her expression that reminded me of the way Blanes looked when he had to ask me for money and then talk of Hamlet: a hint of pity but mainly scorn and dislike.

"That's not the point, Mr. Langman," she said. "Only I wish to see it, no one else, no audience. Myself and the actors, nothing more. I wish to see it once. But that one performance must be done just as I will describe it to you and you must do just as I say, nothing else. Agreed? Well then, please tell me how much it may cost and I shall pay you."

It was hopeless to continue babbling on about experimental drama or similar stuff, face to face with this madwoman who now opened her purse and pulled out two fifty-peso bills. "With this you can hire the actors and take care of our preliminary expenses; later on you can let me know how much more you need." So, I, starving for money, unable to escape that damned hole until someone in Buenos Aires answered my letters and mailed me some pesos, put on my best smile, nodded several times and folded the bills carefully before putting them away in my jacket pocket.

"Don't worry, Madame. I believe I understand the sort of thing you . . ." As I spoke I couldn't look at her; I was remembering Blanes, how I hated seeing that same humiliating scorn on her face. "I'll take care of the matter this very afternoon and if we could meet again . . . tonight? Yes, right here. By then we'll have our leading man and you can explain the scene in greater detail and we'll get it all arranged; just how *Dream, A Dream Come True* . . . ?"

Maybe she was simply mad or maybe she also knew, as I knew, that I was incapable of taking off with her hundred pesos, because she didn't ask for a receipt, it didn't seem to cross her mind, and after shaking my hand, she left. She moved out of that dining room with her skirt swirling and braking against the motion of each step, walking tall and out into the heat of the street as one returning to the warmth of a sleep which had lasted countless years and which had shielded her tainted youth from collapsing into rot.

I found Blanes in some dark, messy room, whose brick walls showed through the paint, sprawled behind some green plants, in the damp heat of the late afternoon. The hundred pesos were still in my pocket; until I found Blanes, until I got him to help me give that madwoman her money's worth, I wasn't going to spend one cent of it. I woke him up and waited patiently while he bathed, shaved, lay down and then once more got up to drink a glass of milk which meant he had gotten drunk the night before. Collapsing once again on his bed, he lit a cigaret, still refusing to listen and even after I had pulled up the remains of some dresser chair I'd been sitting in and leaned forward seriously, prepared to present my plan, he stopped me, saying: "First, take a look at that ceiling."

The ceiling, held up by two or three moldy beams, was made of mud tiles and long dried-up bamboo of unknown origin.

"Okay. Let's have it," he said.

I described the whole thing but Blanes kept on interrupting, laughing, insisting it was either all a lie I had made up or else someone had sent the woman as a joke. Then he asked me to explain all of it and the matter was finally settled when I offered half of whatever was left over after expenses. I told him that I really didn't know what the deal was, what it involved nor what the hell that woman wanted from us, but the fifty pesos were ours and now we could either both take off for Buenos Aires, or at least I could go alone if he chose to stay and go on sleeping. He laughed, quieted down and then asked for twenty out of the fifty pesos I told him I had received. So right there I was forced to hand over ten, something I soon regretted because that evening when he appeared in the dining room of the hotel, he was already drunk. Leaning his head over a little plate of ice and smiling, he said: "You never learn, do you? The millionaire patron of B.A. or anywhere in the world where a whisper of art is heard. A man, bankrupted a hundred times staging Hamlet, is now gambling everything on an unknown genius—in a corset."

But when she arrived, when that woman appeared from behind my shoulders, all dressed in black, veiled, a small umbrella hooked on her wrist and a watch hanging from a gold chain around her neck, and stretching her hand out to Blanes said hello with that special smile, gentler under those electric lights, he stopped nagging me and said: "Ah, Madame, the very gods have guided you to Langman. A man who has sacrificed hundreds of thousands just to give us Hamlet in its true form."

Now, as she looked from one to the other, it seemed she was the one mocking; then she became thoughtful and said she was in a hurry, that she would explain everything until the smallest doubt was cleared up and would only return when everything was ready. Beneath the soft yet clear light, the woman's face and everything that glowed on her body, parts of her dress, the nails on one ungloved hand, the umbrella handle, the watch on its chain, all seemed to return to some reality, protected against suffering the brilliant sunshine. It all made me feel relatively relaxed and throughout the rest of the evening I ceased thinking of her as mad, I forgot the pervading odor of fraud in the whole business, and I felt quite calm as if we were in the middle of some every-day, normal business matter. In fact, there was little for me to worry about now that Blanes was there, acting polite, still drinking, and talking to her as if they had already met several times, ordering her a whiskey which she changed for a cup of linden tea. So that finally, whatever she had come to tell me, she ended up telling him, and I made no objection: with Blanes as the leading man the more he understood of the play, the better it would all work out. The woman's instructions were the following (her voice sounded different as she talked to Blanes and although she never looked at him but spoke with her eyes lowered, I felt she was speaking to him in a very private way, as if confessing to something intimate to her life, which I had heard already but which had to be repeated, as when you stand in an office asking for a passport, something like that).

"The set must show houses and sidewalks, but all thrown together, the way it is in a big city, all shoved one on top of the other. I come out, that is, the woman I'm playing comes out of a house and sits down on the curb, near a green table. Near the table, a man is sitting on a kitchen bench. That's your part. He's wearing a knit shirt and a cap. Across the street there's a vegetable store with crates of tomatoes beside the door. Just then a car crosses the stage, and the man, that's you, gets up to cross the street and I'm afraid, thinking the car will hit you. But you get across before the car passes and reach the other side just as a woman comes out, dressed to go walking, and carrying a glass of beer in one hand. You then drink it all down and come right back just as another car speeds by, this time from the opposite direction. Once again, you get across just in time and sit down on the bench. Meanwhile, I've laid down on the curb like a child, and you come and lean over a little and caress my head."

The play was easy enough to stage but I mentioned that now after having thought it through I felt only one problem remained: that third character, that woman who leaves her house for a walk with a glass of beer.

"Pitcher," she told me. "It's an earthenware pitcher with a handle and a cover."

Blanes nodded and said to her, "Of course, it has some design on it—painted on."

She answered yes and it seemed as if his words had calmed her; she looked content, with that expression of happiness that only women get, a look that makes me want to discreetly close my eyes and not look. We discussed the other woman again and finally Blanes stretched out his hand and said he had everything he needed and there was nothing further for us to worry about. I decided that insanity was contagious because when I asked Blanes whom he had in mind for the woman's role, he answered "La Rivas," and even though I had never known anyone by that name, I caught Blanes glaring at me and said nothing. As it turned out everything was arranged, settled by the two of them, and there was no need for me to think any further about it. I went right off and found the theater owner, who rented us the place two days for the price of one after I gave him my word that no one but the actors would be admitted.

The next day I got hold of some sort of electrician who, for a day's wage of six pesos, helped me paint and move around the scenery. By nightfall, after working nearly fifteen hours, everything was ready. Sweating and in shirtsleeves, I was having some beer and sandwiches while listening with one ear to the man retelling some local gossip. He paused and then continued.

"Your friend was in good hands today. This afternoon he was with that lady you were with last night at the hotel. Nothing is private around here. She isn't from this area; they say she's here during the summers. I don't like to meddle but I saw them going into a hotel. Yes, I understand, you also live in a hotel. But the one they went into this afternoon was different . . . You know the kind I mean?"

A bit later Blanes arrived and I mentioned the famous actress Rivas was still missing and the business of the cars had to be organized since only one was available. It belonged to the man who had been helping me and for a few pesos he was willing to rent it out and drive it. Actually I had already figured out a solution since the car was an old beaten-up convertible, and all one had to do was drive it by first with the top down and afterwards with the top up, or vice versa. Blanes was silent; he was completely drunk and I hadn't the faintest idea where he had gotten the money. Moments later, it struck me that he was probably cynical enough to have accepted money directly from that poor woman. The thought sickened me and I went on eating my sandwich in silence while he walked about drunk and humming as he mimed and leapt around the stage like a photographer, a spy, a boxer, a football player. With his hat tipped back on his head and humming away, he looked everywhere, from every angle, searching for God knows what. I had no stomach for talking to him; with every passing second I felt more and more convinced that he was drunk on money he had practically stolen from that poor sick woman. So after finishing my sandwich, I sent my man out for six more and another bottle of beer. Meanwhile, Blanes had tired of prancing about and he came over and sat down on some crate near me, still drunk but now sentimental, his hands in his pants pockets, his hat on his knees, and looking glassy-eyed at the stage. Nothing was said for a while and I could see that he had aged and that his blond hair was dull and thinning. He hadn't too many years left as a leading man, or for taking women to hotels, or for much else really.

"I haven't wasted my time either," he blurted out.

"Yes, I can imagine," I answered indifferently.

He smiled, became thoughtful, pulled his hat down and got up again. He continued talking, pacing back and forth, as he had often seen me do at my office while dictating a letter to the secretary, surrounded by personally autographed photos.

"I've been checking that woman out," he said. "It turns out she or her family once had money but later she had to teach. Nobody, you know, nobody says she's crazy. Sort of strange, yes. Always has been but not mad. I don't know why I'm talking to you, oh Hamlet's most sad adopted father, with your snout smeared in sandwich butter. Talking about this to you."

"At least," I told him calmly, "I haven't taken up spying into other people's lives. Nor playing the Don Juan with strange women." I wiped my mouth with my handkerchief and turned toward him with a bored look. "And I also don't get drunk on who knows what sort of money."

As he now stood, hands on hips, looking seriously back at me and spouting insults, no one could have guessed that he was thinking about that woman, that he really didn't mean what he was saying, that it was just something to do while he thought about her, something to keep me from guessing his mind was fixed on her. He walked back to me, squatted down and quickly straightened up again holding the bottle of beer and drank it slowly down, his mouth glued to the opening. He walked around the stage a while longer, and then sat down again, the bottle between his feet and his hands covering it.

"I've talked to her and she's told me," he said. "I wanted to know what it was all about. I don't know if you understand it's not just a matter of pocketing some cash. I questioned her about what we have to perform and then I knew she was mad. Do you want to know? The whole thing is a dream she had, get it? But what's really insane is that she says the dream means nothing to her. She doesn't know the man sitting down and wearing the blue shirt, nor the woman with the pitcher, she's never even lived on a street like this idiotic mess you've dreamed up. So, in the end, why? She says that while she was asleep and dreaming she was happy, the word isn't happy exactly, something else. So she wants to see it all again, afresh. It's crazy, but there's some reason in it. Something else I like about it is there's no cheap sex in any of it. When we were going off to bed, she kept stopping on the street—the sky was so blue, it was so hot—she kept grabbing me by the shoulders and lapels and asking if I understood. I still don't. It's something still unclear to her, too, because she never finished explaining it."

At ten on the dot, the woman arrived at the theater, wearing the same black dress with the watch and chain, which to me seemed out of place on that painted slum street and not the thing for lying down on a curbstone while Blanes stroked her hair. But it didn't matter: the theater was empty; only Blanes was involved, still drunk, smoking and dressed in a blue shirt with a gray cap folded down over one ear. He had arrived early with the young woman who was to appear in the doorway of the vegetable store and then give him a pitcher of beer. The girl also seemed wrong for her role, at least as I had imagined it, although the devil alone knew what the role really was. She was sad and thin, badly dressed and made-up, someone Blanes had probably picked up in some cheap little café, taking her off the streets for the night with some absurd story; this was obvious because right away she started strutting around like some great star, and it was pitiful to watch her stretching her arm and holding the pitcher of beer; I felt like throwing her out right then. The moment the other one, the mad one, got there dressed in black, she stood for a while looking at the stage, her hands clasped in front of her and she seemed to me tremendously tall, much taller and thinner than I remembered. Then, without a word to anyone, with that sick smile fainter but still making me bristle, she crossed the stage and hid herself in the wing of scenery from which she was to appear. I don't know why, but my eyes followed her, absorbing the exact shape of her long body, closely outlined by her tight-fitting black dress. I watched her body until the curtain's edge blocked it from my view.

Now it was I who stood stage-center and since everything seemed ready and it was now past ten, I lifted my arms and clapped to signal the actors. But just then, unaware of what was going on exactly, I began to sense that we had gotten ourselves into something I could never speak of, just the way we may know the soul of another and yet find words are useless to describe it. I gestured to them to start, and when I saw Blanes and the girl he had brought begin to move towards their places, I fled into the wings, where the man was already sitting behind the wheel of his ancient car which now began to shudder and quietly rattle. I perched on a crate, hoping to hide since I wanted nothing more to do with the insanity which was about to begin. I could see how she stepped out of the door of the small run-down house, her body moving like a young girl, her hair thick, almost gray and loose down her back where it was tied in a knot with some bright-colored ribbon. She was striding out, just the way a young woman does after she has finished setting the table and decides to step outdoors for a moment to quietly watch the end of the day without thinking of anything. I saw her sit down near the bench where Blanes was and rest her head on her hand, her elbow leaning on her knees, letting her fingertips fall on her half-parted lips; her face turned towards some distant point beyond me, beyond even the wall behind me. I saw Blanes get up to cross the street, crossing precisely before the car, with its top up and belching smoke, passed by and quickly disappeared. I saw Blanes' arm and the young woman's in the facing house joined by the pitcher of beer, and saw how the man drank it all down at once, left the pitcher in her hand and saw how she then slowly and without a sound sank back into the doorway. Once more I saw the man in the blue shirt cross the street an instant before a car with its top down raced by and came to a stop near me, its motor shutting off immediately, and as the bluish smoke from the engine cleared, I made out the young woman on the curb, yawning and then lying down on the pavement, her head resting on an arm which hid her hair and with one knee bent. The man in the shirt and cap then leaned over and stroked the young woman's head. He began caressing her, and his hand moved back and forth, catching in her hair, reaching over to stroke her forehead, tightening the bright ribbon holding her hair; he kept on repeating the caresses.

I got down from my crate, heaved a sigh and feeling calmer, quietly crossed the stage. The car man followed, smiling, intimidated, and the thin girl Blanes had brought came out of her doorway to join us. She asked me something, a short question, a single word and I answered without taking my eyes off Blanes, the woman lying down and his hand still stroking her forehead and her thrown-back head, untiring, unaware that the scene was over, that this last thing, caressing her hair, couldn't go on forever. Blanes' body was bent over; he was still stroking her head, stretching his arm so that his fingertips could run down the length of her hair from her forehead to where it spread over her shoulders and her back resting on the ground. The car man was still smiling, he coughed and spat to the side. The girl who had given Blanes the pitcher of beer began walking over to him and the woman. I turned to the owner of the car and told him he could take it away so we could clear out early. I walked over to him, digging into my pocket for a few pesos. Where the others stood on my right, something strange was going on and as I realized this, I bumped into Blanes, who had taken his cap off and stank of liquor, and he jabbed me in the ribs and shouted:

"Don't you realize she's dead, you animal."

I felt alone, broken by the event, and as Blanes paced drunkenly around the stage like some madman and the girl of the pitcher of beer and the car man leaned over the woman, I understood what it was all about, what it was the woman had been searching for, what it was Blanes had stalked the previous evening, rushing back and forth across the stage like one possessed: it was all clear, like one of those things you know as a child but later on find words are useless to explain.

TRANSLATED BY INES DE TORRES KINNELL

Lectura de John Cage

Leyendo
        Fluyendo
Music without measurements,
Sounds passing through circumstances.
Dentro de mí los oigo
                        Pasar afuera
Fuera de mí los veo
                        Pasar conmigo.
Yo soy la circunstancia.
Música:
        Oigo adentro lo que veo afuera
        Veo dentro lo que oigo fuera.
(No puedo oírme oír: Duchamp.)
                                Soy
Una arquitectura de sonidos
Instantáneos
                Sobre
Un espacio que se desintegra.
                        (*Everything*
We come across is to the point.)

Octavio Paz

On Reading John Cage*

Reading
            Flowing
Music without measurements,
Sounds passing through circumstances.
I hear them within me
                        Outside they pass
I see them outside me
                        Within me they pass.
I am the circumstance.
Music:
            I hear within what I see outside
            I see within what I hear outside
(I can't hear myself hearing: Duchamp.)
                                        I am
An architecture of sounds
Instantaneous
                On
A space that disintegrates itself.
                        (*Everything*
We come across is to the point.)

---

* Cage's books are *Silence* (1961) and *A Year from Monday* (1967). The italicized quotations are from the latter. 'Nirvāṇa is Saṃsāra/Saṃsāra is not Nirvāṇa': in Mahayana Buddhist literature, we find the formula: Nirvāṇa is Saṃsāra, Saṃsāra is Nirvāṇa, which sums up one of the central ideas of the Madhyamika school: the ultimate identity of phenomenal and transcendental reality, of the world of reincarnation and the void (śūnyatā).

                    La música
Inventa al silencio,
               La arquitectura
Inventa al espacio.
                   Fábricas de aire.
El silencio
          Es el espacio de la música:
Un espacio
            Inextenso:
                 No hay silencio
Salvo en la mente.
                 El silencio es una idea,
               La idea fija de la música.
La música no es una idea:
                 Es sonido,
Sonidos caminando sobre el silencio.
(*Not one sound fears the silence*
               That extinguishes it.)
Silencio es música
             Música no es silencio.
Nirvana es Samsara
              Samsara no es Nirvana.
El saber no es saber:
              Recobrar la ignorancia,
Saber del saber.
            No es lo mismo
Oír los pasos de esta tarde
Entre los árboles y las casas
                Que
Ver la misma tarde ahora
Entre los mismos árboles y casas
                  Después de leer
Silence:
        Nirvana es Samsara

Music
Invents silence,
                    Architecture
Invents space.
                    Factories of air.
Silence.
          Is the space of music:
Space
        Unextended:
                      There is no silence
Save in the mind.
                    Silence is an idea,
                    The idée fixe of music.
Music is not an idea:
                        It is sound,
Sounds walking over silence.
(*Not one sound fears the silence*
                        That extinguishes it.)
Silence is music
                    Music is not silence.
Nirvana is Samsara
                    Samsara is not Nirvana.
Knowing is not knowing:
                            Recovering ignorance,
Knowledge of knowing.
                          It is one thing to hear
These afternoon-footsteps
Between trees and houses
                            Another to see
Between same trees and houses
These afternoon-footsteps
                            After reading
Silence:
            Nirvana is Samsara

                          Silencio es música.
(*Let life obscure*
            The difference between art and life.)
Música no es silencio:
                No es decir
Lo que dice el silencio,
                    Es decir
Lo que no dice.
                Silencio no tiene sentido
                Sentido no tiene silencio.
Sin ser oída
            La música se desliza entre ambos.
(*Every something is an echo of nothing.*)
En el silencio de mi cuarto
                    El rumor de mi cuerpo:
Inaudito.
            Un día oiré sus pensamientos.
                            La tarde
Se ha detenido:
                No obstante—camina.
Mi cuerpo oye al cuerpo de mi mujer
                        (*A cable of sound*)
Y le responde:
                Esto se llama música.
La música es real,
                El silencio es una idea.
John Cage es japonés
                    Y no es una idea:
Es sol sobre nieve.
                    Sol y nieve no son lo mismo:
El sol es nieve y la nieve es nieve
                        O
El sol no es nieve ni la nieve es nieve
O

　　　　　　　Silence is music.
(Let life obscure
　　The difference between art and life.)
Music is not silence:
　　　　　It is not saying
What silence says,
　　　　　It is saying
What it doesn't say.
　　　　　Silence has no sense
　　　　　Sense has no silence.
Without being heard
　　　　　Music slips between both.
(Every something is an echo of nothing.)
In the silence of my room
　　　　　The murmur of my body:
Unheard.
　　　One day I shall hear its thoughts.
　　　　　　　　The afternoon
Stands still:
　　　　Yet—it walks.
My body hears the body of my wife
　　　　　　　(A cable of sound)
And responds to it:
　　　　This is called music.
Music is real,
　　　　Silence is an idea.
John Cage is Japanese
　　　　　And is not an idea:
He is sun on snow.
　　　　Sun and snow are not the same:
Sun is snow and snow is snow
　　　　　　　Or
Sun is not snow and snow is not snow
Or

John Cage no es americano
(*U.S.A. is determined to keep the Free World free,
U.S.A. determined*)

O

John Cage es americano
                    (*That the U.S.A. may become
Just another part of the world.

                    No more, no less.*)
La nieve no es sol
                    La música no es silencio
El sol es nieve
                    El silencio es música
(*The situation must be Yes-and-No

                    Not either-or*)
Entre el silencio y la música
                    El arte y la vida
La nieve y el sol
                    Hay un hombre
Ese hombre es John Cage
                    (*Committed
To the nothing in between*)
                    Dice una palabra
No nieve no sol
                    Una palabra
Que no es
        Silencio:
A year from Monday you will hear it.

La tarde se ha vuelto invisible.

*Delhi
a 14 de diciembre de 1967*

John Cage is not American
(*U.S.A. is determined to keep the Free World free,*
U.S.A. determined)
                    Or
John Cage is American
                    (*That the U.S.A. may become*
Just another part of the world.
                    No more, no less.)
Snow is not sun
                    Music is not silence
Sun is snow
                    Silence is music
(*The situation must be Yes-and-No*
                    Not either-or)
Between silence and music
                    Art and life
Snow and sun
                    There is a man
This man is John Cage
                    (*Committed*
To the nothing in between)
                    He says a word
Not snow not sun
                    One word
Which is not
                    Silence:
A year from Monday you will hear it.

The afternoon has become invisible.

Delhi
December 14th, 1967

                    TRANSLATED BY MONIQUE FONG WUST
                    AND GUY AROUL

Blanco
(1966)

NOTE*

Blanco: the color white; blank left in writing; void, emptiness; mark to shoot at (blank: the central white spot of a target); aim, object or desire.

Blanco is a composition which allows the following variant readings:

(*a*) in its totality, as a single text;

(*b*) the central column, with the exclusion of those to the left and right, is a poem whose theme is that of the passage of the word from silence before speech to silence after it;

(*c*) the left-hand column is a love poem, divided into four moments which correspond to the four traditional elements;

(*d*) the right-hand column is another poem, counterpointing the erotic one and composed of four variations on sensation, perception, imagination and understanding;

(*e*) each one of the four parts made up of the two columns can be read, without worrying about previous divisions, as a single text: four independent poems;

(*f*) the central column can be read as six isolated texts and the right- and left-hand columns as eight.

---

* Since this selection is exactly half of the poem, divide by two the numbers in the Note.—*ed.*

Blanco

By passion the world is bound, by passion too it is released.

The Hevajra Tantra

Avec ce seul objet dont le Néant s'honore.

Stéphane Mallarmé

el comienzo
            el cimiento
la simiente
            latente
la palabra en la punta de la lengua
inaudita   inaudible
            impar
grávida   nula
            sin edad
la enterrada con los ojos abiertos
inocente   promiscua
            la palabra
sin nombre   sin habla

Sube y baja,
Escalera de escapulario,
El lenguaje deshabitado.
Bajo la piel de la penumbra
Late una lámpara.
                    Superviviente
Entre las confusiones taciturnas,
                            Asciende
En un tallo de cobre
                    Resuelto
En un follaje de claridad:
                            Amparo

Blanco

By passion the world is bound, by passion too it is released.
                                        The Hevajra Tantra
        Avec ce seul objet dont le Néant s'honore.
                                        Stéphane Mallarmé

    the fountain
                the founding
    the seed
            latent
    word on the tip of the tongue
    unheard   unhearable
            indivisible
    gravid   void
            ageless
    she they buried with open eyes
    innocent   promiscuous
            the word
    nameless   speechless

    It ascends descends
    Stairs of the mine-shaft.
    Uninhabited language:
    Under penumbra's skin
    A lamp throbbing.
                    Survivor
    Among taciturn confusions,
                        It ascends
    On a copper stalk
                Dissolved
    In a foliage of clarity,
                    Refuge

De caídas realidades.
                                O dormido
O extinto,
                        Alto en su vara
(Cabeza en una pica),
                                Un girasol
Ya luz carbonizada
                                Sobre un vaso
De sombra.
                        En la palma de una mano
Ficticia,
                Flor
Ni vista ni pensada:
                                Oída,
Aparece
                Amarillo
Cáliz de consonantes y vocales
Incendiadas.

en el muro la sombra del fuego   *llama rodeada de leones*
en el fuego tu sombra y la mía   *leona en el circo de las llamas*
                                                   ánima entre las sensaciones
el fuego te desata y te anuda
Pan Grial Ascua   *frutos de luces de bengala*
                Muchacha   *los sentidos se abren*
tú ríes—desnuda   *en la noche magnética*
en los jardines de la llama
                        La pasión de la brasa compasiva

                Un pulso, un insistir,
                Oleaje de sílabas húmedas.
                Sin decir palabra
                Oscurece mi frente
                Un presentimiento de lenguaje.

Of fallen realities.
            Asleep
Or extinct,
         High on its pole
(Head on a pike)
            A sunflower
Already carbonized light
                 Above a glass
Of shadow.
          In the palm of a hand
Fictitious,
        Flower
Neither seen nor thought:
                Heard,
It appears
      Yellow
Calyx of consonants and vowels
All burning.

on the wall the shadow of the fire   *flame surrounded by lions*
in the fire your shadow and mine   *lioness in the circus of flames*
                                   soul among sensations

the fire unties and ties you
Bread Grail Ember   *firework fruits*
              Girl   *the senses are opening*
you laugh—naked   *in the magnetic night*
in the gardens of the flame

            Passion of the compassionate ember

   A pulse, an insistence,
   Swell of humid syllables.
   Without uttering a word
   A presentiment of language
   Darkens my forehead.

Patience patience
(Livingston en la sequía)
River rising a little.
El mío es rojo y se agosta
Entre sableras llameantes:
Castillas de arena, naipes rotos
Y el jeroglífico (agua y brasa)
En el pecho de México caído.
Polvo soy de aquellos lodos.
Río de sangre,
                    Río de historias
De sangre,
                    Río seco:
Boca de manantial
Amordazado
Por la conjuración anónima
De los huesos,
Por la ceñuda peña de los siglos
Y los minutos:
                    El lenguaje
Es una expiación,
                    Propiciación
Al que no habla,
                    Emparedado
Cada día
          Asesinado,
El muerto innumerable.
                              Hablar
Mientras los otros trabajan
Es pulir huesos,
                    Aguzar
Silencios
          Hasta la transparencia,
Hasta la ondulación,

Patience patience
(Livingston in the drought)
River rising a little.
Mine is red and is scorched up
Among blazing sand-hills,
Sand-castles of Spain, torn pack of cards
And the hieroglyph (water and embers)
Fallen on the breast of Mexico.
I am the dust of that mud.
Blood river,
          River of histories
Of blood,
        Dry river:
Mouth of the source
Muzzled
By the anonymous conspiracy
Of bones,
By the grim rock of centuries
And minutes:
          Language
Is an expiation,
          Propitiation
To him who does not speak,
            Immured,
Each day
       Assassinated,
The dead, one and innumerable.
              To speak
While the others work
Is to polish bones,
        To sharpen
Silences
      To the point of transparency,
To undulation,

El cabrilleo,
Hasta el agua:

los ríos de tu cuerpo	*el río de los cuerpos*
país de latidos	*astros infusorios reptiles*
entrar en ti	*torrente de cinabrio sonámbulo*
país de ojos cerrados	*oleaje de las genealogías*
agua sin pensamientos	*juegos conjugaciones juglarias*
entrar en mí	*subyecto y obyecto abyecto y absuelto*
al entrar en tu cuerpo	*río de soles*
país de espejos en vela	*'las altas fieras de la piel luciente'*
país de agua despierta	*rueda el río seminal de los mundos*
en la noche dormida	*el ojo que lo mira es otro río*

Me miro en lo que miro	*Es mi creación esto que veo*
como entrar por mis ojos	*la percepción es concepción*
en un ojo más límpido	*agua de pensamientos*
me mira lo que miro	*soy la creación de lo que veo*

delta de brazos del deseo	*agua de verdad*
en un lecho de vértigos	*verdad de agua*

La transparencia es todo lo que queda

Paramera abrasada
Del amarillo al encarnado
La tierra es un lenguaje calcinado.
Hay púas invisibles, hay espinas
En los ojos.
            En un muro rosado
Tres buitres ahítos.
No tiene cuerpo ni cara ni alma,
Está en todas partes,
A todos nos aplasta:
            Este sol es injusto.

The foaming,

To water:

The rivers of your body	*the river of bodies*
land of heart-beats	*stars infusoria reptiles*
entering you	*torrent of somnambulant vermilion*
land of closed eyes	*tide of genealogies*
thoughtless water	*games conjugations juggleries*
entering me	*subject and object abject and absolved*
while entering your body	*river of suns*
land of mirrors in vigil	*'the tall beasts of glittering hide'*
land of water awake	*games conjugations juggleries*
in the sleeping night	*the eye that sees it is another river*

I see myself in what I see	*It is my creation I see*
like entering through my eyes	*perception is conception*
into another more limpid eye	*water of thoughts*
what I see looks at me	*I am the creation of what I see*

delta of the arms of desire	*water of truth*
in a bed of vertigo	*truth of water*

All that remains is transparency

Charred moorland
From yellow to flesh colour
Earth is a burnt-out language.
There are invisible prongs, there are
Thorns in the eyes.
On a pink wall
Three surfeited vultures.
It has no body, nor face nor soul,
It is everywhere,
It crushes us all:
This sun is unjust.

La rabia es mineral.
                    Los colores
Se obstinan.
                    Se obstina el horizonte.
Tambores tambores tambores.
El cielo se ennegrece
                    Como esta página.
Dispersión de cuervos.
Inminencia de violencias violetas.
Se levantan los arenales,
La cerrazón de reses de ceniza.
Mugen los árboles encadenados.
Tambores tambores tambores
Te golpeo cielo
                    Tierra te golpeo
Cielo abierto tierra cerrada
Flauta y tambor centella y trueno
Te abro te golpeo
                    Te abres tierra
Tienes la boca llena de agua
Tu cuerpo chorrea cielo
Tremor
                    Tu panza tiembla
Tus semillas estallan
                    Verdea la palabra

Rage is mineral.
           The colours
Are obstinate,
           Obstinate the horizon.
Drums drums drums.
The sky blackens
           Like this page.
Dispersion of crows.
Imminence of violet violences.
Sands arise,
Darkness of beasts of ashes.
Trees roar in their chains.
Drums drums drums
I beat you sky
           Earth I beat you
Open sky closed earth
Flute and drum lightning and thunder
I tear you open I beat you
           You are opening
Earth your mouth full of water
Your body dripping with sky
Tremor
           Your belly trembles
Your seeds burst
           The word grows green

TRANSLATED BY CHARLES TOMLINSON
AND GUY AROUL

Juan Rulfo

The Day of the Landslide

"This happened in September. Not in September of this year but last year. Or was it the year before last, Melitón?"

"No, it was last year."

"Yes, yes, I remembered it right. It was in September of last year, around the twenty-first. Listen, Melitón, wasn't September twenty-first the exact day of the earthquake?"

"It was a little before that. Come to think of it, it was around the eighteenth."

"You're right. I was in Tuxcacuexco around the time. I even saw the houses collapsing as if they were made of molasses, they just twisted up like this, screwing up their faces, and whole walls crumbled to the ground. And people came out of the rubble terrified, running straight for the church, screaming. But hold on: listen, Melitón, it seems to me there's no church in Tuxcacuexco? Don't you remember?"

"There's none. All that's left there are some cracked-up walls they say was the church something like two hundred years back, but nobody remembers it, or what it was like. It's more like an abandoned farmyard infested with castor-oil plants."

"You're right. Then it wasn't in Tuxcacuexco the earthquake caught me; it must have been in El Pochote. But isn't El Pochote a ranch?"

"Yes, but it has a little chapel they call the church around there, it's a little ways past the Los Alcatraces hacienda."

"Then it was right there the quake I'm telling you about caught me and that's when the ground buckled like it was being whipped up from down inside. Well, a few days later, because I remember we were still propping up walls, the governor got there. He was coming to see if he could help with his presence. You people know that all the governor has to do is show up, and once people get a look at him, everything is fixed up. The thing is he should at least come and see what's happening, and not stay put at home, just handing out orders. As soon as he comes, everything gets fixed up and people, even if their homes cave in on top of them, are real happy they got to know him. Isn't that right, Melitón?"

"That's a fact."

"Well, as I was telling you, in September last year, right after the tremors the governor turned up to see how the earthquake had treated us. He brought along his geologist and experts, don't think he came alone. Listen, Melitón, about how much money did we lay out to feed the governor's followers?"

"Something like four thousand pesos."

"And they only stayed one day, at that, and as soon as it got dark they left, otherwise God knows how deep in the hole we would have wound up. Anyhow, we had a very good time: people were breaking their necks straining them so much to see the governor and talking about the way he'd eaten the turkey and had he sucked on the bones and how fast he was scooping up one tortilla after another and spreading them with guacamole sauce. They noticed everything. And him so calm, so serious, wiping his hands on his socks so as not to mess up the napkin he only used to whisk his moustache from time to time. And afterwards, when the pomegranate punch went to their heads, they all started singing together. Listen, Melitón, what was the song they kept singing over and over like a scratchy record?"

"It was one that went like this: 'You don't know how many hours the soul mourns.' "

"You're good at remembering things. No doubt about it, Melitón. Yes, that was it. And the governor just kept laughing; he asked to know where the bathroom was. Afterwards he sat down at his place again; he smelled the carnations that were on the table. He was looking at the people singing and he was moving his head to the beat of the music, smiling. No doubt about it, he felt happy, because his people were happy, you could even read it on his face. And at speechtime one of his followers got up, his face was raised and kind of cocked to the left. And he talked. And no doubt about it, he knew how to deliver the goods. He talked about Juárez whom we had put up there in the town square, and it was only then we found out it was the statue of Juárez, because nobody had ever been able to tell us who the person on top of that monument was. We always figured it might be Hidalgo or Morelos or Venustiano Carranza, because that's where we used to hold the celebration on each of their anniversaries. Until that dude came along to tell us it was Don Benito Juárez. And the things he said! Isn't that right, Melitón? You've got such a good memory you must remember well what that guy recited."

"I remember all right, but I've repeated it so many times it's getting to be a pain in the neck."

"All right, it's not necessary. But these gentlemen are missing something good. Better yet, you'll tell them what the governor said."

"The thing is, instead of being a visit to the suffering and to those who had lost their homes, it turned into a real drunken brawl. And you can imagine when the band from Tepec came into town, it got there late because all the trucks had been used to bring the governor's people and the musicians had to make it on foot, but they made it. They came in swinging out hard on the harp and the bass drum, going tatachoom, choom, choom, with the cymbals, putting all they had into the *Wet Turkey Buzzard*. It was something to see, even the governor took off his jacket and loosened up his tie, and it went on to become a real wingding. They brought out more demijohns of punch and got busy roasting more venison, because even if it's hard for you to believe this, and they didn't even realize it, they were eating deer meat, the kind that's plentiful around these parts. We laughed every time they said the barbecue was very good—isn't that right, Melitón?—because around here we don't even know what this barbecue thing is all about. The truth is, each time we just about finished serving them one helping, they wanted more and of course we were there to serve them because, as Liborio, the collector of

Revenue, who between you and me was always a big tightwad, as Liborio said, 'Let this reception cost what it costs; after all, what's money for,' and then you, Melitón, who were mayor at the time, and you didn't even sound like yourself to me when you said it: 'Let the punch run, a visit like this has to be celebrated big.' And the punch sure did run, that's the honest truth. Even the tablecloths were red. And those people never seemed to have enough. The one thing I noticed was that the governor wasn't moving from his seat, he didn't even have to stretch out a hand, and all he did was eat and drink anything they put in front of him. And that bunch of asskissers did all they could to keep his table full till there wasn't even room for the saltshaker, which he kept in his hand and whenever he was through with it, he stuck it in his shirt pocket. Even I myself went up to say to him: would you like some salt, my general? He laughed and showed me the saltshaker he had in his shirt pocket, that's how I found out.

"The real good part was when he started to speak. We all broke out in goose pimples from sheer emotion. He raised himself up gradually, slowly, very slowly, until we saw him shove back his chair with his foot, put his hands on the table, lower his head as if he were about to take off the ground, and then his cough, which hushed us all up. What was it he said, Melitón?"

" 'Fellow citizens,' he said. 'Recalling to mind my trajectory, reviving the undeviating performance of my commitments. Here in this land which I visited as the anonymous companion of a presidential candidate, tirelessly cooperating with a man who represents you, whose honesty has never strayed from the context of his political utterances and which, indeed, on the other hand, is a firm commentary on the democratic principles in the supreme linking that ties him to the cause of the people, uniting the austerity he has already demonstrated and the crystal-clear synthesis of revolutionary idealism never until now fully realized and made actual.' "

"There were cheers at this point, right, Melitón?"

"Yes, lots of cheers. Then he went on.

" 'My line of action is still the same, fellow citizens. As your candidate, I was sparing with promises, choosing to commit myself only to that which I could fulfill and which, as it crystallized, was to be converted into the collective, not subjective, benefit, nor am I a member of one generic family of citizens. We are present here today, at the scene of this paradoxical upheaval of nature, unforeseeable within my program of administration . . .'

" 'Exactly, my general!' someone out there yelled. 'Exactly! You said it!'

" '. . . In this case, I say, when nature has punished us, we have come with our understanding presence into the center of the telluric epicenter which has devastated homes that might have been ours, that are indeed ours; we have come to your assistance, not with the Neronian desire to take pleasure in someone else's misfortune, what's more, imminently determined to utilize our munificent effort towards the reconstruction of the destroyed homes, determined, like a big brother, to bring consolation into the homes stricken by death. This place which I visited years ago, ambitions to power so foreign to me then, this place so happy yesteryear, and in mourning today, fills me with pain. Yes, fellow citizens, I am tortured by the wounds of the living for their lost goods and by the plight of human beings crying out to heaven for their dead, unburied under these ruins we now stand before.' "

"There were cheers at this point too, weren't there, Melitón?"

"No, the big-mouth who yelled before sounded off again at this point: 'Exactly, mister governor! You said it!' And then some other guy closer up said: 'Somebody make that drunk shut up!' "

"Ah, yes. And it even looked like there was going to be a real brawl down at the very end of the table, but everybody calmed down when the governor spoke again."

" 'People of Tuxcacuexco, I must insist once again: your misfortune fills me with pain, for despite the words of Bernal, the great Bernal Díaz del Castillo: "The men who died had been recruited for death," and I, considering the basis of my ontological and human concept, I say: It fills me with pain! with the pain brought on by the sight of the tree felled in its first efflorescence. We shall help you with all our strength. The living forces of the State clamor from their faldstool for help for the victims of this hecatomb never foreseen or desired. My regency will not come to an end before I make good my promises to you. On the other hand, I do not believe it has been God's will to bring bereavement on you, to strip you of your homes . . .'

"And it ended there. I didn't memorize what he said after that because the racket they kicked up at the rear tables got louder and it got to be real tough making out what he went on to say."

"That is very true, Melitón. It was something to see. That's about the only way I can put it. And the thing is the same guy from the committee started to yell again: 'Exactly! Exactly!' hollering till they could hear him out in the street. And when they tried to shut him up, he pulled his pistol and started to fire wild over his head, emptying it into the ceiling. And the people who were there looking on began running when the shooting started. And they knocked over tables in their scramble and you could hear the plates and glasses breaking and the bottles they were throwing at the guy with the pistol to quiet him down, and all they did was smash up against the wall. And he still had time to put another clip in his weapon and emptied it again, while he bobbed and weaved, dodging the blows of the flying bottles they pitched at him from all over the place."

"You should have seen the governor standing there, very serious, with a frown on his face, looking to where the rumpus was, as if he could have stopped it with his look."

"Who knows who went to tell the musicians to play something, but they let go with the National Anthem giving it all they had, till the one on the trombone almost popped his cheeks he was blowing so hard; but the ruckus kept up all the same. And as it turned out, the fight had spread to the street too. They came and told the governor that some guys were going at each other with machetes out there, and come to think of it, it was true, because you could hear women's voices this far, saying: 'Break them up or they'll kill each other!' And a little later another scream saying: 'They've killed my husband! Grab him!'

"And the governor didn't even budge, he went on standing there. Listen, Melitón, what's the word for it?"

"Impassive."

"That's it, impassive. Well, with the row going on outside, things seemed to be calming down inside. The drunk who'd yelled 'exactly' was asleep. They had finally scored a hit on his head with a bottle and he had been left sprawled out on the floor. Then the governor went up to the guy and took away the pistol he was holding in one of his hands, clutched stiff when he passed out. He gave it to somebody else and told him, 'Take care of him and make a note that he is unauthorized to carry arms from now on.' And the other one answered: 'Yes, my general.'

"For some reason the band went on playing and playing the National Anthem, until the dude who had spoken in the beginning held up his arms and requested silence for the victims. Listen, Melitón, what victims did he ask us all to be silent for?"

"For the victims of the epifocal area."

"Okay, for those. Afterwards everybody sat down, they straightened up the tables again and they went on drinking punch and singing the song about 'how many hours the soul mourns.'

"Now I'm beginning to remember that the roughhouse was around the twenty-first of September: because my wife had our boy Merencio that day, and I got home very late at night, more drunk than sober. And she wouldn't talk to me for weeks arguing, that I had left her alone with her predicament. Once she got over it she told me I hadn't even had the decency to call the midwife and she had to go through her ordeal trusting in God and hoping for the best."

TRANSLATED BY HARDIE ST. MARTIN

La Palabra

Entonces afluían las palabras
del hechizo de las cosas, o saltaban
en un oscuro borbotón como de sangre,
o sus hogueras ávidas mordian
las manos que querían atraparlas,
o cruzaban como aves o venados
en el fulgor del sol, entre los bosques.

Ahora, cuando llega una palabra
—sola, inmensa, única, perdida,
mensajera que ha logrado atravesar
las más vastas y desnudas extensiones—
es preciso recibirla regiamente,
abrir las puertas, encender las lámparas,
y quedar en silencio hasta que ella,
incapaz de mentirnos, se ha dormido,
y otra vez se confunde con las rocas.

15 de julio de 1961.

Cintio Vitier

The Word

Then, words flowed
from the bewitchment of things, or spouted
in a dark bubbling, blood-like,
or their avid bonfires bit
the hands trying to trap them
or they crossed like birds or deer
in the sun's radiance, through the woods.

Now, when a word comes
—alone, immense, unique, lost,
a messenger successful in traversing
the most vast and naked of spaces—
we must welcome it regally,
open doors, light lamps,
and remain silent until,
incapable of lying to us, it falls asleep
and once again converges with the rocks.

July 15, 1961

TRANSLATED BY ELECTA ARENAL

La Noticia

Una mañana
usted se asomó a mi celda de trabajo, y dijo,
veladamente:
"el olor de los libros
ya me golpeó
con el polvillo del asma"

Recuerdo el tono, lo indecible.

Yo lo vi
joven, grave,
un poco remoto por lo que estábamos
los dos pensando, sin saberlo:
por lo que tajantemente nos separaba
y nos unía.

Sobrio el encuentro. Palabras, pocas.
La Biblioteca, levemente agreste,
adquiría neblinas como un bosque.

Ahora usted ha caído, dicen,
en el bosque americano
(en la puna, la selva, el palmar,
fraternos).
allí
donde la muerte suya, la del héroe,
lo estaba esperando, inaplazable.

¡Qué duro es el amor
a lo que no podemos totalmente compartir, y sin embargo
nos parte el alma, nos divide
el ser!

                ¡Qué ardiente
el arte del respeto

The Notice

One morning
you looked into my work cell, and said,
obliquely,
"the smell of books
has already hit me
with asthma dust."

I recall the tone, what words can't say.

You looked
young, grave
a bit remote because
of what we both
were thinking, without knowing:
because of what separated us
trenchantly and united us.

Reserved encounter. Words, few.
The Library, slightly rustic,
acquired mists like a forest.

Now you have fallen, they say,
in the American forest
(in puna, jungle, palm-forest,
fraternal),
there
where your death, the hero's,
awaited you, undeferable.

How hard, our love
for what we can't share totally, and yet
it breaks our heart, divides
our being!

How ardent
this art of respect

que yo le rindo, difícil, como nota viva
de una cuerda en tensión!

Es lo que puedo darle, sin engaño,
ahora que, en mi celda de trabajo,
los libros huelen como hojas,—tan amargas!

11 de octubre de 1967.

I render you, difficult, like a vibrant note
from a taut string.

It is what I can give you, without deceit
now when, in my work cell,
the books smell like leaves—so bitter!

October 11, 1967

TRANSLATED BY ELECTA ARENAL

René Marqués

There's A Body Reclining On The Stern

. . . Son of man
You can not say, or guess, for you know only
A heap of broken images, where the sun beats
T. S. Eliot (The Waste Land)

In spite of the merciless sun, the eyes remained wide open. Now, with this piercing light, the pupils took on the transparency of honey. The nose, turned up to the sky, and the taut neck seemed to be carved in wax: the creamy whiteness of wax, the dull glow of the beehive converted into candle. What a pity the necklace of red silk was so tight around the flesh. The red looked good on the creamy whiteness of the skin. But it gave him the uneasy feeling that it was uncomfortable, almost anguished.

The nude body was reclining gently, almost gracefully, on the stern of the boat. Not nude. Its breasts, drooping a little because of the position of the torso, managed to hide halfway behind the top of the blue bathing suit.

He was rowing slowly, rhythmically. He was not in a rush. He didn't feel tired. Time was stationary there, stubbornly motionless, set on ignoring its destination, eternity. But the boat moved on. It moved on weightlessly, as if the half-nude body reclining gently, almost gracefully on the stern, had no weight . . .

The boat weighs less than the meaning of my life with you. And the oars transmitted the lightness of the weight to his hands. His muscles, flexing rhythmically, were barely emphasized at the biceps, mere bamboo canes, slightly knotty, without the envied form of other arms, in spite of the vitamins in the newspaper ad guaranteeing a body like Atlas, an athlete's at any rate.

He noticed his own sunken chest. *I have to do some exercise. It's awful.* The narrow stretch of black hairs barely separating his small nipples. *I'll give up smoking next month. I'm killing myself.* He didn't feel the sweltering sun on his back. Maybe it was the breeze. It was a stroking, soft, cool breeze and, instead of brine, it seemed to bring with it the moisture of the plantain leaf or the dew of ferns. It was strange. None of his sensations corresponded to immediate reality. But the boat moved on. And his own flabby belly formed creases above the woollen shorts. And below, between his legs, the bulge sticking out despite the tightness of the elastic.

Because there is a cruel absurdity in the sense of equilibrium of that someone responsible for all things, and it's not equilibrium, it's not the same as keeping the boat afloat with two bodies or making the world go round on an imaginary axis, because I didn't ask to be here, just as I never asked for anything. But they exact, ask, demand of me, of me alone. You're such a child. And you already have certain things like a man. *And I didn't know if she was saying it because I wrote on the sly or because of the other. But she shouldn't have said it. Because a mother would do well to weigh her words carefully in her heart before coming out with them. And you never know. But in order to find out, I agreed to go with Luis to the house with the broken-down balcony where old Leoncia lived with the nine girls. And they all made sure that yes, I did have certain things like a man, and they had a great time, especially the short one with the firm thighs and a look soft as a medlar in her eyes. But, you know, being a man is not that. Because to be a man is to have a meaning of your own. And it was she who had mine:* Don't marry young, son. *And the meaning was not in love itself. Because love was always in a black or mulatto or penniless girl or one who was too generous with her own body. And that wasn't the meaning she intended for me, but a white girl or one of good family. And it wasn't in writing either:* Leave that nonsense alone, son, *but in a profession, any at all, which could only be a teacher's, because there isn't always the means to study what you desire most. And she died when I took her the diploma; I don't know if it was of pleasure, although the doctor assured me it was of a heart attack. Anyway, she died. And I believed that at last my life would have a meaning. But a life empty of meaning can't be filled the way a pillow is stuffed with wadding, or goose feathers, or swan's-down which is softer. Because I was a teacher now. And I would not have to suffer want, since I had a career, as she had assured, and I would never do any more writing again. And I knew you, who promised to put love into my life, softness into my life, like swan's-down. And I married you, whose small breasts were erect then, and you were from a good family, and I thought that I'd be a dependable family man from now on, never going back to the old house with the broken down balcony (after that I only saw Leoncia on Good Fridays carrying the Sepulcher in the four o'clock procession) and I dedicated myself to work with meek resignation and loved you like someone with an old hunger for love, for that's what I had, because there's no human being that lives with less love than the son of a mother who guides his destiny with her rough hands and is her son's slave. And that hunger for love I carried in me since childhood, that the girls (there were nine girls) in the old house could not satisfy, was in me for you to satisfy, and so I didn't write any more, and all that only to have you there now, motionless, on the stern of the boat, as if you couldn't hear or feel anything, as if you didn't know I'm here, steering the boat, I, heading anywhere I please, for the first time, without consulting anyone, not even you, nor my mother because she's dead, nor the headmistress of that school where they say I'm a teacher* (Mister, Mister, you're cute and I like you and the sky is falling), *nor the lady senator who demands that I vote for her, nor the lady mayor*

who asks me to keep her city clean, nor the woman pharmacist
who exacts of me that I, precisely I, pay her the outstanding
bill, smiling, like those people who always hold life or death in
their hands, nor the female doctor who attended the baby, nor all
those women who exact, and compel, and wheedle, and smile,
and leave you empty, without knowing that another had already,
from the beginning, emptied of meaning the man who didn't ask
to be here, who never exacted anything of anyone, don't you un-
derstand?, of anyone.

Why was the coast growing so thin? The tops of the coconut trees
were already fusing with the cactuses and the sea-grapes. It was a green
brushstroke, long-drawn out, like an eyebrow someone has plucked over
the half-closed eyelid of the sand. *The sea looks blue from the coast,* but
it is green here, only green. Wasn't there some reality that was unalter-
able in spite of distances?

Each oar went *chass* as it dipped into the water, and then a quick
glug-glug. And although there were two oars, the sound was simultane-
ous, as if there were only one. The body on the stern went on exerting a
fascination beyond words. It wasn't that the breasts seemed to droop a
little. No doubt it was because of her position in front of him. But the
belly wasn't as smooth as on the wedding night.

"No, I don't want it that way. Children ruin one's figure."

Right there, where the bottom of the blue bathing suit edged into the
flesh tightly, that's where her belly had been disfigured.

"Oh, my poor body. It's your fault."

And it had grown there, right there, at the part that had been so
smooth and he had kissed as passionately as a moon lost in a futile search
for its night. Till it couldn't grow any more and it broke open its foun-
tainhead of blood and cries.

"It's a boy."

He's so weak and frail! Boys are always like that. But the boat's frail-
ness did not stop it from carrying the weight of two bodies, ripping
through the restless green of the sea. The sun had pity on no one. And he

rowed unhurriedly, with infinity at his back. *How frail infancy is!* And how frail a body reclining gently, almost gracefully, on the stern of the boat.

He didn't feel the weariness of those nights and those mornings now.

"The baby's crying."

"You get up. I'm tired."

He rowed rhythmically, almost without effort, without tiring, the breeze spraying the inside of the boat with foam.

"For me, dear, a television set."

"I don't know if I can. This month . . ."

"Life has no meaning without television."

Life had no meaning, but the sun was quickly evaporating the delicate sea-drops on her skin.

"The payment on the washing machine is due tomorrow."

Each oar went *chass* as it dipped into the water, and then a quick, fleeting *glug-glug.* But it was slow, agonizing, maddening, as it came from the incision in the baby's throat, through the rubber tube that gave off a smell of disinfectants.

"If the tube becomes obstructed, the child will die." (*My child, she meant, the child who was my son.*)

Black coffee and benzedrine. *Go away, sleep, go away.* Clean the tube, keep the tube clear of any obstructions. *Glug-glug,* in unison, the oars lifting out of the water. *Glug-glug,* the clock with the black face, on the night table.

"Daddy, mummy's crying because she burned the rice." (*Ay, she burned the rice. She burned the rice again.*)

Glug-glug, the foam in the tube that had to be cleaned. *Carefully. Carefully,* with the wad of disinfected gauze.

"Daddy, am I going to get married too, when I'm big?"

Black coffee and benzedrine. Why were the oars suddenly beginning to feel heavy and difficult in his hands? *Black coffee . . .*

"I just can't any more. You stay with the baby now."

"Not me. My nerves are killing me. I'm only a weak woman."

Glug-glug. Glug-glug. Minute after minute. *Glug-glug,* in the clock on the table. *Glug-glug,* at the tips of the oars. *Glug-glug,* in eyelids heavy with sleep. *Glug-glug. Glug-glug. Glug* . . .

"Late again. And you were absent from class yesterday."

"I buried my little boy yesterday."

The land couldn't be seen now. The horizon was identical to his left and to his right, in front and behind him. Now it was only a boat in the unrest of the sea. And now that it was only this, now that limits and horizons were not important, the oars were beginning to lose their slow rhythm and move with sharp, feverish, irregular blows.

"This neighborhood has turned into a hell."

"It was good enough when we moved in."

"There's a thing called time, dear. And it moves on. But we . . ."

We're just a couple like so many others, the husband a teacher and the wife comes from a good family, and it would have been worse if I were a writer, but I'm not sure of that. The principal is a woman, and the mayor is a woman, and the senator is a woman, and my mother was a woman, and I am only a teacher, and in bed I am a man, and my wife knows it, but she's not happy because good things made in factories are what bring happiness, as they brought it to the supervisor of the English class, and to others as adept as she at drawing happiness to her. But not my wife. Still, Anita, over on Luna Street, is happy when she enjoys me, or pretends to enjoy me, even if she's older than the girls in the old house with the broken-down balcony (there were nine girls and the youngest had firm thighs and the soft look of a medlar), but she doesn't ask for absurd things, only for what I give her, which in a way is a lot, but she doesn't have to have a new outfit for the Rotary Club party on the same day they foreclose my mortgage, and what about the forty dollars they deduct from my pay for the last loan and fifteen more for the Retirement Plan, because the law the lady senator passed is good and forces me to think about old age (my wife's is what the law means, because there is no law to protect a man), even if, before we reach the old age the law indicates, we don't have enough for the back payment on the television set (no one can live without a TV set, ay, no one can), *and she insists I pull it out in time so as to keep her pretty shape and show off the new outfit* (not that one, the last one, the one with the skirt embroidered with rhinestones), *if it were only in order to enjoy it* (her body, I mean), *but she hardly lets me, leaving we with the anguish of incompleteness, and all because she won't use the little sponge, as the social worker said, the one from Public Welfare which is really* Private Hellfare *or else with that business of no, it hurts me, that Anita doesn't say to me because she is satisfied with drinks at the bar and five dollars, plus two more for the room we use that night, and she doesn't complain, and it doesn't hurt her, because she doesn't come from a good family and I'm not sure she's white either.*

"Don't you have any shame or pride, dear? Nowadays decent people live in the new suburbs. But we . . ."

The ends of the red kerchief that was so tight around her neck floated in the air happily uttering *flap-flaps*. He was sure he had tightened the knot firmly when he noticed it was too loose (that's why it looked like a silk necklace now), but he had done it with gentle hands so as not to make her uncomfortable, so that the graceful position of the body against the stern would not be altered the least bit. Anyhow, the boat moved on.

"If I were a man I'd make more money than you. But I'm only a weak woman . . ."

A weak woman destined to be her husband's slave because I am the husband and she the slave. My mother was also a weak woman. And if my son hadn't died, he would have been the master of two slaves, and he's better off dead. A teacher doesn't die, but everything he owns has to be electric, because there are no servants and how can there be when the country girls go into the factories or the bars on Luna Street (not to Leoncia's house because she died on a Good Friday, while carrying the Sepulcher in the four o'clock procession), and they refuse to go into service, which is an agony in time because they think they are free, and they are not if they hope to leave the factory later on and to have, and to demand and the husband to go into a slow death because the electric stove is good, and the pressure cooker too, but the rice gets lumpy, or burns, and the beans get smoked, and the sandwiches at The New Dawn can't nourish a work-ing man, and you have to spend money on vitamins the pharma-cist sells you with her eternal smile, and sometimes I'm tempted to ask her for poison, but there are no rats at home, but I do have a kind of rash in my groins, and there must be something for that trouble (I wonder if the pharmacist would also smile when I talk to her about the itch in my groins), some powder that's white and poisonous because now in the summer it's worse (the rash, I mean), and I have to take her to the beach and she'll give me a headache talking to me about the new car I ought to buy, and about the miseries she's going through, and about be-ing a weak, humiliated woman, until my head explodes and I feel like pouring melted lead into all the holes in her body, but I won't pour anything into her because I teach innocent children (Mister, Mister, the janitor knocked up that little girl), *and in order to feel alive I have to go to Luna Street, but of course I wouldn't hurt Anita because at home is where I am the master, until I drop dead.*

He saw his own naked feet at the bottom of the boat: the long, twisted toes, climbing on top of one another. *They're tight on me, mother. That size is right for you, son. But they're tight on me, mother. You'll soon break them in; they're pretty,* as if they were trying to protect one another from the cruelty of the world. And then he looked at her feet forming almost perfect ovals, with soft little toes, the nails a bright coral.

"Why are you sharpening that beat-up old knife?"

"For tomorrow. To cut open some coconuts at the beach tomorrow."

"It sets my teeth on edge."

He watched a sea bird flying over the boat: its plumage so white, its movements so graceful, its whole form so beautifully lit up by the sun. And the bird dived toward the water and climbed again with a fish in its claws. And they were powerful claws, unsuspected in the fragile beauty of that aerial form.

"We have to change the old balcony curtain, dear. It's disgraceful! We're the laughing-stock of the neighborhood."

The neighborhood laughs, and I hear it laughing, and it owes its bills in the same drugstore. The pharmacist handing me the small package: the red skull and cross-bones. 'For external use.' *Rat poison?* Smiling, forever smiling.

The old knife was at his feet, at the bottom of the boat, the black stains shading its cutting-edge.

"Careful, coconuts leave a stain!"

"That's all right, darling. Taste it. It's cool and sweet." (*Not for external use; internal, internal.*)

"It tastes too tart."

"That's all right, darling. We're going for a boat ride. And we won't have any water handy for a good while. Drink."

He was rowing furiously now, aimlessly. Inexplicably, the boat described large circles, larger . . .

"I'm not mean, dear. But I was born for a different kind of life. Is it my fault if money . . . ?"

The circles, neatly cut out despite the water's unrest, gave him the feeling that there was a definite purpose in it. But was there? The boat was going around crazily, beginning to narrow down the circles. *What's the boat looking for, what's the boat looking for?*

"Mummy says you're a good-for-nothing. Why are you a good-for-nothing, daddy?"

The sweat on his forehead was rolling down his eyelids in big drops, crossing his eyelids and making the world look like an objective out of focus.

"Do you know, dear? A real man gives his wife what she doesn't have."

And the nicotine on his bronchials, sticking there to obstruct his breathing. His weak chest was a bellows full of pain and noises, the narrow stretch of hairs barely separating his small nipples. And the flexion of his arms handling the oars was irregular, exasperating.

The boat was trimming down the circles, making them smaller, but always useless, infuriatingly useless, like a whirlpool that seems to have a hidden meaning and has none, except its coiling, coiling around itself with all that rage, devouring its own concentric movements.

Suddenly, he stopped rowing. Without bearings or steerage, the boat pitched dangerously. The sweat still gave his pupils the vision of a world out of focus. But order reigned because now, suddenly, there was the white-haired old woman, half-nude, disgusting in her blue swimming suit, her body exposed to the merciless sun.

"You're too young to think of marriage. Don't think of it *yet,* son."

"I'm not thinking of it, mother. I swear it. I'm not thinking of it *any more.*"

He was puffing with exhaustion, although his arms remained motionless, limp, aching, the abandoned oars floating and slipping out of his hands, moving away inevitably, in time, over the green . . .

"Daddy, mummy says you shouldn't . . ."

But I should have done it years ago. I should have done it. Because there is something gnawing at her insides, demanding, exacting of me, who can't be blamed for having what she doesn't have and I never asked anyone for. To live in peace, that's all, looking for some meaning to my life. Or in anxiety, never managing to find it. But without the horrible pressure of her envy, without the crying need always to fill her life with things I don't understand. They took away the washing machine yesterday.

Because she thinks that being a man is only that. The new house, dear. *But being a man is to know at least why you are in a boat on the green waters that seem to be blue from far off. And yet, if she asks for it.* If you ask for it . . .

That radiant and youthful creature, of otherworldly beauty, in the blue bathing suit, reclining on the stern was asking for it. *A dance at the Rotary Club, dear.* The sun had pity on no one. *Do I look good in red, dear?* The knife at his feet gave off a blinding flash in spite of the blackish stains on its cutting-edge. *Don't even dream about another child. And with your salary . . . !* As he bent over to take it, his eyes slid over the bulky mound between his legs. *Ay, no, dear, you're hurting me.*

Hurting a man deep down, who asks nothing except to look for the meaning of his life. Urgent call from the bank. *My son wouldn't have found it either.* Urgent call . . . *And he's better off dead.* They have already foreclosed . . . *But I can't. Because first I must know why I am here.* Without an extension . . . *And they haven't given me time.* Dear sir, we regret . . . *They've left me no peace to look for it.* Telegram from the Department. Telegram . . . *Anything you gentlemen want as long as I have some peace!* We regret . . . *And to know. To know . . .*

"Certain things like a man, son."

"Yes, mother, the man you never knew."

He got to his feet. The boat pitched brusquely, but he managed to keep his balance. There was a body on the stern. Motionless now, it was true. But the world back there, on the beach, continued to be a world of man-eating females and male slaves. And here, it was a one-way voyage. He inserted the knife between his flesh and the bathing shorts. He turned the cutting-edge outward. He slit the cloth. He did the same on the left side and the chunks of wool fell with the elastic strips to the bottom of the boat between his bare feet.

The boat was alone between the sky and the sea. Nothing had

changed. The sun was the same. And the breeze kept on tearing happy *flap-flaps* from the ends of the red silk kerchief. But time, motionless before, was beginning to head toward eternity. And now he was naked in the boat's belly. And there was a body reclining on the stern.

"A man gives his wife . . ."

Yes, darling, you said that before. With his left hand he grabbed that whole thing made of spongy tissue and pulled it away from his body as far as he could. He raised the knife into the sunlight and, with a tremendous, horrifying slash, he lopped right down to the black hairs. The howl, together with the bleeding scraps, smashed up against the motionless body that remained propped up gently, almost gracefully, on the stern of the boat.

TRANSLATED BY HARDIE ST. MARTIN

Yo Jehova Decreto

que se termine todo de una vez
hago la cruz al sistema solar

hay que volver al útero materno
doy por finiquitada la cosa

que no se escape nadie
que se termine todo de golpe
para qué vamos a andar con rodeos

está muy bien la Guerra de Viet-Nam
está muy bien la Operacion a la Próstata
yo Jehová decreto la vejez

ustedes me dan risa
ustedes me ponen los nervios de punta
sólo un cretino de nacimiento
se arrodilla a venerar una estatua

francamente no sé que decirles
estamos al borde de la Tercera Guerra Mundial
y nadie parece darse cuenta de nada

¿si destruyen el mundo
creen que yo voy a volver a crearlo?

Nicancor Parra

I Jehovah Decree

that they get it over with once and for all
I'm giving the solar system the slip

everything back into the womb
I'm saying it's over finished and done with

nobody's escaping
everything over with in one stroke
why beat around the bush

great thing the Vietnam War
great thing the Prostate Operation
I Jehovah decree old age

you people make me laugh
you people give me the creeps
only a born moron
could get down on his knees and worship a statue

frankly I don't know what to tell you
we're on the brink of the Third World War
and nobody seems to have noticed

if you destroy the world
do you think I'm going to create it over again?

TRANSLATED BY W. S. MERWIN

La Trampa

Por aquel tiempo yo rehuía las escenas demasiado misteriosas.
Como los enfermos del estómago que evitan las comidas pesadas,
Prefería quedarme en casa dilucidando algunas cuestiones
Referentes a la reproducción de las arañas,
Con cuyo objeto me recluía en el jardín
Y no aparecía en público hasta avanzadas horas de la noche;
O también en mangas de camisa, en actitud desafiante,
Solía lanzar iracundas miradas a la luna
Procurando evitar esos pensamientos atrabiliarios
Que se pegan como pólipos al alma humana.
En la soledad poseía un dominio absoluto sobre mí mismo,
Iba de un lado a otro con plena conciencia de mis actos
O me tendía entre las tablas de la bodega
A soñar, a idear mecanismos, a resolver pequeños problemas de
    emergencia.
Aquellos eran los momentos en que ponía en práctica mi célebre método
    onírico,
Que consiste en violentarse a sí mismo y soñar lo que se desea,
En promover escenas preparadas de antemano con participación del más
    allá.
De este modo lograba obtener informaciones preciosas
Referentes a una serie de dudas que aquejan al ser:
Viajes al extranjero, confusiones eróticas, complejos religiosos.
Pero todas las precauciones eran pocas
Puesto que por razones difíciles de precisar
Comenzaba a deslizarme automáticamente por una especie de plano
    inclinado,
Como un globo que se desinfla mi alma perdía altura,
El instinto de conservación dejaba de funcionar
Y privado de mis prejuicios más esenciales
Caía fatalmente en la trampa del teléfono

The Trap

During that time I kept out of circumstances that were too full of
        mystery
As people with stomach ailments avoid heavy meals,
I preferred to stay at home inquiring into certain questions
Concerning the propagation of spiders,
To which end I would shut myself up in the garden
And not show myself in public until late at night;
Or else, in shirt sleeves, defiant,
I would hurl angry glances at the moon,
Trying to get rid of those bilious fancies
That cling like polyps to the human soul.
When I was alone I was completely self-possessed,
I went back and forth fully conscious of my actions
Or I would stretch out among the planks of the cellar
And dream, think up ways and means, resolve little emergency problems.
It was at that moment that I put into practice my famous method for
        interpreting dreams
Which consists in doing violence to oneself and then imagining what one
        would like,
Conjuring up scenes that I had worked out beforehand with the help
        of powers from other worlds.
In this manner I was able to obtain priceless information
Concerning a string of anxieties that afflict our being:
Foreign travel, erotic disorders, religious complexes.
But all precautions were inadequate,
Because, for reasons hard to set forth
I began sliding automatically down a sort of inclined plane.
My soul lost altitude like a punctured balloon,
The instinct of self-preservation stopped functioning
And, deprived of my most essential prejudices,
I fell unavoidably into the telephone trap

Que como un abismo atrae a los objetos que lo rodean
Y con manos trémulas marcaba ese número maldito
Que aún suelo repetir automáticamente mientras duermo.
De incertidumbre y de miseria eran aquellos segundos
En que yo, como un esqueleto de pie delante de esa mesa del infierno
Cubierta de una cretona amarilla,
Esperaba una respuesta desde el otro extremo del mundo,
La otra mitad de mi ser prisionera en un hoyo.
Esos ruidos entrecortados del teléfono
Producían en mí el efecto de las máquinas perforadoras de los dentistas,
Se incrustaban en mi alma como agujas lanzadas desde lo alto
Hasta que, llegado el momento preciso,
Comenzaba a transpirar y a tartamudear febrilmente.
Mi lengua parecida a un beefsteak de ternera
Se interponía entre mi ser y mi interlocutora
Como esas cortinas negras que nos separan de los muertos.
Yo no deseaba sostener esas conversaciones demasiado íntimas
Que, sin embargo, yo mismo provocaba en forma torpe
Con mi voz anhelante, cargada de electricidad.
Sentirme llamado por mi nombre de pila
En ese tono de familiaridad forzada
Me producía malestares difusos,
Perturbaciones locales de angustia que yo procuraba conjurar
A través de un método rápido de preguntas y respuestas
Creando en ella un estado de efervescencia pseudoerótico
Que a la postre venía a repercutir en mí mismo
Bajo la forma de incipientes erecciones y de una sensación de fracaso.
Entonces me reía a la fuerza cayendo después en un estado de postración
          mental.
Aquellas charlas absurdas se prolongaban algunas horas
Hasta que la dueña de la pensión aparecía detrás del biombo
Interrumpiendo bruscamente aquel idilio estúpido,
Aquellas contorsiones de postulante al cielo

Which sucks in everything around it, like a vacuum,
And with trembling hands I dialed that accursed number
Which even now I repeat automatically in my sleep.
Uncertainty and misery filled the seconds that followed,
While I, like a skeleton standing before that table from hell
Covered with yellow cretonne,
Waited for an answer from the other end of the world,
The other half of my being, imprisoned in a pit.
Those intermittent telephone noises
Worked on me like a dentist's drill,
They sank into my soul like needles shot from the sky
Until, when the moment itself arrived
I started to sweat and to stammer feverishly,
My tongue like a veal steak
Obtruded between my being and her who was listening,
Like those black curtains that separate us from the dead.
I never wanted to conduct those overintimate conversations
Which I myself provoked, just the same, in my stupid way,
My voice thick with desire, and electrically charged.
Hearing myself called by my first name
In that tone of forced familiarity
Filled me with a vague discomfort,
With anguished localized disturbances which I contrived to keep in
          check
With a hurried system of questions and answers
Which roused in her a state of pseudoerotic effervescence
That eventually affected me as well
With incipient erections and a feeling of doom.
Then I'd make myself laugh and as a result fall into a state of mental
          prostration.
These ridiculous little chats went on for hours
Until the lady who ran the pension appeared behind the screen
Brusquely breaking off our stupid idyll.
Those contortions of a petitioner at the gates of heaven

Y aquellas catástrofes tan deprimentes para mi espíritu
Que no terminaban completamente con colgar el teléfono
Ya que, por lo general, quedábamos comprometidos
A vernos al día siguiente en una fuente de soda
O en la puerta de una iglesia de cuyo nombre no quiero acordarme.

Antes Me Parecía Todo Bien

ahora todo me parece mal

un teléfono viejo de campanilla
bastaba para hacerme el sujeto más felíz de la creación
un sillón de madera—cualquier cosa

los domingos por la mañana
me iba al mercado persa
y regresaba con reloj de pared
—es decir con caja del reloj—
o con una victrola desvencijada
a mi cabañísima de la Reina
donde me esperaba el Chamaco
y su señora madre de aquel entonces

eran días felices
o por lo menos noches sin dolor

And those catastrophes which so wore down my spirit
Did not stop altogether when I hung up
For usually we had agreed
To meet next day in a soda fountain
Or at the door of a church whose name I prefer to forget.

TRANSLATED BY W. S. MERWIN

Everything Used to Look Good to Me

now everything looks bad to me

an old telephone with a little bell
was enough to make me the happiest creature alive
an arm chair—almost anything

Sunday mornings
I'd go to the flea market
and come back with a wall clock
—anyway with the case—
or with a pensioned-off victrola
to my shack at la Reina
where Chamaco was waiting for me
and the lady
who used to be his mother in those days

those were happy days
or at least nights without pain

TRANSLATED BY W. S. MERWIN

Esto Tiene Que Ser Un Cementerio

de lo contrario no se explicarían
esas casas sin puertas ni ventanas
esas interminable hileras de automóviles

y a juzgar por estas sombras fosforescentes
es probable que estemos en el infierno

debajo de esa cruz
estoy seguro que debe haber una iglesia

This Has To Be a Cemetery

nothing else can explain
these houses without doors or windows
these interminable lines of automobiles

and judging by these phosphorescent shadows
it's more than likely that we're in hell

under that cross
I'm sure there must be a church

TRANSLATED BY W. S. MERWIN

Gabriel García Márquez

Balthazar's Marvelous Afternoon

The cage was finished. Balthazar hung it under the eave, from force of habit, and when he finished lunch everyone was already saying that it was the most beautiful cage in the world. So many people came to see it that a crowd formed in front of the house, and Balthazar had to take it down and close the shop.

"You have to shave," Ursula, his wife, told him. "You look like a Capuchin."

"It's bad to shave after lunch," said Balthazar.

He had two weeks' growth, short, hard, and bristly hair like the mane of a mule, and the general expression of a frightened boy. But it was a false expression. In February he was thirty; he had been living with Ursula for four years, without marrying her and without having children, and life had given him many reasons to be on guard but none to be frightened. He did not even know that for some people the cage he had just made was the most beautiful one in the world. For him, accustomed to making cages since childhood, it had been hardly any more difficult than the others.

"Then rest for a while," said the woman. "With that beard you can't show yourself anywhere."

While he was resting, he had to get out of his hammock several times to show the cage to the neighbors. Ursula had paid little attention to it until then. She was annoyed because her husband had neglected the work of his carpenter's shop to devote himself entirely to the cage, and

for two weeks had slept poorly, turning over and muttering incoheren-
cies, and he hadn't thought of shaving. But her annoyance dissolved in
the face of the finished cage. When Balthazar woke up from his nap, she
had ironed his pants and a shirt; she had put them on a chair near the
hammock and had carried the cage to the dining table. She regarded it in
silence.

"How much will you charge?" she asked.

"I don't know," Balthazar answered. "I'm going to ask for thirty
pesos to see if they'll give me twenty."

"Ask for fifty," said Ursula. "You've lost a lot of sleep in these two
weeks. Furthermore, it's rather large. I think its the biggest cage I've ever
seen in my life."

Balthazar began to shave.

"Do you think they'll give me fifty pesos?"

"That's nothing for Mr. Chepe Montiel, and the cage is worth it,"
said Ursula. "You should ask for sixty."

The house lay in the stifling shadow. It was the first week of April
and the heat seemed less bearable because of the chirping of the cicadas.
When he finished dressing, Balthazar opened the door to the patio to
cool off the house, and a group of children entered the dining room.

The news had spread. Dr. Octavio Giraldo, an old physician, happy
with life but tired of his profession, thought about Balthazar's cage while
he was eating lunch with his invalid wife. On the inside terrace, where
they put the table on hot days, there were many flowerpots and two cages
with canaries. His wife liked birds, and she liked them so much that she
hated cats because they could eat them up. Thinking about her, Dr. Giraldo went to see a patient that afternoon, and when he returned he went
by Balthazar's house to inspect the cage.

There were a lot of people in the dining room. The cage was on
display on the table: with its enormous dome of wire, three stories inside,
with passageways and compartments especially for eating and sleeping
and swings in the space set aside for the birds' recreation, it seemed like a
small-scale model of a gigantic ice factory. The doctor inspected it care-

fully, without touching it, thinking that in effect the cage was better than its reputation, and much more beautiful than any he had ever dreamed of for his wife.

"This is a flight of the imagination," he said. He sought out Balthazar among the group of people and, fixing his maternal eyes on him, added, "You would have been an extraordinary architect."

Balthazar blushed.

"Thank you," he said.

"It's true," said the doctor. He was smoothly and delicately fat, like a woman who had been beautiful in her youth, and he had delicate hands. His voice seemed like that of a priest speaking Latin. "You wouldn't even need to put birds in it," he said, making the cage turn in front of the audience's eyes as if he were auctioning it off. "It would be enough to hang it in the trees so it could sing by itself." He put it back on the table, thought a moment, looking at the cage, and said:

"Fine, then I'll take it."

"It's sold," said Ursula.

"It belongs to the son of Mr. Chepe Montiel," said Balthazar. "He ordered it specially."

The doctor adopted a respectful attitude.

"Did he give you the design?"

"No," said Balthazar. "He said he wanted a large cage, like this one, for a pair of troupials."

The doctor looked at the cage.

"But this isn't for troupials."

"Of course it is, Doctor," said Balthazar, approaching the table. The children surrounded him. "The measurements are carefully calculated," he said, pointing to the different compartments with his forefinger. Then he struck the dome with his knuckles, and the cage filled with resonant chords.

"It's the strongest wire you can find, and each joint is soldered outside and in," he said.

"It's even big enough for a parrot," interrupted one of the children.

"That it is," said Balthazar.

The doctor turned his head.

"Fine, but he didn't give you the design," he said. "He gave you no exact specifications, aside from making it a cage big enough for troupials. Isn't that right?"

"That's right," said Balthazar.

"Then there's no problem," said the doctor. "One thing is a cage big enough for troupials, and another is this cage. There's no proof that this one is the one you were asked to make."

"It's this very one," said Balthazar, confused. "That's why I made it."

The doctor made an impatient gesture.

"You could make another one," said Ursula, looking at her husband. And then, to the doctor: "You're not in any hurry."

"I promised it to my wife for this afternoon," said the doctor.

"I'm very sorry, Doctor," said Balthazar, "but I can't sell you something that's sold already."

The doctor shrugged his shoulders. Drying the sweat from his neck with a handkerchief, he contemplated the cage silently with the fixed, unfocused gaze of one who looks at a ship which is sailing away.

"How much did they pay you for it?"

Balthazar sought out Ursula's eyes without replying.

"Sixty pesos," she said.

The doctor kept looking at the cage. "It's very pretty." He sighed. "Extremely pretty." Then, moving toward the door, he began to fan himself energetically, smiling, and the trace of that episode disappeared forever from his memory.

"Montiel is very rich," he said.

In truth, José Montiel was not as rich as he seemed, but he would have been capable of doing anything to become so. A few blocks from there, in a house crammed with equipment, where no one had ever smelled a smell that couldn't be sold, he remained indifferent to the news of the cage. His wife, tortured by an obsession with death, closed the doors and windows after lunch and lay for two hours with her eyes opened to the shadow of the room, while José Montiel took his siesta.

The clamor of many voices surprised her there. Then she opened the door to the living room and found a crowd in front of the house, and Balthazar with the cage in the middle of the crowd, dressed in white, freshly shaved, with that expression of decorous candor with which the poor approach the houses of the wealthy.

"What a marvelous thing!" José Montiel's wife exclaimed, with a radiant expression, leading Balthazar inside. "I've never seen anything like it in my life," she said, and added, annoyed by the crowd which piled up at the door, "But bring it inside before they turn the living room into a grandstand."

Balthazar was no stranger to José Montiel's house. On different occasions, because of his skill and forthright way of dealing, he had been called in to do minor carpentry jobs. But he never felt at ease among the rich. He used to think about them, about their ugly and argumentative wives, about their tremendous surgical operations, and he always experienced a feeling of pity. When he entered their houses, he couldn't move without dragging his feet.

"Is Pepe home?" he asked.

He had put the cage on the dining-room table.

"He's at school," said José Montiel's wife. "But he shouldn't be long," and she added, "Montiel is taking a bath."

In reality, José Montiel had not had time to bathe. He was giving himself an urgent alcohol rub, in order to come out and see what was going on. He was such a cautious man that he slept without an electric fan so he could watch over the noises of the house while he slept.

"Adelaide!" he shouted. "What's going on?"

"Come and see what a marvelous thing!" his wife shouted.

José Montiel, obese and hairy, his towel draped around his neck, appeared at the bedroom window.

"What is that?"

"Pepe's cage," said Balthazar.

His wife looked at him perplexedly.

"Whose?"

"Pepe's," replied Balthazar. And then, turning toward José Montiel, "Pepe ordered it."

Nothing happened at that instant, but Balthazar felt as if someone had just opened the bathroom door on him. José Montiel came out of the bedroom in his underwear.

"Pepe!" he shouted.

"He's not back," whispered his wife, motionless.

Pepe appeared in the doorway. He was about twelve, and had the same curved eyelashes and was as quietly pathetic as his mother.

"Come here," José Montiel said to him. "Did you order this?"

The child lowered his head. Grabbing him by the hair, José Montiel forced Pepe to look him in the eye.

"Answer me."

The child bit his lip without replying.

"Montiel," whispered his wife.

José Montiel let the child go and turned toward Balthazar in a fury. "I'm very sorry, Balthazar," he said. "But you should have consulted me before going on. Only to you would it occur to contract with a minor." As he spoke, his face recovered its serenity. He lifted the cage without looking at it and gave it to Balthazar.

"Take it away at once, and try to sell it to whomever you can," he said. "Above all, I beg you not to argue with me." He patted him on the back and explained, "The doctor has forbidden me to get angry."

The child had remained motionless, without blinking, until Balthazar looked at him uncertainly with the cage in his hand. Then he emitted a guttural sound, like a dog's growl, and threw himself on the floor screaming.

José Montiel looked at him, unmoved, while the mother tried to pacify him. "Don't even pick him up," he said. "Let him break his head on the floor, and then put salt and lemon on it so he can rage to his heart's content." The child was shrieking tearlessly while his mother held him by the wrists.

"Leave him alone," José Montiel insisted.

Balthazar observed the child as he would have observed the death throes of a rabid animal. It was almost four o'clock. At that hour, at his house, Ursula was singing a very old song and cutting slices of onion.

"Pepe," said Balthazar.

He approached the child, smiling, and held the cage out to him. The child jumped up, embraced the cage which was almost as big as he was, and stood looking at Balthazar through the wirework without knowing what to say. He hadn't shed one tear.

"Balthazar," said José Montiel softly. "I told you already to take it away."

"Give it back," the woman ordered the child.

"Keep it," said Balthazar. And then, to José Montiel: "After all, that's what I made it for."

José Montiel followed him into the living room.

"Don't be foolish, Balthazar," he was saying, blocking his path. "Take your piece of furniture home and don't be silly. I have no intention of paying you a cent."

"It doesn't matter," said Balthazar. "I made it expressly as a gift for Pepe. I didn't expect to charge anything for it."

As Balthazar made his way through the spectators who were blocking the door, José Montiel was shouting in the middle of the living room. He was very pale and his eyes were beginning to get red.

"Idiot!" he was shouting. "Take your trinket out of here. The last thing we need is for some nobody to give orders in my house. Son of a bitch!"

In the pool hall, Balthazar was received with an ovation. Until that moment, he thought that he had made a better cage than ever before, that he'd had to give it to the son of José Montiel so he wouldn't keep crying, and that none of these things was particularly important. But then he realized that all of this had a certain importance for many people, and he felt a little excited.

"So they gave you fifty pesos for the cage."

"Sixty," said Balthazar.

"Score one for you," someone said. "You're the only one who has managed to get such a pile of money out of Mr. Chepe Montiel. We have to celebrate."

They bought him a beer, and Balthazar responded with a round for everybody. Since it was the first time he had ever been out drinking, by dusk he was completely drunk, and he was talking about a fabulous project of a thousand cages, at sixty pesos each, and then of a million cages, till he had sixty million pesos. "We have to make a lot of things to sell to the rich before they die," he was saying, blind drunk. "All of them are sick, and they're going to die. They're so screwed up they can't even get angry any more." For two hours he was paying for the jukebox, which played without interruption. Everybody toasted Balthazar's health, good luck, and fortune, and the death of the rich, but at mealtime they left him alone in the pool hall.

Ursula had waited for him until eight, with a dish of fried meat covered with slices of onion. Someone told her that her husband was in the pool hall, delirious with happiness, buying beers for everyone, but she didn't believe it, because Balthazar had never got drunk. When she went to bed, almost at midnight, Balthazar was in a lighted room where there were little tables, each with four chairs, and an outdoor dance floor, where the plovers were walking around. His face was smeared with rouge, and since he couldn't take one more step, he thought he wanted to lie down with two women in the same bed. He had spent so much that he had had to leave his watch in pawn, with the promise to pay the next day. A moment later, spread-eagled in the street, he realized that his shoes were being taken off, but he didn't want to abandon the happiest dream of his life. The women who passed on their way to five-o'clock Mass didn't dare look at him, thinking he was dead.

TRANSLATED BY J. S. BERNSTEIN

Cada Poema

Cada poema un pájaro que huye
del sitio señalado por la plaga.
Cada poema un traje de la muerte
por las calles y plazas inundadas
en la cera letal de los vencidos.
Cada poema un paso hacia la muerte,
una falsa moneda de rescate,
un tiro al blanco en medio de la noche
horadando los puentes sobre el río,
cuyas dormidas aguas viajan
de la vieja ciudad hacia los campos
donde el día prepara sus hogueras.
Cada poema un tacto yerto
del que yace en la losa de las clínicas,
un ávido anzuelo que recorre
el limo blando de las sepulturas.
Cada poema un lento naufragio del deseo,
un crujir de los mástiles y jarcias
que sostienen el peso de la vida.
Cada poema un estruendo de lienzos que derrumban
sobre el rugir helado de las aguas
el albo aparejo del velamen.
Cada poema invadiendo y desgarrando
la amarga telaraña del hastío.
Cada poema nace de un ciego centinela

Alvaro Mutis

Every Poem

Every poem a bird fleeing
from the claim staked by the plague.
Every poem a burial suit
in the lethal wax of the defeated
through flooded streets and squares.
Every poem a step toward death,
a false ransom payment,
a shot at a target in the middle of the night,
riddling the bridges over the river,
whose sleeping waters are travelling
from the old city toward the country
where the day is setting its bonfires.
Every poem a stiff touch
from the one lying on the clinic slab,
a hungry fish-hook on its way
through the smooth mud of the tombs.
Every poem a slow shipwreck of desire,
a creaking of the masts and rigging
that take the weight of life.
Every poem a rumble of canvas letting fall,
over the frozen roar of the waters,
the white cordage of the sails.
Every poem invading and tearing
the bitter cobweb of disgust.
Every poem is born to a blind sentry

que grita al hondo hueco de la noche
el santo y seña de su desventura.
Agua de sueño, fuente de ceniza,
piedra porosa de los mataderos,
madera en sombra de las siemprevivas,
metal que dobla por los condenados,
aceite funeral de doble filo,
cotidiano sudario del poeta,
cada poema esparce sobre el mundo
el agrio cereal de la agonía.

La Muerte de Matías Aldecoa

Ni cuestor en Queronea,
ni lector en Bolonia,
ni coracero en Valmy,
ni infante en Ayacucho;
en el Orinoco buceador fallido,
buscador de metales en el verde Quindío,
farmaceuta ambulante en el cañón del Chicamocha,
mago de feria en Honda,
hinchado y verdinoso cadáver
en las presurosas aguas del Combeima,
girando en los espumosos remolinos,
sin ojos ya y sin labios,
exudando sus más secretas mieles,
desnudo, mutilado, golpeado sordamente
contra las piedras,
descubriendo, de pronto,
en algún rincón aún vivo
de su yerto cerebro,

who shouts in the deep hollow of the night
the password of his wretchedness.
Water of dream, fountain of ash,
porous stone from the slaughterhouses,
wood shaded by immortelles,
metal ringing for the condemned,
two-edged funeral oil,
the poet's daily shroud,
every poem scatters over the world
the sour grain of agony.

TRANSLATED BY W. S. MERWIN

The Death of Matías Aldecoa

Neither quaestor in Queronea,
nor lecturer in Bolonia,
nor cuirassier in Valmy,
nor prince in Ayacucho;
in the Orinoco an empty-handed diver,
a seeker for metals in the green Quindío,
a travelling pharmacist in Chicamocha canyon,
a carnival magician in Honda,
bloated and greenish corpse
in the rapids of Combeima,
revolving in the frothy eddies,
without eyes and without lips,
oozing his most intimate honeys,
naked, mutilated, knocking softly
against the stones,
discovering all at once
in some still living corner
of his stiffened brain,

la verdadera, la esencial materia
de sus días en el mundo.
Un mudo adiós a ciertas cosas,
a ciertas vagas criaturas
confundidas ya en un último
relámpago de nostalgia,
y, luego, nada,
un rodar en la corriente
hasta vararse en las lianas de la desembocadura,
menos aún que nada,
ni cuestor en Queronea,
ni lector en Bolonia,
ni cosa alguna memorable.

the true, the essential substance
of his days in the world.
A mute good-bye to certain things,
to certain vague creatures
already confused in the final
lightning flash of nostalgia,
and then, nothing,
a drag in the current
until stranded in the lianas of the river mouth,
even less than nothing,
neither quaestor in Queronea
nor lecturer in Bolonia,
nor anything memorable.

TRANSLATED BY W. S. MERWIN

Adriano González León

The Rainbow

> I establish my covenant with you that never again shall
> flesh be cut off by the waters of a flood and never again
> shall there be a flood to destroy the earth.
>
> * * *
>
> And he drank of the wine and became drunk and he lay
> uncovered in his tent.
>
> *Genesis 9.11, 21*

The sparkle of light from the swampy highway sets the forest animals
stirring.

There is a shred of mist before his eyes. The scene goes on changing
as if someone, by chopping at a tree with sharp blows, were forcing the
light to open a passage. The shabby black truck advances by a route
which leads nowhere or else to hell. Because of the glitter, the man can
scarcely see the mud, or the slender trees fluttering spectrally on the
riverbank. At times he closes his eyes and the truck falters with shrill
shrieks of ungreased springs and a rumble of wooden planks. The wheels
skid, slide, finally overcome mud and water-filled ruts and once more the
truck, with its two bright eyes, rumbles over the heights, bellowing like
an ox, and sinks into the depressions of the highway which leads nowhere or to hell.

For some hours he has not been a man or a driver, nor does he seem
to have the wheel in his hands. For hours he has gone on like this,
planted on the seat with its bouncing springs, one more item of cargo.

He is not a man. He is something attached to the accelerator, he is a wire clasping the shift lever, he is a box which accumulates discharges and suddenly fires them at distant targets, unable to think clearly, unable to remember what route he follows and what curious forces are running this network of cables, cogwheels, boards, noises and worn-out spark plugs in his brain. Five hundred miles non-stop. Once in a while, a brief pause at a gasoline station. Two days and a night of turns and bends, of asphalt highways and soggy roads, of dragging out his body at villages and of being nothing now but a journey without beginning or end, a roaring, a crazy roaring of the gearshift. He, a skilled chauffeur, is a driver shaken up by those roads; a man of bolted meals and miserable couplings with wretched women of the road, endowed with starving children, so that as years go by he will never know them, never know at this moment what the descendents of Camilo Ortíz are doing, yet surely they are as crazy and have souls purulent as his and this would not be their fault any more than his syphilis, his drunken sprees, and his bad bargains are his fault.

Behind it all, far behind it all, with his enormous years on his back, was the old man, spouting curses and saying that Camilo would never have peace or any property, that his grandsons would scratch the earth like animals and be thrown out of everyone's house, beaten, and mocked by all men. To this day Camilo still does not know what went on in the old man's head back in those days when he was already failing badly and his brothers, Semelio and Jacinto, brought their father a blanket to keep out the cold. He let go with all sorts of filth and said everyone was becoming corrupt. He said, too, that everything had been for nothing and, worst of all, one of his sons did not respect him or treat him as he deserved. Semelio and Jacinto gave him enough to buy clothes because in those last days he was very drunk all the time. His eyes were always bloodshot and his curses could be heard three blocks away.

Crops were no good at all and the workers didn't want to lift a finger; they were too big for their boots, puffed up with dirt and laziness, nor was the old man the boss any more. There wasn't anything he could do nor could his laborers go on taking advantage of his age to come whining, asking how to take grubs out of the back of cattle and what did he think was the best way to clear coffee plantations. In the past, Semelio and Jacinto helped the old man work things out with so many people asking for advice and he was well satisfied; his eyes flashed, and he coughed until his breath gave out. But nowadays everything was very different and the old man had lost his patience. He hit himself in the chest and said that too many years weighed upon his shoulders for him to weather another calamity and that everything would be ruined because Camilo was shameless and good for nothing. Everyone would be damned and scattered over the face of the earth.

Now that the truck is standing still on a hilltop, the landscape can be seen, very cold and desolate. Or rather, it can't be seen because darkness consumes the trees, the other roads and the distant ranges, and not a single light reveals a window or door or a place to get a drink or spend a good long time getting warm. There is not even a bird in sight, those birds which suddenly sing in the night, making a racket in the branches. Time, the wind, everything is quiet now and Camilo sees this dark form-less dough extending in all directions, instead of stones or land or fields of corn. Farther on there should be a river and animals should be dis-pelling their fevers in the pools. Camilo sees nothing, observes nothing; his eyes are blurred by mist and his hands tremble when the truck jolts and begins to roll.

"They should all rot down there, let the worms eat them," he had either thought or said two or three hours ago on the edge of the ravine. One by one he was unloading the bags of coffee and lining them up. One by one he was pushing them down the slope, furious, scarcely seeing the letters stamped on the sacking: "Jacinto Ortíz, Commission Merchant-Consignee." He heard the beans bounce and the dull noise of the bags as they struck against the stones at the bottom. "Let the devil have them or the soul of my brother can pick them out of hell." And he went on pushing down the rest of the load with fury and curses. "Let Semelio send one of his trucks or come himself and pick it up bean by bean. . . . Fuck both of them and the old man, too, and all the rest of our genera-tion." Afterwards, when not a single bag was left, he stood on the edge rubbing his hands and spitting into the darkness.

He put the key in and the truck, lightened, went round the hills at top speed, losing itself among the curves.

Even before the ravine and the bags, the urge had mastered him. It happened around two o'clock with a sun that made zinc cans hiss and set a kind of vapor rising from the middle of the highway. The truck groaned heavily and greasy fumes escaped through the cracks of the cab and around the accelerator. It was hot, very hot. He stared drowsily at the road signs and at one or another Vepaco billboard advertising rentable space or painkillers. Suddenly there were spots like water which disappeared as fast as the truck approached. And, suddenly, only the blacktop and that glasslike image in front of his eyes and the piercing sun. Then the old man's face appeared. At first the image was far off, as if staggering down the middle of the highway. Afterwards it came near, just the face, his enormous face, bearded and swollen with the years, just the eyes, accusing and malicious, filling the windshield, fixed right there in the middle of the glass and then projected in front of the truck, and multiplied in the distance. Then one of the old man's eyes, bloodshot and rheumy in the face of the man in the advertisement. One of the old man's eyes, crossed and wrinkled in the trunk of a ceiba. The old man's phosphorescent eyes in the holes in the blacktop, phosphorescent, dancing in the unreal mist. Eyes suspended in the air, grim, dry, two stones with eyelashes, two aggressive spots which came back to install themselves in the windshield and make the truck shudder.

When the old man's eyes went out, Jacinto Ortíz came with his wife and children, each one spreading his foolish face over the windshield, and that of Jacinto also had the look of a satisfied dog who has gnawed its bone until nothing is left, the face of an established citizen who has profited enough from his ten acres of land to start the valise and trunk business and afterward to have a store in which to sell yard goods and leather, and later move to the capital of the state and buy two houses, manage a drug store and open a shop on the Calle Real and send his sons to take over all the businesses of the city, one by one. They built them up and sold them, doubling their profits and now were thinking of importing machinery and going into the tractor business. Jacinto said he was

feeling a little tired and that he would only take charge of the least demanding businesses and that was why he had those letters, "Commission
Merchant-Consignee," painted on in truncated letters, a way of unifying
the work of other people and watching over it with a silent smile, never
offering anything to him, Camilo, not a single opportunity for fear he
might hurt the business or corrupt the employees. And besides, Jacinto's
wife hated him with all her might and saw him as a danger, for Camilo,
according to her, might some day wake up from his vagrancy and his
craziness and begin to demand the land by law, although the old man
had done nothing but curse him before he died. The curses and the eyes
of the old man returned to the windshield, then disappeared and gave
place to Semelio, for he was one who turned up everywhere rapidly.
Semelio always moved fast from the very moment he left the village and
began to work with a pickup truck in the East. In two years he already
had three more vehicles and then went into the transportation business
with a powerful fleet of red GMC trucks bearing on the doors the distinc-
tive trademark, "Ortíz Brothers, Trucking," because Jacinto smoothed
the way for business and thus got more profit from his consignments and
sales since he could offer to transport the products. Maybe because the
sign said Ortíz Brothers, for after all he, too, was an Ortíz, Semelio
called him in now and then to offer him temporary work and gave him
one of the oldest trucks—like this one, echoing and groaning over the
sunny highway—so that he could pick up a little money—so that, even
though it was only a lie, the family would remain united.

The fortress, the unity of the Ortízes, the wives and the children of
the wives, was a unity forged by the old man when he built his house on
the highest part of the range. He called them all together and told them
to apply themselves to work because times were about to be hard and it
was better to get together and save the fields and the livestock he had
succeeded in accumulating. At least they had built good fences and barns
to take care of the grain and cattle. It would be better if they all paid
attention and came with their wives and children and helped enlarge the
house.

The leaves began to be filled with poison, a white tracery consumed the sap, and then the plantations became covered with caterpillars. Blackbirds did not spare a single ripe fruit.

They were all in the house when the violent and prolonged thunder came, thunder that seemed to split the sky, followed by more thunderstorms which broke the fields up into countless fragments and the water poured down in lashing torrents. The animals and chickens stamped, shook their wings, or milled around in the stalls. The water continued to drum heavily and the ravines began to fill. Day and night, the storm grew worse, and for many days and nights it never stopped raining. They knew that the neighboring houses had cracked or roofs had flown off and there was no place to shelter animals or children and the water had swept everything away. The broken dams of the lakes released more water into the valley and from above the flashes of lightning fell implacably upon the trees, splashing the old man's house with red lights as it stood firm and solitary on the top of the range.

One day the rain stopped falling from the sky and the flooding waters began to subside. The earth revealed was an immense mudflat and the flesh and hides of animals floated all about with no one anywhere trying to save anything. Now and then the old man looked out of the window and began to take an interest, using the same tone of voice and gestures as he had when he was building the house and putting the children and livestock in order. One day he announced that it was time to return to work and to see what could be done. Then he went down from the hill and ordered the others to come down, too, as he looked over the ravaged fields. Then he spoke up and told them it was time to sow again because he saw some live shoots and the earth could again be fruitful.

In the night the truck is a mass of iron and wood. Its bellowing is the only sound to be heard in the long-enduring country silence. Shadows and blinded owls fly across in front of it. Camilo's eyes hurt from so much staring into the darkness, from so much peering within himself in search of the dirty face of his boy, kicked and beaten in Puente Villegas because he had no one to defend him from the drunks who attacked him. He sets himself to search out the faces of the others, in a hamlet on the highway to Pampanito, but he cannot see them because they have been disfigured by squalor and hunger. He does not know what became of the son he had with Manuela Pernía, nor if the swollen bellies of Josefa, La Negra, and María Rosario were all successful pregnancies, or if the children came to a bad end. Camilo asked himself now why he didn't stay home with the others and wait for his share of the land and the money. Camilo does not know why his evil star has led him into these worlds and made him sleep on rotted mats and shoot dice on dirty burlap and grease the cards so as to distinguish the aces at a glance. Who? . . . what drunken hand flung him headlong into that house crowned with red lights, reeking of vomit and alcohol, called La Conga? Why did he stay there for so many days? What did that blonde Colombian put in his beer, the one who spoke with exaggerated eses and made the word Bucaramanga sound like a bad word? Camilo had started helping out at the bar and the women had shown him a lack of respect, calling him by nicknames. It got so the little Colombian refused to stay in the room with him because business was business. At times Camilo went to the nearby ravine and washed clothes for them in exchange for food. One night when he was very drunk and began to remember things and to call himself a bum, the women made fun of him and then he threw a glass of beer at them and splashed some of them. In a moment he was running down the highway with fourteen dishevelled whores pelting him and shouting insults at him.

There had been other days and other episodes which he could not grasp clearly. A bound book and a black suit smelling of medicines. The little man seemed half off his head . . . half something . . . The little man talked slowly and behaved very politely. But he stank of . . . it seemed that he had pissed in his pants . . . Yes, definitely, the little man passed the whole day with the book and Camilo became acquainted with him on a bench in the square. The little man was nice to him and told him that if he had no place to sleep he could stay in his room for a few days, in the district called La Plata. But he didn't let him sleep. Every night he took up the book and, passing his finger along the print, read, "All that moves and lives shall be yours for your sustenance: likewise the grass and plants, all of this I give unto you." Camilo had not eaten for

days. Days without vegetables or anything else. Neither did the little
man have much and the only thing he prepared once was a soup made of
spaghetti and cornmeal. The little man said that God had spoken thus:
"And your fear and trembling shall be upon every animal of the earth
and on all of the birds of the air and all that creeps upon the earth; they
are delivered into your hands." But Camilo thought that at that moment,
cold as it was, he had nothing, nothing on earth except for the fear and
trembling which at times overcame him. The little man explained that
he must not create scandals and that he ought to prepare himself for
eternity and that those who were full of anger would not be saved. After
that he began to ask questions about Camilo's life and where he came
from. All of this until very late. Morning was the only time when he was
let alone because the little man began to sing hymn 243—as he heard
him say—and did not concern himself with Camilo. "He gave you do-
minion over the work of your haaands . . . And all creation laid beneath your feeet . . . Oxen, sheep, likewise beasts of the feeeeld . . .
Birds of the air and fishes of the seees . . ." On other days he went too
far, like that last time when he asked too many questions and urged
Camilo to confess the truth. The little man supposed he was wanted and
began with his strange words to say, "He who sheds the blood of a man,
his blood shall be spilled." Camilo didn't understand, didn't answer, and
the little man said he could not keep him in his room any longer but that
he should go in peace, take these oranges and always remember the Lord
had said, "I shall place my bow in the skies, which shall be for a sign of
the covenant between me and the earth."

Everything turns dark again except for the headlight beams. The
truck makes *my . . . my . . .* on the slope, and Camilo's hands are
trembling, the gearbox rumbles so that it is difficult to shift into first.
Why didn't he stay home that time? What time? What home? Oh . . .
yes . . . the old man very red with swollen veins, covered with the
garment Jaquín and Semelio had brought him. The old man clutched
the blanket with one hand to hold it closed at his chest and shook the
other threateningly, spouting curses, his words broken by hiccups.
Camilo had gone out into the patio and heard the insults. It had never

been like that before. During the final months there were many drunken bouts but none like that afternoon when Camilo found him naked, flung down on the floor tiles of the room. The old man's face was wretched, a squalid face, the eyes of a dog, the nails of a tapir. The old man had been vomiting and each time he tried to get hold of the bottle, he slipped in the filth, soaking his beard. The beard and the eyes were there in the windshield, obscuring the highway. Eyes, accounts, seeds, the coffee beans of his brother Joaquín, his brother Semelio's receipts, fear, dirty hair and face, the eyes of his sons, eyes of those he thought were his sons, markets, people, the man who attacked him and whom he made run pell-mell with a razor, a shabby valise and the door of the Pension Continental, those three nights in jail and those two lying on a shawl which seemed to be girls; they gave him Cafenol with nothing in it to dope himself with, winds, highways, hungers, encounters, sonsofbitches, bosses who wanted to suck him dry, the yankee who offered him money in the oil field if he would go down on him on the office sofa, the police, the administration, the official with a frogface and a chip on his shoulder who didn't want to give him his papers, the menacing drunks, the dust, the sweat, the fear and trembling which began to moisten the seat of the truck.

Two days and nights of going over and over the same thing, a period of years squeezed into this desperate journey in order never again to see those stamped papers which said "Jacinto Ortíz, Commission Merchant-Consignee." Nor the bookkeeper with his malarial face and his account book where he wanted to account for money as if accounting for his soul. Camilo had to sit on the wooden bench until it suited them to approve his expenses, because they checked him right to the last cent. Now it's the truck from Semelio Ortíz's fleet. This black donkey with double wheels in the rear which, for the first time, was not going to give vent to its metallic braying in the immense entrance to the garage, waiting its turn to be let in. This hoarse animal that was now eating the straightaways and the curves with no specific destination, driven recklessly as he himself had been driven by his crazy career during which he could never organize ideas, sensations, control of his affairs, his desire to snatch at everything and at the same time drop everything, his slow rise and his dizzy fall, his fatal urge to submerge himself completely in memories, papers, curses, the interstices of a life so poverty-stricken that it swallowed up the traffic signs, and highway signals were forgotten. The signals . . . the signal . . . there isn't any, nowhere does the rainbow of which the little man spoke appear; the only rainbow in his future is patches of darkness and legs tired of leaving always very transitory footprints in villages and offices, quick, like someone who is always stepping on the accelerator and the brake fluid or the fluid of the heart which is now used up and then he has to throw himself confusedly against the rocks to survive.

Again the faces crowd in upon him. They come in a troop. They hide the highway, he can scarcely go on. The eyes and the old man's twisted mouth, the oily vomit-covered beard, the eyes and the mouth of Semelio and Joaquín. The eyes and the knife-wound of his son in Puente Villegas, the bellies of La Negra and María Rosario, his father again corraling the animals, and the streaks of lightning suddenly lighting the house and the interior of the truck. Then the hands, the accusing fingers of Semelio and Joaquín, the old man's hand gesturing curses, the man he chased with a razor, the queers in the jail, the voice of the little man again speaking to him about eternity, the shadows, the bulging sacks, the wings of an owl or bat, the dough which begins to cover the machine in front, the water which has lasted for many days and is now beginning to boil in the radiator, the fourteen painted women gathering stones in the middle of the highway to keep him from passing, and he, breathing deeply, and he dries the perspiration because the voice of the little man is heard again, "And it shall come to pass when clouds shall cover the earth, then my rainbow shall be seen in the clouds."

Camilo Ortíz, the third of the Ortízes, suddenly stops the truck. He gets out on the highway and goes to the edge of the gorge. Camilo Ortíz is sweating and he spits because he can't stop. He turns to measure the distance between the edge and the truck. Having made his decision, he returns and with a jump is at the wheel. The gearbox rumbles and the reverse finally goes in with a noise like wood splitting and the truck moves backward, roaring as never before, over twenty-five feet of high-way. Camilo clashes the gears, shifts again furiously, with the wheel aimed at the ravine. Just at the edge Camilo jumps out onto the highway, keeping clear of the darkness as the truck falls into the ravine with its faces, its eyes, its specters, its lettering, its stones, its beards, its heap of shadows on the windshield. A tremendous explosion can be heard on the rocks at the bottom. "Let it rot down there and let the worms eat them . . . let the soul of my brother come and pull it out of the depths."

Camilo waves his hands before his eyes, as if to get rid of the last of the shadows. He raises his face to the sky above, brilliant, cloudless, all the stars pricking it from one end to the other. There is no rainbow, no shadow, no sound. Camilo has no covenant with anyone and he begins to walk over the earth's back.

TRANSLATED BY H. R. HAYS

Uno se despierta con canonazos
en la mañana llena de aviones.
Pareciera que fuera revolución:
pero es el cumpleaños del tirano.

Epitafio Para la Tumba de Adolfo Báez Bone

Te mataron y no nos dijeron dónde enterraron tu cuerpo,
pero desde entonces todo el territorio nacional es tu sepulcro;
o más bien: en cada palmo del territorio nacional en que no está tu
cuerpo, tú resucitaste.

Creyeron que te mataban con una orden de ¡fuego!
Creyeron que te enterraban
y lo que hacían era enterrar una semilla.

Ernesto Cardenal

Waking up to cannon shots
in the morning full of airplanes
it would seem to be the revolution
but it is the tyrant's birthday.

TRANSLATED BY JANET BROF

Epitaph For The Tomb of Adolfo Báez Bone

They killed you and didn't tell us where they buried your body
but since then all our land is your tomb,
or let's say: you came back to life
          in each inch in which your body is not.
They thought they killed you with an order "fire!"
They thought they buried you
and what they did was bury a seed.

TRANSLATED BY JANET BROF

2 A.M. Es la hora del Oficio Nocturno, y la iglesia
en penumbra parece que está llena de demonios.
Esta es la hora de las tinieblas y de las fiestas.
La hora de mis parrandas. Y regresa mi pasado.
"Y mi pecado está siempre delante de mí"

Y mientras recitamos los salmos, mis recuerdos
interfieren el rezo como radios y como roconolas.
Vuelven viejas escenas de cine, pesadillas, horas
solas en hoteles, bailes, viajes, besos, bares.
Y surgen rostros olvidados. Cosas siniestras.
Somoza asesinado sale de su mausoleo. (Con
Sehón, rey de los amorreos, y Og, rey de Basán.)
Las luces del "Copacabana" rielando en el agua negra
del malecón, que mana de las cloacas de Managua.
Conversaciones absurdas de noches de borrachera
que se repiten y se repiten como un disco rayado.
Y los gritos de las ruletas, y las roconolas.
"Y mi pecado está siempre delante de mí"

Es la hora en que brillan las luces de los burdeles
y las cantinas. La casa de Caifás está llena de gente.
Las luces del palacio de Somoza están prendidas.
Es la hora en que se reúnen los Consejos de Guerra
y los técnicos en torturas bajan a las prisiones.
La hora de los policías secretos y de los espías,
cuando los ladrones y los adúlteros rondan las casas
y se ocultan los cadáveres. Un bulto cae al agua.
Es la hora en que los moribundos entran en agonía.
La hora del sudor en el huerto, y de las tentaciones.
Afuera los primeros pájaros cantan tristes,
llamando al sol. Es la hora de las tinieblas.
Y la iglesia está helada, como llena de demonios,
mientras seguimos en la noche recitando los salmos.

2 A.M. It is the hour of the Night Service
and the church in shadows seems filled with demons.
This is the hour of darkness and night life.
My time out on the town. And my past comes back to me.
            "And my sin is before me always."

And while we are reciting psalms, my memories,
like radios and juke boxes, interfere in my prayer.
Bits of old movies, nightmares, lonely hours
in hotels, bars, dances, journeys, kisses come back to me.
And forgotten faces turn up. Sinister things.
Assassinated Somoza steps out of his tomb. (With
Sihon, king of the Amorites, and Og, king of Basan.)
The lights from "Copacabana" shimmer in the black
bay water which flows from the sewers of Managua.
Absurd conversations on drunken nights
which play over and over like a scratchy record.
And the shrieks at the roulette and juke boxes.
            "And my sin is before me always."

It is the hour when the lights shine
in brothels and barrooms. The house of Caifas is jammed
with people. The lights in Somoza's palace are on.
It is the hour when War Trials get under way
and the torture experts go down to the holes.
The hour of secret police and spies
when thieves and adulterers prowl houses
and corpses are hidden. A bulk falls in the water.
It is the hour when the dying go into their last agony.
The hour of the sweat in the Garden, and of the temptations.
Outside the early birds sing sadly
calling to the sun. It is the hour of darkness.
And the church is frozen, as if it were filled with demons.
While we go on reciting our psalms into the night.

TRANSLATED BY JANET BROF

Detras del monasterio, junto al camino,
existe un cementerio de cosas gastadas,
en donde yacen el hierro sarroso, pedazos
de loza, tubos quebrados, alambres retorcidos,
cajetillas de cigarrillo vacías, aserrin
y zinc, plástico envejecido, llantas rotas,
esperando como nosotros la resurrección.

≈§

Ha venido la primavera con su olor a Nicaragua:
un olor a tierra recién llovida, y un olor a calor,
a flores, a raíces desenterradas, y a hojas mojadas
(y he oído el mugido de un ganado lejano . . .)
¿O es el olor del amor? Pero ese amor no es el tuyo.
Y amor a la patria fue el del dictador: el dictador
gordo, con su traje sport y su sombrero tejano,
en el lujoso yate por los paisajes de tus sueños:
él fue el que amó la tierra y la robó y la poseyó.
Y en su tierra amada está ahora el dictador embalsamado
mientras que a ti el Amor te ha llevado al destierro.

Behind the monastery, down by the road
there's a graveyard of used up things,
with rusty iron lying there, pieces
of china, broken piping, twisted wires,
empty cigarette packs, sawdust
and zinc, worn out plastic, ripped tires
waiting, like us, for the resurrection.

TRANSLATED BY HARDIE ST. MARTIN

Spring has come with its smell of Nicaragua:
a smell of newly rained earth and a smell of hot weather,
flowers, upturned roots and wet leaves
(and I have heard an animal lowing off somewhere . . .)
Or is it the smell of love? But that's not your love.
And love of country belonged to the dictator: the fat
dictator, with his sports clothes and ten-gallon hat,
crossing the landscapes of your dreams in his plush yacht:
he it was that loved, stole and possessed the land.
And now the embalmed dictator lies in the earth he loved
but Love has carried you into exile.

TRANSLATED BY HARDIE ST. MARTIN

Me contaron que estabas enamorada de otro
y entonces me fui a mi cuarto
y escribí ese artículo contra el Gobierno
por el que estoy preso.

Los insectos acuáticos de largas patas
patinan sobre el agua como sobre un vidrio.
Y patinan en parejas. Se separan
y se persiguen y se emparejan otra vez.
Y pasan toda su vida bailando en el agua.
Tú has hecho toda la tierra un baile de bodas
y todas las cosas son esposos y esposas.
Y sólo Tú eres el Esposo que se tarda
y sólo yo soy la esposa sola sin esposo.
Los tálamos de los pájaros están verdes
y las parejas de grajos vuelan jugando,
las parejas de grajos negros, jugando
y gritando: ¡A A A A! ¡A A A A!

Someone told me you were in love
with another, another man
and so I went to my room
and wrote that article
against the government
for which they then
put me in jail

TRANSLATED BY QUINCY TROUPE
& SERGIO MONDRAGÓN

Long-legged aquatic insects skate
on the water as if over glass.
They skate in pairs. They separate,
follow each other and pair up another time.
They pass their whole lives dancing in water.
You have made the whole earth a marriage dance
and all things, brides and grooms
and only You—the Bridegroom come late
and only I—the bride, waiting, alone.
The bird beds are green
and crows, in couples, fly by—playing—
the coupling of black crows, playing
and crying, A A A A! A A A A!

TRANSLATED BY PHILIP LAMANTIA

Ricardo Ocampo

The Indian Paulino

Bouncing across the desolate pampa in the midst of a cloud of dust over an almost imaginary road, the truck advanced toward the city. It was early morning and very cold. The wind blowing along the land pushed up a delicate curtain of mist which had stretched over the high plateau during the night. The sun lit the vast scene; the flat lonely landscape broken only by small scattered hills between which plunged the earth-colored ribbon of road. As far as the eye could see, there was not a single tree. From time to time, a kind of blunt yellowish grass clung to the ground. Some leafless branches of shrubs endured the punishment of the icy wind. Further ahead, to the right, becoming faint near the horizon, the lake gleamed like a sheet of blue glass.

Paulino was squeezed between other Indians, not speaking to anyone, trying to maintain his balance. They had picked him up in the morning as he was beginning to work, bent over the wooden plow which an ox was stubbornly dragging, and they had ordered him to get in without giving an explanation. Piled together in the bed of the truck, doubt and fear in their eyes, were others like him. All were trying to stay clear of the tailgate which bent in the curves, threatening to break and spill out the truck's cargo onto the highway. The Indians maintained their balance with nothing solid to hold on to, and with each turn in the road they swayed in a solid mass from side to side, compensating for the steep inclines with their weight.

The small piece of tilled land, the inert frame of the plow, the idle ox, the barren earth of the pampa were left behind with their houses. The

Indians looked at each other, unseeing, silent. Their eyes passed quickly across the crush of hard faces and frightened expressions. No one seemed to know where he was going or who was taking him there. Dust accumulated on their faces, in their noses, dried their mouths and hurt their eyes. Pointed just above their hats and dusty heads were the three rifle barrels. "The land reform," Paulino thought, "will it be again?" The truck rolled along, bumping and creaking, in the direction of the city. His feet and back ached with the effort of keeping his balance and avoiding the tailgate. The armed men in city clothes, wearing ties and shirts of indefinable color, spoke among themselves in a language Paulino did not understand.

Ahead, the road became the entry to the narrow streets of a small village. The length of the poorly cobblestoned streets was lined with uniform houses with dark straw roofs, all of clay, windowless, with only a door in the center. Somber women, clad in multicolored dresses and carrying children on their backs, stealthily crossed the half-deserted village. A man was driving three mules loaded with kindling toward the city. Most of the doors were shut.

The truck entered a square and, with a great squeaking of brakes, stopped at the door of a tavern. The driver and his helper got out first, followed by three armed men. A laconic warning was tossed up from the ground.

"Shit! No one get out!"

With the five men gone, the Indians looked at one another, relieved. Paulino used the moment to question a man passing near the truck.

"Where are they taking us?"

"To the demonstration. They're going to parade. Our leader is going to speak."

"Is it the land reform?"

"No. They say the revolution has failed."

"And when are we going to return?"

"I don't know. They say that the trucks are going to bring you there."

"And what are we going to eat?"

"They say they're going to give you ten thousand bolivianos."

"And where are we going to meet the trucks to bring us back?"

"That they'll tell you after the demonstration."

The mention of ten thousand bolivianos lit a small light in Paulino's heart. The other Indians had followed the conversation and were pleased. The idea of going to the city fascinated them, especially now that they knew it was only a question of the parade for ten thousand bolivianos. The tension disappeared; there was embarrassed laughter amid a murmur of conversation.

The five men appeared in the tavern door and came toward the truck, one behind the other. The three armed men got into the back, giving off the fierce odor of liquor.

Again the trucks went on bumping along the twisting roads. Throat dry and feet aching, Paulino thought about the strange things that had happened in the last years. One day Old Man Bautista had gone away, never to return. A short time after, some men came from the city with banners and notebooks, and they assembled all the Indians to speak to them of things no one understood. They asked for their names and painted their fingers, which they then had them press on the pages of the notebook. At night, the oldest men and those who knew a little Spanish got together, trying to remember what the men from the city had said, but not much could be made clear. Another time, some armed men came to the big house of Old Man Bautista and asked many questions.

"Who is your boss?"

"Young Bautista."

"What Bautista?"

"Young Bautista."

"Did he beat you?"

"Your boss, young Bautista."

"You don't understand. I'm asking you if your boss beat you."

"You don't understand."

"Was your boss a good man?"

"He was good."

"But he beat you."

"He beat you."

"Then he was bad."

"He was bad."

They didn't ask Paulino more. After the men left, he wanted to know what they were after, and he asked Marcos Nina who knew something of Spanish. Marcos told him that the interrogators wanted to know if Old Man Bautista was bad because the revolution had triumphed and the old man was hiding. And he said that the government was going to hand the land over to the farmers, and later they would give them schools, seeds, medicine, tools and money. "It's the land reform," Marcos Nina said. The men came back at various times and the second time Marcos Nina went away with them.

From then on, it was Marcos Nina who gave them explanations, speaking in *aymará*. His appearance had changed. He didn't wear his poncho now and he wore sneakers instead of sandals. In time, he came to wear a tie and dark glasses with white tortoise-shell rims. He became fat and life in the city robbed him of strength of character. The callouses disappeared from his hands and one day Paulino's envy was provoked when he saw a ring with a blue stone on Marcos Nina's finger. With the changes in his body and clothes, his soul had also changed; he had turned bad, as bad as Old Man Bautista. Finally, the men no longer came; only Marcos Nina appeared occasionally, assembled the Indians and again explained the land reform to them. "The land," he said, "ought to be for those who work it. And as the revolution has triumphed, the earth is now for the farmers. Soon we are going to have titles of ownership signed by our leader, who is the President of the Republic. And then we are going to have schools and they will give us money, seeds and farm machines. But the government does not have money now because the crooks took it before the revolution, and we have to help. Those who do not help will not be given their title, nor will they get money, nor will their children go to school."

Paulino always contributed because Marcos Nina was their chief, he was the one who carried the money to La Paz. One day, after explaining the land reform, Marcos had told them he was their chief, and this no one doubted. Thus, when he had no money, Paulino borrowed some or sold a sheep in order to help the land reform, and when Marcos Nina called him to put his painted finger on the notebook, he did not refuse. Schools, roads, money, title, seeds and machines would be denied to those who would not help. Paulino always kept it in mind. Finally, Marcos Nina no longer explained the land reform but just took the money he collected and went away again.

While Paulino was thinking, the truck went on its way. Suddenly, at the turn of a small hill, the silhouette of the city appeared in the distance. Some scattered buildings indicated the airport. Further ahead there were some enormous silvery balls with steps that rose in a spiral. At the entrance to the city, under an arch with large letters, there were other trucks, all loaded with Indians who had come to the demonstration. In each truck there were armed men; in some a flag was fluttering in the wind. Ahead, from the entrance to the city on, the high plateau was divided and opened as if it had been given a great slash. The truck descended interminable curves, crossed through miserable slums, and passed before large factories with their erect chimneys belching smoke. Paulino looked at everything, eyes wide with curiosity. They swung into a wide avenue. Trucks surged out of the side streets loaded with Indians and armed men who, from time to time, fired their guns in the air; it smelled like the fireworks at fiesta. Groups of people, men and women, carried banners rolled around poles, some of them with a gun on their shoulder, all going in the same direction as the trucks. Up ahead, the military band could be heard. At last the truck stopped at the door of a building. It was the Ministry of Farmers' Affairs, that same place where Paulino had gone years before to collect his legal title signed by the leader.

During one of Marcos Nina's visits, Paulino had asked when the titles to the land which had been Old Man Bautista's would be handed over to them, and Marcos said that Paulino had to go to La Paz and ask for himself at the Ministry of Farmers' Affairs. He had sold four sheep to make the trip, and when he got there, he lodged at an inn where he slept on the ground next to a pile of oranges, his face to the stars and his money-belt so tight that he could scarcely breathe. They had not given him his title that time, but they had told him the man who had the papers signed by the President would soon visit Old Man Bautista's land. That had been many years ago.

Since then, Paulino had given money for the land reform, for the revolution, for the school, for the union, for the cooperative and for the road, but things went on the same as always. The man with the documents never appeared on Old Man Bautista's land. There was no school, nor road, nor cooperative, and the union only met when Marcos Nina came to collect money.

In front of the door of the Ministry, the trucks unloaded the Indians, thousands of them. Everyone looked around, trying to appear calm and not as if this were his first time in La Paz. They spoke to each other in *aymará* and the hard dry words, without a trace of melody, blended into a single murmur. Indians sat on the sidewalks or leaned against the Ministry walls chewing coca, passing the leaves from one side of the mouth to the other.

An automobile stopped suddenly and several city men stepped out. They spoke rapidly among themselves and then all of them got into an empty truck. The Indians stopped speaking and turned around to look at them. One of the men began shouting. Paulino watched his gestures, the blunt movements of his arms, the way he used his hands, but he did not understand what he was saying. When he finished his speech, an Indian who very much resembled Marcos Nina got up, and Paulino was happy because now he would know what was going on. But the new speech was also in Spanish. When it ended, the men got down from the truck and left in the automobile. Paulino approached a group circling a tall Indian, whom he asked, "What did he say?"

"He says the revolution has failed."

"Then the land reform has ended?"

"No. That was a revolution of the crooks."

"Then we're not going to parade for the land reform?"

"No. We're going to march for the revolution."

"Have they already given you the ten thousand bolivianos?"

"Not yet. They say after the parade."

"Who's firing guns?"

"The militia. They've come from the mines."

"What for?"

"To march in the demonstration."

"There is also the land reform in the militia?"

"No. They have the nationalization of the mines."

"And have they already given them their documents?"

"Yes, but don't question me more, comrade."

The conversation was interrupted by the arrival of a truck carrying the military band. Paulino went toward a line which was forming and took his place. The time had come to march in the demonstration. Many Indians like Marcos Nina appeared and helped organize the columns, giving loud commands. At last the parade began. Paulino marched mixed in among other Indians whom he had never seen. At one corner, everybody stopped and from a truck they began to lower long pairs of poles joined by a band of white cloth on which there were letters. They gave one of the poles to Paulino, standing on one side of the column, and they gave the other pole to an Indian across the street. Something was written in large red letters on the white cloth. The column again moved forward. Ahead, the military band played a march, but each Indian walked any way he wished; only those who had been in the army marched in step.

The parade lasted a long time. Paulino walked through unfamiliar streets, trying to remember the location of the Ministry where, at the end, he would be given ten thousand bolivianos and a place in a truck so he could go home. In a large square with churches and tall buildings, there were many men on a balcony making signs with raised arms, and many people in front of the building looking at them. The bands were in front of the crowd, deafening the air with their pounding rhythms. The militia passed, firing their rifles and machine-guns in the air, but Paulino wasn't afraid. Everybody went on marching, leaving the square.

The column paraded for several blocks; then, unexpectedly, it broke apart. Some, guided by the noise of the bands, went back to the square where the men on the balcony were; others roamed up the side streets.

Paulino decided to return to the Ministry and wait for the truck. Down the street, many Indians were walking about. He followed after them and when he understood that the parade was still in progress, sought out a place to wait. Sitting on the grass in the shade of a scrawny tree, he took out a handful of leaves which he chewed parsimoniously. In the distance, he could hear the military bands. It was a long while past lunch time.

None of the Indians waiting there were from Old Man Bautista's land, but Paulino didn't feel like talking anyhow. He sat in the shade with his legs stretched out, the sweet juice of the coca calming and lulling his insides. He wasn't worried. Even more people were getting out of the loaded trucks which were passing. People crossed in front of the Ministry without stopping to glance at the Indians waiting for the trucks to take them back—some sitting on the ground, others in the flower gardens, still others standing around in groups or off by themselves. The militia returned from the parade with a tired air, rifles in hand, pointing downward. All the doors were closed, although some stores had not lowered the metal curtains over the glass doors.

Hours passed. A cold wind from the high plateau began to sweep down into the city. Paulino thought of his never-ending problems and tried to understand. Where would Old Man Bautista be now? Why continue land reform if the revolution had failed? Why did the militia from the mines have their documents and not the Indians? Where could the man be, the one who had the documents for Old Man Bautista's land, the documents signed by the President? When would the trucks come to take him back?

He thought of home. He would get back at nightfall, time to eat near the hearth, seated on his bed in the one-room hut where he lived with his wife and children, sheltered from the cold wind. Very early the next morning, he would begin the work interrupted today so that he could attend the demonstration.

One after the other, the Indians were leaving the square in front of the Ministry. Paulino decided he would still wait for the truck. Above his head, the light of a streetlamp suddenly flared and a long red luminous sign shone on the door of a store. Automobiles began to pass with head-lights on, the great beams of light skimming across the pavement like antennae. It was very cold again. He thought of the last time, when he slept at the inn, and then remembered he had no money.

Step by step, retracing the truck's route, he began to walk the road back home. He recognized the tall chimneys, the dirty streets, the doors and signs he had seen on arriving. Music drifted out from some houses with open doors, and light bulbs cast yellowish stains on the street. In-doors, men and women were drinking and dancing. Drunkards passed, bumping into each other, singing and weeping, miraculously keeping their balance. Down below the city glittered.

When Paulino arrived home, it was early morning. His feet were swollen from so much walking. His head and stomach ached with thirst and hunger. His hands and face were blue with cold. All night he had walked with a steady stride down the road which led home, passing through deserted villages with not a light shining and long stretches which, in the dark, seemed sadder and more desolate than ever. He didn't even have a cigarette and he had chewed his last coca leaf waiting for the truck in front of the closed doors of the Ministry. Through the night, more than one truck had passed along going his way. Paulino had not even made a gesture to stop them since he had no money to pay for a ride. Raising clouds of dust, breaking the silence with the noise of their motors and rickety frames, loaded almost to the top with bundles on which other Indians like himself were sitting, the trucks had gone on without stopping.

In the doorway of his house, his wife waited for him with fright-ened eyes. Standing next to her, a boy wrapped in multicolored rags watched him in silence. No one spoke when Paulino crossed the thresh-old and dropped heavily on the bed. Before sinking into sleep, he heard his wife say, "Where did they take you?"

"To La Paz."

"What did you do?"

"I marched. It was the demonstration."
"And did you go to the Ministry?"
"Yes."
"And did they give you the document?"
"Not yet."

TRANSLATED BY HORTENSE CARPENTIER

Testamento Ológrafo

Dejo mi sombra,
una afilada aguja que hiere la calle
y con tristes ojos examina los muros,
las ventanas de reja donde hubo incapaces amores,
el cielo sin cielo de mi ciudad.
Dejo mis dedos espectrales
que recorrieron teclas, vientres, aguas, párpados de miel
y por los que descendió la escritura
como una virgen de alma deshilachada.
Dejo mi ovoide cabeza, mis patas de araña,
mi traje quemado por la ceniza de los presagios,
descolorido por el fuego del libro nocturno.
Dejo mis alas a medio batir, mi máquina
que como un pequeño caballo galopó año tras año
en busca de la fuente del orgullo donde la muerte muere.
Dejo varias libretas agusanadas por la pereza,
unas cuantas díscolas imágenes del mundo
y entre grandes relámpagos algún llanto
que tuve como un poco de sucio polvo en los dientes.

Acepta esto, recógelo en tu falda como unas migas,
da de comer al olvido con tan frágil manjar.

Sebastián Salazar Bondy

Olographic Testament

I bequeath my shadow
a sharpened needle wounding the street
examining, sad-eyed, the walls,
the latticed windows where inept trysts were kept,
the skyless sky of my city.
I bequeath my spectral fingers
which have perused keys, bellies, waters, honied eyelids
& through which writing came down
like a virgin in a threadbare soul.
I bequeath my ovoid head, my spider paws,
my clothing burned by the ash of prophecies,
discolored by the fire of a nocturnal book.
I bequeath my wings half spread, my typewriter
which galloped, year after year, like a little horse
seeking the fountain of pride where death dies.
I bequeath various books, wormholed by sloth,
a few intractable images of the world
and a wailing I carried like a little dirty dust
in my teeth among great lightning.

Accept them, gather them in your skirt like crumbs,
feed this so fragile meal to forgetfulness.

TRANSLATED BY TIM REYNOLDS

Pregunto por la Tierra Perdida

¿Cómo me busco en este recipiente,
en este barro derramado por los cráteres,
en este inmenso puerto donde duermen barcazas sin luz
cercada por la peste y la redondez de la carne,

y cómo me he de hallar en el ocaso despoblado
de la montaña y el mar
si tan sólo escucho un aleteo de plumas negras
y no hay pájaros en el impuro delantal del cielo,

y cómo sabré si ese rumor es la súplica de otro recluso
o mi propio corazón que se desvive,
que se despoja de su sangrienta ropa enamorada
y baraja sus naipes pues quiere ganar la partida,

y cómo entenderé las palabras de la política
y las trajetas de visita de las relaciones públicas,
y las conciencias explayadas en su viscoso domingo,
o el sarcerdocio, la epidemia, el rocío, la conferencia económica,
en síntesis, el mundo abochornado que no me cabe en la frente,

y cómo seré capaz de tomar un mapa escolar y encontrar
en sus minucias el lugar tórrido de la inocencia,
la tierra que perdí bajo los pies antes de irme,

y cómo, al fin, he de aceptar sin ira mi plato de lentejas?

Question for the Lost Land

How did I get here, in this hole,
in this mud slopping through the craters,
in this vast port where lightless barges sleep
surrounded by pestilence & the rotundity of the flesh,

& how will I find myself in the desolate sunset
of sea & mountain
if I am alone hearing the whir of black feathers
& there are no birds on the sky's soiled apron.

& how know if that sound is the moaning of another recluse
or my own disheartened heart
stripping off its amorous bloody cloths
& shuffling its cards, wanting to win the game,

& how should I understand the words of politics
& public-relation visiting cards,
& the consciences extended in their slimy Sunday,
or the ministry, the epidemic, the dew, the economic conference,
in short, the shameful world I can't fit into my head,

& how be able to take a scholarly map & locate
in its minutiae the warm place of innocence,
the country I lost under my feet before I set out,

& how, finally, accept without indignation my plate of lentils?

TRANSLATED BY TIM REYNOLDS

Daniel Moyano

Vaudeville Artists

When he first came to the city, Ismael wanted so many things. He almost wanted even to change his face. In the beginning, finding it somehow hard to believe he was really there, he still thought of himself in terms of the small-town kid who had stared at the train tracks, imagining that at the end of that long road a city of glass lay shimmering under the sun waiting to welcome him. Once arrived, no door would be closed, and to live in the city would mean to live in a world brimming over with possibilities.

The city turned out to hold a limited number of wonders, which, seen a few times, were soon exhausted. This was disappointing, but nonetheless—like a faint hope—Ismael knew he could still be awed should some new wonder appear.

After living in the city a few months, he became vaguely aware that of his former world of feelings only symbols remained. He threw himself into different things, into different kinds of work, and in this compulsion to try his hand at the most unlikely jobs he sensed time passing. To the sadness he was born with, another unexplainable sadness was added. He wanted to be something or at least to amount to something he could show, but he felt he hadn't yet found his way. In a rooming house once, somebody had told him that the one really essential thing in the world was a vocation. The word came as a revelation to him. A vocation was exactly what he had.

At some point, it began to seem to him that in this fabulous city people were only plodding along, indifferent to any wonder or to any attempt at salvation. For in the end only marvels saved one from the risk of a city destiny. It seemed to him that all the good things of this world were really there, it was just that they were not for the city's inhabitants, who were condemned only to look and not to touch. It was a rat race. The good things, the wonderful things, existed for others—for someone like him, for example—who had come from elsewhere to reap them. Nonetheless, for a long time he had noticed that he was no different from the rest and that the arrival of a chosen person, as in his moment he had been, now stood for little. But he had his eyes, at any rate. His capacity for being awed was still intact, and, even if his idols were all to tumble, he was ready to take the great step that would save him.

Several years passed. In rooming house after rooming house, others always imposed their habits on him, and so there were months of soccer matches, Saturday night dances, the racetrack, and other types of attachments. Each new person he met had one or the other of these tastes, and Ismael would adapt himself completely to them, feeling that if he didn't these friends would look down on him.

For a long time, he lived passively, waiting for a glimpse of marvels. He never went out or spoke to anyone. Holidays he slept or spent sprawled on his bed in his rooming house as if waiting for something to happen. An acquaintance of his, who stayed home Sunday afternoons when he was short of money, used to hang over the balcony rail paying compliments to the women on the street. Once in a while, Ismael joined in—but too shy to speak, figuring that women were something he also had to do without. Led on by a thin, moustached room-mate who knew about these things, his contact with girls was strictly limited to housemaids from the better side of town. It was easy to go to those attractive neighborhoods where an hour or two was enough for a fleeting skirmish that gave him the illusion of love.

One night after one such quick affair, the girl told him to take her out somewhere for a little fun. Ismael pleaded that he had no money, but the girl said it didn't matter. What she wanted was to walk, to learn something about him, to hold hands, to justify what they had just done with some simple, everyday fact. They walked for an hour and, at around ten o'clock, they came to an open-air bar in a park. On an improvised stage a vaudeville act was taking place. Leaning against a chain link fence that enclosed the area, Ismael and the girl watched the show—she, having seen it several times already, with little interest; he, all eyes.

The master of ceremonies, a tall thin man dressed in a white suit, ended each of his presentations plugging the merchandise of some store or other. His final word each time was always "terrific." Coats were terrific, refrigerators terrific. He pronounced the word in a strange way, lowering his voice and trying to create mystery. For Ismael, he opened up a world of presentiments, creating the atmosphere essential for the beholding of marvels.

The first to take the stage was a juggler. He worked with plates, glasses, eggs, and other breakables. Ismael was dumbstruck. Two frail, dwarfish men, one with an accordion and the other a set of drums, marked the highpoints with swelling flourishes. Ismael was impressed that nothing got dropped, so much so that he might have accepted a blunder, a smashed plate, without its tarnishing the juggler's reputation in the least. Ismael clapped noisily. Of all those outside the fence, he was the only one to applaud. Next came a gaucho, wearing a blindfold, who danced a *malambo* between several rows of bottles without knocking over a single one. Then a man with four prancing dogs.

Ismael's heart pounded away. Here at last was something really first-rate, something meaningful. Here were the people he would have liked to meet when he first came to the city. Had that only happened, he'd be just like them now—a vaudeville trouper. He had always felt a bit lost in the city, a straggler like everyone else, but now he was discovering something that might possibly save him, something real and true that was linked to the kind of salvation he'd envisioned for himself all along. Deep down, his journey to the city began to justify itself; he could now remain there without his dream being destroyed.

Following the dogs came a team of acrobatic sisters who, after bowing to the audience, came down off the stage to where a trapeze had been set up. For minutes on end, light and airy and brilliant in their scarlet tights, they captured Ismael's elated heart. While the drum kept rolling, they entwined themselves together, then all at once came twirling and spiraling down around a post, looking like some delightful two-headed animal. Even Ismael's indifferent girl friend, who told him her name was Rosa, the same as one of the acrobats, was now all eyes. Their act over, the sisters returned to the stage, bowed quickly and modestly, and disappeared behind the backdrop. Ismael would have liked them to have gone on taking bows, to have said something. He was saddened to see them go off.

At this point his girl friend, who for some time had been insisting that they leave, began tugging at Ismael's clothes. First she begged to be taken somewhere else, then she said she felt ill and that if she got home late she'd be locked out. She pleaded forcefully, almost demanding, although her actual words were little more than whining. The new situation bothered Ismael, but just then the needle man took the stage, announced by the man who used the word "terrific" and whose impeccable white suit, showing not a single wrinkle, appeared to be made of cardboard.

The needle man said he had traveled the whole world over and that he would now perform something he had learned in Tibet that would be brand-new to his audience. He took twenty or so needles and placed them in his mouth. Next, from a spool, he snipped a long strand of thread, placed one end of it in his nostril, and began breathing it in. After a minute or two, the length of thread had disappeared up his nose and then, to Ismael's utter amazement, he drew the thread out of his mouth with all the needles threaded.

Ismael began clapping before the man had even finished, but trying to restrain him, his girl friend told him not to be a fool, for these were nothing more than simple tricks after all. But in Ismael's head ran one idea alone—to become a vaudeville artist. Overlooking the difficulties he would no doubt have to train to overcome, he could think only of becoming a performer all at once. He would have liked telling the girl this, but she nagged and whined to be taken away or else she would have to cross the park by herself in the dark. They were pressed to the fence, she leaning against it, he straightening up only to clap. Then and there the girl suddenly stood erect, told him she was leaving, and said he would be to blame for anything that happened to her. Ismael begged her to stay a minute longer to see the man with the thousand faces, who had just been announced. Her reply was that she was not about to let herself be taken in by such a pack of foolishness. While she went on with her nagging, and pulled and tugged at him, Ismael thought about how hard it would be to become a vaudeville artist, to climb up on a trapeze or thread needles in his mouth. These weren't just tricks, there was no question about it; these things took a lot of skill to perform. To a certain degree, he was worried about what might happen to the girl. Barely aware of it, Ismael had backed away from the fence and was beginning to leave. Thinking now about how hard it was to achieve what he had always set his sights on, he resigned himself to the fact that though he could not be like these vaudeville people at least they existed.

The two of them walked a few steps, she complaining worse than ever, while he turned his head for one last look back at the stage. When they had gone some distance, walking hurriedly, Ismael turned completely around and, between the branches of a tree, he was still able to catch a slight glimpse of the man with a thousand faces.

TRANSLATED BY NORMAN THOMAS DI GIOVANNI

Una mosca anda cabeza abajo por el techo,
un hombre anda cabeza abajo por la calle
y algún dios anda cabeza abajo por la nada.

Tan sólo tú no andas esta tarde,
a menos que las ausencias puras
inventen otra forma de andar que no sabemos:
andar cabeza arriba.

Exploraremos el encuentro del amor y la piedra,
el viaje de la mano a su duelo,
la playa de banderas con que sueña la sangre,
la fiesta de ser hombre cuando el hombre despierta
y se cae en el hombre,
la fábula que se convierte en niño,
la mujer necesaria para amar lo que amamos
y hasta lo que no amamos.

Y exploraremos también el espacio vacío que dejaste en tu poema,
el espacio vacío que dejaste en cada palabra
y hasta en tu propia tumba
para alzar el futuro.

Allí te encontraremos
y juntos echaremos a andar cabeza arriba

(*A Paul Eluard*)

Roberto Juarroz

A fly is walking head downward on the ceiling,
a man is walking head downward in the street,
and some god is walking head downward through nothing.

You're the only one who's not walking this afternoon,
unless pure absences can invent
another form of walking which we don't know:
walking head up.

We will explore the meeting of love and stone,
the voyage of the hand to its pain,
the beach of flags the blood dreams of,
the celebration of being a man when a man wakes
and falls into manhood,
the fable that turns into a child,
the woman who's needed so we can love what we love
and even what we don't love.

And we will explore besides the empty space you left in your poem,
the empty space you left in each word,
and even in your tomb,
to build the future.

There we will meet you
and together we'll break into walking head up.

(*To Paul Eluard*)

TRANSLATED BY W. S. MERWIN

En alguna parte hay un hombre
que transpira pensamiento.
Sobre su piel se dibujan
los contornos húmedos de una piel más fina,
la estela de una navegación sin nave.

Cuando ese hombre piensa luz, ilumina,
cuando piensa muerte, se alisa,
cuando recuerda a alguien, adquiere sus rasgos,
cuando cae en sí mismo, se oscurece como un pozo.

En él se ve el color de los pensamientos nocturnos
y se aprende que ningún pensamiento carece
de su noche y su día.
Y también que hay colores y pensamientos
que no nacen de día ni de noche,
sino tan sólo cuando crece un poco más el olvido.

Ese hombre tiene la porosidad de una tierra más viva
y a veces, cuando sueña, toma aspecto de fuego,
salpicaduras de una llama que se alimenta con llama,
retorcimientos de bosque calcinado.

A ese hombre se le puede ver el amor,
pero eso tan sólo quien lo encuentre y lo ame.
Y también se podría ver en su carne a dios,
pero sólo después de dejar de ver todo el resto.

(*A Octavio Paz*)

Somewhere there's a man
who sweats thought.
On his skin are drawn
the moist contours of a finer skin,
the wake of a navigation without a vessel.

When that man thinks light, he shines,
when he thinks death, he becomes polished,
when he remembers somebody, he acquires their features,
when he falls into himself, he grows dark like a well.

In him the color of night thoughts is visible,
and it's obvious that no thought is without
its night and its day.
And also that there are colors and thoughts
that are not born of day nor of night
but only when oblivion grows a little bigger.

That man is porous, like an earth with more life in it,
and at times when he dreams, he looks like a fire:
splashes of a flame that feeds itself with flame,
writhings of calcined woods.

In that man love can be seen,
but only by someone who meets him and loves him.
And also in his flesh one could see god,
but only when one had stopped seeing all the rest.

(*To Octavio Paz*)

TRANSLATED BY W. S. MERWIN

Llueve sobre el pensamiento.

Y el pensamiento llueve sobre el mundo
como los restos de una diezmada red
cuyas mallas no aciertan a encontrarse.

Llueve adentro del pensamiento.

Y el pensamiento rebalsa y llueve adentro del mundo,
colmando desde el centro todos los recipientes,
hasta los más guardados y sellados.

Llueve bajo el pensamiento.

Y el pensamiento llueve bajo el mundo,
borrando los cimientos de las cosas,
para fundar de nuevo
la habitación del hombre y de la vida.

Llueve sin el pensamiento.

Y el pensamiento
sigue lloviendo aun sin el mundo,
sigue lloviendo sin la lluvia,
sigue lloviendo.

It's raining onto thought.

And thought is raining onto the world
like the remnants of a decimated net
whose cords can't manage to mesh.

It's raining inside thought.

And thought dams up and rains inside the world,
filling all the containers from the middle,
even the best watched and sealed.

It's raining under thought.

And thought's raining under the world,
wiping out the foundations of things
to build anew
the lodging of man and of life.

It's raining without thought.

And thought
goes on raining even without the world,
goes on raining even without the rain,
goes on raining.

TRANSLATED BY W. S. MERWIN

Salvador Elizondo

Bridge of Stone

"You must come to the picnic," he urged her. "It will be the true test of your feelings." She had not wanted to be alone with him there in the country, but she could not refuse. Many times since they had known each other she had told him, "I'd like to be alone with you in a room and see how you are in an intimate setting, just sitting in an easy chair, reading or smoking." For this reason the picnic was a kind of compromise. Alone, but not alone in the clutter of some doubtful apartment, small and motley, with the inevitable posters of Paris and a Picasso exhibition, the reproduction of an abstract painting, the record player, dried-up cigarettes, books nobody reads and cheap furniture. Rather they would share a solitude open to the treetops and the mountainside in the morning. "We'll be together in the midst of nature," he said, to commit her and at the same time reassure her. Nevertheless, both liked being enclosed. They loved movies and cafés and driving around the block in his automobile; then they were always under a roof. At night it was as if the stars made them uneasy; they would stop on some lonely corner and talk for a long while, sitting in the car. Only the midday sun exhilarated them and at noon they liked to meet downtown amid the hubbub of office workers and tourists, isolated in the shade of the trees in the park. Then she would say to him, "How many times I've been here, but it was never like this!" Perhaps she was mistaken, but in that remark was the essence of what he loved most in her. He was frightened by the possibility that their break-up might occur amid the honking of automobiles or in a tawdry bachelor apartment. The picnic struck a neutral note, but one that could be remembered as a perfect setting for that parting scene. She had accepted. He hoped to keep her forever, but she, after saying yes, went home that night and wept as usual, locked in her room while her parents and little brothers watched television. She was like a child or an old lady, tottering between illusion and disillusion, always fearful of losing her emotional balance. But her intuition, which usually troubled her, now assured her that this day in the country would not be of the slightest importance, and so she did not think she had made a mistake in accepting.

He placed all his hopes in that outing. The truth is he hated nature. Above all he hated that unruly countryside where hungry dogs invariably devoured leftovers of a meal and where one always saw those fat women—the same ones you saw on the beaches—wearing shorts, those depressing office workers playing soccer with their boys, and those teenagers strumming the latest tunes on their guitars. In the following days, he made a precise inventory of the different locales and possibilities a day in the country offered. The hot lowlands were not sufficiently serene to be the background for the dialogue he imagined. He thought that perhaps in that heat wine would produce an effect too violent or too oppressive. Yes, they would have to go north, to that mountainous landscape close by, with its cliffs of fir trees and pebbly brooks, with its promise of providing a lingering moment when they could stop to pick up a pine cone and exclaim, "Look, it's full of pine-nuts!" as if those words revealed a great feeling for nature. And that mild soft air always justified a bottle of wine, strong cheese and bread, a primal expression of lyrical feeling in the midst of the quiet broken only by the sound of the running brook.

Would it rain? In the afternoon, maybe. If it rained early, it would be a good opportunity to sequester themselves in the car, listening to the radio, snug under a roof; a good chance to kiss or just be quiet watching the rain slide down the windshield and windows, not saying a word. Everything had to be thought out in advance. It would help to call the Observatory Saturday or consult the afternoon papers to check the weather forecast for the next day. The realization of his dream depended on the perfection of a moment. His decision was governed by a prejudice against brightness, against the overwhelming euphoria of sun and summer. Their relationship had been maintained during rain showers, blizzards that hit against the doors; it had been sheltered from heavy storms and enlivened by races to the car at the first drops of a sudden storm. That was why he had even been careful to load the camera with a supersensitive film for weak sunlight. Saturday afternoon he scrupulously consulted the hourly radio broadcasts: ". . . 12:30 P.M., Italian songs; 1:00 P.M., Chopin Preludes . . . ; 4:00 P.M. *The Girl of the Golden West* . . ." So it went . . .

But in reality, it was an outing like any other. How many times he had seen her as if they were never going to see each other again. Their relationship had been one long farewell which somehow went on and on, their feelings never crystallizing, their intimacy never creating a bond which could affirm a truth only sensed, but never proven. This trip through the countryside, shrewdly conceived and shrewdly accepted, like a foregone conclusion, would define all those formless and awkward feelings. They had imposed on themselves a discipline governed by caution. Their date would take place after several days had passed without seeing each other. "You must think a great deal about us," he had told her. And she had gladly accepted this separation, for in her heart she was uneasy about the closeness already established between them. "Our true relationship will be decided Sunday and then we'll have to face it."

When he saw her coming out, wearing slacks and a flimsy blouse, he felt a momentary disenchantment. "The way women look on the outside seldom has much to do with the feelings they arouse inside us," he thought, not knowing how to respond to the half-affectionate, half-ironic greeting which she gave in a smile from the doorway of a strange house—that of a girlfriend—where they had arranged to meet. He would have preferred a plaid skirt, a tweed jacket, some reddish leather mocassins that hinted at thoughts of a pine forest. The blouse especially suggested the south. At the same time that he was taking inventory of his preferences, he could only say by way of greeting, clumsily, without his usual playfulness, "Good day, Your Highness . . . ," but that familiar phrase sounded so false, he bit his lower lip in reproach. From the beginning, the date was not going well. She got into the car; he had trouble starting it.

"North or south, which would you prefer?" he asked when they arrived at the boulevard where it was necessary to decide their direction.

"North," she answered. "It's closer. Let's go to the Bridge of Stone."

He was pleased her choice coincided with his own, but it seemed to him her answer revealed a desire to complete this sacrifice with a minimum of ceremony, vacillation and enthusiasm.

They scarcely spoke during the first part of the ride. She was uneasy at times, in that absolute animal way women feel before physical danger. "Don't go so fast," she said. A sharp curve, a careless cyclist, a startled dog trying to cross the highway among all the automobiles and crowded buses, made her start involuntarily, a nervousness which lessened only as they approached the country. When the last houses were left behind, a meaningless chattering took possession of her, and she began to expound her favorite subject: the talent she had for solving girlfriends' problems without ever being able to solve her own.

"I don't know . . . I suppose I'm immature," she said, not noticing the first pine trees that could be seen from the highway. "I suppose I'll never grow up . . . I feel there's something basic in life I'm missing, but I do what I can . . . I'm 'blocked,' as they say. Malú, on the other hand . . . I just don't understand it . . . even though Freddy is a darling . . ."

Her conversation was irritating him. He had always believed that nothing could evoke the true wisdom of women more than alcohol or love. "Why don't you talk about other things," he thought, ". . . of us, your feelings toward me, what is happening now, on this ride . . ."

At last they arrived. It was a deserted spot under a cloudy sky. He let her guide him almost there, pretending he didn't know the place, she hadn't noticed that and, taking him by the hand, she offered to show him the beautiful spots she already knew.

"Down there is a brook and a waterfall," she told him.

They descended the slope laboriously, jumping from one rock to another, dodging the pine branches weighed down by the rain which had fallen during the night. When they reached the bottom, the brook and the waterfall had disappeared. A riverbed of pebbles, of round smooth stones, was all that remained.

"The river is dry, poor thing!" she said.

He didn't know how to answer, but in that moment he felt they scarcely knew each other. In that hollow, in the closeness of a memory which was only hers, they had separated until there was a distance between them, like two meaningless scrawls on a blank sheet of paper. Afterwards they climbed up the hill, grasping the fallen branches, and arrived breathless at the car.

"Let's take out the things."

"No, wait. It's early yet."

He wanted to get the most out of every moment.

"It's cold, isn't it?" he asked.

"Yes, it's going to give me rheumatism."

Each time he thought her sickly, he loved her more. In that moment he would have liked to take her hand, caress it, express in some way the pleasure he felt in the compassion she inspired in him. The climb up the cliff had tired them. She opened the car door and sat on the front seat, her feet dangling out, her head resting on her arm on the back of the seat. He looked at her, repeating to himself, not daring to say it aloud, "How beautiful you look that way! How beautiful you look that way . . . !"

Finally, he said, "I've never understood what rheumatism is."

"It's terrifying. I've had it since I was a girl," and then she smiled sadly, adding, "The stone bridge is just ahead."

"We'll eat there if you like . . ." and he opened the rear door to sit a moment, like her. Soon he stretched out his arm to caress the nape of her neck, while she pressed her head firmly against his hand.

"I'm very hungry."

"Wait; let's stay here a little while. I'll take some photos of you."

"I look terrible in these clothes."

"Hand me the light-meter. I'll see if we can take them here, inside the car."

She extended her arm toward the small case and gave him the light-meter. As he took it, he regretted having to break that motionless caress.

"I'm going to take a picture of you like the ones in *Vogue*. Pass me the camera."

He scrutinized her face a long while through the ground glass while she made serious and funny faces. He was enjoying focusing and blurring her image, making it appear from the mist, then obscuring it, and again making it sharp.

"I love you," he said suddenly. She was upset. And in that moment he pressed the shutter.

"That's no good," she said. "It's a trick. I hate you."

But he continued looking at her through the camera lens.

"Let's go eat something, I tell you."

"And I tell you to wait a minute. Another picture."

"No, no more. I look horrible."

"You're very beautiful today."

"It's impossible; I'm dying of hunger."

They walked toward the small stretch of flat plain, to the ruins of the stone bridge. When the car was almost lost to sight, they heard a tiny cry, almost imperceptible in the distance, like a very sharp moan, perfectly defined in miniature. They stopped. He turned to look toward the car, next to which he could distinguish the dim figure of a child. It was the first person they had seen since their arrival. The child made a slow, vague sign to them with his arm raised so that it seemed to point toward the car.

"Keep an eye on it," he shouted to him, signaling in the general direction of the car and making a quick circle in the air with his index finger extended. "We'll be back in a little while!" he added, and they went on walking toward the flat land.

"What solitude!" one of them said when both were seated in the dry pasture near the ruined arches. Everything they said was commonplace.

They decided to eat in silence, in silence made of unimportant phrases.

"Hmmm . . . this wine is good!"

"I should have brought some martinis in a thermos for a cocktail."

"I don't like martinis."

"The truth is I prefer a gibson."

"What's a gibson?"

"It's like a martini, but with a little onion."

"The camembert is perfect . . . and then with this wine . . ."

"It really is good."

"What year is it?"

"Fifty-nine; one of the best."

"Pity there's no dessert."

"There are kisses . . ."

She smiled and he turned on the transistor radio but there was only static.

They had not brought coffee either. After eating, they stretched out side by side and stayed that way for a long while, smoking and watching the clouds pass by slowly massing to make rain. A faint sleepiness was overtaking them but, tenaciously they resisted sleep. They must talk. They had to resolve things, balance the account of this experience. He sat up and, leaning on his elbows, caressed her hair, removing the blades of dry grass; he barely touched her cheeks and forehead with his fingertips, then put his forearm under her head to be her pillow. He took her by the shoulders and pressing her fervently, rested his head on her breast, listening to her breathing. He wished he could hear her pulse. Then he sat up again and looked fixedly into her eyes.

"You're mine, aren't you?"

She did not answer. She closed her eyes smiling, feigning sleep.

"Tell me that you're mine . . ."

In the distance, as if it were coming from a very remote world, they heard the sound of trucks on the highway. She lifted her arm and gently tugged at the hair hanging over her forehead. "Why do you ask me that? Why . . ." she thought, not daring to open her eyes, not daring to meet that look which fell on her with the weight of lead.

"Why do you ask me that?" she said, putting her hand on his shoulders and passing it slowly to his neck, pulling him lightly toward her without succeeding in bringing him close enough to kiss.

"Tell me you love me," he said.

She sat up with her eyes closed, leaning toward him, offering him her lips. They kissed. But no sooner had their lips touched when a scream like a gush of blood, like a loud laugh in a nightmare, separated them. She was pale and her lips trembled in spasm from that explosive scream, a scream like an evil bird flapping in the topmost branches of the pines, losing itself in the mountain slopes. The nails of her rigid hands dug into his arms, her horrified eyes fixed on an invisible, disturbing point close by.

"Look," she said, her voice trembling, hiding her face against his chest, ". . . there . . . behind you . . ."

Still holding her, he turned his head. His embrace froze in a shudder that crossed his face like a whip. He wanted to scream too, but could not.

A few steps away from them stood the child. He was an albino, deformed and demented. His unadorned gaze, tenacious, albino, flowed from the reddened eyelids like pus coming out of a wound, and his tiny skull, covered with grey wool, rose slowly only to fall like lead over his chest covered with rags, with a formless precarious rhythm which made his tongue come out of his toothless half-opened mouth. His smile was an obscene smirk. His rosy idiot's hands were drawing an incomprehensible foul gesture, pointing scalded fingers toward them.

The return was long and silent. It was pouring when they arrived at her girlfriend's house, and she waited in the car a few minutes till it subsided. Then she got out and turned toward him from the gate.

"Good-bye," she murmured, making a slight gesture with her hand. She was still pale, and he would remember her this way always.

"Good-bye . . ." he said as if he were talking to himself, making a movement of his hand behind the blurred glass of the car window.

But both were thinking of something else.

TRANSLATED BY HORTENSE CARPENTIER

DE *La Señal*

De la esperanza

Entreteneos aquí con la esperanza.
El júbilo del día que vendrá
os germina en los ojos como una luz reciente.
Pero ese día que vendrá no ha de venir: es éste.

De la noche

En la amorosa noche me aflijo.
Le pido su secreto, mi secreto,
la interrogo en mi sangre largamente.
Ella no me responde
y hace como mi madre, que me cierra los ojos sin oírme.

De la ilusión

Escribiste en la tabla de mi corazón:
desea.
Y yo anduve días y días
loco y aromado y triste.

De la muerte

Enterradla.
Hay muchos hombres quietos, bajo tierra,
que han de cuidarla.
No la dejéis aquí,
Enterradla.

Jaime Sabines

FROM *The Signal*

On hope

Occupy yourselves here with hope.
The joy of the day that's coming
buds in your eyes like a new light.
But that day that's coming isn't going to come: this is it.

On night

In the amorous night I pine.
I ask it its secret, my secret,
I question my blood in detail.
It doesn't answer
and acts like my mother, who shuts my eyes without hearing
me.

On illusion

On the tablet of my heart you wrote:
desire.
And I walked for days and days
mad and redolent and dejected.

On death

Bury it.
There are many silent men under the earth
who will take care of it.
Don't leave it there.
Bury it.

Del mito

Mi madre me contó que yo lloré en su vientre.
A ella le dijeron: tendrá suerte.

Alguien me habló todos los días de mi vida
al oído, despacio, lentamente.
Me dijo: ¡vive, vive, vive!
Era la muerte.

DE *Diario Semanario*

A medianoche, a punto de terminar agosto, pienso con tristeza en las hojas que caen de los calendarios incesantemente. Me siento el árbol de los calendarios.

Cada día, hijo mío, que se va para siempre, me deja preguntándome: si es huérfano el que pierde un padre, si es viudo el que ha perdido la esposa, ¿cómo se llama el que pierde un hijo?, ¿cómo, el que pierde el tiempo? Y si yo mismo soy el tiempo, ¿cómo he de llamarme, si me pierdo a mí mismo?

El día y la noche, no el lunes ni el martes, ni agosto ni septiembre; el día y la noche son la única medida de nuestra duración. Existir es durar, abrir los ojos y cerrarlos.

A estas horas, todas las noches, para siempre, yo soy el que ha perdido el día. (Aunque sienta que, igual que sube la fruta por las ramas del durazno, está subiendo, en el corazón de estas horas, el amanecer.)

On myth

My mother told me that I cried in her womb.
They said to her: he'll be lucky.

Someone spoke to me all the days of my life,
into my ear, slowly, taking their time.
Said to me: live, live, live!
It was death.

TRANSLATED BY W. S. MERWIN

FROM *Weekly Journal*

At midnight, exactly at the end of August, I think sadly of the leaves falling incessantly from the calendars. I feel that I am the tree of the calendars.

Every day, my child, going away forever, leaves me asking myself, "If someone who loses a parent is an orphan, if someone who loses a wife is a widower, what is the name for someone who loses a child? What do you call someone who loses time? And if I myself am time, what can I call myself, if I lose myself?"

Day and night, not Monday or Tuesday, not August or September, day and night are the only measure of our duration. To exist is to continue—to open your eyes and close them.

At these hours, each night, forever, I am he who has lost the day. (Even though I feel, in the heart of these hours, the dawn, like the fruit in the branches of the peach tree, climbing.)

TRANSLATED BY W. S. MERWIN

Tengo ojos para ver . . .

Tengo ojos para ver en esta noche
algo de lo que soy, tengo el oído oyendo.
Estoy en este cuarto, están mis sueños.

Detrás de cada sombra hay algo mío.
Sentado en cada silla hay uno, obscuro,
y a mis pies, en la cama, me están viendo.
Creo que son como yo, llevan mi nombre,
y salen de las cosas como espejos.

Hace ya mucho tiempo
que no nos congregábamos.
Ahora los aposento
humildemente,
les doy mi cuerpo.

Me reúno en la noche, abro mis ojos,
los mojo de esta obscuridad con sueño.
Solo mi corazón sobre la sábana
queda latiendo.

Desde los cuerpos . . .

Desde los cuerpos azules y negros
que a veces andan por mi alma,
vienen voces y signos que alguien interpreta.
Es tan obscuro como el sol
este deseo. Tan misterioso y grave
como una hormiga llevando a rastras el ala de una mariposa,
o como el sí que decimos cuando las cosas nos preguntan:
"¿quieres vivir?"

I have eyes to see . . .

I have eyes to see in this night
something of what I am, my hearing is hearing.
I am in this room, so are my dreams.

Back of each shadow there's something of mine.
There's one sitting on each chair, dark,
and at my feet, in bed, they're seeing me.
I believe they're like me, they bear my name
and they emerge from things like mirrors.

It's already a long time
since we last assembled.
Now I give them lodging
humbly,
I give them my body.

I come together again at night, I open my eyes,
I wet them with this darkness full of dream.
Only my heart on top of the sheet
still beating.

TRANSLATED BY W. S. MERWIN

From the bodies . . .

From the blue and black bodies
that walk at times through my soul
come voices and signs that someone interprets.
It's dark as the sun
this desire. Mysterious and grave
as an ant dragging away the wing of a butterfly
or as the yes that we say when things ask us
—do you want to live?

TRANSLATED BY W. S. MERWIN

Enrique Lihn

Rice Water

He raced up the first three floors of the building, and the building took him in with a hostile shiver, as it might let in an undesirable tenant, and then, like an agile passenger, finally resigned to missing the train, he counted off the last flight with a slow and uncertain step. It was only eleven-thirty in the morning, a good hour for a Sunday, but not for him, not on this special day.

The door confronted him coldly and unobligingly closed. A number in metal, another carved by hand. All his doubts pounded down upon him. The bell was sure to be out of order. Should he knock, or should he use "his" key to this wrong purpose?

It flung open finally as if he were leading a police raid: breaking and entering. He felt like a private detective, deep into some shameful case, two persons in one, proven efficiency. But the whole of his depravity was greater than the sum of its parts.

"Is that you . . . ?"

In dreams, the identifying of a second person is no guarantee against a third. She will have to be interrogated. And in that reality, when we wake from nightmares. . . .

"I . . ." he held back his words, to gain time.

For a moment it seemed as if they both were in the same situation. Not similar, nor equal: identical. There had been no one in the ante-room. Norma had just run up the other stairs, opening and closing the back door to the apartment with a careful violence. A city, unfolded as if it lay against a mirror, was the vast setting for this symmetrical scene.

"I've been waiting."

Fantasies of assaulting her filled his mind again, as they almost always did.

He gazed deeply at everything, not to see himself. A divided look, from pole to pole.

A conventional order reigned in the room: Norma's order. It rose up, proudly impeccable, in the midst of all the poverty, almost comic, like an exaggerated dignity. In that bed she had guarded her secrets as if she were in the tomb; the water stains on the walls had been a part of the room's decoration, and each of those objects, useless then, troublemakers, was now in its proper place, reduced to natural size. Only her books kept whatever disorder she might leave them in. They were a population apart, in a seditious, lamentable isolation.

As for her, she had re-established herself in all the covetousness of the marriage, pallid at first but filled with a future health. She was a hothouse plant exposed to a sun that illuminated everything, from beginning to end. A meaty plant, compact and resistant. She had poisoned the atmosphere herself, because she couldn't breathe it.

"Attention—," he reproached himself as he worked free of his overcoat with the precise and careful movements of a man caught in a slow motion camera, "you can't go back to an old and rotten story, to rescue the innocent and condemn the guilty. We are adults, not comic strip heroes. This is the only way, for me to come by once a week and let her go out to visit someone, no matter whom. She gets on my nerves if she stays here." And she knew how to do it, too. Anyone could see that.

"I thought you'd prefer to be alone with her, so . . ."

"That's fine. You don't have to explain. Thanks."

A pleasant exchange, but the tone of voice undid the words. An old song with different lyrics.

Norma came back from the kitchenette with some writing in her hand. Another sample of her famous writing.

"Here are the directions."

"I see."

"Can you understand what I've written?"

Already he had understood too well what she had written. Every time she gave up trying to communicate with speech, she would make a declaration in writing, with a logic as absurd as it was unyielding. She was particularly effective in that genre: "I know, I saw everything very clearly last night, where that friend of yours you can't live without . . ." or better: "I was a fool. I thought at least you repected me as another human being. I waited all evening to tell you good-bye."

"How do you like it?"

"A teaspoon. A teaspoon and a half."

Plus which she printed the words and spaced the lines with an unassailable rectitude and put one or two lines, as the case demanded, under the important passages, and her prurient obsession for clarity was a pitiful thing, as if she were a lost child trying to tell an adult where she lived, or a medium in a trance reciting a revelation or an agonized newcomer in some boarding house. As if she were—nobody by-passes that moment, though it's never the same moment for any two people—when a person is thrown spinning back into the womb of his private pit and touches the depths of that inescapable and unnamed solitude. There is no way to break the parched and suffocating silence. We are all lost, side by side in an immense place of small abysses.

The writing had such an exaggerated officiousness about it, that it was easy to read between the lines: a psychological document. But it was something else that got to him now: that ink of a green ingrate, acid, recalcitrant and inexhaustible, which she persisted in using.

"Is it clean?"

The living voice surprised him. Relics don't talk.

"I think so." He looked for some place to fix his gaze. "The penmanship is perfect;" he allowed himself an irony, "you could punish it." He fastened his gaze beyond her.

"You know a baby is terribly delicate."

"Thanks. This isn't the first time I've . . ."

"Please. Just pay attention to it. There are some things that are different. She's six months old now."

"All right. I can read: Rice water. Just go on, and relax."

Norma didn't move. Then she turned away from him with difficulty. They both acted like fish in an aquarium where the water was too heavy to flow.

"There's wine. A bottle in the kitchen. And a little pisco if you want it."

She decided finally to go ahead and offend him. He hardened his look to hide it, peered into her face, as vacant as his, with no particular expression.

They were two blind people, lying in ambush for each other, in a vibrant silence.

"On top of everything else, he drinks," she enjoyed complaining to her increasingly numerous friends.

She had said vino and pisco, stretching out the *i*'s, after a certain fashion of pronunciation.

Afterward she drank rarely, and never alone. She limited herself to the toleration of the vices of others; discreetly pigeon-holing them, reserving the right to condemn later, as if somehow they had not yet been practiced. At least that was the way she acted when she was with him. A trick for the careless clerk who believes he has broken in an ideal helper, in the best of circumstances, when in fact he has given himself over to an experiment in the chambers of his future wife. To know men, one has to know their weaknesses. To break him down for analysis, Norma had left him suspended in a solution of humorous spirits.

In any case, the bottles told him that some family friend had been there often enough. The vacancy had been filled completely. And that was exactly what Norma was telling him now, with that blank look.

"There's wine, a bottle in the kitchen. And a little pisco, if you want it."

For the moment he saw himself standing—he had sat on the edge of the bed—with a hand raised toward that facial eclipse and he heard filthy sounds as if someone were screaming far away, out of time. An oasis. A game of the imagination, violent. Actually everything passed calmly, in a natural crescendo. The silence hummed. That was natural, too. That he should be replaced completely. It was natural. It was the very measure of what was natural. His point of concentration.

Saved.

"Thanks for offering. I'll take it on account."

There had been no betrayal and now there was nothing to betray.

"Good . . ."

This was so absurd that she would probably offer him her hand.

"Good . . ."

". . . I'll be back at eight. . . ."

Almost, almost she had offered it.

"Fine."

After all, there were only a few glasses of wine.

Norma hurried toward the door as if someone had yelled fire or earthquake.

He was sure the child wouldn't recognize him but she might just not know him or simply miss her mother and see nothing in her place but an opaque vacuum, nebulous, concentrating on its turn here, menacing probably, like all indeterminants: the usurper, trying to mimic the real thing. It wasn't necessary for her to call up memories of anyone, or anything; it was more than not necessary; it was dangerous that she might, and it was monstrous of him to wait for a sign of recognition from her; consummately dangerous, that in that tiny head—just large enough to fit in the palm of the hand—there should be a fissure leading to the inside and that it should focus into a point, to bring about the pious and melancholy operation of memory. The sum-totaler of that other world where this end is the ultimate end.

Still he could not resign himself to being a stranger, to seeming like one. Anyway, the child—an absurd idea—would not realize when she awoke that he was here *as a visitor,* even when she saw him for the first time. She would never know—how was she going to know one thing or the other?—what had been one Sunday, as if babies did more than delicately vegetate in a perpetual, unnamed Sunday, a Sunday unremembered and irretrievable. He wanted to cover up, to change his Sunday self, like one of those poor circus artists whose elegance, ragged though it is, will always be superior to what it seems in public, under the lights.

He was, to put it simply, the circus clown.

And his child was one of those imponderable ladies who ironically help out now and then in some grotesque act.

He was perfectly capable of these extremes of sentimentalism. And not only in fantasy. But that wasn't the worst of it. Out of what strange mixture of sentiments had he fashioned this chemically pure paternal love?

He hunted his slippers in the closet, creating a chaos there in his own image and likeness.

In this unimaginable but real setting, he had not been his true self. OK, he was a little drunk. But what was unusual about that?

The chaos spread to the bathroom. The slippers weren't there, either.

He had argued with Norma about the baby. In a moment when he had seemed to himself most logical, she took the point.

And in a moment of even greater confusion he had fought with her —physically. Nothing more than a few light jolts passed in a swinging of arms, but not entirely held back, either. There was the sort of noise a person makes screaming in silence, as if the body were charged with a centrifugal force. But the baby had let loose a flood of tears, more eloquent (relatively) than any scream.

The slippers.

Then he had renounced "his" right.

Until the twelfth year—he recalled—the children of a broken marriage belong legally to the mother—a sarcastic phrase—at least. . . .

And he was only the father of the creature. *Only* the father. But the boundaries fell once and here he was, in someone else's place, the seventh day of creation. He thought of the other man, running furiously ahead of him. He was not even an animal. Something more bestial even than a little scorpion hidden in the mud. The mud itself crawling marvelously, bristling at the fear and the cruelty. Without age, without sex, without condition, without anything.

A depressing sight.

He had not renounced his right in order to make an absurd scene for the faces you catch by surprise when you gaze distractedly into the windows of a neighboring building. Those faces whose feelings will always escape us. His look strayed from the room and searched out another one of unequivocal significance: a woman undressing in front of a mirror.

How they sleep, how finely, how preciously they sleep, the newly born. A blank sleep where just the film of an image begins to form, like the cream in a bucket of milk. Deep, but tuned to the slightest sound, as if sleep were made of light itself. A sleep almost invisible, to be touched from a distance. A folding and an unfolding.

What solitude was his! Absolute, sensate, passive. He seemed to radiate solitude: a sign of sanctity: warning of a terrible disgrace.

He stretched out on the bed beside the cradle, in his coffin. He wore an old bathrobe he shared with his wife, an essential part of the disguise with which she barely managed to trick time. Something smelled like a smouldering cigarette. He had warned Norma repeatedly not to smoke around the child. But that was something left over from other days, a little smoke in the rooms, the dissipation of his old obsessions in an imperceptible flow of dead sunlight in dead air.

Where would she be, she who had never managed to afflict him with jealousy, while he waited here?

For him, nowhere. In whatever place, with no matter whom.

And here too, somehow, at his side. Reduced to her most tender words. He summoned all his strength to remember her; it was not the simple replaying of a few painless, empty and lustrous images.

They ran into each other at first by accident. Later, casually. Finally, deliberately. But always, a little proudly, by accident. The truth is that mistrust was the one constant quality of the union. Too free. A struggle to break it now and then. A war of nerves.

They had married to prolong the battle on more solid ground, where the blows could be felt more deeply. To keep her to himself.

When he was so poor, of course, that he couldn't have bought the dirt to cover his coffin. And the intercession of her family who arrived at that inhospitable land was never any help. A mission to a savage island.

She moved her bed to the other side of the room and set them at different angles. She was able to keep her silence for a whole week together.

He began returning late to their rooms in that damned boarding house and knocking the lamp over with such force he didn't know himself. To break the silence. Or for any reason.

At dawn, an exchange of words in a blue-black air, air like damp clay, and insults from those that only heard him passing down some doubtful street.

It had been a game at first, to fight body to body from midafternoon until three in the morning, while a possessed rooster crowed, someplace too close by. But the game had begun to take on an absurd, ridiculous seriousness, like a nightmare you wake from screaming.

And all the other things.

All reduced to simple images, precisely separated once but hanging together like the pieces of a new puzzle, then falling apart into a jumble no one was meant to solve.

Symbolically yawning, he crushed his cigarette out on the floor. He had been sleepy for months; it had taken root in his body like a sickness.

So why not sleep, now that he was at peace? Some skirmishes, nothing more, and they even liberated him a little here and there. Any battle fought now was between enemies so decimated they no longer recognized themselves.

The child was hunting him with her eyes.

He felt a quick weight pass the mouth of his stomach. A strangeness in his breathing. An alarm.

The small basket creaked again, full of life, and miniature hands moved along the edges, grasping, until with an incredible force there rose into view the head and almost a shoulder of his daughter, looking at him with a slow and intelligent look.

Standing, the giant covered the crib now, leaning over it, his arms spread to the wall. The bathrobe seemed like the ragged wings of an old guardian angel that had come to a poor end. He tried to smile naturally, as if he had always been there, in that place. He was happy in a dull way, as if he had indeed committed unpardonable errors in the fulfilling of his task and should be called, nevertheless, to take charge here, undeservedly clean of all guilt.

Apparently the child had recognized him now. There was not the least gesture of strangeness or rejection. She emitted an informative sort of talking song. Then she set out on a metaphorical flight, folding and unfolding her arms.

They are like glad birds at that age—he had heard someone say it—happy as long as everything is on schedule. But they are pitiful when they are hungry, and when the wetness gnaws at them, or when they are hot or cold or when a fly with warped instincts sits cruelly in the same spot on the skin or when they hear the cry of another baby in the next room. All these small accidents brought to bear against that enormous happiness, against a joy as light and fragile as thistledown.

And the big accidents, unforeseeable always, no matter what kind they are.

What right did she have to be so helpless?

She became repentantly serious.

Both of them were serious, absorbed in one another in very different ways, but with that same amazement we show at any wordless reflex.

On the seventh day of creation.

In the prehistory of thought.

On the eve of the invention of language.

Against all logic, he reproached himself. Probably she had no idea who he was and would have greeted any other good-willed giant in the same way.

She had taken possession of one of his hands, pulling it away from the rest of his body, and seemed to want to examine the internal mechanism of her edible toy.

Establish with her a "unique, essential, unsubstitutible" relationship.

He bent the finger the baby had managed to get into its mouth, so she could chew the knuckle. Hygiene. You never stop washing your hands when you're the father of a family.

He would guard the memory of that bite. One never knows what level of insensibility one can come to when one has a monster inside.

The child looked at him out of the corner of her eye, with malice. Where did that intelligence come from? (Norma and he had been a pair of fools while they were waiting for her.) He thought up a question: Are you hurting? An answer: I believe so, most of the time. A request: Can I keep on doing it? A threat: I will, anyway. And a condescending doubt, mocking: But perhaps, if you're sure you can't resist it . . .

He was increasingly doting as he approached his thirtieth year. He, who had never wanted a child himself. Probably it was simply the problem of new friendships. But that emptiness in the room when he got home late was worse than nothing.

With the child in his arms he walked a circle of miles. He had a sense of going nowhere, running from who knows what. Of exploring a new and untilled planet. Where he walked, familiar objects rolled across the floor. Things that had lost their usefulness and begun to live lives of their own, as pointless as his was. His travelling companion insisted on stopping now and then to take charge of some accident-scene along the roadside. There was nothing to put into its mouth. Fruits that were only stains in the wallpaper, photographs that reminded neither of them of anything.

He came to a halt so that she could quiet his rider. A delicate operation when one has hooves in place of hands and a sickly fear of breezes.

He was not embarrassed to talk out loud to her; they had come together to a strange planet.

But when he was preparing her bottle—the instructions didn't seem so precise now, it was all so hazy in his mind—it came on him suddenly. A horrible weariness. A slip-up. He came down to reality, a forced landing with no sense of destination.

A teaspoon. A teaspoon and a half.

Lemon. Where had he left it last time?

Meanwhile, his wife. . . .

And it was a Sunday afternoon. For him too, who was never disposed to—less than anyone—to . . .

Worthless, indispensible objects, hiding among the dirty dishes. Milk was splattered everywhere, as if some one carrying it had passed by, again and again.

She had said wine and pisco, stretching the *i*'s insidiously.

Well, no matter. Wine for him. To toast his uncountable errors. To bring his old fantasies to life.

Don't let her look like either one of us. He was still able to frame one clear desire.

Let her look like her father, slyly, in one sense only. To have his irreducible astonishment before all things, a grand quality, even if he couldn't control it. That dark feeling of exultant impotence toward all knowledge that does not have its roots in the heart, at the mercy of all his contradictions, dark and exultant.

Rice water, two hundred grams.

The hard ground of reality. The constant danger of the abyss of our own unique certitude, found spinningly, as in dreams. It exposes us to reality, that species of weakness one discovers when logic is put to the test, pushed to its final consequences. Terra Firma.

He swayed into consciousness, lightly.

He would die, in any case, before his time.

Children must bury their parents and take up their own lives.

All in all, the child would gain nothing by looking like either one of them.

Only that something of his should pass to her. He was still capable of framing a clear desire.

What to call it?

The bare buzzing of an unlocalized and uncertain impulse, by which he would break open that murmuring Sunday silence, somehow prejudicial to him, not in its right place either, as he was turned by grace and works from his uncountable errors into a poor man who relieved his wife, a male babysitter, while she . . .

He had broken a plate; it seemed to scream at him: "Stupid!"

The baby began to cry from hunger. Understandably.

Fatherhood.

A good subject for a justly forgotten painter. He posed for the painter across a distance of a century, the baby on his lap, as he gave it the inexhaustible bottle. The child's eyes were an inexpressive blue, mated to a milky breath. It didn't see him at all. It was lost in the pleasure of suction. Only the flaring and wincing of the nostrils eternalized the avid and secret activity.

What solitude this was. The solitude of an old toy in the attic. He seemed to radiate it. A mark of uselessness, the sign of absurdity.

Thanks to the bottle of wine it was five-thirty in the afternoon.

His inventions failed, one after another. He was distracted by them and the child searched for some way to entertain itself. The boredom with worn-out tricks: making the sound of a sleigh-bell, drawing things in the air, standing on his head. She wanted to throw breakable things to the floor or suck on metal objects or tear up important papers. She seemed irritated with him, when he interfered with her fancies, and she managed to get her hands on his face and pull his nose, his lips, purposefully, as if she meant to take them off. She was not going to stop fondling him. She would build her relationship to the world by little clouts, full of feeling. She was irritated. Maybe she was sleepy. He didn't care.

He put her down gently. She slipped slowly into sleep and he turned quietly from the crib, as an inopportune visitor is turned tactfully away. Why not devise some unforgettable diversion for her, something that would call up all the genius he was capable of?

Absurd, absurd.

He drank deeply now, immoderately, desperately.

Night came heavily, the dark crept in, pillaging, trying to make everything disappear before he was forced to turn on the light. It did not occur to him to move, paralyzed by the temptation to become part of the darkness, helping it to erase him.

What was the thought that kept trying to take shape, to have something done? He re-read her writing until he grew tired, and each time he did it seemed less purposeful, less intelligible. One of those poems of his, born dead, in which all the words were laboriously strung into a spider's thread, pulled out finally to be shown in all its miserable excess. No sign of life, nothing at all but a way to pass the time, exercises, events, something to feed his vanity and help him overcome his obsessions.

But how could he resolve all this when his time was nearly up? He would not be back for days, and those days were years.

All because of Norma.

Right. Right. There had been innocence and guilt too in that old putrid story, a comic strip. And he was *innocent, he had to be.* She had him at a disadvantage.

Her stupid jealousies, her demands, the pretension that she was always right. That nobility of feeling she wore so proudly, in a rancorous silence, to wear him down. Her "feminism," as if man and woman were occasionally one and then the other, and fought with the same arms, battled over the same chunk of ground, hand to hand. Her face. Everything became a part of the game when the rules were suspended. Even the things around them took part.

He passed the room like an animal in a cage. It was unfair. It had to be. His hands flew in all directions.

As if he had started out to run in the darkness, he stumbled violently into the bed and sprawled across it, breathless. He tore the covers loose, piling them up as if he wanted to give his enemy a body. He beat it senseless with his fists, throwing its remains in the air. He stomped it on the floor, silently. But he had disturbed the child and she was moving in the cradle. A loose monster floating in the air. He could not approach her now. He kneeled softly on the floor, holding his breath. Until finally he heard again nothing but the voices in his conscience, the laughter of the strangers that had managed to get inside of him, by some wrong door, to taunt him. And far off, that kind of consolation one believes he hears, when he wants no more than a little peace, no matter at what price.

He cried.

And why shouldn't he?

The game was over.

TRANSLATED BY MILLER WILLIAMS

Cementerio de Punta Arenas

Ni aun la muerte pudo igualar a estos hombres
que dan su nombre en lápidas distintas
o lo gritan al viento del sol que se los borra:
otro poco de polvo para una nueva ráfaga.
Reina aquí, junto al mar que iguala al mármol,
entre esta doble fila de obsequiosos cipreses
la paz, pero una paz que lucha por trizarse,
romper en mil pedazos los pergaminos fúnebres
para asomar la cara de una antigua soberbia
y reírse del polvo.
Por construirse estaba esta ciudad cuando alzaron
sus hijos primogénitos otra ciudad desierta
y uno a uno ocuparon, a fondo, su lugar
como si aún pudieran disputárselo.
Cada uno en lo suyo para siempre, esperando,
tendidos los manteles, a sus hijos y nietos.

Graveyard at Punta Arenas

Not even death could turn these men to equals
who give their names on separate tablets of stone
or scream them into the wind that erases them:
a little more dust for a new gust of air.
Here rules, together with the sea that levels the marble
between this double row of obsequious cypresses
peace, but a peace that strains to shatter itself,
to break into a thousand pieces the dark diploma
to show the face of an old arrogance
and laugh at the dust.
This city was being built
when its first-born sons built another deserted city
and one by one, they took their places deeply
as if there were those who might not let them stay.
Each one within his own forever, waiting,
the table spread, for his sons and grandsons.

TRANSLATED BY MILLER WILLIAMS

Gallo

Este gallo que viene de tan lejos en su canto,
iluminado por el primero de los rayos del sol;
este rey se plasma en mi ventana con su corona viva, odiosamente,
no pregunta ni responde, grita en la Sala del Banquete
como si no existieran sus invitados, las gárgolas
y estuviera más solo que su grito.

Grita de piedra, de antigüedad, de nada,
lucha contra mi sueño pero ignora que lucha;
sus esposas no cuentan para él ni el maíz que en la tarde lo hará besar el
polvo.
Se limita a aullar como un hereje en la hoguera de sus plumas.
Y es el cuerno gigante
que sopla la negrura al caer al infierno.

Rooster

This rooster, come from some far place singing,
brightened by the first rays of the sun,
this king that molds himself at my window
with a living crown
hatefully
neither asks nor answers
screams in the Banquet Room
as if his guests the gargoyles did not exist
and he were more alone than his cry is.

He cries of stone, of antiquity, of nothing,
fights my sleep, ignoring what he fights.
His wives count for nothing, nor the corn
that in the evening he will kiss the dust for.
He howls like a heretic in the bonfire of his feathers.
His a gigantic horn blowing the darkness to hell.

TRANSLATED BY MILLER WILLIAMS

José Lezama Lima

FROM *Paradiso* (A NOVEL)

"Your interest in knowing the circumstances of Foción's life," Fronesis said, smiling, "makes me think he should have spoken to you of mine since these sorts of familiar acquaintances are generally verified by pairs; you should learn something of Foción's life through me after having learned something of mine through him. And thus the Aristotelean analogy functions in social intercourse.

"Well then, the story of Foción's life is sufficiently interesting to fill a morning—all the mornings in the world, for that matter, since it is the history both of a reality and a surreality. Our friend Foción's father, Nicolas Foción, had a brother, Juliano, two or three years younger. They lived on Industria near the corner of Neptuno. One side of the house faced a busy street, crowded from early morning on; the other side faced a neighborhood of really remarkable silence. I mention these details only because of their relevance to the following events. On the side which faced these remarkably silent streets there lived a girl who had moved there shortly before, and both brothers became much aware of her. She was finishing high school and in the afternoons, after classes, she would attend to her toilette with all the care characteristic of her seventeen years. The brothers were attracted by the tranquility of her skin texture, the tiny flowers that appeared to float in her chestnut hair, hair sensitive to every change of light. Nicolas and Juliano watched her, and her image sank deeper into their eyes every day. They never discussed the matter between them. Neither ever said a word of the girl in the window across the street, of her flowers, of the noble serenity of her skin.

"The brothers were utterly opposed as types, but always tending toward closeness, tending toward brotherhood. Nicolas was the sort to whom it would never occur to speak to the girl with flowers in her hair until one day, without thinking of it, he would go to her and say what was to be said. Juliano was the sort who, face to face with the girl with flowers in her hair, would dream of saying what was to be said, day after day, and never say a word of it—not even caught with her under an awning one rainy day. And so Nicolas finishes his medical preparation, working since he was a child, and marries the girl with flowers in her hair, while Juliano finished nothing he undertakes, can't find a job, and the hair and the flowers become the substance of an anguish that howls at midnight.

"Celita, despite the flowers that so transfigured her, was the product of her specific home environment, as the deterministic statisticians put it. Her father, decisively worn out at fifty, half lawyer and half journalist, was excessive only in the three packages of hacking smoke he devoured daily. Her mother was typical Cienfuegos, come to La Habana to fill a teaching post. They viewed the wedding with the fledgling doctor as the rise of the morning star. Celita's father came late that night; he'd been at the home of another journalist, a friend, so that he could be the first columnist to announce it. The three pencils in the Cienfuegan teacher's vase danced an antic hay over the tapestry of that jubilant morning.

"After the Pauline ceremonies, everything was arranged in the usual way. In the living room, the bookcase full of comfortable wisdom, the four easy chairs, the classic sofa for romantic vulgarities, the mirror disquieting in its inability to capture any living reflection. In the first room, Celita and Nicolas—shutting windows and doors when their passion overcame their need for ventilation, opening doors and windows at midnight, when their need for ventilation overcame their extinguished passion. In the second room, the journalist and the Cienfuegan teacher, locating their breakfast orange preserve along the line of their horizon. And then the servants' quarters—the only poetic precinct of the house, curiously, when, at midnight, the shower would drizzle for almost a quarter of an hour without anyone's having turned it on. And then the kitchen, where occasionally a small mouse carried its tiny flame in its tail. And then we arrive at a more interesting region, a room on the roof, and in that room the bed of the Eternal Dreamer, Juliano—still seeing, after years, those moist flowers (more clearly than wasted opportunities on rainy days) in Celita's hair.

"Nicolas spent more time away, studying or on consultation in special cases; his clientele increased constantly, foaming. Juliano, on the contrary, increased only his beery disgust. When the foam of his beer reached a level equalling his brother's foaming clientele, he exchanged it for a cheap somnolence, with illustrations to the accompaniment of a Moorish harp, of laudanum. Lights burning within paper houses, pagodas with trembling peaks would cross the roof before he fell asleep, softer than the breeze. After such a rest he would peer out down the staircase, Celita's skirt would sway to the wave of the bells of San Pedro, he would see her extend her hand to turn the dial, begin to hear a firmly founded lecture by the President of the Academy of Science of Connecticut concerning abnormalities of the pituitary gland. That wave would go on ringing in his head until it drove him to dive back into his bed again. The creak of springs was the final echo of the enormous dignity of that metallic sound.

"The doctor's medical outings became constantly more frequent. Juliano, wrapped in the coral mass of his somnolence, no longer moved from his rest to the staircase; but Celita, irritated by these scientific absences, began to ascend, trembling, that sleepy spiral. Her trembling was due only to the calming presence of the journalist and the nervous absence of the Cienfuegan teacher.

"The hecatomb was provoked by the coincidence of the teacher's search for a hatband, a serious case of typhus in Mayabeque Valley for the doctor, and certain signatures for a petition, to the journalist's delight. It was four-thirty in the afternoon when Celita woke from her siesta, four baby fawns at the four pillars of her bed. The house, in its solitary rectitude, was sweating ornaments of imitation marble. The lock of the street door, newly polished, let a bit of light pass unfiltered—a light meant to smear the senses, cracking them, making mouths of them.

"When the doctor arrived at Mayabeque, the time for consultation as well as extreme unction had passed; it was time for whispering among the spectators. After attending the first moments of the sorrowing family's eloquence, he handed out sleeping pills to the children and claxoned back toward La Habana. On his arrival, the house breathed a pure and uninhabited ambience. Unluckily, this absence was less a sensation than a pendulum, a glass of water right at the edge of the table; it was an absence something like matter's first contradictions, the silence of a body disentangling itself from another, the drop that indicates huge underground waterways. He waited, in the living room, for the arrival of the others. A breeze moved about; the doorbell, immutable in its bland sluggishness (nothing) courted information. The hours passed. Only the sudden start of the bell did not occur.

"The boredom of waiting brought him to think of the staircase which led to his brother's room. But at the end of that labyrinth he was to meet a blow that would destroy his life as a reasoning creature. I am stressing what must be stressed; at the end of the labyrinth he met Nicolas, the bull that did not kill him, but carried away his sanity on its horns. The bull, this time, did not bury his horns in the man's groin, as though seeking out and shrouding the secrets of his seed—it triumphed, rather, in carrying off on its horns the trophy of his reason, that which kept its horns from piercing the equilibrium of the constellations.

"To go back a bit. This same boredom had previously goaded Celita into attempting the labyrinth and staircase that led to Juliano's high room. That afternoon he had increased his dosage of laudanum, on his bed, surrounding his nakedness with dreams, as though he were lying sleeping beside a river, exhibiting a body diseased by the timidity of his adolescence, infinitely amorous of this exchange of an external world for a vegetable one, his eyelids a lock secured by laudanum, providing him his rejection of any sumpter in the interior of an egg painted by Bosch, the slow voluptuousness of a Cranach figure asleep near a fountain.

"Silently Celita commenced her divestiture. She avoided even the most subterranean noises. She felt that even the sliding of silk over her body might touch the sleeping root of Juliano, wake him with an intractable start, letting all that cascade fall over her neck. The scales were still; she put her hand on the headboard to avoid any indiscretion in the room through new proportioning of its mutations, through her arrival in the ambit of this aroused sleep. Touching the scale, she seemed, waking Juliano, to be asking him not to wake. Naked, Celita was seeking the naked dream of one who had never dared to praise the scarlet flowers of her hair. She began to surround the sleeper. He awoke with his body between her hands. The two donors, the two salivas, the two moist essentials annihilated themselves in their complimentaries. Juliano was swallowed in her sleepy profundities, and opening his eyes he found Celita, smiling, with a pleasurable and a little demoniacal malice, who slid her lips over his with liquid movements, seeming to extricate themselves from a sedge and advance, guarded, over moist ferns. And Juliano, having ascended from dream to the configuration to the ship which sailed with scarlet flowers in the hair, and had to die. The seaweed of his dream allowed that bird to escape for a moment; and then it faded away above the river slime, vanishing. Celita, at the center of her tree, felt the weight of imposing distances, agglomerations of ants, shadowy distributions of mongol emigrations, the howling voices of morning tide rose one colossal wave that rolled over the moans and all the bits of the splintered moon. And Celita was closing her eyes in sleep; moments later, Juliano opened his in death. Both had been incorporated into some eternal felicity. Celita had ascended, via ecstasy, to dreams. Juliano had descended, having seen that face, to the chilly grottos of Proserpina.

"Perhaps a third figure, that of madness, was still lacking in that tragic composition. The doctor correctly interpreted his brother's pallor. Celita woke to see her husband Nicolas at her side, brother's pulse in his hands, shaking his head, confronting the occurrence with an incomprehensible scientific seriousness. He turned to her and, almost with his ordinary voice, said: 'Eudoxia (it was the name of his nurse) this patient has died during consultation, his heart failed; speak to the patients who are waiting, tell them I'm feeling indisposed, and then we'll notify his relatives.' He had lost his mind.

"Following Juliano's death, Celita had to carry out her role as the nurse Eudoxia perfectly. The insanity of the doctor was this: each morning he would begin to receive a nonexistent clientele. Shut up in his consultation room at ten, he would address Celita, now always as Eudoxia, the nurse, saying to her: 'Show in the first patient.' He began his consultations: 'You seem better,' 'Blood pressure seems to be normalizing,' 'Keep taking the pills,' 'Above all no salt in your diet,' 'Come back at the end of the week.'

"He would shake hands with nothing and say goodbye with the smiling ceremony of a doctor. And would then say to Celita/Eudoxia: 'Show in the next patient.' He had ten such consultations in the morning and ten more in the afternoon. There was no one in the waiting room. He gave these consultations to patients to whom only his madness gave body. Twenty nonexistent persons per day filed through, he spoke with the air, gave prescriptions to the wastebasket, become human. Celita/Eudoxia had to comply precisely with the minutiae of this madness. At seven or eight at night, depending on the length of the day's consultations, he recovered his reason. At that time Eudoxia became Celita again.

"The other doctors had warned Celita that she had to be most cautious in following the alternations of the mad doctor. One error, the penetration of any light into that wandering mind, could bring on a terrible attack, with an axe, or the interrogation with a scalpel of that rosy flesh. Celita would arrange the waiting patients on the sofa and on chairs; as they entered the consulting room, these figures created by her lunatic husband, she would guide them. She listened as he advised his patients, whatever mass of air stood before him, and as the last syllables were being spoken, she would prepare for the entrance of the next nonexistent patient. As soon as his professional duties were finished, he would turn to the pseudo-Eudoxia and say: 'Let's get out for a breath of air, Celita. Why don't we eat out tonight; I'd rather like an onion soup.' Having finished his duties, he would recover his sanity. All this time he was living on a decorous pension granted him, in view of his unfortunate disorder, by the Medical College. And so it went for twenty years, consultations with creatures of his lunatic imagination, changing Celita into the nurse Eudoxia from ten in the morning to eight in the evening, changing nurse into wife the rest of the time, substituting for the starched cap those flowers in Celita's moist hair.

"After twenty years of this consultation with shadows, he reached the age of retirement. At this time, no longer having to give consultations, his lunacy and his sanity became indistinguishable. He would play chess, he supervised Foción's education with extreme acuity, he gave himself over to the literature of the Alexandrine gnostics.

"When Celita became pregnant, she couldn't be sure which of the two brothers was father. Foción grew up seeing the unreal, the nonexistent, shut up, many hours each day, in his room. The nurse's cap and the flowers in the hair served him as sort of clock, advising him of alienation and return, silence and speech, reason scrupulously placed at the service of lunacy and lunacy working with such accuracy, with such parsimonious precision, as though having arrived at that plenitude of reason achieved by the Greeks."

TRANSLATED BY TIM REYNOLDS

Sonata para Pasar Esos Días y Piano

A Lisandro Otero

Que realmente fue tremendo,
Entre bombas que casi seguro que llegaban
Y cohetes que finalmente se fueron,
Y que si sí y que si no.
El kennedi hasta habló de cenizas en los labios,
Y los pedantes dijeron: Eliot, Eliot.
Pero la mayoría no dijo casi nada
(O se limitó a decir a los amigos: "Fue bueno haberte conocido"):
Se puso el uniforme de miliciano,
Y a ver qué es lo que había que hacer.
Cada mañana, cuando se abría los ojos,
Venían y le decían a uno: anoche pasamos un peligro tremendo,
Estuvimos a punto de termonuclearnos todos en el planeta.
Uno se sentía contento de haber amanecido.
El día empezaba a estirarse lenta, lentamente.
Cada hora, cada minuto eran preciosos,
Y en cada hora pasaba un montón de cosas.
Entre las seis y las ocho llegaban los periódicos, el café con leche y las
                    primeras llamadas.
A las ocho era despedirse a lo mejor para siempre.
A la tercera o cuarta vez de hacerlo, la imagen de Héctor y Andrómaca
                    se había debilitado mucho.
Entre las ocho ye las diez, rodeados de gente que llegaba, llamadas,
                    saludos, mensajes,

Roberto Fernández Retamar

Sonata for Surviving Those Days & Piano

To Lisandro Otero

It was really scarey
what with bombs coming practically for certain
& rockets that finally left
& yes one minute no the next.
El kennedi as much as spoke with ashes on his lips,
& the pedants said: Eliot, Eliot.
But most of us hardly said anything
(said, at most, to friends: "Nice to have known you.")
You put on your uniform
& went to look for something needing to be done
Every morning when you opened your eyes
They'd come to tell you: Last night we just about had it.
They were on the edge of thermonuclearing everybody on the planet.
You felt you were lucky to wake up at all.
The day stretched out, slowly, slowly,
Every hour of it, every minute, precious,
& so many things happening every hour.
Between six & eight the papers came, cafe con leche, the phone started
           ringing.
At eight you said goodbye to the world, maybe permanently.
The third or fourth time around, the Hector-&-Andromache bit was
           becoming tattered
Between eight & ten flocks of people arriving, calls, greetings, messages.

Las noticias más frescas empezaban a desbordar las redacciones:
Se conversaba, no se conversaba, si se conversara.
Conversación, sinversación, verconsación.
A la hora de almuerzo, se había delantado muy poco y se comía sin
        apetito.
Después había una reunión, otra reunión, la misma reunión.
Alguien llegaba con nuevas noticias: cartas cruzadas, palabras cruzadas,
        dedos cruzados.
Los que entraban y salían iban oscureciendo el día
Hasta que era de noche nuevamente.
El periódico de la tarde por una vez tenía noticias distintas a las de la
        mañana.
A la hora de acostarse (aunque fuera sobre una dura mesa de palo)
Parecía que, en fin, según, sin, so, sobre, tras.
Con esa esperanza copiosa se dormía,
Aunque sabíamos que a la mañana iban a decirnos
Que por la noche habíamos corrido un peligro mortal.
Era necesario dormir ese peligro, como el viajero del avión
Que se entera, al llegar a tierra,
Que durmió la noche sobre el Pacífico con un solo motor en el aparato,
Y recuerda que se había olvidado de asustarse.
A las setentidós horas, ya se conocía el ritmo:
Peligro mortal—amanecer—pesimismo—poco almuerzo—posibilidad
        —dormir—
Peligro mortal—etc.
Entonces vino lo que vino y lo que se fue
Y vino que,
Entonces,

—El piano, por favor.

Stop-press items were overflowing the print-shops.
Talked, no didn't talk, yes talked
Conversation, nonversation, bombservation.
By lunch it had slowed down, a little, you ate without appetite.
& then a meeting, another meeting, the same meeting.
Somebody came with fresh news: letters crossing, crosswords, crossed
                      fingers.
They came & they went, darkening the day,
Until it was evening once again.
For once the evening paper's news was different from the morning's.
At bedtime (even with bed a hard wood table)
It looked like, all things considered, depending on, unless, beneath, over,
                      behind.
& with this ample consolation you slept,
Even knowing that in the morning they'd come to tell you
How last night we'd just about had it.
You had to sleep this danger like an air passenger
Learning, as he disembarks,
How he'd slept all night over the Pacific with one engine shot,
Remembering he'd forgotten to be afraid.
By seventytwo o'clock you'd settled into the rhythm:
About had it—morning—bad prospects—light lunch—possibility—
                      sleep—
About had it—etc.
& then what came came & what left left
& so it came to pass
& then

—A little piano, maestro, please.

TRANSLATED BY TIM REYNOLDS

Los Feos

La mano o el ojo inmortal
Que hizo el cielo estrellado, esta bahía,
Este restorán, esta mesa
(Y hasta hizo el tigre de Blake),
También la hizo a ella, y la hizo fea.
Algo en los ojos, en la nariz,
En la boca un poco demasiado pequeña,
O en la frente interrumpida antes de tiempo
Por cabellos de color confuso;
Algo insalvable para siempre,
Que resiste al creyón de labios y al polvo,
Hace que esta noche, junto a la bahía,
En el restorán El Templete,
Esta noche de suave brisa marina
Y vino tinto y amistad,
Ella esté sola en una mesa,
Mirando quizás en el plato de sopa
La imagen movediza de su cara,
De su cara de fea, que hace vacilar
El orden de todo el universo,
Hasta que llega un hombre feo
Y se sienta a su mesa.

The Uglies

The immortal hand or eye
that framed this starhung sky, this bay,
this café, this table
(& framed the burning Tyger) framed
her too; & framed her ugly.
Something about the eyes, the nose,
the a little too pinched mouth,
the forehead chopped off too low
by hair of indeterminate color—
something eternally unsalvageable
no lipstick or powder can reconstruct
so arranges it that tonight, by this bay,
in the El Templete café,
on a night of easy ocean breezes,
red wine, amigos,
she is alone at her table,
watching maybe in her plate of soup
the shifting reflection of her face,
her ugly face, unhinging
the entire order of this & any universe
until he comes, the
ugly man, &
sits at her table.

TRANSLATED BY TIM REYNOLDS

Usted Tenía Razón, Tallet: Somos Hombres de Transición

Entre los blancos a quienes, cuando son casi polares, se les ve circular la sangre por los ojos, debajo del pelo pajizo,

Y los negros nocturnos, azules a veces, escogidos y purificado a través de pruebas horribles, de modo que sólo los mejores sobrevivieron y son la única raza realmente superior del planeta;

Entre los que sobresaltaba la bomba que primero había hecho parpadear a la lámpara y remataba en un joven colgando del poste de la esquina,

Y los que aprenden a vivir con el canto *marchando vamos hacia un ideal,* y deletrean Camilo (quizás más joven que nosotros) como nosotros Ignacio Agramonte (tan viejo ya como los egipcios cuando fuimos a las primeras aulas);

Entre los que tuvieron que esperar, sudándoles las manos, por un trabajo, por cualquier trabajo,

Y los que pueden escoger y rechazar trabajos sin humillarse, sin mentir, sin callar, y hay trabajos que nadie quiere hacerlos ya por dinero, y tienen que ir (tenemos que ir) los trabajadores voluntarios para que el país siga viviendo;

Entre las salpicadas flojeras, las negaciones de San Pedro, de casi todos los días en casi todas la calles,

Y el heroísmo de quienes han esparcido sus nombres por escuelas, granjas, comités de defensa, fábricas, etc.

Entre una clase a la que no pertenecimos, porque no podíamos ir a sus colegios ni llegamos a creer en sus dioses,

Ni mandamos en sus oficinas ni vivimos en sus casas ni bailamos en sus salones ni nos bañamos en sus playas ni hicimos juntos el amor ni nos saludamos,

Y otra clase en la cual pedimos un lugar, pero no tenemos del todo sus memorias ni tenemos del todo las mismas humillaciones,

Y que señala con sus manos encallecidas, hinchadas, para siempre deformes,

You Were Right, Tallet:
We Are Transitional People

Between the whites (the near-polar ones) whose blood you can see
  circulating through the eye, under the straw-colored hair
& the nocturnal blacks, blue at times, selected & purified by unspeakable
  trials, only the best surviving, making them the only truly superior
  race on this planet;
Between those frightened by the bomb which first made the lampflame
  leap and finished with a young man hanging from the post at the
  corner,
& those who learn to live with the song "Marching Towards an Ideal,"
  & spell out Camilo (younger, perhaps, than we) as we did Ignacio
  Agramonte (old already as the Egyptians when we were in first
  grade);
Between those who had to wait, palms sweaty, for work, any work, &
  those who can choose & reject work without humiliation, without
  lies, without keeping their mouths shut, & there are jobs no one
  wants to do for money & voluntary workers have to do them (*we*
  have to do them) for the continued life of the country;
Between the spattered weaknesses, the St. Peter denials common every
  day in practically every street,
& the heroism of those who have shed their names on schools, farms,
  defense committees, factories, etc.
Between a class we don't belong to, since we couldn't go to their schools
  or believe in their gods
Or administrate in their offices or live in their houses or dance in their
  ballrooms or swim on their beaches or make love to them or say
  good morning to them,
& that other class where we seek a place, though we do not wholly share
  the same memories, or the same humiliations,
& who make signs with their hard swollen hands, deformed forever,

A nuestras manos que alisó el papel o trastearon los números;
Entre el atormentado descubrimiento del placer,
La gloria eléctrica de los cuerpos y la pena, el temor de hacerlo mal, de
 ir a hacerlo mal,
Y la plenitud de la belleza y la gracia, la posesión hermosa de una mujer
 por un hombre, de una muchacha por un muchacho,
Escogidos uno a la otra como frutas, como verdades en la luz;
Entre el insomnio masticado por el reloj de la pared,
La mano que no puede firmar el acta de examen o llevarse la maldita
 cuchara de sopa a la boca,
El miedo al miedo, las lágrimas de la rabia sorda e impotente,
Y el júbilo del que recibe en el cuerpo la fatiga trabajadora del día y el
 reposo justiciero de la noche,
Del que levanta sin pensarlo herramientas y armas, y también un cuerpo
 querido que tiembla de ilusión;
Entre creer un montón de cosas, de la tierra, del cielo y del infierno,
Y no creer absolutamente nada, ni siquiera que el incrédulo exista de
 veras;
Entre la certidumbre de que todo es una gran trampa, una broma des-
 comunal, y qué demonios estamos haciendo aquí, y qué es aquí,
Y la esperanza de que las cosas pueden ser diferentes, deben ser difer-
 entes, serán diferentes;
Entre lo que no queremos ser más, y hubiéramos preferido no ser, y lo
 que todavía querríamos ser,
Y lo que queremos, lo que esperamos llegar a ser un día, si tenemos
 tiempo y corazón y entrañas;
Entre algún guapo de barrio, Roenervio por ejemplo, que podía más que
 uno, qué coño,
Y José Martí, que exaltaba y avergonzaba, brillando como una estrella;
Entre el pasado en el que, evidentemente, no habíamos estado, y por
 eso era pasado,
Y el porvenir en el que tampoco íbamos a estar, y por eso era porvenir,
Aunque nosotros fuéramos el pasado y el porvenir, que sin nosotros no
 existirían.

To our hands, which slid papers around or manipulated figures;
Between the tormented invention of pleasure,
The electrical glory of the bodies & the shame, the fear of messing it up,
    of being sure to mess it up,
& the fullness of beauty & grace, the lovely possession of a woman by a
    man, of a girl by a boy,
Chosen, each by each, like fruit, like truths in the light;
Between the insomniac masticated by the clock on the wall,
The hand that can't sign the examination paper or raise the damn
    spoonful of soup to the mouth,
The fear of fear, the tears of heavy impotent fury,
& the exultation of a man filling his body with the fatigue of a day's
    work & the earned rest of a night,
Of a man easily handling tools & weapons, as well as a loved body
    trembling with anticipation,
Between believing in a mass of things, earth-things, sky-things, hell-
    things,
& believing absolutely nothing, not even that the doubter truly exists;
Between the certainty that it's all a great trap, a monstrous joke, &
    what in God's name are we doing here, & what *is* here,
& the hope that things can be different, must be different, will be
    different;
Between what we don't want to be any more, would have preferred not
    to be, & what we still want to be,
& what we want, what we hope to succeed in being some day, if we have
    the time & the heart & the guts;
Between some neighborhood hotshot, Toughnuts for example, who
    could whip your ass, what the shit,
& José Martí, who exalted & shamed you, burning like a star;
Between the past in which, clearly, we hadn't been, which is why it
    was past,
& the future, in which we are also not going to be, which is why it was
    future,
Although we were the past & the future, without us they wouldn't be.

Y, desde luego, no queremos (y bien sabemos que no recibiremos) piedad ni perdón ni conmiseración,
Quizás ni siquiera comprensión, de los hombres mejores que vendrán luego, que deben venir luego: la historia no es para eso,
Sino para vivirla cada quien del todo, sin resquicios si es posible
(Con amor sí, porque es probable que sea lo único verdadero.)
Y los muertos estarán muertos, con sus ropas, sus libros, sus conversaciones, sus sueños, sus dolores, sus suspiros, sus grandezas, sus pequeñeces.
Y porque también nosotros hemos sido la historia, y también hemos construido alegría, hermosura y verdad, y hemos asistido a la luz, y alguna vez a lo mejor hemos sido la luz, como hoy formamos parte del presente.
Y porque después de todo, compañeros, quién sabe
Si sólo los muertos no son hombres de transición.

&, of course, we don't want (& know we won't get) pity or pardon or
    compassion,
Maybe not even understanding, from those better men who will come
    later, who must come later: that's not what history's for,
But to be lived fully by each, if possible without gaps
(& always with love, probably the only truth.)
& the dead will be dead, with their clothes, their books, their conversa-
    tions, their dreams, their sorrows, their signs, their grandeurs, their
    pettinesses.
& because we have also been history, & have also built happiness, beauty
    & truth, & have served the light, & sometimes perhaps have been
    the light, as today we form part of the present.
& because after all, compañeros, who knows,
maybe only the dead are not transitional people.

TRANSLATED BY TIM REYNOLDS

Julio Cortázar

Silvia

How in the world can anyone know how something could have ended that didn't even have a start, that began in the middle and stopped without any precise shape, growing hazy and disappearing into the edge of another cloud; in any case, we have to start by saying that a lot of Argentinians spend the summer in the valleys of Luberon; we veterans of the region frequently hear their deep voices that seem to bring more open spaces with them, and along with the parents come the children and that's Silvia too, trampled crusts of bread, lunches with pieces of beef on forks and cheeks, terrible wails followed by reconciliations of a markedly Italian cut, what people call a family vacation. They don't bother me too much because I'm protected by my well-deserved fame of being rude; the filter only opens up enough to let Raúl and Nora Mayer pass through, and, of course, their friends Javier and Magda, which includes the children and Silvia, the barbecue at Raúl's a couple of weeks ago, something that didn't even have a start and still is Silvia most of all, this absence that now inhabits my bachelor house, brushing my pillow with her gold medusa, making me write what I'm writing with the absurd hope of a spell, of a soft golem of words. In any case, we also have to include Jean Borel, who teaches the literature of our countries in a university in western France, his wife Liliane, and tiny Renaud, in whom two years of life have piled up all in a tumult. So many people for a small barbecue in the garden of Raúl and Nora's house under a broad linden tree that did not seem to be of much use as a sedative during the moments when there were children's fights and literary arguments. I arrived with a few bottles of wine and a sun that was withdrawing behind the hills; Raúl and Nora had invited me because Jean Borel had been wanting to meet me and didn't feel like doing it on his own; during that time Javier and Magda were also staying at the house, the garden was a battlefield, half Sioux, half Gallo-Roman, feathered warriors battled without quarter with soprano voices and balls of mud, Graciela and Lolita allied against Alvaro, in the midst of the uproar poor Renaud staggering along with his gaucho breeches full of maternal cotton and a tendency to spend all his time going back and forth from one side to the other, an innocent and cursed traitor whom only Silvia looked after. I know that I'm piling up names, but the order and genealogies were also a little slow in coming to me; I remember getting out of the car with the bottles under my arm and a few feet away among the bushes I saw Winning Buffalo's feathered headdress appear, his suspicious frown as he confronted a new Paleface; the battle for the fort and the hostages was taking place around a small green tent that was evidently the headquarters of Winning Buffalo. Guiltily neglecting an offensive that could have been decisive, Graciela dropped her sticky ammunition and finished wiping her hands on my neck; then she sat down indelibly on my lap and explained to me that Raúl and Nora were up above with the other big people and that they'd be right along, details that had no importance next to the fierce battle in the garden.

Graciela always felt the need to explain things to me, working under the principle that she considered me stupid. For example, that afternoon the Borels' child wasn't of any importance, don't you realize that Renaud is two years old, he still makes caca in his diapers, it happened a while back and I was going to tell his mommy because Renaud was crying, but Silvia took him over to the faucet, washed his behind, and changed his clothes, Liliane didn't find out about anything, because you know, she gets very annoyed and gives him a whack on that part, then Renaud begins to cry again, he bothers us all the time and won't let us play.

"What about the other two, the older ones?"

"They're Javier and Magda's kids, don't you know that, silly? Alvaro is Winning Buffalo, he's seven years old, two months older than me, and he's the oldest. Lolita's six, but she knows how to play games already, she's Winning Buffalo's prisoner. I'm the Queen of the Forest and Lolita's my friend, so I have to rescue her, but we'll do it again tomorrow because now they're calling us to take our baths. Alvaro got a cut on his foot, Silvia put a bandage on it. Let me up, I have to go now."

No one was holding her, but Graciela always tends to assert her freedom. I got up to greet the Borels, who were coming down from the house with Raúl and Nora. Someone, Javier, I think, was pouring the first *pastis;* the conversation began with nightfall, the battle changed its nature and age, became a smiling study of men who had just been introduced; the children were bathing, there were no more Gauls or Sioux in the garden. Borel wanted to know why I didn't go back to my country, Raúl and Javier smiled compatriot smiles. The three women busied themselves about the table; curiously, they looked alike, Nora and Magda united by their Buenos Aires accents, while Liliane's Spanish fell from the other side of the Pyrenées. We called them over so they could drink some *pastis,* I discovered that Liliane was darker than Nora and Magda but the resemblance was there underneath, a kind of common rhythm. Now the topic of conversation was concrete poetry, the group of the magazine *Invenção;* common ground was rising up for Borel and me, Eric Dolphy; the second drink lighted up the smiles between Javier and Magda, the other two couples were already living in the time in which group conversation loosed antagonisms, aired the differences that intimacy keeps quiet. It was almost nighttime when the children began to appear, clean and bored, first Javier's, arguing over some coins, Alvaro obstinate and Lolita petulant, then Graciela, leading Renaud by the hand, his face dirty again. They gathered together near the small green tent; we were discussing Jean-Pierre Faye and Philippe Sollers; the night invented the fire of the grill, until then barely visible among the trees, and it became daubed with golden and changing reflections that tinted the trunks of the trees and extended the limits of the garden; I think that at that moment I saw Silvia for the first time, I was sitting between Borel and Raúl, and at the round table underneath the linden tree were Javier, Magda, and Liliane in that order; Nora was coming and going with plates and silverware. That they should not have introduced me to Silvia seemed strange, but she was so young and perhaps wanted to stay on the fringes that I understood the silence of Raúl and Nora; evidently Silvia was at the difficult age, not wishing to enter the game of the adults, she preferred to impose her authority or prestige on the children grouped around the green tent. I had only managed to get a glimpse of Silvia, the fire was violently lighting up one of the sides of the tent and she was there, squatting down beside Renaud, cleaning his face with a handkerchief or piece of cloth; I saw her tanned thighs, thighs that were vague and well-defined at the same time, like the style of Francis Ponge, about whom Borel was speaking to me, her calves were in the shadows, the same as her torso and face, but her long hair suddenly glowed with the fluttering of the flames, hair also of old gold; all of Silvia seemed to have the tone of fire, of thick bronze; her miniskirt revealed her thighs to the very top, and Francis Ponge had been undeservedly ignored by young French poets until now, with the experiments of the *Tel Quel* group, he was recognized as a master; it was impossible to ask who Silvia was, why she wasn't with us, and besides, fire is tricky, perhaps her body was ahead of her age and the Sioux were still part of her natural territory. Raúl was interested in Jean Tardieu's poetry, and we had to explain to Javier who he was and what he wrote; when Nora brought me the third *pastis* I was unable to ask her about Silvia, the discussion was too lively and Borel was drinking in my words as if they were worth all that. I saw them bring out a small, low table near the tent, preparations so that the children would dine separately; Silvia was no longer there, but the shadows were half-erasing the tent and perhaps she had sat down farther off or was strolling through the trees. Obliged to air opinions concerning the attainments of Jacques Roubaud's experiments, all I could manage was surprise at my interest in Silvia, in the fact that Silvia's sudden disappearance made me feel ambiguously restless; when I finished telling Raúl what I thought of Roubaud, the fire was fleetingly Silvia once more, I saw her pass by the tent leading Lolita and Alvaro by the hand; behind came Graciela and Renaud, jumping and dancing in one last avatar of the Sioux; Renaud fell on his face, of course, and his first howl aroused

Liliane and Borel. Graciela's voice rose up out of the group: "It's all right, it's all over now!" and his parents went back to their conversation with the kind of ease that comes from the everyday monotony of blows from a Sioux tomahawk; now it was a matter of finding meaning in Xenakis's aleatory experiments in which Javier showed an interest that seemed extreme to Borel. Between Magda's and Nora's shoulders in the distance I saw Silvia's silhouette, squatting beside Renaud once more, showing him some toy and trying to console him; the fire laid her legs and profile bare, I could imagine a thin and anxious nose, the lips of an ancient statue (but hadn't Borel just asked me something about a statue from the Cyclades which called for a response from me, and hadn't Javier's reference to Xenakis turned the discussion towards something more worthwhile?), I felt that if there was something I wanted to know at that moment it was Silvia, know her close at hand and without the enhancement of the fire returning her to the probable mediocrity of a timid girl or confirming the fact that the silhouette there was too beautiful and alive to be nothing but a spectacle; I felt like talking about it to Nora, with whom I had an old confidence, but Nora was setting the table and laying out paper napkins and telling Raúl that he had to buy a Xenakis record right away. Out of the realm of Silvia, invisible once more, came Graciela, the small gazelle, the know-it-all, I offered her the old place to hang her smile, hands that helped her settle on my lap; I took advantage of her excited news about a hairy beetle to slip out of the conversation without Borel's thinking me discourteous, as I asked her in a low voice if Renaud had hurt himself.

"Of course not, silly, it wasn't anything. He's always falling down, he's only two years old, you know. Silvia put some water on the bump."

"Who is Silvia, Graciela?"

She looked at me with surprise.

"A friend of ours."

"Is she the daughter of any of these people?"

"You're crazy," Graciela said in a reasonable way. "Silvia's a friend of ours. Isn't that right, Mama, Silvia's a friend of ours."

Nora sighed, placing the last napkin beside my plate.

"Why don't you go back with the children and stop bothering Fernando? If she starts telling you about Silvia, God knows how long you'll have her there."

"Why, Nora?"

"Because ever since they invented her they've got us all confused with their Silvia," Javier said.

"We didn't invent her," Graciela said, grasping my face with her hands to turn me towards the adults. "Ask Lolita and Alvaro, you'll see."

"But who is Silvia?" I repeated.

Nora was already too far away to hear and Borel was talking with Javier and Raúl again. Graciela's eyes were fixed on mine, her mouth pouting, half-mocking and half-wise.

"I already told you, silly, she's a friend of ours. She plays with us when she feels like it, but not Indians, she doesn't like that. She's too big, you see, and that's why she takes such good care of Renaud, he's only two years old and he makes caca in his pants."

"Did she come with Mr. Borel?" I asked in a low voice. "Or with Javier and Magda?"

"She didn't come with anybody," Graciela said. "Ask Lolita and Alvaro, you'll see. Don't ask Renaud, because he's too little and he doesn't understand. Let me go, I have to go now."

Raúl, who always seems to have some kind of radar working for him, pulled himself away from a comment on *léttrisme* and made a sign of pity for me.

"Nora warned you, if you follow their train you'll go mad with their Silvia."

"It was Álvaro," Magda said. "My son's a mythomaniac and he infects everybody."

Raúl and Magda kept on looking at me, there was a fraction of a second when I could have said: "I don't understand," in order to force an explanation, or, more directly: "But Silvia's there, I just saw her." I don't believe, now that I've had more than enough time to think about it, that Borel's absent-minded intervention stopped me from saying it. Borel had just asked me something about *The Green House;* I began to talk without knowing what I was saying, but in any case, I wasn't speaking to Raúl and Magda anymore. I saw Liliane go over to the children's table and make them sit down on stools or old boxes; the fire illuminated them and made them look like the prints in novels by Hector Malot or Dickens; the branches of the linden tree crossed for moments with a face or a raised arm in between, laughter and protests could be heard. I was talking about Fushía with Borel, letting myself be carried downstream on that raft of my memory where Fushía was so terribly alive. When Nora brought me a plate of meat I whispered in her ear: "I don't understand too well what the children are up to."

"There you go, you fell for it too," Nora said, looking at the others with a pitying expression. "It's just as well that they're going to bed right after they eat, because you're a natural-born victim, Fernando."

"Don't pay any attention to them," Raúl put in. "It's easy to see that you haven't had any practice, you take what kids say too seriously. You should listen to them the way you listen to the rain, old man, or else you'll go out of your head."

Perhaps it was at that moment that I lost any possible access to Silvia's world, I'll never know why I accepted the easy hypothesis of a joke, that my friends were spoofing me (not Borel, Borel was still going down his road and was getting close to Macondo); again I saw Silvia, who had just appeared out of the shadows and was leaning over between Graciela and Alvaro as if to help them cut their meat or perhaps to eat a mouthful; the shadow of Liliane, who came to sit with us, was interposed, someone offered me some wine; when I looked again, Silvia's profile seemed to be lighted up by the embers, her hair fell over one shoulder, slipping down and blending with the shadow of her waist. She was so beautiful that I was offended by the joke, the bad taste, and I began to eat with my face over my plate, listening out of one ear to Borel, who was inviting me to take part in some university round-tables; if I told him that I couldn't make it, the fault was Silvia's, because of her involuntary complicity in my friends' needling fun. That night I didn't see Silvia again; when Nora went over to the children's table with fruit and cheese, she and Lolita were busy making Renaud eat as he was falling asleep. We began to talk about Onetti and Felisberto, we drank so much wine in their honor that a second warlike wind of Sioux and Charrúa Indians enveloped the linden tree; they brought over the children to say good-night, Renaud in Liliane's arms.

"I got an apple with a worm in it," Graciela told me with enormous satisfaction. "Good night, Fernando, you're awful mean."

"Why, sweety?"

"Because you didn't once come over to our table."

"That's true and I apologize, but you had Silvia, didn't you?"

"Of course, but just the same."

"He's keeping it up," Raúl said, looking at me with something that must have been pity. "It's going to be hard on you. Wait'll they catch you with their famous Silvia when they're wide awake, and then you'll be sorry, fellow."

Graciela wet my chin with a kiss that smelled strongly of yogurt and apple. Much later, after a conversation in which sleep had begun to take the place of opinions, I invited them to dinner at my place. They came last Saturday around seven o'clock in two cars; Álvaro and Lolita brought a cloth kite and with the excuse of flying it, immediately put an end to my chrysanthemums. I let the women take care of the drinks, I knew that nothing could stop Raúl from taking charge of the grill; I showed the Borels and Magda the house, made them comfortable in the living-room across from my oil painting by Julio Silva, and drank with them a while, pretending to be there and listening to what they were saying; through the large window one could see the kite in the wind and hear Lolita and Álvaro shouting. When Graciela appeared with a bouquet of pansies, put together presumably at the expense of my best flower bed, I went out into the darkening garden and helped them get the kite even higher. The shadows were bathing the hills on the other side of the valley and coming forward through the cherry and poplar groves, but there was no Silvia. Álvaro had not needed Silvia to fly the kite.

"It sways nicely," I told him, trying it, making it go back and forth.

"Yes, but watch out, sometimes it nosedives and those poplars are tall," Álvaro warned me.

"It never falls for me," Lolita said, jealous of my presence perhaps. "You pull the string too hard, you don't know how to do it."

"He knows more about it than you do," Álvaro said in a quick show of male solidarity. "Why don't you go play with Graciela, can't you see you're in the way here?"

We were alone, feeding string to the kite. I waited for the moment when Álvaro would accept me, know that I was as capable as he to guide the green and red flight that was becoming dimmer and dimmer in the half-light.

"Why didn't you bring Silvia?" I asked, pulling on the string a little.

He looked at me out of the corner of his eye, half-surprised, half-mocking, and took the string from my hands, subtly degrading me.

"Silvia comes when she feels like it," he said, pulling in the string.

"Well, then she didn't come today."

"What do you know about it. She comes when she feels like it, I tell you."

"Oh. And why does your mother say that you invented Silvia?"

"Look how it spins," Álvaro said. "Boy, that's what I call a kite, the best there is."

"Why don't you answer me, Álvaro?"

"Mama thinks I invented her," Álvaro said. "And you, why don't you think so?"

Suddenly I saw Graciela and Lolita beside me. They had heard the last words and were there staring at me; Graciela was slowly twirling a purple pansy between her fingers.

"Because I'm not like them," I said. "I saw her, you know."

Lolita and Álvaro exchanged a long look, and Graciela came over to me and put the pansy in my hand. The kite string gave a sudden tug. Álvaro let it out and we saw it disappear into the shadows.

"They don't believe because they're silly," Graciela said. "Show me where the bathroom is and come with me while I pee."

I took her to the outside stairs, showed her the bathroom and asked her if she could find her way down. At the bathroom door, with an expression in which there was a recognition, Graciela smiled at me.

"No, you don't have to come any farther. Silvia will stay with me."

"Oh, good," I said, fighting against the devil knows what, the absurdity, the nightmare, or the mental retardation. "So she finally came."

"But of course, silly," Graciela said. "Can't you see her there?"

The door to my bedroom was open, Silvia's naked legs were outlined on the red bedspread. Graciela went into the bathroom and I heard the bolt close. I went over to the bedroom, I saw Silvia sleeping on my bed, her head like a gold medusa on the pillow. I closed the door behind me, approached in some way, there are hollows and whiplashes at this point, a water running across the face that blinds and bites, a sound like one coming from noisy depths, an instant without time, unbearably beautiful. I don't know whether Silvia was naked or not, for me she was like a poplar tree made of bronze and dream, I think I saw her naked even though afterwards I didn't, I must have imagined her under what she was wearing, the line of her calves and thighs was outlined on one side against the red spread, I followed the soft curve of her rump, abandoned in the advance of a leg, the shadow of her sunken waist, the small breasts, imperious and golden. "Silvia," I thought, incapable of any words, "Silvia, Silvia, but then . . ." Graciela's voice exploded through the two doors as if she were shouting in my ear: "Silvia, come get me!" Silvia opened her eyes, sat up on the edge of the bed; she was wearing the same miniskirt as on the first night, a low-cut blouse, black sandals. She passed by without looking at me and opened the door. When I went out, Graciela was running down the stairs and Liliane, carrying Renaud in her arms, passed her on the way to the bathroom and the mercurochrome for the seven-thirty bump. I helped her cure and console him, Borel came up, worried about his son's howls, reproached me smilingly for my absence, we went back down to the living-room to have another drink, everybody was on Graham Sutherland's paintings, phantoms like that, theories and enthusiasms that got lost in the air along with the tobacco smoke. Magda and Nora were concentrating strategically on the children so that they would eat separately; Borel gave me his address, insisting that I send him the piece I promised for a magazine in Poitiers, he told me that they were leaving the next morning and that they were taking Javier and Magda along to show them the region. "Silvia will be going with them," I thought darkly, and I looked for a box of shiny fruit, a pretext for going over to the children's table, to stay there for a moment. It was not easy to ask them, they were eating like wolves, and they snatched away the fruit in the best tradition of the Sioux and the Tehuelches. I don't know why I asked the question of Lolita, at the same time cleaning her mouth with the napkin.

"How should I know?" Lolita said. "Ask Álvaro."

"And I don't know any more than she does," Alvaro said, trying to decide between a pear and a fig. "She does what she feels like and maybe she'll go along."

"But which one of you did she come with?"

"None of us," Graciela said, giving me one of her best kicks under the table. "She was here and now, who knows, Álvaro and Lolita are going back to Argentina, and you can see that she won't stay with Renaud because he's too small, this afternoon he swallowed a dead wasp, ugh."

"She does what she feels like, just the way we do," Lolita said.

I went back to my table, I saw the evening end in a fog of smoke and brandy. Javier and Magda were going back to Buenos Aires (Álvaro and Lolita were going back to Buenos Aires) and the Borels were going to Italy the following year (Renaud was going to Italy the following year).

"We oldtimers are staying here," Raúl said. (Then Graciela was staying but Silvia was the four of them, Silvia was when the four of them were there and I knew that they would never come together again.)

Raúl and Nora are still here in our valley of Luberon, last night I went to visit them and we chatted again under the linden tree; Graciela made me a gift of a doily she had embroidered, I learned of the best wishes that had been left for me by Javier, Magda, and the Borels. We ate in the garden, Graciela refused to go to bed early, she played riddles with me. There was a moment in which we were alone. Graciela was trying to get the answer to the riddle of the moon, she couldn't and her pride was suffering.

"What about Silvia?" I asked her, stroking her hair.

"Don't be silly," Graciela said. "Do you think she's going to come tonight just for me alone?"

"That's good," Nora said, coming out of the shadows. "I'm glad that she's not going to come for you alone, because we've had just about enough of that fairy tale."

"It's the moon," Graciela said. "What a silly riddle that was."

TRANSLATED BY GREGORY RABASSA

El Noche

Aquí llega el noche
el que tiene las estrellas en las uñas,
con caminar furioso y perros entre las piernas
alzando los brazos como relámpago
abriendo los cedros
echando las ramas sobre sí,
muy lejos.

Entra como si fuera un hombre a caballo
y pasa por el zaguán
sacudiéndose la tormenta.

Y se desmonta y comienza a averiguar
y hace memoria y extiende los ojos.

Mira los pueblos que están
unos en laderas y otros agachados en barrancos
y entra en las casas
viendo cómo están las mujeres
y repasa las iglesias por las sacristías y los campanarios
espantando cuando pisa en las escaleras.

Y se sienta sobre las piedras
averiguando sin paz.

Ramón Palomares

Night

Here comes night
who has the stars in his nails,
at a furious pace and with dogs between his legs,
raising his arms like lightning,
opening the cedars,
throwing the branches over himself,
very far away.

He comes in like a man on a horse
and runs though the entry
shaking off the storm.

And he dismounts and starts to inquire
and remembers and extends his eyes.

He looks at the towns that are placed
some on slopes and others crouched in ravines
and he enters the houses
seeing what the women are like
and he goes through the churches by way of the sacristies and the belfries
terrifying when he treads on the stairs.

And he hunches down in the stones
inquiring without rest.

TRANSLATED BY W. S. MERWIN

Para contar que estoy en un octavo piso
no tendría necesidad de escribir este magnífico poema
Me bastaría con saltar por la ventana.
Pero soy todavía un poeta de papel.
Pero ya vendrán los días en que me siente sobre tu boca
oh mundo!
Oh mundo mío que me oyes desde el octavo piso
como una maldición
viejo mundo podrido—y su octava maravilla—
miro reír los árboles y la baba de los pájaros
que me empaña las gafas.
Martirizado y hueco soy en tí como una naranja olvidada
en el jardín de los cerezos
oh mundo
no comprendo este sol en las pestañas.
Te toco con las uñas y se me parten
saco la lengua a la luz y se me carboniza.
Pero ya vendrán los días en que me siente sobre tu boca
oh mundo!

Eduardo Escobar

To say that I'm on the eighth floor
I've no need to write this magnificent poem.
I could just jump out the window.
But I'm still a paper poet.
But the days will come when you'll feel me against your mouth
o world!
My world, listen to me from the eighth floor
like a curse
poor old stinking world—I your eighth wonder—
I watch the trees laughing and your birds driveling
until my glasses are filthy.
I'm harassed and spongy
hanging inside you like an orange for-
gotten in a cherry orchard   .   o world,
I do not understand this sun on my eyelashes.
I touch you with my nails and they fall off
I reach my tongue toward the light and it burns to a crisp.
But there'll be days, o world, soon
you'll feel me against your mouth!

TRANSLATED BY PAUL BLACKBURN

Como las gotas de agua resbalan por el muro
—y el diente roto no crecerá—
el tiempo atrás todo ha sido perdido.
El vestido de paño nos oprime los hombros
como un pájaro de rapiña.
Ya no tendremos resurrección.
Está bien la vida
pero que viva también la muerte.
Tiene derecho
e izquierda.
Yo madrugo a limarme las uñas con una larga paciencia.
Cada día soy menos y menor.
Ojalá fuera un punto.
Niños, guardad vuestros padres en la nevera!
No sea que el mundo se canse de su edad
y nuestra edad sea la edad de piedra.
Destruíd las neveras!
No busquéis el camino
el camino es una vía sin obstáculos.
El camino no es nada
ni verbo ni sustantivo.
No hay que caminar:
sólo caer como las gotas de agua que resbalan por el muro
desplomarse como el plomo.
Nada me convence:
ni el sueño ni la embriaguez
ni las palabras.
Destruíd las palabras, académicos!
Y a cada mico dad su abanico.
Para que gesticule.
La verdad es una larga mentira convincente!

Like waterdrops that skid along the wall
    —and the broken tooth won't
            grow out again—all
of time past has been lost.
The expensive suit pinches our shoulders like
                a bird of prey.   No more
resurrections for us.   That's life, that is
life is   Let death be also.   You've got
right
and left.

I get up early and file my nails with enormous patience.
                Everyday I'm worse and less.
                Would to God I were a speck.
Kids, keep your parents in the icebox!
May be the world won't get tired of your age
                and our age
                be the stone age.
Bust the refrigerators!
Don't look for the road
the road is a way without obstacles.
The road is nothing, neither
                noun nor verb.
                Who has to walk? Just fall
like waterdrops that skid along the wall
. like lead—thud.
Nothing convinces me, not
dream or drunkenness,
nor words.
Destroy the words, you academics!
Give every monkey his fan.
                To gesticulate with.
Truth is a long-winded convincing lie!

TRANSLATED BY PAUL BLACKBURN

Jaime Espinal

Migraines and Phantoms

The migraine almost always hit him when he arrived at home. It began ten minutes before leaving work, sharpened on the corner where he waited for the bus, and reached its climax in that moment when he opened the door. At first he paid it no attention. He thought of his nerves, always tense since his father's death; always as tight as the strings of a *tiple,* they caused him to jump with fright at the slightest thing: a cigarette lighter dropped on the floor, a car slamming on its brakes, the turning of his neighbor's lock. When the head pains became frequent and then unfailing, he decided to see a doctor and demand some good pills. The doctor prescribed rest, cold drinks and light reading which, of course, included the stories of Salgari or comics and the sports page of the daily newspaper, and made him seem fifteen years younger. From then on, his co-workers at the office began to throw paper wads at him and to make sly jokes about his gray suit while Renato, the same introverted bookkeeper as always, chewed his pencil and pretended that none of this had anything to do with him. However, in spite of the expensive prescriptions, the eucalyptus leaf vapors, and the strict diet of fish and green vegetables, the headaches persisted until they were one long whistle, the continuous jab of a diaper-pin, and Renato began to feel different, to imagine his desk was an immense cloud with little holes. He became careless with his clothes and surprised himself in dingy brothels looking for an insatiable whore, and more than three times he, Renato, fell to his knees in the Cathedral praying from a remote guilt.

He opened the door and discovered by the light in the patio that today it was pink. Yesterday it had been yellow and Wednesday afternoon perhaps green. The truth was that that damned migraine did him dirty whenever it could. Color and distance were distorted by the slightest touch of light on an object, the lightest trace of shadow in the corner. The dining-room was further away than ever from the front door, and it certainly wasn't pink.

"How's the baby?" he asked, even before he was all the way in the door, and from somewhere inside Marcela answered, "Fine." Renato threw his hat on the sofa and heard Marcela's voice shouting at him not to leave it in such a bad place. Looking for her, his glance stopped at the bathroom door, behind the plants in the hall and among the clothes hung in the back patio to dry; while tossing his jacket next to his hat, he again heard Marcela's voice telling him from who-knows-where not to undress in the living-room, that every day he was becoming more and more like his father. It was a phrase she used when she wanted to squash him or to praise him if he were holding three-month-old Renatico in his arms; to resemble his father because of a quiver in the eyelid, or a finger slipping down from the bridge of the nose, or the wide-brimmed hat worn in a manner which could be tender or ironic. Renato's eyes kept looking for Marcela. Suddenly Renato saw *him* coming down the hall, looking at him harshly and with each step forward the cuffs of his trousers swaying in their peculiar way. He stopped in front of Renatico's room and made a defiant gesture. It was his father.

Renato massaged the pain in his head and paled. Six months earlier Marcela had yelled at him to get a move on or he would be late for the funeral, and he struggled with his black tie in front of the mirror. The news took him by surprise; he thought that his father's will to live was much greater, that bronchitis at the age of fifty was a small thing for a man of his size. He remembered those hundred and ninety pounds shoving him against the front door the first time he stayed out late without permission, the fists pounding on his face. He remembered being next to his corduroy jacket at Abbott and Costello movies; he remembered him entering through wide doors and even in his sleep. The eve of the funeral he had lacked the courage to look at his father's face, but he kept vigil at a distance all night long like an enemy, shooing off the flies which lighted on the wreaths close by. Neither did he see his stepmother. Exhausted by sorrow, she preferred to leave him alone, shutting herself in with her prayers and her desires to touch the corpse just so. "Poor dear, I told you to take care of yourself!" Renato did not even get up to go to the bathroom, and at dawn the maid emptied his full ashtray. She offered him yet another of the endless cups of coffee, thus distinguishing him with an honor only achieved in mourning, and touchingly reminded him that the funeral would be in three hours. Renato went to change clothes, to wash away the odor of wax and pollen, and he took his first aspirin. His migraine had begun: first a belt of fire around his forehead, then a drill penetrating the scar above his right eyebrow, and finally a spinning top in his stomach. He returned to the funeral with two boxes of pills, but refused to carry the coffin and only accompanied it for a distance. He did not want to know in which vault or in what plot of earth his father would rest. Killing once and for all any temptation to offer him an occasional bouquet of tulips, discreetly he left the procession.

Now he almost felt his way down the hall. He did not see the more distant objects and as for those near him, it was already too late. Upon touching it, he dodged the large vase in the entrance hall. He felt the emptiness of the open door to the small sitting-room, but stumbled over the flowering geranium in the corner of the patio. *That's the last straw!* The flowerpot fell to the floor and bounced two or three times before flying into pieces. Renato waivered, waiting for Marcela's shout which refused to come out of anywhere, and he pushed aside the magenta fragments of the petals, the bits of pottery and a crystal marble which lay buried in the dark soil. He saw it roll over the tiles and fall on the stones of the patio before coming to rest.

"Go see who went into the baby's room!" he heard Marcela say, as if there were a third person in the house. Her voice came from the scorpion-filled closet, and from the moth-eaten wardrobe in their bedroom which he could not see, and from the door leading to Renatico's room. She mended her husband's socks sitting on the edge of their marriage bed, silently, emptying the house of spirits so that the child might sleep.

Renato pulled himself together and tried to return to earth by telling himself that not everything was a result of his migraine because even Marcela had seen his father, or felt him; impossible not to feel his weak cough in the child's room, that cough which reeled and staggered between tuberculosis and alcoholism to which the doctors had listened, that cough which the patient emitted celebrating a goal or the winning card with a chorus of buddies. Marcela did not hear the cough but to Renato it sounded like a gong. He remained stunned and thought he had fallen on his face striking a wicked blow on the migraine; his father's cough in the baby's room sounded intermittent and encapsuled. Renato had chosen the sky-blue paint for the walls and he himself had painted them one weekend, harassed by a headache and Marcela's laughter. She would not stop scoffing at his underpants of a Peruvian center forward nor at the splatterings of paint on the parquet floors. He had dared to buy a crib at a junkyard and had bathed it with paint at intervals, waiting for four sunny Sundays, every other one. Renato identified with panic the brilliant room which he would occupy seven years later in New York, the barking of watchdogs and the heavy truck traffic. The yellow crib was in the place of the bathtub next to the window overlooking Houston Street. It seemed to have been painted by a foreign hand just three minutes earlier, the cans and brushes were still dripping. He saw the television next to the closet, the shortwave radio, the aquarium with piranas illuminated by the neonlight of the tombstone shop below, and Marcela's shoes scattered on the floor forming strange pairs: talisman red, warrior green, old bread ivory, saintly black. The shadow of his father was slipping towards the room where Marcela ought to be.

Renato went to the crib, pulled back the net, and the boy's eyes shone against the satin sheet. Four purple stripes cut across his face and hemp-colored curls bounded from under his sleeping cap. In spite of everything he was smiling into space, hitting his chest with his corroded hands. Renato sensed an odor of old parks in the blankets and the crackle of pustules bursting to the rocking of the crib. He had deposited his drunken stagger and the musky odor of his cough there before going in search of Marcela. Renato let out an incoherent curse and the child unleashed a one-note monologue when Renato placed his hands beneath him to lift him up and toss him over his shoulder as if he were a dead deer. Before going to the other room, he turned off the light in order to speak to his father from the darkness, and to prevent the contagion of that now sarcastic little cough in possession of his nuptial alcove and possibly something more, which Renato suspected was a consequence of the migraine. The baby's blue room, as Marcela so solemnly called it, became magenta, a magenta of nervous neutrons but slower than those Renato crushed when he squeezed the child against his chest and heard the voices from the other room. Before it had been a whisper from one end of the bed to the other; now the whisper interrupted the haughty voice of his father wrapped in a fur-collared Prince Albert. Renato recognized the creaking of his marriage bed and the tone of rejection in Marcela's whisper, but he could not look. He held the child more tightly and stuck to the wall like a lizard to shadow.

"Don't come near me!"

"Why not? Cough, cough. Why not, Treasure, cough?"

"If you come any closer I'll call Renato!"

Suddenly the child began to cry and the whispers stopped. Feeling denounced, Renato remained glued to the wall but this time decided to slither like a lizard always, always on the defensive and in the shadow when it came to talking with him. He stopped on the magenta without reaching the light, two inches past the dark copper color chosen by Marcela for their bedroom, sprayed on by a machine of transparent plastic which, as Renato tired of telling her, would ruin his collection of daguerreotypes. His eyes passed over his father's back, inexplicably undermined by the cough. He was sporting an English-cut jacket with three buttons, a wide-brimmed hat and an impeccable crease in his woolen pants as if he had not come from Hell and were not going back.

"I told you to stay away!" Renato yelled. His father turned to smile while continuing to chew his cigar. He had three coughing fits; the cigar fell to the floor but the aroma of Prince Albert persisted and the old man kept looking at him with his red, pupil-less eyes. Little by little he was recovering his confidence, the authoritarian gesture, the wrinkle in the corner of his burning forehead. He had been drinking again but had the prudence to belch as if from the first few drinks. Renato rubbed his head while thinking, *he looks like a Giacometti.* After mentally ridiculing him, he discovered that his feet, although on a different color, were also on the ground; and that his father's ghost would not cross the line either. It was then that he began to insult him by using his first name familiarly, infuriatingly. Renato stamped his feet and pointed to the street-door with his index finger, but the old man continued dragging himself towards his wife.

Marcela had her head between her legs but Renato recognized her bent giraffe-like neck, the birth of her breasts beneath her bare arms. His father had unbuttoned her blouse and had begun to work on her brassiere as if he had not been discovered, absolutely uninterested in whether he might break a leg if he had to run. Renato bluffed a threat, shouting, "Respect my wife!" and felt how the floor loosened. His feet slipped in a bland, shaky cheese which made movement impossible. To make matters worse, the old man stopped him by holding up his hand western style; he didn't say anything; he opened his mouth to talk but he was overcome by a coughing spell that only allowed him to exhale a little smoke. Then he pointed to the woman who was now raising her head, throwing back the hair which hung to the floor in strands, and Renato calmed down. It was not Marcela. Wrapped in a beige burial dress, the bloated, large-eyed monster assented with the crown of its head to something which Renato did not understand, something rehearsed like a migraine with six months of training and three championships coming up; a nice cool monster, while his father breathed as if a night train were parching his insides and allowed his putrid fingers to play with a limestone nipple.

No clock saw them remain so for several minutes, the one listening, the other making his fingers sound on the humid limestone of the Thing. Neither dared to step on the enemy color nor to retreat from one millimeter of conquered space, as if both were only slivery remnants of light. Renato felt Renatico gurgle on his right shoulder. He felt him spit up the sticky shellac on his starched collar, felt his little frog ribs stuck to the lapel of his shirt; the look of his father struck his head like a stone. It

was then that he began to vanish: little by little his father and the monster lost themselves in a fog worthy of London, shrinking as if Renato
were looking at them backwards through binoculars. Blinded by the
headache, he saw the monster disintegrate before disappearing from view
and his father's changeless expression, as if he were still in the fore-
ground. Cynical, laughing, with his cigar and the cold stare of one who
knows everything, he kept looking at Renato until Renato had no one to
look at, only a minuscule larva on the horizon doubled over with laughter at Renato, who was holding a kite.

TRANSLATED BY MARCIA ESPINAL

El Juego en que Andamos

Si me dieran a elegir, yo elegiría
esta salud de saber que estamos muy enfermos,
esta dicha de andar muy infelices.

Si me dieran a elegir, yo elegiría
esta inocencia de no ser un inocente,
esta pureza en que ando por impuro.

Si me dieran a elegir, yo elegiría
este amor con que odio,
esta esperanza que come panes desesperados.

Aquí pasa, señores
que me juego la muerte.

Costumbres

no es para quedarnos en casa que hacemos una casa
no es para quedarnos en el amor que amamos
y no morimos para morir
tenemos sed y
paciencias de animal.

Juan Gelman

The Game We Play

If they'd let me, I'd choose
this wholesomeness of being quite sick
this happiness of going on very unhappy.

If they'd let me, I'd choose
this innocence of not being an innocent
this purity through which I pass for impure.

If they'd let me, I'd choose
this love with which I hate
this hope which eats desperate bread.

There you have it, gentlemen
I toss my life on the table.

TRANSLATED BY JANET BROF

Customs

we don't build a house to stay at home
we don't build love to stay in love
and we don't die in order to die
we are thirsty and
have the patience of animals.

TRANSLATED BY HARDIE ST. MARTIN

La Victoria

En un libro de versos salpicado
por el amor, por la tristeza, por el mundo,
mis hijos dibujaron señoras amarillas,
elefantes que avanzan sobre paraguas rojos,
pájaros detenidos al borde de una página,
invadieron la muerte,
el gran camello azul descansa sobre la palabra ceniza,
una mejilla se desliza por la soledad de mis huesos,
el candor vence al desorden de la noche.

Hechos

yo quisiera saber
que hago aquí bajo este techo a salvo
del frío del calor quiero decir
que hago
mientras el Comandante Segundo otros hombres
son acosados a morir son
devueltos al aire al tiempo que vendrá
y la tristeza y el dolor tienen nombres
y hay tiros en la noche y no se puede dormir

Victory

In a book of verses splashed
with love, with sadness, with the world,
my children drew yellow women,
elephants advancing over red umbrellas,
birds held back at the edge of a page,
they invaded death,
the huge blue camel rests on a sooty word,
a cheek slides along the solitude of my bones,
candor wins over the jumble of the night.

TRANSLATED BY JANET BROF

Deeds

I would like to know
what I am doing here under this roof safe
from the cold the heat I mean
what am I doing
while el Comandante Segundo* other men
are hounded to death are
returned to the air to kingdom come
and sadness and pain have names
and there are shots in the night and you can't sleep.

TRANSLATED BY JANET BROF

* Ricardo Jorge Masetti, a noted Argentine journalist who disappeared from public life in 1961 and organized the E.G.P. (People's Guerrilla Army). He was captured in 1964 in a government surprise attack in the Argentine N.W. that wiped out the entire nucleus of guerrillas. Masetti was imprisoned and tortured and died at the age of 35. He was called El Comandante Segundo; Che Guevara was to have become El Comandante Primero.

Norberto Fuentes

Captain Descalzo*

The plowed land sagged down into a mountain canyon, bordering a choked jungle where the marabou was entwined with the lemon tree and the lemon tree with the mastic and the mastic with the bindweed and the bindweed with the marijuana and the marijuana with the cigüelon and the cigüelon with the coffee tree and the coffee tree with the marabou.

A machete-hacked train connected the plowed field with Captain Descalzo's house. The Condado road crossed in front of the house. Descalzo halted the oxen. The animals, freed momentarily from the goad and the shouting, knew the respite was only momentary and so continued masticating their miseries and their cud.

Descalzo sat down on the border of jungle and plowed land. His lunchsack lay at his side—a slab of creole bread, his water-jug. Descalzo began to chew the bread, pushing each mouthful along with a swallow of water. He wore a work-shirt, pants of irridescent blue hitched up at the waist with a rope and, on his head, a fatigue cap. His feet stuck out beyond the frayed edges of his pants. Enormous feet, their soles calloused and dirty.

"They're after me," someone said. Descalzo dropped a hand to his machete, sat up straight and turned to the speaker. "They're after me," the man said again. He carried a Garand; a holster hung from his right hip.

"I'm not a thief," the man assured him.

* This story, and the two which follow, are from Fuentes' "Condenados de Condado."

"If you're on the run, don't mix me up in it," Descalzo said. The man looked up and back, toward the spot where a tumult of red dust, torn up from the earth, was surely and calmly approaching.

"That's the Militia," Descalzo said.

"They're coming for me, but I'm all worn out." The man sat beside the jug and the slab of bread.

"Will you give me a piece of bread and a little water?"

"Help yourself," Descalzo ordered. "But as quick as you can. I won't get my family in trouble."

The man emptied the jug with three swallows, quenching the thirst he'd held at the junction of tongue and throat.

Descalzo asked him, "What sort of weapon's that?"

"A Luger," the man said.

"Any good?"

"The best."

"It looks a bit old, eh?"

"The trigger's rusted," the man explained. "Still, it shoots well. It's a noble pistol."

"This is the weapon I prefer personally," Descalzo said, flourishing his machete.

"A Collin?"

"Yes," Descalzo answered, "a Collin I've carried with me more than ten years."

"May I see the trademark?" the man asked. Descalzo handed him the machete; he looked below the haft, where the rooster and trademark were engraved: COLLIN.

"It's a Collin, all right," and he returned the machete to Descalzo. "Take care of this machete, it's the best there is, the best steel."

"You don't have to tell *me,*" Descalzo exclaimed.

The man halved the bread and Descalzo ran the blade over the veins of his wrist, drawing blood which flowed down to his palm, soaking into the lump of bread.

"Why are you doing this to me?" the man asked.

Descalzo struck again, precisely; the machete buried itself in the stock of the Garand the man held across his thighs. His hand fell to the ground, clutching the bread. The man reached to pick his hand up, but a final blow of the machete, this time to the neck, smothered his cry in the gusts of blood coagulating in his mouth.

Descalzo collected the Garand and the Luger, returned to his house, entering by the kitchen door, snarling at the children running about the house, left the weapons on his bed, and came out onto his front porch just as the caravan stopped in the front yard.

Bunder Pacheco stepped down from the first jeep. The soldiers waited, seated in their vehicles.

"How goes it with our Captain Descalzo?" Bunder Pacheco greeted him.

"As you see me, *comandante.*" Descalzo fetched two stools and brought them onto the front porch. They sat down.

"And what have you to tell me, Captain?"

"I'm doing poorly these days, miserably," he answered. "My woman's run off and left me with this litter of kids."

"So I've heard, Captain."

"I pleaded with her till the blood came, not to go, but you know how she is, how stubborn."

"I don't enjoy seeing you like this, Captain."

"Anyway, she's gone."

"Now I too am unhappy, Captain."

"Don't upset yourself about me, *comandante.* Will you have a cup of coffee?"

"If it's no trouble . . ."

Descalzo called to one of the children, told him to make coffee.

"And how is your work coming along?"

"Not well, not at all well. The corn has gone bad with the drought and coffee is selling for next to nothing. No, I'm not doing well. And then I'm old and my furrows don't run straight."

"Listen, Captain, why don't you go to Habana? There, surely, you can get a house, a car, a decent salary."

"No, no, I can't do that, *comandante.* You know how these things work. The regulations state that the wearing of boots is mandatory. And there's no way I can get around that. Wait a minute, look at this," and he rose from his stool, entered the house, and reappeared in a moment with a pair of boots in his hand.

"You see? Brand new, just like when they gave them to me six years ago. But no matter how I try, I can't walk in shoes. I don't know, something happens, it's as though I can't breathe."

Bunder Pacheco smiled.

"Don't laugh, don't laugh. I tell you, these are the best boots to be had," and he showed his enormous feet. "The day I wear these out I won't need another pair."

The boy brought out the heated-up coffee; after drinking a cup, Bunder Pacheco rose and prepared to leave.

"You are leaving, *comandante?*"

"I must, Captain. We are on duty, the soldiers are waiting."

"You don't have to hurry," Descalzo told him. "Who are you hunting so seriously?"

"We're after Magua Tondike, he was seen in this area yesterday."

"Ah," said Descalzo, surprised. "And could you spare a little tobacco?"

Bunder Pacheco searched his pockets and found two cigars. He gave them to Descalzo.

"Well, Captain, I must go."

"You don't have to hurry, you don't have to hurry," Descalzo repeated. "I tell you you don't have to hurry, as I have just recalled that Magua Tondike is stretched out rotting under the sun in my field."

For The Night

Beyond Condado, where the Sierra is masterless, the hanged men re-volved on the trees, swinging aimlessly, and a white horse trotted along the boundaries seeking vengeance; and farther still, after one leaves the Lomo Perea road and enters the plain of Los Cócoros, there are some roof-poles with blackened points, stifling night by night in the spring underbrush.

But here in Condado there is a yellow light provided for the body's song of Virgen María, until eleven in the evening when the local elec-tric plant shuts down, and then only Virgen María knows she's there, huddled in her bed, breathing tobacco smoke burning in the ashtray, thinking of those abandoned roof-poles and of how the underbrush shouldn't ravage over what was once an earth floor, well-trodden down, well-swept, covered with walls of jocuma wood.

Still, the roof-poles will vanish in less than a year; the fire was fierce and no one hindered it. The roof thatch curled up and burned the mo-ment the candle licked it, and it seemed maddened rats and spiders were raining from the sky, their backs in flames.

There was no choice for Narey and Virgen María. They had to leave the house. Outside was Realito Quiñones, for he himself said:

"I am Realito Quiñones."

"You wouldn't kill me, friends," Narey said.

"Where is your rifle?" asked Realito.

"I left it inside."

"Left it?"

"Listen, friends, honestly, I left it inside. I don't want to be killed."

"No, Narey Becerra. You left the rifle on purpose, so as not to hand it over," Realito announced, lightly pressing the trigger of the M-3. A small red mouth opened above the fly of the cream pants. Narey was astounded. Virgen María was about to scream, her legs were weak and she fell fainting, but her scream was drowned in the explosion of the struck powder.

"I don't want to be killed," Narey repeated, as his fly became soaked.

"Finish it," they said to Realito, and another man approached Narey, who was by then falling with his eyes turned up white. The man fired into his chest.

Virgen María recovered consciousness. Five paces from her, Narey's skull had crumpled; he had died like a candle, dwindling slowly into a white and cream mass soaking into the ground.

Realito Quiñones said:

"Stool pigeon," and spit on the blood-spattered skin.

Then Realito Quiñones ordered:

"Let's go!," and all the men went off toward the plain.

Behind them they left the woman, who bit the ground and struck herself in the stomach and clawed at the rocks and threw herself against Narey and again struck herself in the stomach and again bit the earth. Until dawn.

Later came the house in town the Party gave her and the primary school named after Narey Becerra; the hours she tried to fill with work for the community dining-hall, as secretary of the Women's Federation, in visiting the Narey Becerra School.

The day they captured Realito Quiñones, Virgen María requested that the *comandante* permit her to be present at the execution. She was permitted. But nothing within her changed, not when Realito recognized her, not when Realito pleaded with her for mercy, not when Realito exploded against the stake in Bramadero; she had thought that somehow, from that day on, things would be different.

Now, every night, Virgen María lights a cigar and lets it burn out in the ashtray, caressing her nipples, clutching her thighs, weeping.

Order #13

To all officers and enlisted men:

Comrades:

As you will recall, one month ago we successfully executed an encircling operation against the Chano Borrego band. The spotted cow belonging to citizen farmer Elviro Bertolo perished during this heroic operation. The cow perished as a result of fire directed against Chano Borrego, who had hidden himself precisely behind the aforesaid cow. As this cow was already senile and practically made into steaks, this Superior Command ordered the Quartermaster Corps to use the meat for military rations.

However, this Supreme Command has since received extremely disturbing information:

During operations in the past two weeks no less than eighteen further accidents have come about, involving mishaps to fifteen cows and three pigs. The eighteen animals died as a result, and my informants testify that some received the *coup de grace.*

As these animals must be paid for and I must justify the incurred expense to the Estates-Major for purposes of indemnity, I order, from this moment:

1. It is absolutely prohibited to accidentally kill animals belonging either to private individuals or to the State.

2. As no spoils of war are taken by this army, to be immediately dismantled are the corrals constructed in the barracks-yards of the 3rd and 4th Motor Transport Battalions, the 5th Support Battalion, and the 9th Light Shock Battalion; it is understood that the birds now kept in said corrals are to be returned *ipso facto* to their original owners.

3. Violators of this order will be tried and condemned by the Revolutionary Tribunal.

Given in Condado, to be posted on company bulletin boards and strictly observed, 8 October 1961, "Year of Education."

/s/Bunder Pacheco,
Comandante

TRANSLATED BY TIM REYNOLDS

De nuevo la cárcel, fruta negra.

En las calles y las habitaciones de los hombres, alguien se quejará en estos momentos del amor, hará música o leerá las noticias de una batalla transcurrida bajo la noche del Asia. En los ríos, los peces cantarán su incredulidad acerca del mar, sueño imposible, demasiada dicha. (Hablo de esos peces en realidad azules llamados Lirio-Negros, de cuyas espinas hombres violentos y veloces extraen perfumes de gran permanencia.)

Y, en cualquier lugar, la última de las cosas hundidas o clavadas será menos prisionera que yo.

(Claro, que tener un pedazo de lápiz y un papel—y la poesía— prueba que algún orondo concepto universal, nacido para ser escrito con mayúscula—la Verdad, Dios, lo Ignorado—me inundó desde un día feliz, y que no he caído—al hacerlo en este pozo oscuro—sino en manos de la oportunidad para darle debida constancia ante los hombres.

Preferiría, sin embargo, un buen paseo por el campo.

Aun sin perro.)

Algunas Nostalgias

Encallecido privilegio este orgulloso sufrir,
no se rían.

Yo, que he amado hasta tener sed de agua, luz sucia;
yo que olvidé los nombres y no las humedades,

Roque Dalton

Jail again, dark fruit.

In the streets and rooms of men, someone at this moment will be moaning in love, will be making music or reading news of a battle happening under the Asian night. In the rivers, fishes will sing of their disbelief in the sea, impossible dream, too good to be true. (I speak of those fish, in reality blue, called Lily-Blacks, from whose spines violent and swift men extract perfumes of great durability.)

And, in whatever place, the least of sunken or nailed down things will be less prisoner than I.

(True, my having a piece of pencil and paper—and poetry—proves that some puffed-up universal concept, born to be written in capitals— Truth, God, The Unknown—flooded me one happy day, and that I have not fallen—fallen into this dark well—but into the hands of opportunity in order to give proper evidence of it before mankind.

Nevertheless, I would prefer a walk in the country.

Even without a dog.)

TRANSLATED BY TIM REYNOLDS

Some Nostalgias

Horny privilege this proud suffering, don't laugh.

I, who have loved until thirsty for water, dingy light;
I who forgot the names and not the wetness

ahora moriría fieramente por la palabrita de consuelo
    de un ángel,
por los dones cantables de un murciélago triste,
por el pan de la magia que me arrojara un brujo
disfrazado de reo borracho en la celda de al lado . . .

El Gran Despecho

País mío no existes
sólo eres una mala silueta mía
una palabra que le creí al enemigo

Antes creía que solamente eras muy chico
que no alcanzabas a tener de una vez
Norte y Sur
pero ahora sé que no existes
y que además parece que nadie te necesita
no se oye hablar a ninguna madre de ti

Ello me alegra
porque prueba que me inventé un país
aunque me deba entonces a los manicomios

Soy pues un diosecillo a tu costa

(Quiero decir: por expatriado yo
tu eres ex patria)

now would die fiercely for a small word of consolation
>from an angel
for the singable talents of an unhappy bat
for the magic bread thrown to me by a warlock
disguised as a drunken criminal in the next cell. . . .

TRANSLATED BY TIM REYNOLDS

At the Bottom

Country of mine you don't exist
you are only my poor silhouette
a word I believed from the enemy

Before I thought it was just you were very small
you didn't manage to have at once
North and South
but now I know you don't exist
and besides it seems no one needs you
one doesn't hear any mother speak of you

That makes me happy
because it proves I've invented a country
though I might then owe myself to the asylums

I am therefore a little god at your expense

(What I mean is: me being expatriated
you are ex patria)

TRANSLATED BY TIM REYNOLDS

Antonio Skármeta

The Cartwheel

> "Crush me. I have been yours;
> Unmake me, for I made you . . ."
> *Gabriela Mistral*

Now, Rucia, now that the floorboards are arching and the heels spit saw-dust and the sawdust flies off the stage in a stampede of angels and the dogs and the birds smash into the winecasks and the wine makes your eyes rebel and fills your fleshy breasts and with your ardent fingers you tear at my neck as if it were a dark, ripe bunch of grapes, curl up into this leather chair, grab another glass of wine, and free my lips, while I go searching for the image you want until I murder your language and become a man, for the same reason that I was in New York the summer of fifty-seven and you were fifteen, vacationing with your boyfriend and there was that huge harvest of peaches on your father's farm and you got sick with them when the men carted them to Papudo, and two months later they took out your appendix and you read Rojas' *Son of a Thief,* and started to write songs, and it was there where your pale skin which frightened your mother, began to turn golden, your calves and your thighs got tanned, became flattering and overwhelmed the kids in your neighborhood, your classmates, the university teachers, when I interrupted my literature class that month of November when you walked in with your cotton print and the chalk turned to dust in my fingers. But that summer I was far away, that November I was bitter-tongued, long-haired, and twenty-three. My eyelids were swelling, I sold a pint of blood for five dollars to a hospital so as to eat for a week, I got so weak that styes were bursting out all over me like flowers in the spring. I wrote home asking for money and my mother told me to come back. My mother sent me fifty dollars, and asked me to come back. I thought she was right, I went to the Consulate to ask them to send me back. The underlings showed me their teeth, drummed on the table-top in the office, deepened the voices in their throats, raised their eyebrows, laughed heartily during endless waits in the consul's offices; when they learned I was a writer, they asked to see my publications, but I hadn't published anything, I hadn't even taken one damned manuscript to a publisher to get it read, I thought it was enough to be a writer in order to get by as easily as air.

And, one September afternoon, between the habitual boredom of back numbers of the *Mercurio,* of torn *Ercillas,* while it was lunchtime and the elegant employed opened boxes of *Planella* wines and went out, loud-mouthed, down to the restaurants near the harbor, I met the old woman. I sharpened the creases in my pants with my nails, with my eyes popping out, Rucia, as if the old woman were asking for them back, even as if my matted, filthy hair was crushing me to the ground. Her face was so grave, almost dark; the cheekbones stood out like a guitar, Fernando said that all she needed to look like a real peasant were potato peelings stuck all over her forehead; I asked myself what the hell was happening to us, who is it that lets us scatter all over the world like ripe fruit crushed to the pulp in foreign lands; what the hell had that particular space, those tourist ads, the ridiculous racket of the freight elevators on Broadway, to do with us; and her hair was scattered about placidly, loose, and gray, and her glance was like a harsh, mean hand and like another, friendly hand, and I stood up with my hands in my pockets, with a cigarette in my hands, with my hands grabbing hers, with my hands made into fists, and I smiled and looked serious, and my voice squeaked like a good Chilean when he doesn't want to be heard, wary of offending the air around him with conventional words, knowing all the time I was going to fail, that she would never know my name, that the wind was going to turn solid and separate us, to make us know what absence means, the great distance of the flesh, the weight of an arm. I saw death dancing on the old woman's cheeks, I saw it creeping up the almost straight hips. I wished I had a full orchestra in my veins, an archangel in my throat (don't pay any attention to me), I wished I smelled like the sea of the place where I was born, and that she could then sniff me, making her laugh by flapping my arms like a clumsy pelican, get her to see that I wasn't young in vain, and that she didn't have to die so much, I would have battered my way through and carried her off by her stubborn angel's head, instead of lighting a blasted cigarette and remaining always awash in ashes. Then I called her by her name,—go on, babe, have some of that wine!

She put her hand on my head and asked my name; but instead I told her I was a writer, but I needed something to eat right then, I wanted to get rid of the hallucinations that were sucking at me like snakes, and when we shook hands my nails were shining feverishly and she had triumphed over her death, she had torn it apart like a luxury cat, had got it drunk until it was bent over, and I instead was no more than one single defeat, I was twenty-three, I still hadn't read Hemingway's last book, I hadn't mentioned my name, I had to get something to eat and have a shower, give me some of that wine.

That was a vicious autumn, Rucia, not like this autumn in Santiago where you drink wine in the artists' studios, where you welcome the first rain taking cover in the thighs of a lover, where you take part in those great demonstrations against the injustice that rides us hard anyway; that was the autumn of two bums walking among the frying smells of the harbor, cracking the crystal frost gathered in the curbs, the old woman's big shoes looked like my grandfather's, I had nothing but my breath, and my wool scarf and my beggar's belly, and the old woman slowly whistled something or other between her teeth; she put her hand in my pocket, and her paw was frozen; we stumbled like a couple of cripples through Canal St. and the Bowery, and once in a while she would stop to hear the birds, to chat with the Virgin, to knead the wrinkles that barked on her face, to pray before some incredible saint, to wait for some miracle. A Jewish cabdriver took us over the bridge, and she wanted me to translate what he was saying, and the driver had said that it was going to be a bad winter, that the radiators were cracking, that a ship had gone under way out at sea.

She took me to her place, made me read my stories to her, found every trite thing great, but I knew she wasn't listening, or that she was hearing on another, inaccessible channel, that my words were going to improve themselves in another country with which she was secretly in touch; I knew perfectly well she only heard that poetry, which was why she'd praised so much mediocrity, that in the statesmen's greeting ceremonies, Rucia, her fingertips were dampened by the lips of princes, of medieval bards, of hungry, hallucinating saints, of archangels announcing apocalypses and catastrophes; she didn't give me bread, the bread dozed dying on a marble table-top; she didn't give me milk, its crystal texture showing in the ice-chest; the cheese was a distant nation; she poured me a Scotch, promised me a hearty dinner with vegetables and hot coffee, I said no thanks, I wasn't hungry, I couldn't care less if I died, I couldn't feel my feet, the flesh had become one with the shoe leather, the liquor had sunk down my spine turned to a mad herald, a raging tiger; it flashed in my teeth, burst into fire between words, my eyes stung like a dagger blow and the old woman had disappeared behind an armchair where the dark of the window screens made her look like a plaster saint yelling in a church, except that the yells were mysterious, voiceless, only the grimace, the attitude of pain; I became a child, the liquor made the skin of my belly stick to the skin of my back, I leaned over the edges of chairs to stop from fainting, I could see her shadow lengthen along a wall like a drunken bat; she was talking, I stumbled on a rug or a cat or a mad canary, the gloom began to enclose us like a tango, the tiny lamp was absurd. On my knees on the floor, sticking to her legs, hard as kicks, I drank a second glass, I was the one who was singing and she was laughing; I said I don't care if I die, ma, I'm ashamed, and she said go on singing, and I said I am singing, ma, and she, don't cry, and I striking my fists on the wall, scattering a knot of birds of ill omen, and she, you're feverish, and I, make me rebel, ma, tear apart once and for all this silence that fills me like the plague, like a malign growth, an abyss, and she, put

your head on this pillow, and I choked my sobs between the pawings of
the feathers, I said I'm laughing, ma, that's good, she said, get some sleep,
I'll watch over your knowing night of wakeful flesh, go on, let me rock
you in the air, come close to the fire my son that's great, mama, whew, oh,
oh, oh.

And then came the breakfasts, the fever would leave me in the mornings and the sofa would awake bathed in sweat; at night we would share
our terror of medicines like a bottle of Scotch or a pack of cigarettes; just
by feeling my thighs I could tell how much weight I'd lost; my nose
would grow sharper while she served me an egg dropped into a silver
cup, it scared me to hear my wrists in my ears. Over the first meal we
faced each other pale and smiling, like bride and groom after a successful
nuptial night; the old woman was polite, she put some devilled ham on
my bread, she let a knitted wool shawl drop over a profusion of lace, her
blouse with a wide collar. On the first page of *The New York Times* a
second snowfall was forecast for the afternoon; I had to refuse her invita-
tion to pray at St. Patrick's, one because I never knew how to do it, two
because my feet were as drunk as sailors ashore. I saw her go out, but
holding back as if a piece of herself were being left behind, or as if she'd
forgotten a speech in the attic, or to write a letter, or to show me once
and for all the real body beneath that Prussian officer's uniform, that
milliner's enigma, the best metaphor once and for all, the beautiful one,
the one that made us so alike, that Saturday morning, so much raging
poetry. I don't mean to say, Rucia, that she was better than you, or than
me, or than all of us together, because being alive is better than being a
glorious corpse, it's better to drink this wine, eat this pie, claw this breast,
bite this tongue. And I was the one who was going to buy her the flag,
but that's a long story, another bottle, pal, have a cigarette.

She came back home and took off her clodhoppers, the toes showed
through those football player's socks and slowly felt the floor as if looking for some earth, and it snowed that night, and the birds were going
crazy pecking at the windows; let them in she said, and her eyes were
turning gray because her cancer was like a cloud rising from her pan-

creas; then I would arrange the logs in the fireplace, bother the cat with the guitar, whistle jazz tunes and sad Chilean songs.

When the secretary arrived on a luminous Monday, I had to clear out of the living room and seek refuge in the attic. The meal hours grew regular, the painters with scholarships came around to see her, the diplomats would shake handkerchiefs petulantly, the conversation got very toney, it was enough to make you want to shoo some hens into the living room, to fill the sofas with pigs and chickens; what are you writing now, dear lady, which is your favorite work, have you read Robert Lowell, no, she had to answer, a strange being is writing on my hips, is turning the marrow of my bones to dust, leaving them as frail and empty as Indian flutes, my spit is bitter in the mornings; take the trip, dear lady, go towards the raisins and the mangoes, try our wine, air travel is so fast; and the old woman, to cross America, to skirt the Cordillera like a mountain lion, enjoying the stones, one by one, to sweeten the hurricanes and earthquakes with the tameness of a wounded beast, can you imagine, my friend (she was speaking to me) flying over America like an angel, can you imagine the frightened Indians hiding in their huts from the old ghost, from the innocent old woman perfectly dead floating on the cobalt blue sky, whizzing by on ancient wings; and the secretary would slam down her eyeglasses on an onyx stool, and begin to play on the tape recorder the silver trumpets of the Swedish Navy. And the world in New York was a quiet sphere, a wide blue that enlarged your pores, snow that fell without a sound. So my ear got used to the touch of her lips at dusk, I would play any music I felt like and she would go on talking, the saliva almost wetting my earlobes, the air softly sick, slightly drunk.

Now that it grew darker earlier she would start to sink into the sofa and I began my irreverence. As soon as I managed to eat for two days running, I thought that it was me who was going to live and I speculated with the chance of exploiting such a privilege commercially; irony became a pernicious habit with me; my enthusiasm for that Italian edition of her favorite book hardly ceased to seem forced when she gave it to me in that corner dyed with a waning light that settled on a shelf full of plaster saints; while I made my indifference more obvious to the old woman, the more I realized that I was there for some reason, my language still could not spill out with strength the plot of her mystery, the fur of her cat arching under the concave palm could have been more tender than the empty country that I was hiding like a clumsy beast in that North American autumn which turned to winter.

I told her, one night I told her, banging the ice cubes on the side of a glass empty too long, my knees pressed together, withdrawn, shy even, trying to guess at those kneecaps she said were hard under the lap of a wide skirt that mingled with the rug, I told her. It was then that she touched me decisively for the first time. How do you expect me to understand, Rucia, I didn't even know what baptism was, I didn't know that the body was able to stretch like a planet, I didn't understand there was another way to live, I was a Chilean bourgeois plagued by ceremony and servile smiles, my fingers always busy with a cigarette, lazy, illiterate, a glutton, my prose weaker than toilet water; while my touch reduplicated the texture of my skin, the old woman's skin knew how to be an orange, a dove, breadcrumbs for the birds epiphanizing on her lap, a bed to clasp the world, even the nonexistent country, the land of absence which is lighter than an angel. That way of bending was hers, hers that way of making the smoke a wraith around her cheeks, hers that way of looking at a crust of bread on the table as if a birth were taking place there; she touched me with decision, her hand didn't tremble as it crept up my hip, the nails bedded down in my ribs, she was screaming something at me with her hands, her wrists felt my skin like a burr seeking the right ground, all she did was to mesh me in her gestures, it was almost dark and a winging of angels around the room, a procession of dead friends flying into the air with a village band playing Verdi, everything was perfectly painful and enigmatic, except that the old woman wanted something from me, that it was winter in New York, that she would wind up giving me some money the next morning for me to go buy her a flag, let me think.

I haven't forgotten that day spent among Syrian merchants, who seemed to have machine-guns in their fists, while my beard slowly grew and frost became a habit on the cartops and the sky turned gray like a freight train. I spoke to a Greek who didn't dare answer me while he watched the rhythm with which the stove heated the coffee on the street, with a Jew who tried to sell me a similar flag, "who's to know, fella, anyways no one's gonna look at it, fella," who opened immeasurable cardboard boxes and took out flags of countries we'll get to know some-day, Rucia, who would display several yards of Cuba, tear greasy Australian pennants with feverish fingers, always answered that they had one just like that, or almost, that perhaps just the star was missing, that they'd put it on in cloth-of-silver, that they'd sew it on with gold thread, that, depending, it would set me back twelve dollars. They spilled out the flag of Burma, of Yugoslavia, time and again the Cuban, time and again the Australian, finally a black clerk skinned his smile, his teeth flashing like white bullets and shaking his head saying I was mistaken, that "there was no such country," that he'd "never heard of Chile," that "maybe I was mistaken," that "maybe I meant China." Fed up, I bargained with a Jewish tailor who very gravely calculated the design and promised me a Chilean flag that same night.

The rest of the morning I spent lying among the bums in Washington Square. Coming onto the dried-up fountain, I made a place for myself in the sun elbowing the folklore singers, the false students, the pale girls in jarring multicolored vests, the trembling dogs sniffing at their heels, the distant blacks harmonizing Jamaican ballads with an obligato of knuckles; the girls scratched at their thighs trying to get warm, the poets wrote smoking in great drags, once in a while feeling the texture of the pencil as if the words were hiding there, and that sun was too little for so many people, it didn't lavish itself like a star for mortals, it turned to dust as it fell, it turned to a halo of mist over the young people. I crouched smiling among a group of girls, one of them took my arm and brushed her cheek against my incipient beard. Okay, I said, I've eaten for a month, now I can go to another hospital and sell another pint of blood, change my gray shirt for another, Village cowboy style, get hold of a pair of fancy pants, rent an old typewriter and try my luck with my stories in the competitions. Besides, death was a different star then, the planet where the old woman was heading, I couldn't care less; I imagined what the Chilean newspapers would say, I could see a million country girls invading the walks, segmenting the light of Chile, adoring a name which would be remotely tender to them, like a fairy tale told by their parents, like a song that once was well-known, and that girl, Rucia, that plump girl with big teeth and tender lips, of warm and slightly ridiculous arms, who now would lay her head wrapped in a tartan kerchief, who sought to lean on my novel, who tried to say something definite in a language I was beginning not to understand, arched me over into space suddenly as if a howl had burst in my belly, as if something were kicking my forehead. I mumbled some sort of excuse; I was crying as I walked along, I thought I wasn't feeling well, that I was destroying with my heels the wrists and ears of the North American kids who were chasing that bit of sun like lizards, who could drop dead of loneliness into that fountain; in Chile it was spring, it was going to be December, you were getting ready for a holiday with your boy friend in Papudo or some other beach, I walked over to the tailor's, I'd go back home that night with the flag, I'd borrow some money from the old woman.

In the tailor's dingy little room I spent an afternoon sipping bitter coffee while the secretary worked the thread among the silks; I remember the tables were very dusty, that an old woman kept telling her beads and sneezing in a corner. The folds of the flag hung down, turning over at the corners, the old woman was cutting a star out of a bit of white cloth. Of Chile I remembered then the second-hand bookstores of San Diego, the neighborhood dance clubs with their bitter wine, the poetry recitals given by hallucinating poets in the conference room of the University, the concert where a child prodigy wrapped in a yellow wig massacred some Schumann, the success of Lucho Gatica's records, the street parades of the FRAP and the Christian Democrats, Antonio Zamorano galloping at the head of an overcast day lodged between an army of informers, the hotel love and dawns (hounds, tired of biting each other's lips). My God, my hands that day in the tailor's shop!, the letters of a girl friend in the faded jeans, the glory of Chile, in a mansion on Long Island, made of the same flesh and the same fortune, and still I was not really hallucinating, one lived and died in vain, the birds fell so vertically in the air offshore, and what had we got out of it, what had we got out of it for Chile, tailor Isaac Goldstein, with your child's hands and reproachful eye, what Swedish trumpets will raise again the generations consumed in boarding-houses, and the stye-ridden kids who hoist kites aloft and knock their heads throwing themselves off trees to see if they'll fly, and the kids with the dogs' legs; who was to know this was the country that sings; who ordered the poets removed from the hotels in St. Paul to give them a place in court (watch it, I sang, with the skinny brother who sings, give him something to eat or else he'll ridicule you, he'll announce an apocalypse behind your back, he'll hold aloft the dagger of the poor and the holy meal will be made with barrels from the vineyards of perverse petty nobles). There's the flag you're weaving, Hebrew tailor; I'll carry it under my arm for the old woman to wrap the Virgin in, and then the Virgin and her unlikely patrons to wrap her in it like an apostle's baggage; I'll walk with it around the Times Square subway station tonight, I'll sniff the billboards of theaters where unapproachable dolls undress, where an allegory is being plotted, a nation I don't understand, the package will be a burden under my armpit.

Through the half-opened door, I could see the old woman listening to some Jewish music on the record player with her nails clawing at the window panes, as if waiting for a snowstorm, the visit of an organ-grinder with a drum, of a gypsy with a fortune-telling parrot, face to face with an indecipherable zodiac; the music was sensationalistic, it tumbled around the room, it made one as drunk as a barrel of whisky. Then, without disturbing the floors or the tapestries, I placed the flag on an armchair, took clean advantage of the shadows, fished a pair of pants and my best sports shirt out of a closet next to the pantry, and made a parcel with them; I had no foreboding when I felt the doorhandle or stepped on the snow outside. And when I went into the hospital at seven in the morning of a January day in New York, the old woman was as dead as anybody, and an ambiguous young man was inflaming her cheeks with paint and smoothing away her wrinkles with a thick emollient cream, and the women around her were plotting some fancy sorrows; "the great dead do not belong to us," said one of them, "the great dead belong to the people." But years have gone by since, it isn't that I'm forgetting, I was hungry again, I had quarreled again with my girl, I was trying to crash the pad of some painter with a Guggenheim, where I come from no one would have touched the old woman's face except to kiss it, a barrier of officials proved my country was present, you could see a great many hired photographers, behind everybody's glasses you could see the flash of recognition of an important moment in history, the flag was there, wrapped around the Virgin like a red wave, someone had stitched over with silver thread the star's twisted points. I strolled over calmly to a cafeteria to have some breakfast, I smoked the first cigarette, I went around crashing into different walls, going from the weak coffee in the drugstores to the stale beer of the *Engagé* on the lower east side, grabbing the guitar during the matinée hour to strum a *cueca,* much to the enthusiasm of the beatniks; I went to recitals of promising poets who pushed out their teeth and their jaws to massacre society; I lived for two days just waiting for the funeral; I'd circle the newspaper stands like a lame horse; in the midst of my waiting I got to loathe even the drugstores and the pinball machines; something kept spurring me on, I needed to turn time around, wring it like a sweatshirt, reproduce the old woman's death spasms. I needed to stick to the walls of the surly hospital, the bars of the bed slipping away from my touch, I needed to have proof of what I was saying, the hands of Doctor Vogel, the child doctor, overwhelming with sophistries the old woman's modesty, I loved Chile like a saint hallucinating his own death, I needed the old woman's martyrdom so as to be born in my country, I wanted a land in which to burst this lung singing, to set a daring and passionate head thinking, to merit the space which awaited me so much alone; a contact, a short-circuit, a soldering, an amalgamation, a binding, an explosion was needed with that woman who was so absurdly dead, who had been consumed in the devil's exercises between truth and Chile, and I, my companion, my good bed, my friendly wine, didn't want the poetess to die in vain, I needed to replenish my flesh with her voice, I needed a foundation, stronger legs and more tactile paws; it was a question of stripping one's flesh, of undressing before every stone, of letting the fever come from the air and dig into the ear with the names of things; it was necessary to start writing again, to turn the skeleton inside out, to grow weak before each hungry man, to bleed for each treason done to a Chilote*, for each bad mine explosion, to lie on the ground in an earthquake and leap on it, clean, with the sun hot on the nape, the forehead throbbing, the clods of sandy soil bursting like ripe watermelons. I would go to the funeral and I would return to Chile on any boat, on some Liberian freighter, upholstering the officer's chairs, right, Rucia? And I, still hanging around St. Patrick's, my weird stomach between the limousines and the listless Irish cops—how to transform the mist into the flesh of our trees, for you, old woman, to spring a mountain lion from the midst of the temple! I hung around there, squatting between the pillars; the sun kept coming down the vitrial's sieve; it was January 'fifty-seven, and still drunken Santas strolled through the streets with Hindu bells hanging from their necks, and still certain cars would fill the streets with shredded cotton, the motorbikes were wearing steel hooves, you couldn't see a bird flying anywhere, or anything green, or people without a tie; I myself could have been a witness at a wedding, a prosecution witness in a criminal case, someone who enters a church as if it were a lawyer's office; no, my friend; I had to get away as soon as possible, to put up a restaurant at La Quintrala with some guys from the university, to take a trip down to Viña del Mar with a rich mistress, but above all to get away from there fast. I stuck my hands in my pockets, in the deep pockets that allowed me to rub my thighs, and then, Rucia, when it was least expected, when the cityscape gathered all its strength to turn into a cyclone of needles, when the dignified officials were carrying out their duty, when I understood that sorrow was possible even for them, I saw my dead one's coffin, loving, inflating the flag, the one you so roughly made, tailor Isaac Goldstein in the streets of the Bowery, which was wrapped around her like a fur coat on a shivering woman, which swelled out at the belly like a country girl's skirt, like a flight of petticoats in a dance; I had nothing at all to do with the whole thing, a smile began to grow on me, pushed a bit

* A native from Chiloe, an island in the south of Chile—*ed.*

by the grimace the face makes when you're holding back a tear; pity you weren't there then (I'm going to have to write many years into your notebooks, and this story on your hips), the street suddenly burst into flames, the sun of Antofagasta shone down on me, someone looked at me sourly because I was smiling more, or laughing very softly; pity that Alexander Fleming who gave the world penicillin, or Ernest Cheron who again broke the atom, or Johannes Jensen who had to wait so long for the war's epilogue to end, or Howard Florey, or Arturo Virtanen, could not be there wearing their Sunday best, or even now immediately a forest of white schoolgirls' uniforms; and that was what was needed, for the wind to blow, my soul! the wind of New York, the frozen sea of Manhattan to go by cutting off the ears, and my dead one, Rucia, was raising herself up like a bull that won't die, some lines kept going through my head, the little broken shoe for you to come and tell us another one, and I was laughing, I was slapping my thighs in a rage (here in my gut I know well what I'm singing); and then, my Rucia, your dead one went flying off over America, the seven towns beneath were clinging to the mother Cordillera (let me eat, she said to Julio, one of my American potatoes, and now one of my American chickens), and now the Indians could scrutinize the skies to avert the evil omens, the angle of the wings of the birds would foretell the future in cartwheels, and my dead one flew so high over America; and now came a cosmic generation, the night of my birthday I saw the first satellite go by, but still I did not sing, I didn't know my name, I didn't deserve my lover's waist; the old woman had died, what did you expect me to do! I came back to Chile on a Liberian freighter. This is a land of high mountains, lots of sun, there are birds everywhere, and I'm getting ready to have a ball, as they say; so I just set out to write, got hold of the most beautiful woman, accelerated on the road down to liquor.

Well, to hell with it, Rucia; let's dance.

TRANSLATED BY JOHN C. MURCHISON

Arte Poética

En verdad, en verdad hablando,
la poesía es un trabajo difícil
que se pierde o se gana
al compás de los años otoñales.

(Cuando uno es joven
y las flores que caen no se recogen
uno escribe y escribe entre las noches,
y a veces se llenan cientos y cientos
de cuartillas inservibles.
Uno puede alardear y decir
"yo escribo y no corrijo,
los poemas salen de mi mano
como la primavera que derrumbaron
los viejos cipreses de mi calle")
Pero conforme pasa el tiempo
y los años se filtran entre las sienes,
la poesía se va haciendo
trabajo de alfarero,
arcilla que se cuece entre las manos,
arcilla que moldean fuegos rápidos.

Y la poesía es
un relámpago maravilloso,
una lluvia de palabras silenciosas,
un bosque de latidos y esperanzas,
el canto de los pueblos oprimidos,

Javier Heraud

The Art of Poetry

Really, to speak of it really,
poetry is hard work that wins or loses
on the beat of autumnal years.

(When you're young
& the fallen flowers are never picked again
you write and write between nightfalls,
and hundreds and hundreds, sometimes, of useless
pages get filled.
You can brag and say:
"I write, I don't amend,
poems fall from my hand like the spring
they cut down the old cypresses in my street")
But time passes agreeably, and
the years line up between the brows,
poetry goes on becoming
pottery,
        clay that bakes between the hands,
        clay that brisk fires shape.

And poetry is a
marvelous flash of light,
a rain of silent words,
a wood full of throbbing and hope,
the songs of oppressed peoples,

el nuevo canto de los pueblos liberados.

Y la poesía es entonces,
el amor, la muerte,
la redención del hombre.

Madrid, 1961—La Habana, 1962

Palabra de Guerrillero

Porque mi Patria es hermosa
como una espada en el aire
y más grande ahora y aún
y más hermosa todavía,
yo hablo y la defiendo
con mi vida.
No me importa lo que digan
los traidores
hemos cerrado el paso
con gruesas lágrimas
de acero.
El cielo es nuestro.
Nuestro el pan de cada día,
hemos sembrado y cosechado
el trigo y la tierra,
son nuestros
y para siempre nos
pertenecen
el mar,
las montañas
y los pájaros.

the new song of liberated peoples.

And poetry is, then,
love and death,
the restoration of man.

Madrid 1961—Havana 1962

TRANSLATED BY PAUL BLACKBURN

Word of the Guerrilla Fighter

Because my country is fair as
a sword in air
and greater now, even,
and fairer still, I
speak and I defend her
with my life.
Traitors? What
do I care what they say, we
have closed the pass
with bulky tears
of steel.
The sky is ours.
Ours the daily bread, we
have sowed and reaped
the wheat and the earth,
they are ours, and ours
forever are
the sea,
the mountains,
and the birds.

TRANSLATED BY PAUL BLACKBURN

Mario Vargas Llosa

*Literature is Fire**

Approximately thirty years ago a young man who had fervently read Breton's first works lay dying in the mountains of Castille, in a charity ward, driven mad by rage. He left to the world a red shirt and *Cinco Metros de Poemas* (*Five Yards of Poems*), a work of unique visionary delicacy. His name was noble and resounding, that of a viceroy, but his life had been tenaciously obscure, stubbornly unhappy. In Lima, he was a starving provincial and dreamer who lived in a lightless hole in the Market section, and when he was in Central America, on his way to Europe, no one knows why he was yanked off the boat, imprisoned, tortured and turned into a feverish wreck. After his death, his persistent misfortune, instead of ceasing, reached an apotheosis: the cannons of the Spanish Civil War blew his grave off the face of the earth, and during all these years time has been erasing his memory from the recall of the persons who were lucky enough to know him or read him. It wouldn't surprise me at all if the mice have already come across the copies of his only book, buried in libraries that no one visits, or if his poems that no one reads anymore become "dust, wind, nothing," like the insolent colored shirt that he bought to die in. And yet, this countryman of mine was a consummate sorcerer, a witch with a word, a daring architect of images, a blazing explorer of dreams—a complete and obstinate creator who possessed the lucidity and the madness necessary to assume his vocation of a

* On accepting the 1967 Rómulo Gallegos Prize, Caracas, for his novel, *The Green House*.

writer as it must be done, as one must do it: as a daily and furious immolation.

I conjure here tonight his fugitive nocturnal shade to dampen my own celebration, this celebration that has been made possible by the conjugation of Venezuelan generosity and the illustrious name of Rómulo Gallegos. The award to a novel of mine of the magnificent prize created by the National Institute of Culture and Fine Arts as a stimulus and challenge to novelists of the Spanish Language and as a homage to a great American creator, not only fills me with gratitude toward Venezuela, but also and above all, increases my responsibility as a writer. And the writer, as you all know, is the eternal wetblanket. The silent ghost of Oquendo de Amat installed here at my side should make us all remember—especially this Peruvian whom you've dragged out of his hideaway in Kangeroo Valley in London and brought to Caracas and loaded down with friendship and honors—the somber fate which was, and in so many cases still is, that of the creators in Latin America. It is true that not all our writers have been tested to the extreme that Oquendo de Amat was; a few managed to conquer the hostility, the indifference, the scorn that exist in our countries toward literature, and they wrote, published and were even read. It is true that not all could be killed off by starvation, oblivion or ridicule. But these fortunates constitute the exception. In general, the Latin American writer has lived and written under exceptionally difficult circumstances because our societies assembled a cold and almost perfect machinery to discourage and kill in him his vocation. That vocation, in addition to being beautiful, is absorbing and tyrannical and demands of its skilled total involvement. How could they make of literature an exclusive calling, a militant cause, if they lived surrounded by people who in their majority did not know how to read or could not buy books, or who in their minority had no inclination to read? Without publishers, without readers, without a cultural environment that stimulated and pushed him, the Latin American writer has been a man who fought battles knowing full well from the very beginning that he would lose them. His vocation was not recognized by society, it was barely tolerated;

he couldn't live on it, and it made of him a minor, *ad honorem* producer. The writer in our countries has had to split himself, separate his vocation from his daily action, multiply himself in a thousand jobs that deprived him of the time so necessary for writing, jobs that often revolted his conscience and his convictions. For in addition to not admitting literature into its midst, our societies have encouraged a constant mistrust toward this marginal being, a bit anomalous, who, against all reason, set himself to practice an art that in the Latin American circumstance was virtually unreal. This is why our writers have failed by the dozens, deserted their vocation or betrayed it by practicing it in a half-hearted and hidden fashion, with neither diligence nor discipline.

However, it is true that in the last few years things have begun to change. Gradually one senses a more hospitable climate for literature in our countries. The circle of readers begins to grow, the bourgeoisie discover that books matter, that writers are something more than harmless madmen, that they have a function to fulfill among humanity. But then, at the same rate that the Latin American writer begins to be treated justly, or rather, at the same rate that this injustice which has weighted him down begins to be rectified, a threat may emerge, a devilishly subtle danger. These same societies that exiled and rejected the writer may now think it convenient to assimilate him, integrate him, confer on him some kind of official status. Therefore, it is necessary to remind our societies what awaits them. To warn them that literature is fire, that it signifies non-conformism and rebellion, that the writer's very reason for being is protest, contradiction and criticism. To explain to them that there are no half-measures, that societies always suppress that human faculty which is artistic creation and eliminate once and for all that social agitator who is the writer, or that they admit literature into their midst, and in this case, they have no choice but to accept a perpetual torrent of aggression, irony, satire that will range from the descriptive to the essential, from the temporary to the permanent, from the tip to the base of the social pyramid. That's the way things are and there is no way out: the writer has been, is, and will continue to be a non-conformist. No one who is satisfied is capable of writing, no one who agrees with and is reconciled to reality would commit the ambitious folly of inventing verbal realities. The literary vocation is born of a man's disagreement with the world, of his intuition of the deficiencies, vacuums and filth around him. Literature is a form of permanent insurrection and recognizes no straitjackets. Every attempt destined to change its angry, ungovernable nature will fail. Literature may perish but it will never conform.

Only if this condition is fulfilled is literature useful to society. It contributes to the process of attaining human perfection by impeding spiritual swamps of self-satisfaction, immobility, human paralysis, moral and intellectual softening. Its mission is to agitate, disturb, alarm, keep men constantly dissatisfied with themselves: its function is to unconditionally stimulate the will to change and improve, even though in order to achieve this the most deadly and poisonous weapons must be employed. It must be understood once and for all that the more terrible and cruel an author's writings against his country, the more intense the passion that binds him to it. For in the realm of literature, violence is the test of love.

Of course the American reality offers the writer a virtual orgy of motives for being a rebel and living dissatisfied. Societies where injustice is law, these paradises of ignorance, of exploitation, of blinding inequalities, of poverty, with economic, cultural and moral alienation, our tumultuous countries provide sumptuous material, examples galore to demonstrate in fiction, either directly or indirectly, through deeds, dreams, testimonies, allegories, nightmares or visions, that reality is distorted, that life must change. But in ten, twenty, fifty years all of our countries will have reached, as Cuba has today, the time of social justice and all Latin America will have freed itself from the empire that sacks her, from the castes that exploit her, from the forces that today offend and repress her. I want this time to arrive as soon as possible and for Latin America once and for all to reach dignity and modern life; for socialism to free us from our anachronism and our horror. But when social injustices disappear, in no way will the writer have reached the time of consent, subordination or official complicity. His mission will continue; it must continue to be the same one; any compromise in this realm constitutes on the part of the writer a betrayal. Within the new society and along the way that our personal devils and ghosts drive us, we will have to continue as we did before, as we do now, saying no, rebelling, demanding that our right to disagree be recognized, demonstrating in a living magical way as only literature can do, that dogma, censure, abuse are also the mortal enemies of progress and human dignity, affirming that life is not simple nor does it fit into neat schemes, that the way to truth is never smooth nor straight, but often tortuous and brief, demonstrating with our books again and again the essential complexity and diversity of the world, the contradictory ambiguity of human acts. As yesterday, as today, if we love our vocation, we must continue fighting the thirty-two wars of Coronel Aureliano Buendía[1] even though, as he was, we are defeated in them all.

Our vocation has made of us the writers, the professional malcontents, the conscious or unconscious disturbers of society, the rebels with a cause, the world's unredeemed insurrectionists, the intolerable devil's advocates. I don't know if this is good or bad, I only know that it is so. This is the writer's condition and we must claim it for what it is. Now that literature is beginning to be discovered, accepted and patronized, Latin America must also know the menace that hangs over her, the high price that she will have to pay for culture. Our societies must be alerted; for rejected or accepted, persecuted or rewarded, the writer who deserves the name will continue throwing into men's faces the often unpleasant spectacle of their miseries and their torments.

Upon awarding me this prize which I deeply appreciate, and which I have accepted because I consider that it does not demand of me even the slightest shadow of ideological, political or esthetic compromise, and which other Latin American writers with more merits and works than I should have received in my stead (I think of the great Onetti, for example, to whom Latin America has still not granted the recognition that he merits), by showing me so much affection, so much cordiality, since I

[1] Refers to a character in *One Hundred Years of Solitude,* by the Colombian novelist García Márquez.

first set foot in this city in mourning,[2] Venezuela has made a heavy debtor of me. The only way that I can repay that debt is by being, to the utmost of my efforts, more faithful, more loyal to this vocation of a writer, which I never suspected would provide me with a satisfaction as great as the one it has given me today.

TRANSLATED BY MAUREEN AHERN DE MAURER

[2] The city of Caracas was just recovering from one of the worst earthquakes in its history, in which hundreds of persons lost their lives.—*tr.*

BIOGRAPHICAL NOTES

JOSÉ MARÍA ARGUEDAS was born in Peru in 1911, and grew up in predominantly Indian villages. He spoke Quechua before he spoke Spanish, and his vision was shaped by the myth and magic of the Indian world with which he always remained profoundly involved. A writer of novels and stories, his first work, *Agua* (1935), is a collection of stories included in the volume *Amor Mundo y Todos los cuentos de José María Arguedas,* from which the present selection is made. Arguedas died a suicide, in Peru on December 2, 1970.

ROBERTO ARLT was born in Argentina in 1900 and died there in 1942. The son of a struggling immigrant, he left school at an early age, and later, after a variety of jobs, found his way into journalism. He continued to work at that profession while he wrote his stories and novels in which madmen carry to extremes the lessons the world has taught them. The present story is from a collection entitled *El jorobadito* (1933).

MIGUEL ÁNGEL ASTURIAS, Guatemalan author and diplomat; born in 1899. His poems, stories and novels are steeped in the language and imagery of the Mayan people. An ardent anti-imperialist, Asturias' opposition to dictatorial regimes forced him into long periods of exile from his native country. Under more liberal regimes, he has served Guatemala in various diplomatic posts in Spanish America, as well as serving as its Ambassador to France, the country in which he now resides. Of his prose work, his first novel, originally published in 1946, appeared here under its original title, *El Señor Presidente* (New York, Atheneum, 1964), followed by two volumes of a trilogy which attack the economic domination of Guatemala by the United Fruit Company, *Strong Wind* and *The Green Pope* (New York, Seymour Lawrence, Delacorte, 1969 and

1970). His most highly praised novel, *Hombres de Maiz,* has not appeared in English. The present piece is from a collection of stories, *El espejo de Lida Sal* (1967). In 1967, Asturias was awarded the Nobel Prize in Literature.

JORGE LUIS BORGES was born in Buenos Aires in 1899. His many works of labyrinthine thought, in which he deciphers reality and invents it, have renovated the Spanish language and endowed its literature with a masterful corpus of poetry, stories and essays. His published works in English include *Ficciones* (New York, Grove, 1962), *Dreamtigers* (Austin, University of Texas Pr., 1964), *Other Inquisitions 1937–1952* (Austin, University of Texas Pr., 1965), *A Personal Anthology* (New York, Grove, 1967), *Labyrinths* (New York, New Directions, 1969), *A Book of Imaginery Beings* (New York, Dutton, 1969), and *The Aleph & Other Stories 1933–1969* (New York, Dutton, 1970). Borges shared the International Publishers' Prize with Samuel Beckett in 1961. Himself a living library, he has been, since 1955, Director of the Argentine National Library in Buenos Aires. Together with Norman Thomas di Giovanni, Borges is presently translating nine more of his books into English.

ERNESTO CARDENAL was born in Nicaragua in 1925. After joining the resistance in the fight against the notorious dictator, Somoza, father of the present dictator, and suffering persecution and imprisonment, he changed his course and entered the Trappist Monastery at Gethsemany, Kentucky where Thomas Merton was his spiritual director. Now a priest, he lives in a community on an island off Nicaragua where he has built with friends a school and a polyclinic for the islanders. Some of his books of poetry include: *Hora O* (1960), *Epigramas* (1961), *Gethsemani, Ky.* (1965) and *Oración por Marilyn Monroe* (1966).

ALEJO CARPENTIER, writer, journalist, musicologist, and professor of literature, was born in Cuba in 1904. Although for many years he lived in Paris and Caracas, since the revolution he has been in Cuba, where his activities have included teaching at the University of La Habana and, in 1966, a diplomatic mission to France. Carpentier's work is strongly marked by a poetic vision of the Afro-Cuban past, which transforms both place and time in his novels and stories. The French version of his novel, *The Lost Steps* (New York, Knopf, 1956) was awarded the Prix du Meilleur Livre Étranger. *The War of Time* (New York, Knopf, 1970) is a collection which includes a short novel and three stories; one of these, "Journey to the Seed," appeared in J. M. Cohen's distinguished collection *Latin American Writing Today* (Baltimore, Penguin Books, 1967). The story presented here is from *Narrativa Cubana de la Revolución* (1968).

JOSÉ CORONEL URTECHO was born in Nicaragua in 1904. He lived for a few years in California in the 1920's and since then has had an active interest in North American poetry, publishing two anthologies, the second one in collaboration with Ernesto Cardenal. As an early and continuing innovator, a translator of French poetry as well as English, Coronel Urtecho provided leadership for the new poetry of Nicaragua. *Pol-la d'ananta, katanta, paranta* (1970) spans a wide variety of unexpected forms, the most daring of which are untranslatable because of the play of words. He lives far from the city on a farm in Rio San Juan, Nicaragua.

JULIO CORTÁZAR was born in Brussels in 1914 of Argentine parents. When he was four years old, the family moved to Argentina and settled in the outskirts of Buenos Aires. As a young man, Cortázar taught school in isolated towns in the provinces; it was then that he began writing his stories, in many of which the distinction between fantasy and reality is erased. His unique faculty is one of attacking all the conventions of language and life—a hazardous task that he accomplishes with elegance, humor and brilliant intuition. *End of the Game & Other Stories* (New York, Pantheon Books, 1967), includes most of his early work; one of the pieces is "Blow-up," on which Antonioni based his movie. His first novel, *The Winners,* was followed by a truly masterful work, *Hopscotch* (New York, Pantheon Books, 1965 and 1966). Cortázar has also published a book of notes and sketches, *Cronopios & Famas* (New York, Pantheon Books, 1969). The selection in this anthology is from *Último Round* (1969), a collection of poems, commentary and stories. Cortázar has lived in Paris since 1951.

ROQUE DALTON was born in El Salvador in 1933. He studied law and anthropology, was persecuted and imprisoned in his own country and subsequently lived in exile in Guatemala, Mexico, Czechoslovakia and Cuba where he now resides. *Los pequenos infiernos* (1970) contains poems written just prior to another work, *Taberna y otros lugares*, winner of the 1969 Casa de La Americas prize in Cuba, which contains the poems included here.

SALVADOR ELIZONDO was born in 1932 in Mexico City and lives there at the present time. His first novel, *Farabeuf, o la crónica de un instante*, won the 1965 Villarrutia prize. In 1968, a second novel, *El hipogeo secreto*, was published in Mexico. The present piece is from a collection of stories, *Nardo o el verano* (1966).

EDUARDO ESCOBAR born in 1942 in Medellín, Colombia, was a leading member of the Nadaistas, a vanguard group of poets similar to the Beats, who were active in the 1960's in Medellín. He has published four books of poetry, among them *Del embrión a la embriaguez* (1969) and *Cuac* (1970).

JAIME ESPINAL was born in 1940 in Medellín, Colombia. As a young writer, he was for a short time a member of the Nadaistas (see Escobar). In 1965, he came to the United States, lived in Chicago and New York, where he worked at such odd jobs as making plaster "antiques," teaching at a Montessori school, and doing editorial work in a New York publishing house. He returned to Medellín in 1970 and is currently working with the people of the barrios in that city. Espinal's poems and stories have appeared in various Colombian newspapers and magazines, but the present selection is his first story to appear in English.

ROBERTO FERNÁNDEZ RETAMAR was born in Havana in 1930 and was educated there and in Paris and London. He taught at Yale University before the Cuban revolution and now is a professor at the University of Havana and the editor of the literary magazine *Casa de las Americas*. *Poesía Reunida* (1966) contains his poems from 1948 to

1965. *Algo Semejante a los Monstruos Antediluvianos* (1970) is his latest book.

NORBERTO FUENTES lives in Cuba, where he was born in 1943. Before becoming a writer and journalist, he studied the plastic arts. During the post-revolutionary struggle within Cuba, Fuentes was a front-line correspondent whose reportage appeared in Cuban newspapers and magazines. The present selections, based on those experiences, are from a collection of stories, *Condenados de Condado,* which won the 1968 Casa de las Américas prize.

GABRIEL GARCÍA MÁRQUEZ, Colombian novelist and short story writer; born in 1928. At the age of eighteen he was already writing stories and, on the strength of one of them, got a job as a reporter and editor. His long absences from Colombia began in 1954, when an assignment took him to Rome. Despite his wide travels, his stories are rooted in Colombian myth, describing the life and characters in backward or isolated villages. These works appear in a collection entitled *No One Writes to the Colonel & Other Stories* (New York, Harper & Row, 1968), which includes the selection offered here. Extending the intimate scale of these themes to a grand scale with a plurality of meanings, his novel, *One Hundred Years of Solitude* (New York, Harper & Row, 1970) is a truly fantastic metaphoric chronicle of five generations.

JUAN GELMAN was born in 1930 in Buenos Aires, Argentina. He left his university studies in chemistry "to become a poet," and has since traveled widely—in Latin America, China, and Africa—"my best apprenticeship" he calls it. He had worked at odd jobs until starting in journalism ten years ago. As a member of the Argentine left which he joined in 1946, he was imprisoned in 1963. Gelman has published seven books of poems, among them: *Violín y otras cuestiones* (1956), *Fábulas* (1971) and *Colera buey* (1971).

ADRIANO GONZÁLEZ LEÓN, born in Venezuela in 1931, has taught in the University of Caracas and lived in Buenos Aires and Paris. His first novel, *País Portátil,* won the 1968 Biblioteca Breve prize. Previous to this, he published three books of stories, one of which, *Hombre que daba sed* (1967), includes the present selection.

NICOLÁS GUILLÉN, was born in Camaguey, Cuba, in 1904, has been a central figure in bringing the Afro-Carribean tradition into Spanish American poetry. He has been a typographer, journalist and diplomat, and was a delegate to the Intellectuals' Congress of Culture held in Spain in 1937. He was a good friend of another poet of the oppressed, Langston Hughes. Guillén is now director of the Writers and Artists Union of Cuba. Among his books are: *Songoro consongo* (1931), *El son entero* (1947) containing the poem offered here, and *La paloma de vuelo popular* (1958).

JAVIER HERAUD was born in Lima, Peru, in 1942. He studied at the Universidad Católica and wrote two books of poems, *El río* and *El viaje,* published posthumously. He joined the guerrilla movement in Peru and died in 1962 at the shore of the river Madre de Dios, fighting against the police.

FELISBERTO HERNÁNDEZ, an Uruguayan fiction writer, was born in 1902. Hernández was also a concert pianist who performed in modest halls in the provinces of Uruguay and Argentina, and played piano for silent movies. His wry humor and deceptively simple prose style are a thin skin through which the pulsations of absurdity and tragedy are clearly visible. The story in this collection is from *Las Hortensias* (1949). Hernández died in 1963.

VICENTE HUIDOBRO was born in 1893 in Chile. He was a leading figure in opening the poetry of the Spanish language to the avant garde sensibility of early twentieth-century France. As one of the first Spanish American poets in the vanguard of European literature, he collaborated with Apollinaire in the review *Nord Sud* (1916), wrote several books in French, and was acclaimed by the poets in Spain. Through essays, speeches and manifestos, he espoused "creationism"—the return of the poet from his role as imitator of physical reality to his original mission of creating new realities. ("Poets why sing of the rose?/Make it bloom in your poem!") In *Altazar,* a key poem, Huidobro speaks for contemporary man who denies God in order to take the place of the creator, but finds himself hurled into the abyss of existential nothingness. Huidobro's complete works, *Obras Completas* were published after his death in 1948.

ROBERTO JUARROZ is an Argentinian poet, born in 1917. Very little is known about his life. His works are: *Poesía vertical, Segunda poesía vertical* (1963), *Poema vertical* (1964), *Tercera poesía vertical* (1965) and *Cuarta poesía vertical* (1969), containing the poems offered here.

JOSÉ LEZAMA LIMA was born in Cuba in 1910, lives there at the present time, and is one of the directors of its Union of Artists and Writers. In 1944, in La Habana, he was one of the founders of the literary magazine, *Orígenes*. His first books of poems were followed by essays and stories, as well as his novel, *Paradiso* (1968), a section of which has been selected for this anthology. Its fullness of poetic vision and richness of language are considered, in the Spanish American literary world, a standard against which past and new works may be measured.

ENRIQUE LIHN, best known for his poetry but also known as a writer of stories, was born in Chile in 1929. The poems included here are from *La Pieza Oscura* (1963), a winner of many prizes. His more recent books of poetry are: *Poesía de Paso,* winner of the 1966 Casa de las Américas prize, *Escrito en Cuba* (1969) and *Musiquilla de las Pobres Esferas* (1969). The prose selection offered here is the title story from a collection entitled *Agua de Arroz* (1964). Lihn resides in Santiago de Chile.

RENÉ MARQUÉS was born in Puerto Rico in 1919 and lives there at the present time. Author of poetry, plays, novels and short stories, Marqués' work reflects a passionate concern with the struggle for identity, personal and national. His play, *Oxcart* (New York, Scribner, 1969), examines the fate of a Puerto Rican immigrant to the United States, and "Give Us This Day" (*New Voices of Hispanic America,* edited by Flakoll & Alegría; Boston, Beacon Press, 1962) is a study of the Puerto Rican nationalist leader, Pedro Albizu Campos.

LUIS PALÉS MATOS was born in 1898 in Guayama in southeastern Puerto Rico. Guayama with its nearness to the sea, its isolation from the north by mountains that detain both inhabitants and clouds, was important in shaping the sensibility of the young poet. Growing up in a poetry-writing family, he found the way to escape isolation and to span great distances was books, and he read whatever fell into his hands. His first published book came out when he was 17, and by the end of his life he had encompassed a major part of the poetic experience of our century. His well-known evocation of Afro-Carribean themes, *Tuntún de pasa y grifa* (1937) is in his collected *Poesía* (1957).

DANIEL MOYANO was born in Buenos Aires in 1930. His novel, *El oscuro,* won the Primera Plana-Sudamericana Prize of 1968, juried by Gabriel García Márquez, Leopoldo Marechal and Augusto Roa Bastos. The present selection is from a collection of stories, *El monstruo y otros cuentos* (1967).

ALVARO MUTIS was born in Colombia in 1923 and now lives in Mexico City. Among his books of poems are: *Los elementos del desastre* (Buenos Aires, 1953) and *Los trabajos perdidos* (1965) from which the present selection was made.

PABLO NERUDA, the pseudonym of Neftali Reyes, was born in Parral, Chile, in 1904. Early recognition as a poet was awarded with consulships to various countries. However as Consul in Madrid he proclaimed his government's support of the Loyalists in 1936 and was removed. The disaster of the Spanish Civil War which he witnessed, changed his poetry. The first two poems offered here are from his surrealist *Residencias en Tierra II* (1935), and the third is from *Tercera Residencia* (1941). The last selection is part of a long poem included in *Canto General* (1950), a book in 15 sections covering the geological, social and political history of Spanish America. In the presidential elections of 1970 Neruda was nominated to represent the Communist Party of Chile. His work has exercised a great influence on North American poets. Translated books are: *Twenty Love Poems and a Song of Despair* (Cape Edition, Grossman, 1968), *Selected Poems of Pablo Neruda* (New York, Grove Press, 1961), *The Heights of Macchu Picchu* (Farrar, Straus, and Giroux and Jonathan Cape, 1966), *Pablo Neruda:*

A New Decade (New York, Grove Press, 1969), *We Are Many* (Cape-Goliard, Grossman, 1968), and *Neruda and Vallejo: Selected Poems* (Boston, Beacon Press, 1971).

RICARDO OCAMPO, born in Potosí, Bolivia, in 1928, is, like so many Latin American writers, a journalist as well as a writer of fiction and was, for several years, editor on the La Paz newspaper, *La Nación*. A series of his stories, as yet uncollected, appeared in the magazine *Momento* (Caracas).

JUAN CARLOS ONETTI was born in Uruguay in 1909, spent his youth in Montevideo, and went to Buenos Aires at about the age of twenty, when he began his long and varied career as a journalist. He returned to Montevideo in 1954 and accepted a library post at the Institute of Art and Letters. Since 1939, Onetti has published seven novels and two collections of stories, in which his strange humor and particular despair often concentrate on themes of urban loneliness. Only a few of these works have appeared in English: his novel *The Shipyard* (New York, Scribner, 1968) and several of his stories, among them "Dreaded Hell" (*Latin American Writing Today,* see Alejo Carpentier above) and "Welcome, Bob" (*Short Stories in Spanish,* edited by Jean Franco; Baltimore, Penguin Parallel Texts, 1966). The present selection is from *Cuentos Completos* (1968).

CARLOS OQUENDO DE AMAT was born in Puno, Peru, in 1901. He was exiled in 1931 for political reasons and imprisoned in Central America while on his way to Spain. As yet there is little information about his life (see epilogue by Vargas Llosa in this book). He died in Spain in 1936 leaving only *Cinco metros de poemas* (1927).

RAMÓN PALOMARES was born in Venezuela in 1935. He has published three books of poems, *El Reino, Paisano, Honras Fuenebres. Paisano* was the Premio Municipal de Poesia, in 1965.

NICANOR PARRA, a poet and physicist, was born in 1914 in Chillán in the south of Chile. He studied mathematics and physics at the University of Santiago, Brown University and Oxford. He has been strongly influenced by the folkloric tradition of his country as evident in *La Cueca*

Larga (1958) named for the celebrated national dance of Chile. Parra prefers being called "anti-poet" and says, "anti-poetry shoots in all directions with the same force." *Poems and Antipoems* (New York, New Directions, 1967) brought attention to his work here. Selections from his collected poems *Obra Gruesa* (1969) will appear as *Problems* (New York, New Directions, 1972). He teaches poetry at the University of Santiago and has been visiting lecturer in poetry in the United States on several occasions.

OCTAVIO PAZ was born in Mexico in 1914. He edited the literary magazine *Taller* and helped to found *El Hijo Prodigo*. In 1943 after returning from a stay in the United States on a Guggenheim grant, he joined the diplomatic service of Mexico which took him to Paris and to the Orient. He resigned his position as Ambassador to India when, in the summer of 1968, the Mexican government violently suppressed the student demonstrators before the Olympics. He has written essays, among them *Labyrinth of Solitude* (New York, Grove Press, 1961), art criticism, *Marcel Duchamp or the Castle of Purity* (Cape Goliard, Grossman, 1970), plays, and over twelve books of poetry. Selections in English are contained in the following: *Selected Poems of Octavio Paz* (Indiana University Press, 1963), *Eagle or Sun* (New York, October House) and *Configurations* (New York, New Directions, 1971), which contains the two poems in this book.

ANGEL RAMA, born in Montevideo in 1926, is a short story writer, playwright, critic and professor of Spanish American literature at the University of Montevideo. For many years he has been critic on the Montevideo weekly *Marcha,* and director of the publishing house Ediciones Arca. He has published several books of criticism, among them *La generación crítica.*

AUGUSTO ROA BASTOS was born in Paraguay in 1917, but has lived in Argentina for many years, an exile from political persecution in his native country. A writer of poetry, novels and stories, Roa Bastos uses the language of the Guarani Indian and archetypal situations or myths to link local realities to broader meanings. His story, "The

Excavation," appeared in *New Voices of Hispanic America* (see René Marqués above), and in 1959, his novel, *Son of Man* (London, V. Gollancz, 1965) won several literary prizes. The present selection is from a group of stories, *Madera Quemada* (1967).

JUAN RULFO, born in Mexico in 1918, was brought up in the village of San Gabriel. Orphaned at an early age, he was fifteen when he moved to Mexico City, where he later attended the University. In simple rhythms of spoken language, Rulfo writes of the bitter resignation and odd candor of the dispossessed who roam the land of their birth haunted by a forgotten past. His important reputation rests on two books: *The Burning Plain and Other Stories* (Austin, University of Texas Pr., 1967), and a novel, *Pedro Páramo* (New York, Grove Press, 1959). The present selection is one of five new works which will soon appear in an expanded collection of Rulfo's stories. Since 1962, Rulfo has worked at the Indian Institute in Mexico City.

JAIME SABINES was born in Chiapas, Mexico, in 1926. He studied literature in Mexico City where he now lives and works as head of a business firm. The poems offered here are from *Recuentos de Poemas* (1962) which contains all his work up to his most recent book *Yuria* (1967).

SEBASTIÁN SALAZAR BONDY was born in 1924 in Peru. Not only did he write plays, poetry, narratives, criticism and essays, but he inspired a whole movement in the arts starting in the 1950's when there was very little interest and support. Among his books of essays is *Lima la horrible* (1964). His last book of poetry, *El tacto de la araña* (1965), contains the poems offered here. All of his writings have been collected in six volumes of *Obras* (1967) published two years after his death, with essays in homage to this well-loved man who died, as have so many other Peruvian writers, at an early age.

ANTONIO SKÁRMETA, short story writer; born in Chile in 1940. In 1964–66, he attended Columbia University under a Fulbright, and he has served as a juror for Cuba's publishing house, Casa de las Américas. A winner of many national contests, his stories have appeared in literary magazines throughout Spanish America. Currently, Skármeta teaches Spanish American Literature at the University of Chile and the Technique of Expression at the School of Journalism of the Catholic University in Santiago de Chile. His first book, *El entusiasmo*, appeared in 1967 and, in 1968, a collection of stories, *Desnudo en el tejado*, from which the present selection was made, won the Casa de las Américas prize.

MARIO VARGAS LLOSA was born in Arequipa, Peru in 1936, and was soon after taken to Cochabamba, Bolivia. When he was nine years old, his family moved back to Peru, and he was eventually sent to the Leoncio Prado Military Academy in Lima. This became the undisguised setting for his first novel, *The Time of the Hero* (New York, Grove Press, 1966) which, in 1962, was awarded the Biblioteca Breve Prize. (At Leoncio Prado, a thousand copies of the book were burned in official outrage at the revelations it contained.) His most recent work to appear in English is the novel *The Green House* (New York, Harper & Row, 1968), which won four important literary prizes, among them the 1967 Rómulo Gallegos Award. Vargas Llosa's speech on accepting that award appears as the epilogue to this anthology. Since 1959, he has lived in Europe most of the time and currently resides in Barcelona.

CÉSAR VALLEJO was born of devoutly Catholic parents in Santiago de Chuco, a small Andean town in Peru in 1892. His maternal grandparents were Indian (Neruda has pointed out that Vallejo's Indian roots show in the subtlety and obliqueness of his poems). *Heraldos Negros* (1919) and *Trilce* (1922) were written before he left for Paris not to return to his homeland again. *Poemas Humanas/Human Poems* (New York, Grove Press, 1968) and *Espana aparta di mí este caliz* (1940) were completed shortly before his death and bear witness to his profound physical and spiritual suffering, to the intense and thwarted hope he had for Spain, and above all, to the depth of his compassion for man. He died in 1938 on a Thursday, a day foretold in one of his poems. *Neruda and Vallejo: Selected Poems* (Boston, Beacon Press, 1971) is a selection of poems from all his books.

CINTIO VITIER, a Catholic Cuban poet and essayist was born in Key

West, Florida, in 1921. He founded the literary magazine *Origenes* in Havana with José Lezama Lima, Eliseo Diego and his own wife, Fina Garcia Marruz. He lives in Havana and does research in the Biblioteca Nacional José Martí. *Visperas* contains his poetry from 1943 to 1953. The poems offered here are from *Testimonios* (1968), his collected poetic work since 1953. Among his critical works are *Cincuenta Anos de poesía cubana* (1952) and *La voz de Gabriela Mistral* (1957).

INDEX OF TRANSLATORS

H. R. HAYS
The Mirror of Lida Sal, by Miguel Ángel Asturias
The Rainbow, by Adriano González León
The Living Tomb, by Augusto Roa Bastos

INES DE TORRES KINNELL
A Dream Come True, by Juan Carlos Onetti

JOHN C. MURCHISON
The Cartwheel, by Antonio Skármeta

GREGORY RABASSA
Silvia, by Julio Cortázar

TIM REYNOLDS
Captain Descalzo, For the Night, and
Order #13, from "Condenados de Condado," by Norberto Fuentes
from *Paradiso* (a novel), by José Lezama Lima

HARDIE ST. MARTIN
The Ayla, by José María Arguedas
The Fugitives, by Alejo Carpentier
There's a Body Reclining on the Stern, by René Marqués
The Day of the Landslide, by Juan Rulfo

MILLER WILLIAMS
Rice Water, by Enrique Lihn

POETRY

ELECTA ARENAL
Vicente Huidobro
Cintio Vitier

GUY AROUL
Octavio Paz

RACHEL BENSON
Luis Palés Matos

PAUL BLACKBURN
Eduardo Escobar
Javier Heraud

ROBERT BLY
Pablo Neruda

JANET BROF
Ernesto Cardenal
José Coronel Urtecho
Juan Gelman
Carlos Oquendo de Amat

NORMAN THOMAS DI GIOVANNI
Jorge Luis Borges

CLAYTON ESHLEMAN
César Vallejo

KATE FLORES
Pablo Neruda

H. R. HAYS
Carlos Oquendo de Amat

PHILIP LAMANTIA
Ernesto Cardenal

W. S. MERWIN
Jorge Luis Borges
Vicente Huidobro
Roberto Juarroz
Alvaro Mutis
Ramón Palomares
Jaime Sabines

SERGIO MONDRAGÓN
Ernesto Cardenal

ALASTAIR REID
Jorge Luis Borges

TIM REYNOLDS
Roque Dalton
Roberto Fernandez Retamar
Sebastián Salazar Bondy

HARDIE ST. MARTIN
Ernesto Cardenal

This book was composed on the linotype in Garamond
by H. Wolff Book Manufacturing Co., New York.
The printing is by Noble Offset Printers, Inc., New York
and the binding by H. Wolff Book Manufacturing Co.
Designed by Jacqueline Schuman.